John Francis H. Claiborne

Life and Correspondence of John A. Quitman

Vol. 1

John Francis H. Claiborne

Life and Correspondence of John A. Quitman
Vol. 1

ISBN/EAN: 9783337399894

Printed in Europe, USA, Canada, Australia, Japan

Cover: Foto ©Raphael Reischuk / pixelio.de

More available books at **www.hansebooks.com**

LIFE AND CORRESPONDENCE

OF

JOHN A. QUITMAN,

MAJOR-GENERAL, U.S.A., AND GOVERNOR OF THE STATE OF
MISSISSIPPI.

BY

J. F. H. CLAIBORNE.

IN TWO VOLUMES.

VOL. I.

NEW YORK:
HARPER & BROTHERS, PUBLISHERS,
FRANKLIN SQUARE.
1860.

TO

THE YOUNG MEN OF THE SOUTH,

THIS MEMOIR

OF ONE WHO BECAME, BY HIS OWN EXERTIONS, EMINENT AT THE
BAR, ON THE BENCH, IN THE ARMY, AND IN THE COUNCILS
OF HIS COUNTRY, AND MAINTAINED THROUGH LIFE
HIS PERSONAL VIRTUE AND POLITICAL
INTEGRITY, IS

Respectfully Dedicated.

INTRODUCTION.

I present these volumes with diffidence to the public. They have been written from a sentiment of duty, under the drawback of ill health, and at intervals snatched from other pressing engagements.

My aim has been to make them, like the man whose acts they recite, plain and frank, without pretension or parade. Wherever it has been practicable, I have preferred original letters to my own speculations, and thus the work may be considered an autobiography.

The difficulty of procuring documents has occasioned some delay, for it is no part of the merit of the South to attach the proper value to the materials of history. The reports made by the field-officers of the first Mississippi regiment of the services of their respective commands at Monterey—a document essential to the glory of the state, and confided to its archives—can not be found, and our Legislature has been vainly appealed to for some provision to preserve the rich but perishable records now in private hands. My own stores, however, and the kindness of friends, have enabled me to complete this work.

Of the war with Mexico, I have, of course, only been able to review so much as was required to illustrate the services of Quitman. The glorious deeds of his comrades are in the records of the country. No complete history of that war has yet appeared. Some military writers have severely criticised the operations of Taylor and Scott, and more than insinuated their incapacity to conduct armies in the field. It is easy to write after a campaign has ended, as it is easy to moralize at the close of a life of error. An ingenious casuist may demonstrate almost any thing on paper. British critics, enraged by party spirit, long contended that Sir John Moore was no general, though Soult, Wellington, and Napoleon, according to Napier, expressed a very different opinion. Military writers for a long time questioned the capacity of Sir Arthur Wellesley, and find fault often with the arrangements of Napoleon. Some of them even charged him with cowardice. Generals Lee, Conway, and Gates, and the officers of their school, habitually sneered at the generalship of Washington.

Taylor and Scott both conducted their campaigns, in a hostile and populous country, under many difficulties. They had not the confidence of their government, and, in that respect, were in the position of Marlborough harassed by Dutch civilians, of the Archduke Charles by military councils, and Wellesley by Portuguese juntas and Spanish regencies. But, like those great commanders, they triumphed over the enemy in front and the "fire in the rear." They conducted their operations, in the main, according to the received principles of war, but neither ever hesitated to adopt any expedient deemed necessary by the emergency of the hour, and this it is that distinguishes the man of resources from the martinet. This was, in fact, the secret of Napoleon's first triumphs in Italy over the Austrians of the old school.

These incompetent generals of ours conquered an

empire older than our own in the course of one campaign!

Such men may defy criticism. Theory and speculation fall before facts.

In another respect—their moderation after victory —they challenge the admiration of the world. Matamoras, Monterey, Vera Cruz, Puebla, Mexico—when before have such capitals been occupied by foreign troops without pillage, outrage, and massacre? The restraint, the discipline, the protection to persons and property, and the free exercise of religious and social duties, were as perfect during our domination as in any city of Europe or America.

The whole campaign was honorable to our arms and country.

In relation to the political events discussed in this memoir, I have endeavored to be impartial, and to assign good motives where bad ones were not obvious.

With a strong attachment and admiration for General Quitman, I have not sought to represent him as infallible. I was his pupil in early life, but afterward differed with him on many important questions, as, for instance, when he supported nullification, and when he opposed that silent acquiescence in the compromise measures which the Democratic party recommended.

I have to acknowledge, however, that the course of events has satisfied me that on both occasions he was right. Carolina stood on doctrines as old as the Constitution, and we have gained no security by a temporizing and conciliatory policy since.

If these volumes are favorably received, they may be followed by a more piquant volume illustrative of parties and public men in the South. I have over two thousand letters not used herein.

In relation to the letters submitted to the reader, I should perhaps observe that they are all on matters of public concern. None of them are designated as private; the parties that wrote them, if living, entertain the same opinions, and if dead, *died* with them; and they are opinions that they never shrank from avowing. I feel that it is right to give them to the world. They illustrate the history of the past, and are applicable to passing events. In political correspondence there should be no secrets, and no false sensibility when they are submitted to the public. Mr. Hume, the English reformer, used to say, that whenever he heard the word "delicacy" mentioned in any argument or public document, he felt certain there was something wrong.

I have now to express my acknowledgments for documents, facts, and dates, to Gov. Gist, Hon. J. W. Hayne, Dr. R. W. Gibbes, and Capt. Stanley, of South Carolina; Col. Thomas Williams, of Alabama; John Marshall, Capt. Rogers, Capt. Duffau, and J. A. Quintero, of Texas. Messrs. A. G. Brown, Jefferson Davis, J. J. M'Rae, John B. Nevitt, J. T. M'Murran, J. S. B. Thacher, R. Elward, W. W. W. Wood, Wm. Cannon, J. S. Holt, W. P. Mellen, J. D. Elliott, Henry Hughes, Thomas Reed, B. W. Sanders, G. V. H. Forbes, J. Roach, E. Whaley, Rev. C. K. Marshall, and particularly my late lamented friends, Hon. Edward Turner and Hon. C. S. Tarpley, and since his death his estimable widow. To this accomplished lady I am under many obligations for valuable papers.

Bay of St. Louis, Mississippi.

CONTENTS OF VOL. I.

CHAPTER XII.

CHAPTER XIII.

LIFE AND CORRESPONDENCE

OF

JOHN A. QUITMAN.

LIFE AND CORRESPONDENCE

OF

JOHN A. QUITMAN.

CHAPTER I.

Ancestors and Parentage.—John Frederick Quitman, D.D.—Settles in Curaçoa.—Effects of the French Revolution on Society.—His Views of Government.—The Constitution of the United States a Problem to Europe.—Washington.—His Character and Career.—Influence upon Immigration and Capital.—Dr. Quitman in Philadelphia.—Interview with Washington.—His Connection with Literature.—Review of his Work on Magic.—His Death.

I AM to record the acts of a man whose whole life was governed by fixed rules of action, maintained with untiring energy and inflexible will. He possessed what Cicero notes as the characteristic of the younger Brutus: *quidquid vult, valde vult.*

"The true test of a great man," says Lord Brougham, "is his having been in advance of his age."

Bearing these things in mind, there will be no difficulty in comprehending the career of John A. Quitman, and the consistency and decision that marked it throughout.

The tradition is, that during the time of Luther, a citizen of Rome, of the famous family of the Marcelli, having adopted the doctrines of the Reformation, sought refuge in Germany, and finally fixed himself at Iserlohe, Westphalia, where he assumed the name of Quitman—a name compounded from the old Saxon, signifying "freeman." One of his descendants settled in Cleves, and from him the Quitman family in the United States have sprung. The grandfather of Gen. Quitman was a man of science and distinction, who held, under the Prussian government, for the greater portion of his life, the important office of Inspector of Harbors, Dikes, and Military Roads. His residence was on a small island in the Rhine, near the city of Cleves, which, having been swept away by an unprecedented flood, gave his son, in after life, occasion to say, when questioned as to the place of his birth, that he had no native place, but was a citizen of the world.

This son, Frederick Henry Quitman, qualified himself at an early age for the University of Halle; indeed, the rules as to age were relaxed on account of his attainments. He soon won the confidence of the professors of that famous institution. Rather against the inclinations of his father, he devoted himself to the study of theology, and soon became distinguished as a dialectician and casuist. Having completed his studies at nineteen years of age, he accepted the position of preceptor to the daughters of the Prince of Waldeck—Count Rantzowe (who afterward made some figure in history) holding the same trust toward the young princes of that house. This engagement lasted two years. Resolving then to enter the ministry, he repaired to Amsterdam, and presented himself to the Lutheran Consistorium of the United Provinces. That learned and influential body had the direction of missions, and other ecclesiastical affairs, in Holland and its colonies. He was ordained, and dispatched to the island of Curaçoa, where he received a cordial welcome. After a residence of twelve months, he married Anna Elizabeth, daughter of John Casper Hueck, one of the most influential citizens of Curaçoa. She was a woman of refined and elegant manners; her mind had been carefully cultivated; her countenance was intellectual and full of character; her disposition gentle and obliging.

The Rev. Dr. Quitman retained his charge some twelve years, faithfully discharging the duties that devolve upon a pastor: to inculcate religious sentiment and social improvement; relieve the distressed, comfort the sick, and support the dying. In our hours of prosperity, the servant of God is often forgotten, sometimes sneered at. But there come periods in the life of every man when pleasure has no charms, wealth no resource, wretchedness no consolation. It is then that we appreciate the beloved pastor, forgetful of neglect, cordial in his sympathies, tender even unto tears!

About this period, the convulsions that had dislocated society in France, and torn up established institutions and the old notions of order and discipline, were felt in the West Indies. Jacobinism, social equality without regard to race, and universal emancipation—more irrational and revolting than the agrarianism imputed to the Romans—began to be recommended in those peaceful and prosperous islands, where the easiest and most remunerative form of domestic servitude had long prevailed, and where crime, and even litigation, were almost unknown. Those monstrous doctrines—chimeras from the brains of infidels and assassins—came trooping, one after another, like bloody spectres, across the Atlantic; and they were followed by scenes of terror, conflagration, massacre, and anarchy, such as had been recently witnessed in the unhappy country of their origin. A false and fanatical notion of liberty began to prevail. Society was rapidly demoralized. After having vainly, and at some personal hazard, resisted the new state of things, Dr. Quitman resolved to seek some other abode. Like the great Earl of Chatham, he believed, "where law ends, there tyranny begins;" and he justly regarded the Christian religion as the only sure basis for civilization and order. In Holland, a pension for life for twelve years of missionary service, and a high place in the Lutheran Church, guaranteed by his learning and eloquence, awaited his return. But the pernicious example of France, as well as her military power, overshadowed all the contiguous nationalities; and, after much consideration, he resolved to fix himself in the United States, the freest country in the world, yet with notions of liberty wholly opposed to the irrational and extreme views of European revolutionists. The philosophers of the Continent did not then, and do not now, comprehend the nature of constitutional government. The whole tribe of encyclopedists, when monarchy was extinguished in France, was incapable of producing a simple Constitution. Their ablest writers, after critical study, and even personal observation, have never yet been able to give a correct definition of our peculiar system. With a thousand years of experience, they are less practical, and more ignorant of the principles of political liberty than the Romans. They conquer kings and demolish aristocracies, but of popular rights and the restraints of law, civil liberty and social order, they have no proper conception. All their theories amplify themselves into impracticable optimism, or degenerate into brutality and blood. Not until, in the fullness of our mission, we teach them common sense and enlightened conservatism, will France, Spain, Germany, Italy, and the nations of this hemisphere that have sprung from them, understand what regulated liberty means, and what blessings it confers. Their absurd transcendentalism—their vulgar and disorganizing radicalism—the strife of factions—the war upon religion—the jealousy of property—the rule of the mob, or imperial despotism, are the only substitutes Europe has yet invented for the evils of hereditary monarchy, privileged orders, and the dominion of the

Church. There must be a general conflagration of ancient and polluted things, and of dangerous modern fallacies, and the Old World and its offshoots to the south of us must be Americanized before they can comprehend real freedom.

The American Revolution gave birth to no anarchy. It spawned no crimes. During the war and after it, old English notions of law and order prevailed. The army, without an effort, melted into the great body of the people, and returned to civil pursuits. It is a remarkable fact, stated by Gouverneur Morris in a letter to Hamilton, Paris, Feb. 16th, 1793, that "a great proportion of the French officers who served in America were either opposed to the revolution in their own country, or felt themselves obliged, by its excesses, to abandon it." They found the people too ignorant and too corrupt to support a legal administration. Habituated to obey, they required a master, and, like the citizens of ancient Rome, the French people had reached a period when Cato was a madman, and Cæsar a necessary evil. That a large portion of the people in *our* Eastern states and frontier territories, from the abuse of the democratic principle of popular sovereignty, have begun to regard liberty as license, and have no adequate conception of constitutional restraint, is not to be denied.

In his island home Dr. Quitman had studied the career and character of Washington; and guarantees for law, order, and stability, derived from this study, induced the staid and order-loving clergyman to seek an asylum in the United States. Washington had conducted our army through a protracted and unequal war. He had been placed at the head of a new and untried government, to be managed without reference to past precedents, and exposed at every step to temptation and danger. False friends, enthusiastic advisers, open or covert

enemies, with plaudits and menaces, beset him.   French
appeals and French intrigue, sustained by a powerful and
popular party in this country—the crash of thrones and
the progress of so-called republicanism in Europe—the
popular recollection of the wrongs we had endured from
Great Britain and the aid we had received from France,
all conspired to influence and embarrass his administration.   With a well-organized British army to encounter
—with a divided country to defend, there having been
"more American Tories in the king's service than the
whole of the enlisted troops in the service of Congress"*
—without money or credit, or any controlling government to supply his necessities, he had maintained his
army in the field by his personal influence, and secured,
by his prudence as much as by his valor, the independence of the country.   Great as were his difficulties during the war, he encountered and subdued more after the
organization of the government.   In opposition to his
personal friends—against public opinion in his own commonwealth—at the hazard of a total loss of popularity,
he maintained the neutrality of the republic between
France and England, and thus preserved the independence he had won by the sword.   His celebrated proclamation of neutrality was the sublime of moral courage,
and may now be regarded as the greatest action of his
life.   He stands like an isthmus in the bloody chart of
history, between despotism on one hand, and the licen-
tiousness of liberty on the other.   Rigid, even austere
in his public and personal virtue, he exacted every thing
for his country that justice demanded—asked little for
himself—and won more glory by self-denial than the
whole race of imperial conquerors by their triumphs and
usurpations !

* Intercepted letter from Lord George Germain to Sir Henry
Clinton.

It was thus that he impressed himself upon mankind at a period when revolution achieved few results that humanity could rejoice at. Thinking men every where regarded him as a guarantee for order and stability, and intellect and capital poured into the country.

Dr. Quitman, soon after his arrival, repaired to Philadelphia to wait upon this illustrious chief magistrate. He was charmed with the dignity of his manners, and the respect he manifested for the clergy.* Soon after

* Of this interview he left the following interesting memorandum:

"A servant in livery conducted me into the presence of President Washington. He was alone, standing in the centre of the apartment. His demeanor was truly royal. He was clothed in black velvet. His bow was very stately and ceremonious. He invited me to be seated. I waited respectfully until he took his chair. I waited until he should choose to break the silence. He asked some questions about the West Indies, but, finding that I was a Prussian subject, he passed immediately to my country, and seemed perfectly informed in regard to our military history. He put some questions to me about the subsistence and compensation of the soldiery, in answering which I fear I betrayed my ignorance. He twice corrected me in the campaigns of the great Frederick. He spoke of Alexander, Cæsar, Epaminondas, Marlborough, Charles XII., Turenne, Condé, Wallenstein, and the great Frederick, but pronounced Hannibal the greatest general of them all. On looking into the authorities, I find his information surprisingly accurate and minute.

"When he became silent I rose. He bowed low, but said nothing, and I withdrew, bowing myself out. His manner was grave and reserved rather than haughty. The countenance in repose was meditative and sad. His conversation was not fluent or very striking, except for its common sense. There was that about him which I can not forget. I can not define it, but I am constantly thinking of him, and seem to be constrained by his presence. There is not so much real grandeur on any throne in Europe.

"The day after I was honored with a note from his secretary, inviting me to tea with the Lady Washington. I found only half a dozen gentlemen and four ladies. The Lady Washington has been handsome. Her manner is stately and dame-like, but cordial. She placed me by her side, and often addressed me. The President said but little, but offered me many civilities at table, and recommended me to visit Virginia. Both of them manifested the utmost respect for my ministry. The refreshment consisted of tea, toast, muffins, salted herring, and Virginia ham, the two last from the President's estate on the Potomac River. At 10 o'clock, after a glass of Madeira, the guests withdrew."

this the doctor took charge of a Lutheran congregation in Schoharie, New York, where he remained until 1798; when he accepted a call to Rhinebeck, an ancient Dutch village on the North River. Six years afterward Mrs. Quitman died, leaving four sons and three daughters. All the former are dead. Two daughters only survive. They reside in Philadelphia. A brother of this lady, Carl Hueck, a bold and adventurous man, in early life attached himself to the fortunes of Admiral Brion, of the Columbian navy, and distinguished himself during the War of Independence. He was promoted to a post-captaincy, and died a few years since in Venezuela. A sister married Admiral De Verien, of the Dutch navy.

Two years after the death of his first wife the Rev. Dr. Quitman married again. He maintained an extensive correspondence with a number of learned men in Europe and the United States, among whom were President Kirkland of Harvard University, and Dr. Channing of Boston. Harvard conferred on him the degree of D.D. When Mr. Edward Everett and Mr. J. Ticknor were going to Europe, he provided them with letters to the most eminent professors. At Gottingen, these American students made so favorable an impression that Professor Eichhorn wrote a special letter of thanks to the doctor for the introduction of "such agreeable young barbarians." His letters to his son show that he was a man of scrupulous integrity, and uncompromising and austere in his notions of virtue. In the Medical Repository, conducted by the learned Samuel L. Mitchill, LL.D., for 1811, there is a review of Dr. Quitman's work on Magic.* He published, likewise, a series of sermons on

---

* *From the Medical Repository.*—"In this enlightened age and country there are, even at this day, many traces of magical delusion. Many persons will not permit themselves to be bled without consulting the almanac to know whether the sign is favorable. The prohibition

the Reformation, which were highly spoken of. He presided for many years over the general synods of the Lutheran Church, and even when his physical and mental powers rendered him incompetent, insisted on perform-

of palmistry, fortune-telling, and such like arts, by a special statute of New York, is an acknowledgment of their prevalence and influence on society. The strong belief in the witchcraft of the Poughkeepsie girl, in the demoniacal music and dancing at Tarrytown, and in the reputed enchantment which secures the treasures buried by Captain Kidd, Blackbeard, and other pirates, are proofs of the popular proneness to superstition. To expose and eradicate these errors, the Rev. FREDERICK H. QUITMAN, professor of divinity, President of the Lutheran clergy, and minister of the Gospel at Rhinebeck, has written a learned and sound treatise on magic, and the supposed intercourse between spirits and men. He inculcates, substantially, the opinions that appear in the writings of Eberhard and Tiedman on the same subject. This curious tract comprehends the definition of magic as the art of producing supernatural effects by spiritual agency; the history thereof as a propensity of the human mind prone to credulity, and curiosity about the future; the accounts extant about it from the Chaldeans, Persians, Egyptians, and Greeks, as also among the Jews and early Christians. The connection of magic with physic is plainly stated, as well as its relations with the civil and theological systems of the Middle Ages. The origin of the black art, and the leagues with Beelzebub in the time of Charlemagne, are explained, and full details of the Theurgists, Theosophists, and Mystics, down to the days of Cagliostro and Swedenbourg, Schröepher, and Gussner. Having traced the natural and literary history of magic thus far, Dr. Quitman proceeds to inquire whether supernatural beings can possibly affect men, or enable them to accomplish supernatural things; whether there is any such intercourse between the natural and spiritual world, and whether there are any certain proofs of witchcraft, sorcery, or magical enchantment. After a very analytical and able examination of each of these propositions, he decides them severally in the negative. This inquiry evinces a logical and perspicacious mind, highly and carefully cultivated. It is worthy of special remark, that his account of the Egyptian sorceries, of the Witch of Endor, and of Simon Magus, are excellent pieces of medical as well as Biblical criticism."

We shall see, in the course of this narrative, the qualified faith that the son of Dr. Quitman had in mysterious influences, or the forces of nature.

ing his pastoral duties.   He died June 26th, 1852.   His remains repose at Rhinebeck, under a tomb erected by his son, the subject of this memoir, who was in youth the bright star in the family horizon, and in mature years its comfort and support.

CHAPTER II.

John A. Quitman.—IIis Boyhood.—Conduct at School.—Tutor at Hartwick.—Letter from Dr. Pohlman.—Goes to Philadelphia.— Assistant Professor in Mount Airy College.—Familiar Letters.— Resolves to remove to Ohio.—The Great West.

JOHN ANTHONY, third son of the Rev. Dr. Frederick Henry Quitman and Anna Elizabeth Hueck, was born at Rhinebeck, September 1st, 1798. "In childhood," says one who knew him then, "he exhibited a bold and self-reliant, somewhat arbitrary temper, especially toward those older than himself, and a disposition to question any authority exercised over him, and to rebel against any sort of restraint. Toward those younger than himself, especially his sisters, he was gentle and forbearing. He was an intelligent lad, always fond of books, and his father early destined him for the ministry, and shaped his studies to that end. Even in boyhood idleness was no luxury to him. If not at his studies, he was always at some athletic sport, or engaged with the knife and saw at some mechanical device, for which he showed much aptitude. He was general lock-mender about the house; constructed the furniture of his own room; and, though not possessed of much talent for music, he fabricated a very respectable violin. He was fond of chess, and from some hard wood cut his set of chessmen. I never saw him unoccupied. He had a large collection of birds, reptiles, and insects. * * * * * Although of such active habits, he had been from childhood subject to attacks of gloom and melancholy, that sometimes lasted several days in succession. Though never morose,

VOL. I.—B

he preferred being alone on these occasions, and would seclude himself. He was sensible of this infirmity, and conquered it by reflection and strength of will."

In 1809 he was placed under the tuition of the Rev. A. Wackerhagen (son-in-law of the second Mrs. Quitman), a German divine of great moral worth, residing in Schoharie. This venerable gentleman, now eighty-nine years of age, recently wrote as follows of his favorite pupil:

"During his two or three years' sojourn under my roof in Schoharie, his conduct was mild, gentle, and courteous, obtaining for him the love of all. He applied himself diligently to the classics, and paid laudable attention to the religious and moral instruction I connected with his daily studies. He was then in his twelfth or thirteenth year, and I do not remember a single instance of improper conduct or disobedience on his part. When he returned home I had the satisfaction to hear his father, who was a good grammarian, say he was well posted in Greek and Latin, and his morals very praiseworthy. He afterward took a high stand in the academy of Hartwick; and, after completing the course of study there, the trustees appointed him assistant tutor in the classical department. His unexpected death, in a most splendid present and prospective career, has left us desolate and overwhelmed with grief. But, blessed be the God of all consolation, for the Christian mourner an eternity is near at hand, when all tears shall be wiped away, and a happy reunion will bring never-ending joys."

While at Mr. Wackerhagen's, John first exhibited the military spirit that distinguished him in after life. A recruiting officer of the United States army opened a rendezvous in Schoharie, with whom he became quite a pet. The lieutenant presented him a drum, fife, and pair of colors, and John enlisted a corps of juveniles, which, by regular drilling in imitation of their seniors, became quite a respectable corps of soldiers. When the lieutenant marched off his recruits at early dawn one morning, the Liliputians had disappeared. They had stolen a march before day, and were found drawn up by the road-side several miles from the village, to accompany the command. With difficulty they were prevailed on to return.

In 1812 he resumed his studies at home, under the immediate supervision of his father. He now began to think for himself; and when he formed an opinion, as he often did, at variance with his father or other members of the family, he argued for it with great tenacity. The venerable doctor was an advocate for strong government, and a warm admirer of Alexander Hamilton. The son early conceived very liberal notions, and soon disclosed the side he leaned to. Their argument usually ended by the old doctor exclaiming petulantly, "Pshaw! John, you are a born Democrat"—in those days, and from his lips, any thing but a compliment.

During this period his hours of recreation were spent in athletic exercises, in which it was his ambition to excel. He was very fleet of foot, and had uncommon strength of arm. He was an excellent hunter and trapper, and, not caring to be dependent on his father, provided his own ammunition, and, in some measure, his wardrobe, by the produce of his expeditions. The skins of his muskrats supplied him with pocket-money.

In 1816, his mind having rapidly developed under the careful instruction of his father, he was invited to become tutor at Hartwick Academy, Otsego county, N. Y., in charge of the Rev. Ernst Lewis Hazelius, who subsequently removed to Lexington Court-House, South Carolina, where he presided over a Southern theological institution, and was still living and in correspondence with his old pupil as late as 1850. Besides securing a small income, this appointment enabled the young tutor to pursue his studies for the ministry.

A letter from the Rev. Henry N. Pohlman, D.D., of Albany, N. Y., says:

"Of the little company that made the journey to Hartwick I am the only survivor—John and Albert Quitman, Rudolph Sutermeister, Allen Sutermeister and myself, and a colored servant of Dr. Quitman's for our charioteer.* A merrier party never took the road. We started from Albany in October, 1816. I was in my sixteenth year, and just about to commence my classical studies. John, though but one year my senior, was already a scholar, and occupied the responsible place of assistant teacher in the academy. I became for a short time his pupil, but was soon transferred to a higher class. We became intimate companions. I never met with a nobler character. He was the soul of honor, truthfulness, and integrity; and, though sustaining toward many of the students the relation of tutor, always an invidious one, especially when the tutor is the junior of many of his pupils, he never failed to acquire their confidence and love. I have before me a faded MS. in his handwriting, which reminds me we were both very fond of the ladies, and often gave more attention to them than to our books. He fancied me seriously in love, and hence the following *jeu d'esprit:*

"Tell me, Pohlman, now, by Jove,
        Igo and ago,
Are you certainly in love?
        Iram coram dago.
Say you so? then is it true?
I sincerely pity you.

"Since you now confess it so,
I advise you straight to woo.
If you think accordingly,
With my form you may make free.

"Emma, mistress of my heart,
I am shot by Cupid's dart.
Can you guess, O nymph divine,
Where he made his treacherous shrine?

"From your pretty eyes so blue,
Twang! his little arrow flew.

* Slavery then existed in New York. Dr. Quitman owned several slaves.

Soon I felt the stinging pain,
Soon the god let fly again.

"(Ah! the little dev'lish elf,
Might he once but prick himself,
I'll be whipp'd if, after that,
He'd even shoot a tabby cat.)

"But, to close my tale too true,
I am deep in love with you;
Happy, then, may Pohlman hear,
Sweetly fall these accents dear:
Henry, I confess to you,
        Igo and ago,
I am shot as well as you,
        Iram coram dago."

The village of Hartwick is four miles south of Cooperstown, hard by where the Susquehanna leaves Otsego Lake. In a letter to one of his brothers, June 28th, 1816, he thus refers to it and his tutor-life:

To his Brother.

"This is a place of mountains, valleys, lakes, and woods. The town sleeps in a low vale. From my window I see the river gliding swiftly through the valley. It is deep and narrow. Mountains—before, behind, and on each side—fence us in from the inquisitive world. It freezes here in June, and the sun rises and sets one hour later than in Rhinebeck. I am sufficiently busy: I rise early, and study till nine. From that hour till 12 M., and in the afternoon from 2 till 5, I hear one Greek, three Latin, two English classes, and one class in arithmetic. The greater part of the pupils are older than myself, and do not like to be instructed by a youngster. They try very hard to catch me by cross-questions; but I have thus far kept ahead of them, and hope I shall be able to continue to do so."

On the 17th of October, 1817, his father thus writes to him:

From his Father.

"The paternal advice I gave you, I hope, has deeply sunk into your mind. You can not be too careful in

guarding your heart against such passions, which have a
tendency not only to destroy your health and peace of
mind, but to blast your future prospects. I know that
your natural ambition, and even the religious principles
you have imbibed, will prevent you from degrading yourself. The thought of a father who loves you affectionately has great influence upon you, but we are all liable
to make a mistake in an unguarded moment. Prudence,
therefore, requires that we should avoid opportunities
and temptations.

"You seem discouraged at the deficiency of scholars.
The faculty should not despond. Constancy is no ingre-
dient in the American character; and, as loss of time is
considered a very little matter in this country, your
scholars may drop in by-and-by.

"Your letter is a little desponding. What reasons
can a young man have for melancholy, unless they be of
his own creation? Occasional propensity to gloom seems
to be a family complaint; but this ought to be counter-
acted as early as possible. It renders man unhappy, and,
when strengthened by suspicion, miserable. Banish sorrow, John, and never brood over vain imaginations.
Have courage and fortitude. We must move forward
without being pushed."

In 1818 he accepted the appointment of adjunct-profes-
sor of the English language at Mount Airy College, Germantown, Pa., an institution established by Mons. ——
Constant, and then very prosperous and popular. His
familiar letters to his family at that period show how
early he learned to rely upon himself, and how resolutely
he was bent on acquiring an independent and honorable
position in the world.

To his Father.

"Philadelphia, August 13th, 1818.
"I arrived here on Tuesday. Next day I went, in
company with Mr. Goodman, to Mount Airy, to see Mr.
Constant, president of the college. I found him a
Frenchman in every respect. The result of our conver-
sation, however, was an agreement, on my part, to stay

a year with him as teacher in the English department for $350, besides boarding, lodging, washing, and fuel. I anticipate, from the regulations of the establishment, pretty tight times. I am not afraid, however, to engage in any thing for *a year*. It will extend my knowledge of the world, and give me some other good opportunities of improvement."

To his Brother.

"Mount Airy, November 8th, 1818.

"My life here is very different from what it was at Hartwick. There I had my sleigh-rides, my skating, my picnics, and evening parties; here my occupation is study, and my amusement is study; nor do I regret it much. I prefer my Spanish to any pleasure. I am usefully employed; but yet I recur with regret to the charming female society I once enjoyed. It seems to be necessary to my happiness that I should have some sweet object for my affections to repose on. As I have none here, I can only sigh for those I left behind me. Germantown is famous for its scandal, not for its sociability. I have been but once to Philadelphia. The interruption to my studies prevents me from going."

On the 23d of November his father addressed to him the following beautiful letter:

From his Father.

"It gave me great satisfaction, my dear son, to see, in your last, that you are content with your present situation. It is true, your task must be tedious on account of its constant sameness, and the little mental employment it affords; but Mungo Park found some heath flowers even on the Desert of Sahara. The social deprivations of which you complain, in your letter to Henry, may, perhaps, be remedied in time. And even if this were not immediately the case, it is profitable to learn early how to dispense with our dearest enjoyments. I am glad that you employ a chief part of your time in studying the Spanish language, and that you have found in Don Merino an excellent friend and instructor. The Castilian tongue deserves attention, not only on account of its sublimity, but it is, in the present state of affairs of our country and the important future, highly to be recommended to young Americans who desire to make a figure in the world.*

"I am happy to be informed that President Constant speaks in terms of great approbation and esteem of you. It is in the character of Southern nations not to be so studious and persevering as the inhabitants of the North, and on this account the north of Germany has produced more learned works and men than all the Southern provinces together."†

His next letter, to a brother, manifests the predilection he early formed for the South, his cosmopolitan spirit, and his punctuality even in pecuniary trifles. He touches upon city manners, and sketches his associate professors.

To his Brother.

"Mount Airy, March 21st, 1819.

"Papa mentions that he has hopes of finding a situation for you in Charleston. May it be so. I should be particularly pleased to see you well settled there, as I know the Carolinians readily foster and promote deserving young men. We have a number from that state. They are liberal, generous fellows, and charm me with their manners.

"Philadelphia is, at present, a dull place for adventures, and it is no wonder. There are so many young men who fancy that when they get off the pavements of the city they are out of the world, and so many merchants live above their means; the counting-houses are overstocked, and failures occur every day. It is folly to remain in these parts when there are such wide fields open South and West, where much can be done with little money. As soon as Congress breaks up I intend to

* The venerable writer seems to have had a presentiment of the future career of his son in Mexico, where his knowledge of the Spanish language proved very useful to himself and to the public service.

† This is amusing. A critical comparison of literary history, and of intellectual and military achievement the world over, would exactly reverse the worthy doctor's position.

write to Col. Brush,* and learn if I can have any encouragement to go there, and if so, I will bid this place a long adieu. Do not understand that I am discontented with my situation; on the contrary, I am every day more pleased with it; but I want something more than a mere support, and my duties here leave me no time for myself. I am engaged in my class-room six hours every day; besides this, on Fridays I keep studies, that is, I rise at 5 A.M. and keep 70 boys at their books for one hour, and then in the evening from 7 to 8. Every morning (except Mondays) I am required to be on duty at 6 o'clock, and I retire at 12 P.M. My leisure moments are spent chiefly with the teachers. Mr. Haslam, the classical teacher, is an English Unitarian minister, a singular, wavering character, fond of nothing so much as roast beef and plum-pudding, and withal a great gallant. Mr. Kaumfout, teacher of mathematics, a lieutenant of marines, is a military martinet in every respect. Mr. Bulkley, my colleague, is a poor sheepish Yankee, afraid of a fly, and the butt of all the others. Mr. Mareno, a Spaniard, is a great politician, familiar with the diplomacy of Europe. Lastly, Mr. Burquese, a Frenchman from Bonaparte's army, a very odd genius. Of such a compound does this fraternity consist. They are all young men, and have many wild schemes; but, upon the whole, they are very amiable, and desire to make my situation agreeable. I wish you could be here one week to see how I live.

"Papa has some money of mine in his hands. Tell him he is welcome to the use of it till next fall. I wish it was much more, that I might, in a measure, repay much that he has done for me. I owe you a trifle on your seal, which you can receive from papa."

He was now finally resolved to exchange the study of divinity for law. For the sacred profession he felt persuaded that he had no vocation, and to assume it merely

---

* Platt Brush, a prominent lawyer, and member of Congress from the Chilicothe district, Ohio. Young Quitman, when a tutor at Hartwick, had met with him in the mail-coach, and had been recommended by him to cast his lot in Ohio.

for a livelihood was to do a thing degrading to the calling and to himself. This conscientiousness and self-ex-
amination was a marked feature of his character through
life. On consulting his father he received the following
qualified assent:

From his Father.

"Rhinebeck, June 22d, 1819.
"The contents of your letter did not surprise me. I
had long anticipated them. You have arrived to years
of discretion, and ought to know what is for your own
good in the choice of your profession. I shall never
compel my children to enter upon any occupation against
their own inclination. I am no friend to the profession
which you prefer, because I am too independent to flatter, or to court popularity by improper means, with a
view to be raised by the people to position, which in re-
publics is too often the case. You have, however, my
consent and blessing to the step which you meditate to
take, under the full persuasion that you will never deviate
from the principles of rectitude and honor. I would, nevertheless, advise you to inform yourself perfectly respecting the character of the person who has promised to patronize you, before you enter into any engagements, and
to be circumspect in the formation of them."

Soon after he received the following:

From Hon. Platt Brush.

"In answer to yours, I will say, the services you can
render to my sons, who are numerous, though young, I
should consider almost a compensation for what your
circumstances require, and for the balance I will be responsible. You shall have your profession and board for
the consideration of teaching a few lads during the time
you are studying in my office."

On the 18th of August following he wrote his last letter from Mount Airy:

To his Brother.

"Mount Airy, August 18th, 1819.

"This is probably the last time I shall write you from this place. I have received a second letter from Mr. Brush. He wishes me to be in Chilicothe in October. Our term will end the last day of this month. I will pay you a long visit at Rhinebeck, and start West in search of fame and fortune. I anticipate much from my visit to you; 'tis a long time since I have been from home a whole year. The next time I leave, it will be for a longer time, perhaps forever!

"Your caution to me concerning going to Ohio I have reflected on. I generally look ' before I leap.' I think there is nothing more fatal to success than delay. Rather be a little rash sometimes, than suffer little circumstances to rule you entirely. 'Nothing venture, nothing gain,' is an old, and, I think, a very good saying."

The month of September he spent with the family at Rhinebeck. His parting with his venerable father was tender in the extreme. The stern old divine shed tears as freely as his boy, who, to the last hour of his life, and on the battle-fields of Mexico, preserved, as a sort of talisman, the written benediction of his father, given to him on that occasion, with a lock of his hair:

"*May the God of power and wisdom preserve thee, my son, sound in body and mind, and his benevolence and favor accompany you through a long series of future years.*"

- How literally and lavishly this prayer was vouchsafed, will be seen in the course of this memoir. "The prayers of the righteous availeth much."

Arriving in Philadelphia early in October, he wrote on the 19th

To his Brother.

"I have just bid farewell to Mount Airy. Mr. Constant has handed me a credential very flattering indeed. Exchanging my funds into U. S. bank-notes has caused

me a great deal of trouble. My Connecticut note, like
sundry other wares from that state, turned out a counter-
feit.   Yesterday I went to the Pittsburg stage-office, and
found I should have to pay 17 cts. per pound for all baggage over 14 lbs.; and, as my trunk alone weighs 120
lbs., I could not afford it. I went to the agent of a train
of transportation-wagons, and got a receipt for its de-
livery in Pittsburg in 16 days. This will give me time
to cross the mountains on foot—a mode of traveling I
do not shrink from, and which squares with the state of
my finances."

And thus, with his gun in hand and knapsack on his
back, he crossed the Alleghanies, and thenceforward
became identified with the *West*—the GREAT WEST!
There is magic in the name. "*We can not fortify the
Atlantic Ocean. The utmost we can do is to become
formidable to the westward.*"

This is one of the most striking sentiments ever uttered by an American statesman. It fell from the pro-
phetic lips of Patrick Henry, in the Convention of Virginia, assembled in 1778, to deliberate on the adoption
of the federal Constitution. It embraces, in a few words,
not only the creed of a great party, but the true solution
of our national progress. The influence of the sentiment may be traced in all the important movements of
our government. Washington conceived it during his
solitary expedition to the Ohio, when he planned the
union of its waters with the Atlantic. It has been practically carried out in every treaty made with the Indians.
Virginia and North Carolina had it in view when they
issued their military land-warrants at the close of the
Revolution, thus colonizing Kentucky, Tennessee, and
Ohio. The persevering negotiations of the federal authorities for the right to navigate the Mississippi, so long
claimed by Spain as an exclusive privilege, show that the
great maxim of Henry was never lost sight of. Mr. Jef-

ferson had it in view when, by a master-stroke of diplomacy, he wrested Louisiana from the miser gripe of Napoleon. The great expedition of Lewis and Clarke to the sources of the Missouri and the mouth of the Columbia was part and parcel of the same policy.

The pre-emption system of Andrew Jackson—a marked and distinctive feature of the Democratic party, and the most beneficent of its measures—was framed upon this injunction of the inspired orator to make ourselves "formidable to the westward." It is the only true principle of successful colonization, and is peculiar to our country. The immense land grants of Spain, the feudal concessions of France, and the proprietary charters of England, locked up whole territories, fostered monopolies, and were, in theory and practice, more or less defective. But the principle of subdividing the country into small tracts, and then conceding the first choice to the first occupant—not rendering him a beneficiary and dependent, but offering a just inducement for enterprise and labor—has achieved miracles in the progress of civilization and empire. Missouri, Indiana, Illinois, Michigan, the upper Territories, and the southwestern states owe their unparalleled strides to opulence and population more to this than to any other cause. The Democratic party early perceived its abstract justice and salutary operation, and steadily adhered to it, and now it has become the established policy of the nation. The pre-emption system, insignificant as the hut and clearing of the settler may seem, practically realizes the fable of Midas. It turns every thing into gold. It scatters roses over the wilderness. It invites the cross-road schoolmaster and the saddle-bags missionary. It has created mighty states in the dim and dusky West. It stocked them with men who were foremost in battle on the frozen wastes of Canada, and who afterward, in the same spirit, crossed the Sabine, and planted with their hands and baptized with their blood the star-gemmed banner of a maiden republic !

The graduation and reduction of the price of the public domain was the next great step to "make ourselves formidable to the westward." Millions of acres, at the old minimum, remained unsold. By the reduction every man gets an interest in the soil. The endearments of home cluster around the household, however humble, and our citizens are bound by an allegiance of the heart stronger than a thousand oaths.

Oregon, California, and the achievements of the war in Mexico, are illustrations on a grand scale of Patrick Henry's celebrated maxim, "*Make ourselves formidable to the westward.*" This is the great American motto. It should be stamped on our national coinage. Amid the strife and vicissitudes of party it should never be forgotten. Under its inspiration splendid cities have leaped up in the frowning wilderness. Great agricultural communities occupy the haunts of the nomadic tribes. States have been created more powerful than the world ever knew before, because they possess within themselves all the resources of subsistence and internal commerce, and are exempt from all possibility of invasion.

This vast empire of the West, stretching along the Ohio, the Missouri, and the Mississippi, is, in this point of view, an historical phenomenon. Its insulated position; its vast distance from the sea, yet direct communication therewith; its magnificent hydrography of lakes and rivers; and its teeming and warlike population, reduplicating every half century, guarantee it against attack; and year after year, epoch after epoch, this process of accumulation and development will go on, unchecked by those vicissitudes to which most other communities are exposed. War will probably never leave its red footprints on the banks of the Ohio or Missouri. Whence . could the invader come ? The most numerous army that any government in Europe could dispatch would perish under the mere weight of the physical power that might be concentrated against it.

The GREAT WEST is, indeed, the backbone of our Union. It is the citadel of our national strength. If the sea-board states be ever overrun and occupied by the conquering armies of the Old World, in this vast interior and unapproachable empire we shall have retreat and security. From the everlasting battlements of the Alleghanies and the Rocky Mountains we may defy their power, and send down living avalanches to expel them from our shores.

Make ourselves formidable to the westward ! The remarkable expeditions of Fremont, and subsequent official reconnoissances, opened new and inviting vistas into our glorious future. The vast region previously mapped down by geographers as a repulsive desert, has been ascertained to be, for the most part, adapted to agricultural purposes, and the finest pastoral region in the world. The impenetrable mountains and interminable wastes which, it was thought, interposed insurmountable barriers to our union with the Pacific, have dwindled away before the wand of scientific and adventurous exploration.

"Look to the westward," said the Demosthenes of Virginia. "Extend the area of freedom," said the dying Jackson. "Warn the committee of public safety to be on their guard," were the expiring words of Jefferson. The great statesman dreaded some attempt to curtail the system of self-government which we had put in operation. Upon these maxims we have extended and consolidated our national Union. Circumscribed com-

munities have expanded into states. We have created
an impregnable centre of power and supply to fall back
upon in great emergencies. We have secured an immense interior empire, where art and science may pursue their labors and human nature reach the highest
point of improvement. No insolent Goth shall tread
upon this soil, nor imperial conqueror enrich his capital
with our spoils. From this great laboratory will go
forth the torch-bearers in every department of human
learning and every avenue of useful industry. From
this point, too, will be commissioned the missionaries of
freedom to preach the lessons of free government to the
downtrodden and oppressed. Here LIBERTY shall find
its permanent home. The GREAT WEST will be its perpetual resting-place. It may be extinguished in the
North by an insane fanaticism; it may perish in the
South from apathy and neglect in the enforcement of
great constitutional rights; but in the mighty valley
of the Mississippi, under God's blessing, it will live forever!

CHAPTER III.

Keel-boating on the Ohio.—Arrival at Chilicothe.—Family Letters.—Dr. Hosack of New York, or Young Physic and Old Physic.
—Removes to the Village of Delaware.—Ohio forty Years since.
—Admitted to the Bar.—Letter from Mrs. Griffith.—Departs for
the South.

OF the young adventurer's voyage down the Ohio
there remains an imperfect diary, from which the following is taken:

Extract from Diary.

"Nov. 2d, 1819. Reached Pittsburg at night, none
the worse for my journey; enjoyed myself on the road,
and had some pleasant flirtations with the girls; found
my baggage, or, as they say here, "plunder," all right;
river very low.

"4th. Mr. Whiting (a young New Englander, on a
trading tour, who crossed the mountains with me) engaged a passage for us on a keel-boat; we furnish our
own kit, and do our own cooking.

"5th. Got off at 3 P.M. Passengers—the wife* and
daughter of Judge Griffith, of Burlington, N. J.; Mr.
Postlethewaite and daughter, of Lexington; Dr. Young,
Whiting, and myself, and some 30 in the steerage. The
accommodations were very rough, but the ladies made it
agreeable. Miss G. played on the flageolet, I on the
flute. I felt like poor Goldsmith when, wandering over
Europe, he fluted for his supper. Our fowling-pieces

* This lady was the granddaughter of Elias Boudinot, LL.D., first
Superintendent of the United States Mint, and President of Princeton
College. Her husband was an eminent lawyer of New Jersey, and
afterward Clerk of the Supreme Court of the United States. This
casual meeting with Mrs. G. on a keel-boat, it will be seen, was the
pivot on which the young adventurer's fortunes turned.

supplied us with game; biscuit and jerked venison were our stand-bys. Whiting and I messed together; a couple of blankets furnished us a bed. At Wheeling, Mrs. and Miss Griffith, charmed with our mess-table, became our boarders. We laid in some tea and loaf-sugar for them, and, to provide more game, we purchased a small canoe, here called a 'dug-out,' or 'man-drowner.'

"16th. Lay by at Point Pleasant, where Whiting and I visited a Virginia 'break-down.' Saw for the first time what are termed 'steam-boats,' 'snapping-turtles,' and 'half-horse half-alligators'—a formidable set of fellows, truly!

"18th. Made fast at night to the Kentucky shore. Nine cheers went up for 'Old Kaintuck,' and Whiting and I had to treat to 'red-eye,' or 'rot-gut,' as whisky is here called. They had made us do the same thing when we first tied to the Virginia shore.

"On the 19th we landed at Portsmouth, Ohio, the nearest port to my place of destination. The captain, in compliment to me, lay there all the afternoon. The cabin passengers determined to spend the evening together at a hotel. We had a pleasant supper, and took a kind leave of each other. That night, when I saw the keel swing off, and looked around in vain for a familiar face, I indeed felt alone in the world. Next day, when preparing to set out afoot for Chilicothe, I fell in with a man who wished to send a horse there. Showing him my 'papers,' he intrusted him to me; and I set out with a light heart, cheered by this piece of good luck. It saved me a long tramp. Deer were so numerous on the way, I shot one with my pistol near Piketown, and with it paid for my lodging and entertainment. On the 22d, at 4 P.M., I dismounted at an inn in Chilicothe, and sung out to the astonished hostler, 'Hic labor extremis, hic meta longarum viarum.' Col. Brush gave me a cordial welcome. Our agreement is that I am to board in his family—fuel, washing, and lights—and have instruction in his office, for which I am to teach him Spanish and his sons the classics.

"30th. I have joined a society, composed chiefly of young lawyers (here called 'Gougers'), of which Edward King, son of the great Rufus, of New York, is president."

This diary was sent to his brother William, a young physician, recently settled in New York. His reply, rather tart upon the celebrated Dr. Hosack, will be read with interest:

From his Brother.

"I parted from you on the Battery, dear John, with sad forebodings for myself, but none for you. You will succeed. Your energy of character warrants your success. Want of energy is my infirmity.* In every part of your journey, save the tour on foot, I should like to have been your *compagnon du voyage*. I could stand your flirtations, the lazy sweep of your boat, and even your concerts. I could fight your snapping-turtles, shoot turkeys, eat your grub, and share your blanket, but I can't walk. I am glad you are at your profession. Although the business of a mere scrivener must be irksome to a man of busy intellect, the study of the principles of jurisprudence is exceedingly interesting, and comprehends all that is sublime in philosophy and ethics. I have read with profound interest the works of Grotius, Puffendorf, and Vattel, Erasmus and Machiavelli, but statutes and reports drove me from the profession. The realities of life, however, require us often to tread an arid track. You may be called from your sage meditations on the social compact to write a deed transferring a dirty acre from Dick to Tom, while I may be summoned from the most intricate investigations of nature by the belly-ache of an infant or the hysterics of an old lady. On these things depend our subsistence, and scholars and sages would get along poorly without them. I am doing quite well for a new-comer. At a late meeting of the faculty, I was appointed secretary and committee-man, notwithstanding the inveterate opposition of my old boss, Dr. Hosack, who vainly exerted his influence to defeat my election to the Medical Society of the city. He at first

* Too true. This young man, the most brilliant and fascinating of his family, gradually sunk into indolence, gave way to the hereditary gloom, and died prematurely; while his brother John, with an intellect substantial but not showy, owed his success mainly to untiring effort and systematic industry. "Perseverance" was his motto through life.

wished me to come into all his views as to the college.
Feeling no inclinations to be one of his subalterns to become his pet, I bolted. He treated me with neglect; I
avenged myself by ridiculing his theory of yellow fever.
He aimed several shots at me in his lectures; I retorted
in essays before the Medico-chirurgical Society. He
warned his pupils against a certain young physician, who,
from ignorance and self-sufficiency, disputed the established dogmas; I warned them against a distinguished
F. R. S. whose classic lore was derived from the transla-
tions of his students, whose literary honors had been purchased with money, and whose popularity and influence
might be traced to a superb table and a well-filled cellar.
At 9 A.M. he lectured on the indespensability of nosolog-
ical arrangement in the practice of medicine; at 9 P.M.
I proclaimed to the society that nosology was nonsense,
and put me in mind of the burlesque examination in Mo-
lière's Malade Imaginaire. So the squabbles of the pill-
boxes at present stand."

In reply, he writes from Chilicothe, March 29, 1820:

To his Brother.

"Had I not been too much interested in the success
of one of the champions, I would have been amused by
your relation of the tournament of the pill-boxes. Permit me to send you a *caveat*, as we lawyers term it.
Your entering into a contest with a man so powerful is
like provoking the great beast of the ancient Sophists.
You rouse him to your certain destruction. You will,
perhaps, laugh at my nice calculations, or suspect me of
having turned Democrat; but a diffidence in my own
abilities, a conscious want of talents, have given me a
kind of cold prudence which I did not possess by nature
more than yourself. A letter received from brother
Henry mentions, with much satisfaction, the news the
family receive of you. May your endeavors be crowned
with success. Had I your gifts I would engage that, in
two years, you would have a governor for your brother,
and, most probably, in twenty years a supreme judge or
a president.

"I was made free as Cæsar; so were you. Thanks to

the patriots of the Revolution, they have left us the fee simple of liberty, an incorporeal hereditament only, but one I would not exchange for a silver mine, for it leaves our opinion free, and our ambition uncontrolled. In a former letter I referred to my situation here, but perhaps it will be gratifying to you to hear something more. Virgil says that 'Fame stalks on the earth, and rears its head among the clouds.' I do not believe the monster is so bulky as he represents, or that such is its method of conveying rumor. In my opinion, it travels in the leather sack that holds the mail. At all events, I have no reason to think that *my* fame will reach you unless I transmit it myself. I rise early, and go to bed late. The greater part of my time is spent in close application to law-books. Sometimes I indulge in a walk before sunrise on the banks of the Sciota, and think of the friends I have left on the Hudson, and the *many* girls I have loved. Sometimes with my gun I ramble through the primitive forest that flanks the town on the northwest. I visit the ancient tumuli that, abound here, and, 'fancy free,' meditate on the mysterious past. Occasionally—not as often as I wish, and as a luxury almost too great for a poor student —I spend an evening with the belles of Chilicothe. They are social and agreeable. Thus, as it respects myself, I am free from care; and, could I but know that my brothers were all in some good business, I think I should be content with the fate Providence has awarded me. I have made several attempts to get a situation for Henry, but so far have failed.

"When I compare myself with some others here, I think I can become a good lawyer, at least, if not an advocate. Should I fail, I will find something else to do. Nature has endowed me with some physical force, to supply the deficiency of mental power. I think I would make a good soldier, or a fur trader in the Rocky Mountains. What think you? If I can not trap *clients*, I know, from experience, that I have a genius for trapping *musk-rats*. Besides, they consider me here a crack shot with a rifle. But enough of my qualifications, or I fear you will fancy I have wrested the trump from the hand of Fame to sound my own praise."

To his Brother.

"Chillicothe, May 1st, 1820..

"For two weeks I have been in attendance at the
Court of Common Pleas of this county, and, with open
eyes and ears, have drawn a good deal of information
from the bench and bar; besides, Mr. Brush gives me
the credit of having suggested some very pertinent hints
to him in conducting his cases. I must mention one indictment made by the grand jury. John Armstrong,
blacksmith, and Warren Johnson, Indian doctor, were in-
dicted for maliciously, feloniously, and unlawfully making
an assault and battery on Platt Brush and John A. Quitman at the corner of Main Street and Bank Alley. They
plead guilty, and were fined accordingly. I was subpe-
naed as a witness in behalf of the state. I stated the fact
to the court that, from our office window, I had seen
those two men fall on Mr. Brush. I ran to his assistance,
and they both turned upon me. After an affray of some
ten minutes they cried, lustily, 'Enough! enough!' I
got, however, a black eye in the conflict. I was sorry
that the prosecuting attorney noticed the affair at all, and
that the poor fellows should be fined after having been
soundly thrashed. They are very strict here as to offenses against the state, and, indeed, it is necessary to
keep the savages in order. A lawyer's vocation in Ohio
is very laborious. He is obliged to attend the various
courts in five or six counties, on a circuit of some 250
miles. The accommodations are exceedingly rough; the
inns are often mere shanties, crowded and filthy; the fare
coarse; two, and even three, lodging in a bed infested
with vermin. By the way, no one seems to notice these
pests. They seem to be thoroughly domesticated, and
regarded in the light of friends and fellow-citizens. The
court-houses on circuit often have no fire-places or stoves,
and the farmers have a strange habit of leaving their
dwellings unfinished. For years they will live in a house
with only half a chimney, and with no shutters to doors
or windows, a bit of blanket being stuck up to exclude
the wind.

"I have a notion of going to Natchez after I shall
have finished my studies, unless I meet with good luck
here, such as a partnership with my boss or some other

respectable lawyer. A young man who enters on the great theatre of life with no more means than his head and hands supply, with no recommendation but an honest heart and good principles, must expect to meet with many obstacles in working out his career. The despondency he feels in leaving, far away, the chosen few whom he loves is but the beginning of sorrow and care. It requires all the energy of the soul, and constant, active employment to sustain his spirits, particularly if he meets, as often he will, with neglect, disappointment, and ingratitude. Although I have been specially favored, have met with encouragement, and been received with a welcome into the most respectable society wherever I have lived, still I often wonder at the wild ambition that induced me to wander so far from home—to prefer honor to happiness, and trouble to ease and obscurity.

"I am glad to hear you are all well and happy, but I wish you were, somehow or other, comfortably settled. I have applied several times at the public offices here to find a vacant clerkship or so, but there are none. I will keep a bright look-out for you all. To have even one of you settled near me, would add much to my happiness.

"You remember the seal I purchased of you for $6. I have just sold it and the key for $13, and an elegant pair of gloves thrown in. I have exchanged my pistols for Cruise's Digest, a set of invaluable books.

"Wheat brings here only 37½ cents per bushel, corn 20 to 25 cents, and other produce cheap in proportion. In the villages board and lodging may be had at $1 to $1 50 per week."

From his Father.

"May 20th, 1820.

"Thank you, dear John, for your kind inquiries. Thanks to God, I now feel a little stronger, and look forward hopefully to warm weather. I am growing old, and my time will probably not be long. Sixty-three years has been the common climax of the life of my ancestors. I am ready whenever it pleases Providence. There has been and is great political excitement here. Last Wednesday there was a great festival, music and cannon, in honor of Clinton's election. The same is to be repeated on Saturday at the Flats. What fools are

men to suffer themselves to be ridden by priests and gulled by demagogues! A very evil demon appears to prevail at present every where among the deluded inhabitants of this world."

To his brother William.

"Chilicothe, June 24th, 1820.

"Yesterday, on my return from a grand wolf and deer
hunt, I received your long-expected letter. My anxiety
to hear from you had been increased by letters from
home complaining of your silence. Your illness, and desire not to give uneasiness to any of us, now accounts for
the negligence of which I had accused you. It appears
to me, dear brother, that, for so young a man, you have
received your share of the blows of adversity, and yet
you can not blame Fortune. Genius smiled on your
birth, and Education assisted your expanding faculties.
True, neither of these can shield us from sickness, but,
prudently managed, they will keep poverty and care at
arm's length. I know you are not so womanish as to require the sympathy of others, yet I shall ever share in
your joys and sorrows. I approve much of your desire
to get a surgeon's place in the navy. My friend, Col.
Brush, has influence at Washington, and is intimate with
the secretary. He has promised to write immediately,
and I will see that he does it. You must not, however,
in the least, abate your exertions in rallying influence
from every quarter. That of Col. Brush, as he only
knows you through the partiality of a brother, will, of
course, be defective, and must not be your dependence.
Write at once, personally, to the secretary, and transmit
all the recommendations you can get. In such a case,
the letter of Col. Brush, coming from this distant and
unexpected quarter, will be like a flank attack, and be
sensibly felt. Dispatch your part of the business quick-
ly, for Col. Brush's letter will be on the way by the 27th.
A brother of Col. B. has received the appointment of
U. S. register for the sale of public lands at Delaware,
seventy miles north of this—a new district, extending
up to Lake Erie. He offers me a clerkship, and ample
time to continue my professional reading. I will go. I
must get away from the fascinating charms of female so-

ciety. My natural inclinations waft me too near the rocks of the sirens. A student must separate himself from the world, hard as the task may be."

To his Sister.

"Chilicothe, June 26th, 1820.

"I am not, my dear sister, so deeply engaged in study, nor so much absorbed with my amusements, as to neglect for a moment your affectionate letter. I know well enough that you and Eliza constantly think of me, yet it is flattering to one's self-love to have actual assurances, when we feel that they are sincere. This is specially the case when we are among strangers, far from the family hearth, and not in such circumstances as secure the attention of a selfish world, which seldom bestows favors unless there be a prospect of some return. It would, however, be ingratitude to Providence in me to complain in this respect. Wherever I have sojourned I have found warm friends, and, without the aid of talents or fortune, have made my way in society. In Cooperstown I might ascribe this to my father's name; in Philadelphia to family friends; but in Ohio I have beaten my own path. I started from home with but one hundred dollars. I traveled one thousand miles, sometimes on foot, but as a gentleman. I dress as well as any young man in town. I have attended the balls and parties; I have not gambled. I owe no man a cent, and I have fifty dollars in my pocket; and, what is better, some prospect of adding a little to it. I shall leave Chilicothe on the 15th of next month, and during the interval will seek the enjoyment of society here. The fashionable circle consists of about twenty families. As much etiquette prevails as I observed in Philadelphia, and the same hours for calls and receptions. The ladies are gay, dressy, sociable, and well-informed. There is quite a circle of distinguished gentlemen, with whom Mr. Ashe, the Englishman, in his recent book of travels, says he dined; but they all agree that they never knew Mr. Ashe.

"Speaking of facetious travelers, I must not omit to say that the famous Capt. Riley, of Arab captivity and shipwrecked celebrity, resides here, and continues to relate some wonderful exploits.

Vol. I.—C

"I have transmitted letters to William to promote his views. Col. Brush has written warmly to the secretary of the navy. To see my brothers well settled, my sisters happy, would remove every care from my heart. As for myself, I have no apprehensions. I can get along without any assistance but the smile of Heaven, and that I will try to deserve. My sanguine fancy anticipates the time when I shall have the happiness of affording an asylum to those of my beloved family who may require it. If Fortune rewards those who deserve her favors, this will never be necessary.

"Delaware, where my new residence is to be, is a very small village, but in a few years, such is the progress of population here, the land-office will probably be removed to Sandusky, on Lake Erie, and then, if the grand canal be completed, I can often drop in to see you. Tell Henry I will try and get him a situation in this country. *Ask him how he would like a captain's commission in the patriot army of Texas.* Tell Walter to push on with his Latin and Greek, and be prepared in two years to enter my office.

"Excuse this hurried letter. I am fatigued, having been diving all day in the river to recover the body of a poor boy who was drowned yesterday."

To his Brother.

"Delaware, Ohio, August 16th, 1820.

"I fear you only think of me, dear brother, on a rainy day, when there is no business, no amusement, no company to occupy your mind. It is not thus with me. In the mild summer evenings, when all nature is tranquil, in my solitary walks I love to think of home and its endearments. Every clear day, every fine prospect, every glimpse of comfort reminds me of them. My feelings are not akin to home-sickness. That boyish disease has ceased to affect me. I came here from choice to better my situation, and from choice I remain here. My theory of life is, let every man follow up good fortune, whether it leads him to the thronged city or the lonely wilderness. Happiness and friends may be found every where. I acknowledge the force of your arguments against a frequent change of residence, yet these changes often

.become necessary. I was much attached to Chilicothe, and had reason to be so. The attention and hospitality I there received, and the friendships contracted, were more than I had a right to expect from my humble circumstances and pretensions, and had I been admitted to the bar I should have remained there. As it is, however, perhaps it is better for me.

"This village is on the very edge of white population, in the district purchased from the Indians a few years since. This purchase embraces about eight thousand square miles. It has been divided into two land-districts, of one of which (the eastern) Mr. Brush is register. It extends fifty miles on the base line, and thus up to Michigan and Lake Erie, including Sandusky River and a great part of the Miami of the Lakes. This vast tract will be offered for sale, in eighty-acre tracts, to the highest bidder, and, if not sold, may be entered at $1 25 per acre. The lands are of the finest quality, the greater part of them plains, with here and there copses of trees in them, like islands in the ocean. Corn, wheat, and grass attain a luxuriance almost fabulous to relate. These noble plains often sweep beyond the range of the eye; here a long tongue or peninsula of timber projecting into them in graceful curves, there clumps of trees clustered together or standing at graceful intervals, without underwood, as though planted and nurtured by the hand of art. The timber consists chiefly of oak, hickory, and black walnut. If your present prospects are not satisfactory, and you like a farmer's life, try and get $400, and buy 320 acres on Sandusky River. You can make a fortune by raising stock and corn. If you can get no money, I have another scheme. The sixteenth section in every township is set apart for schools. It may be leased for thirty-three years, at seven per cent. upon the valuation of the improved land. After the expiration of this term, the lessee may take two more leases on the same terms, and then sell improvements for their apprized value."

To Frederick R. Backus.

"Delaware, September 18th, 1820.
"I will stake every thing on the rapid progress of this region. Fort Croghan is the place from which the scin-

tillations of my genius shall, at some future day, dazzle the aborigines of Ohio. Your moneyed men in Philadelphia would make the best speculation in the world by purchasing lands here. This village has now about fifty well-built houses. In the vicinity is a mineral spring (called a "lick"), where, not many years ago, thousands of buffaloes resorted. The woods now abound with deer, wolves, and turkeys, the streams with geese and ducks.

"I am not yet licensed, but I have made several speeches in court in criminal cases, and gained some reputation. They think me a clever fellow and a *good Republican*, because I turn out to musters and wear a straw hat cocked up behind! I write a little, too, for the Delaware Gazette. Thus my time passes. Though remote from my relatives, I am not unfriended by the world. 'Tis true, I taste not the delights of society or the exquisite pleasures of love, yet I hope I do not live in vain. With good luck, the time will come when I shall reap the reward of my labor. I left Chilicothe with great regret, nor did I know my attachment for it until I was about to leave it. The hospitality and kindness I received there will ever be gratefully remembered."

"Delaware, November 12th, 1820.

"DEAR FATHER,—While the snow-storm is howling without, and nobody within the office to disturb my reflections, I think that an hour can not be better appropriated than in writing to you. I would have done it sooner, I would do it oftener, if I did not know that you regularly hear from me through my letters to the family. Do not think it is negligence, decay of affection, or indolence that influences me. I have feared that you would suppose my incessant engagements in the land-office, the study of law, the novelty of my associations, or speculations on the sources of wealth, had blunted the home feelings of my nature. Conscious of an unabated, nay, growing affection for you all, I desire, nevertheless, not to appear an unobservant traveler on the road of life. At this distance, and in a new country, I wish my letters to contain something more than reiterated assurances of esteem and love.

"Brother Albert, I perceive, is still disposed to try his fortune at sea. If he has fixed his mind upon it and sees no better prospects, I would second his wishes as soon as possible. He has studied no profession, and is therefore right in choosing some occupation in which he may gain an honest livelihood. He should remember, however, that the only path to promotion in that pursuit is the knowledge of mathematics, navigation, and geography. Your influence, and the many favors you have rendered to men now flourishing in the world, should enable you to procure situations for both Henry and Albert. Are you repaid with the proverbial ingratitude of prosperity?

"Col. Brush tells me that, of the many men whom his father assisted in better days, but one has ever befriended him. With the exception of this gentleman, my fortune has been the same. From strangers to me and to my family, I have received the most attention. I trust, however, this will never be used as an argument on which to predicate doctrines opposed to benevolence. I am grateful for the interest Mr. Wackerhagen takes in my welfare.* I know not whether to say I feel most gratitude for his solicitude at the present day, or for the care and attention he bestowed on my early years. I know not a man in the world whom I esteem more, and I am happy that the old age of my father is blessed with the society of such a friend.

"The climate of this country is very unsteady. Two days ago we had warm smoky weather; now the ground is covered with snow. We are in the latitude of the city of New York. Owing, I suppose, to the excessive drought, the lowness of the waters, and the tranquillity of the atmosphere, the autumn has been very unhealthy. A low, nervous, or typhoid fever, prevailed all over the West, frequently fatal. I have lost three of the first friends I made in Ohio, all young men in the bloom of life. One died in New Orleans, one in this place, and one, Mr. Grier, a young lawyer, at Kingston, in your vicinity, several months after he left Chilicothe.

---

* His first instructor, with whom he resided some years at Schoharie.

"When I consider, however, how the majority of the working classes here live, I do not wonder at their sickness. A Dutchess County farmer would consider it certain death to spend twenty-four hours as they do whole years here. With prudence and temperance, I consider this climate as healthy as any.

"I have now been in this state a year. Twelve months more of hard study, and I will be prepared for admission to the bar. What measure of success I may have, I know not. The pressure of the times, and the scarcity of money, will not permit me to flatter myself with brilliant prospects. Yet I trust I have a sufficient store of energy and perseverance to overcome all difficulties. I will spare no pains to perfect myself in my profession, and to deserve the confidence of my clients, and leave the rest to Providence."

"Delaware, Dec. 10th, 1820.

"MY DEAR BROTHER,—Your last letter did indeed surprise me. Poor Albert is really, at this moment, plowing the southern seas. May Heaven smile upon him! May "the angel that sits up aloft" guard the life of "poor Jack!" Most heartily do I pray with you, that "he may return a good sailor and a prosperous man." In every letter that I received from him, I could see his desire daily increase to tempt the boisterous billows. I am pleased that he has found so good an opportunity to test this darling inclination. I know not how it is, now more than ever affection for the beloved playmate of my childhood glows in my heart, and brings apprehension and shadows along with it. Many past scenes revive in my memory. I fancy that I see the little fellow trotting behind us, when we went gunning, with a game-bag upon his shoulder, or, at my side, going to look at the musk-rat traps in the morning, or tugging at the oar in Otsego Lake, until the big drops rolled down his cheeks. When you sailed for the West Indies, my feelings were somewhat the same, yet I had greater confidence in your experience. You had tried the world before, and learned to take care of yourself. Besides, you were going among friends, whose sympathy and assistance would cheer and comfort you. I doubt not, however, that Ap's conduct and noble disposition will soon make all his comrades his friends. When I consider, too, that we must all, sooner or later, act for ourselves in the world, I am well satisfied with this enterprise of his. Like myself, he has little to lose, and every thing to gain. Providence has thought fit to leave the making of our fortunes to ourselves. It is, therefore, necessary that we should make some *bold push*, and, if we are disappointed, whistle it off and try it again. A few years ago, one roof sheltered all our family; now we are scattered as though the winds had done it.

"Give me all the news you get of the vessel in which our brother Albert sailed. Ship news never penetrates this deep interior.

"I am very busy here. Mr. Brush is mostly absent on circuit; the duties of the land-office fall upon me, and my studies consume all my leisure. I have just returned from a trip to Portland on Sandusky Bay, 100 miles from this place. I have now traversed the whole length of the state from north to south, and for the quality of the soil, the size of the timber, the luxuriance of vegetation, in short, for every feature that constitutes a rich farming country, it is not to be surpassed. As I rode over the undulating plains, the islands of timber, the trooping deer, the prairie-fowl, the wild flowers that gemmed the path, the serene and cloudless sky, made an enchanting scene. The trees stood so artistically—here and there the curling smoke of the Indian hunter wreathing around their heads—that I almost looked for the mansion they were-destined to adorn. All these are United States' lands. The method of purchasing, or entering them, is thus: they are surveyed and offered for sale by proclamation of the President to the highest bidder. If not sold, the applicant comes to the office, examines the map of survey on which all the lands are numbered, makes his selection, pays $1 25 per acre to the receiver, and gets two receipts—one of these he delivers to us (the register), the other he keeps. These receipts are recorded, and at the end of every month we transmit them to the General Land-office at Washington, and receive, in due time, patents, signed by the President, to be delivered to the purchaser.

"You ask what farmers here do with their produce. In this part of the state, as yet, there is no regular market. Grain is usually converted into flour, whisky, or stock, and sent to New Orleans, Detroit, or Canada. The current price of pork is $2 50 per cwt.; wheat 40 cents per bushel; corn 25 cents: but they will not command cash even at these prices. A farmer here can raise twenty hogs with no more cost than a Dutchess County farmer incurs for one. In this section, and in these times, agriculture is not a short road to wealth; but if it can any where make a man independent, it will in this district. After the grand New York Canal shall be opened, the produce of this section will seek that market, and the rise of property will be rapid. If a man has plenty of money, he can not do better than by investing it in lands here and waiting for their appreciation; and the small farmers of your state would do well to sell out and remove hither. If one goes in for comfort altogether this is not the country to find it. This is not the place for a wealthy man to enjoy life; it is too democratic.

"I rather hope, dear brother, you may be able to get some good situation near home. We should not all desert papa in his old age.

"I have just received a ticket to a New Year's ball. This reminds me of the day. May you all spend it happily, and I will drink a glass 'to him that's on the sea.'"

To his Brother.

"Delaware, February 23d, 1821.

"Rhinebeck, you tell me, dear brother, is the same quiet place as formerly. Its tranquil shades suit the serenity of age, and I trust our father's years may be peaceful and undisturbed. I trust you have all learned to seek for happiness where alone it is to be found—in your own bosoms. Those who depend upon extraneous circumstances, the charms of society, the resources of opulence, or the state of the weather, are liable to be disappointed by the occurrences of each succeeding day. It is a source of great sorrow to me that William has so wholly given up to the indulgence of an idle disposition. Do your best to rouse him from it. Tell him that, if he would yet exert his energies and be a man, he may gain all that he has lost. I can not conceive how his sober reflection can countenance his present torpor. For my part, I would 'rather be a dog and bay the moon'—even a drayman's hack—than be a sluggard. If I had his talents I would accomplish every thing worthy of human effort. Far inferior to him, I mean to accomplish much by honest perseverance. We can not yet expect to have news of Albert. Every morning when I awake my eyes turn involuntarily to a map of the world that hangs near my bed, and I wonder on what sea he is now trying his adventurous fortunes. Shut up as I am in an interior country, I can not but envy him bounding over the free and ever-rolling waters; and then, like Rasselas, I feel that I am indeed a prisoner.

"I am not, as you suppose, even at this distance, a stranger to your New York politics. We take the American, the most violent of the Bucktail papers. I perceive that your ambitious colts about Rhinebeck, such as Livingston and Shufeldt, who are aiming at popularity, are Bucktails. Pray, what are you? I am, I fear, a decided Swiss.

"Our winter has not been severe, though the thermometer was as low as 18° below 0. Spring has now set in. Great quantities of maple-sugar are made in this section. Sugar, wax, honey, tallow, hides, furs, and linen, are the only domestic articles our merchants will take for goods. Money is very scarce among all classes, and it would be still scarcer if the cunning Yankees among us did not contrive to clutch the greater part of the annual stipend that the Wyandots and Senecas draw from government. Ohio is not all Yankee, but those that are here are the shrewdest of all the race, and could return to Connecticut and make fortunes by skinning whetstones. If I can not say of them *nullum tetigit quod non ornavit,* I can say that every thing they touch turns into gold. The farther they travel, the shrewder they become. Some of them are so sharp their very countenances seem to be whittled and ground down to the point of a needle. Others study an obtuse look and a stupid manner; but look close, and you will detect the proverbial keenness lurking about the mouth, and twink-

C 2

ling slyly and mischievously in the eyes. Their perseverance under difficulties, their dogged resolution, their
versatility, their confidence in themselves and in the
"universal Yankee nation," atone for a multitude of
minor sins. You ask, Yankee-like, whether a speculation
could not be made in furs? I don't think it would pay to
turn trapper or trader in skins. I have never known a
hunter to become rich. As for trading, the Indians have
become so accustomed to high prices, they do not know
how to fall with the times.

"This is not so insignificant a village as you fancy it
is. We have a singing-school, a boxing and fencing
school, a debating society, and a masonic lodge, and parties very often. Most of our citizens have been in the
army, and know something of the world. The land-office brings people here from every quarter and of every
grade. The Normans used to be called the land robbers
of Europe, but in this country all classes share the passion for land. I keep close in my office, and seldom in-
terfere in public concerns, unless specially called on. I
have found this to be the best method of acquiring and
retaining popularity, at least for a fellow of moderate
abilities; he should, like the great Mogul of Tartary,
show himself but seldom, and then look very wise and
solemn!

"I can not help noticing a blunder our wise Legislature made last winter. They are in the habit of enacting and changing laws every session, designating the
time of holding courts, etc. On the 2d instant, the day
before their adjournment, they passed a law *repealing*
all other statutes on the subject, and enacting that the
present law shall take effect and be in force *from* and
after the first day of February *next*. It is contended
that, under this law, no courts can be held this year. It
has been referred to the Supreme Court. If it grants
no relief, the Legislature must be convened, or we lawyers must starve. You ask when I think of making a
visit home? Not, I assure, till I am admitted to the
bar, and probably not for a long time thereafter. Independence and fame first, and then home."

To F. R. Backus.

"Delaware, Feb. 28th, 1821.

"I have been very fortunate, dear Backus, since I came to Ohio, and have even been more prosperous than I merit. I am now nearly through with my legal studies, and must search around for a location. My eyes are turned toward the setting sun. I have an opportunity, by staying here, of a partnership with Mr. Brush; but, if I adopt this plan, a decent support and a career of mediocrity are all I can expect. In this section it is easy to make any kind of property but money. There is scarcely money enough among our farmers to give their babies to cut their first teeth with. Every thing they buy is paid for with produce; consequently, it is no place for lawyers or mechanics. It is so all over Ohio, owing to the pressure of the times and to the relief laws, making it impossible to collect debts. I think, therefore, of Alabama or Mississippi. Money is there more plenty; trade is brisk; their cotton commands cash. The bar is not overcrowded with well-read lawyers, and fees are high. It is bad policy for a young man to move about, but much depends on the location we make when we first set out in life.

" You dazzle me with your account of the holidays in Philadelphia. Ours were more primitive, but we had our ball and our kissing-parties. It is now twelve at night. *You* are perhaps just returning from your stewed terrapins, your chicken salad, your confectionery and ices; on *my* table stands a small pyramid of maple-sugar, our only luxury, a present from one of our neighboring belles. Your dressy dolls of Chestnut Street are washing off their rouge, to wake up pale and nervous in the morning, while my Ohio belle sleeps with her roses, and rises with them, blooming and fragrant, on her cheeks.

" Pray tell your lazy city astronomers that I discovered a comet last night. Let them brush up their cobwebbed telescopes and look due west about 7 o'clock P.M., 14 degrees above the horizon."

To his Father.

"Delaware, May 7th, 1821.

"I hope, my dear father, that, with the return of spring,

you have recovered full health and vigor. I know that the winter, particularly the last, must be disagreeable and dreary to one who has spent the most happy seasons of his life in a climate where eternal spring prevails; yet the return of our glorious summer compensates for the inclemencies we have endured. In winter, too, mental trials and depression of spirits are apt to annoy us more, and, in spite of philosophy or religion, we too often despond. All this is dissipated by the bloom of the year.

"I am pained to hear that William continues to idle away his time. If he would rouse himself at once, he might yet recover the past. Do urge him to remove at once to Mississippi or Alabama. I will vouch for his success, not only in acquiring position, but, by industry and prudence, a large fortune. From the papers I perceive that our whalers in the South Seas have met with unparalleled success. This argues favorably for dear Albert.

"I have now been in Ohio eighteen months, have nearly completed my studies, and have formed a very extensive acquaintance. When I first came to this place, the prospects for business appeared so flattering that I extended my views no farther, and expected to remain here. Since then I have had ample opportunities of learning more. This is a flourishing part of the state, rapidly increasing in population, but the people are poor, and money, the life of a professional man, is very scarce. The little that there is is drained off by the merchants and the land-office. In fifteen or twenty years, I doubt not, ease and plenty will be found here, but the prospect is too remote and slow for me. I have determined, therefore, to look elsewhere for an abode, being sensible of the great advantage to a young man to make a good choice first, and then settle down permanently. I think I might in time expect here the honors which are in the gift of the people, but they are not profitable; indeed, they are injurious to a poor man who seeks eminence in his profession. The Southern States hold out golden prospects to men of integrity, application, and good acquirements. Money is there as plenty as it is scarce here, and a good reason for it; for while not a single article of our produce will command cash, their cotton, sugar, tobacco, and rice are always in demand, and the world will not do without them. They have, besides, facilities for transportation and avenues to market at all seasons of the year; and as to the climate, balancing all things, it is quite as healthy as this. My design is to remain here until I am admitted to the bar, and then go to Natchez or to St. Stephen's. I even think a warmer climate will lengthen my life. The consumption here destroys more than all the various diseases at the South. Dissipation there is the great source of mortality. The only thing that chills my expectations is the want of a little money to convey me there and set me up. I could do sufficient business here to earn it, but my fees would be paid in corn, or wheat, or pork, or land, and none of these can be converted into cash. The move, however, will not cost much. With the little I have, I must try and borrow a little more, and rely on that good fortune which has accompanied me ever since I left your roof. I have full confidence in making enough after I once take a start. At all events I will try."

To his Brother.

"Delaware, June 10th, 1821.

"You complain, dear brother, of the brevity of my letters. I believe the study of the law makes one's mind logical, but not inventive; it is therefore necessary that I should have facts to reason upon, or I am at a loss what to write about. I have determined to go South, where, at least, more than a fourth part of the year may be enjoyed. The wintry rigor here is intolerable to me. I agree with you that, in general, it is best for a young man of no fortune, when he starts out in the world, to circumscribe his views, and not suffer himself to fall into a wandering, restless habit. It is, therefore, the more necessary that he should weigh every thing well before he makes his choice. Afterward he should allow no trifling disappointments, mortifications, or even deprivations, to affect him, but persevere and hang on, come weal or woe. I mean to live by the practice of law, not by clerking in a land-office. After considering well, I think prudence and good sense recommend my going

South. As you request it, I will enlarge upon the subject; and then give your opinion. I will not commence
by dividing my subject, as Stephen Burrows did his ser-
mon, into seven heads and ten horns; but, by way of
preamble, will recall to your mind my floating down the
Ohio on a keel-boat, in company with the wife and
daughter of Judge Griffith, of New Jersey, who were on
their way to Natchez, to visit her sons, both eminent
lawyers. Mrs. Griffith, who is a lady of great accomplish-
ments and good sense, advised me to select Mississippi
instead of Ohio, spoke of the success of her sons, and
promised me their friendly encouragement. A short
time before her return to New Jersey, in April last, she
honored me with a letter, from which I now quote:

"'You express something like an intention of removing to this country. I am able to give you the information you desire, but I can not incur the responsibility of
advising you one way or the other. The advantages and
disadvantages of a residence in this country are so equally balanced that I can do nothing more than state them.
An attorney from other states is not obliged to wait for
any thing but an examination; he can be licensed immediately. It is an excellent place to make money.
There is a good opening here for men of talents. Men
of that description are much wanted, and the general
profligacy and idleness that prevail render young men
of talents, morality, and application to business, objects
of public confidence and esteem. Society is improving
every year. It is not very refined, and by no means literary, but gay and fashionable. In winter Natchez affords much amusement; in summer it is almost deserted.
I must now, in justice, present the reverse of the picture.
If you come here, come prepared to strike the word comfort out of your vocabulary, during the summer months
at least. You must be either sufficiently romantic to
despise it, or stoical enough not to sigh for it; though
my stoicism, on which I plume myself, soon failed before
the combined attacks of heat and musquitoes, which last
constitute the greatest annoyance of the two. Then
there is the sickly climate and the depravity of morals.
I should severely reproach myself if, by my advice, you
should come here and fall a prey to either of them. By

prudence and self-denial one may, perhaps, live as long and as innocently here as in any other country. Mary and myself have not had a day's illness here. My eldest son has resided here four years without suffering. The great mortality may be traced to imprudence, exposure, and high living. Although it would give me pleasure to see you the friend and companion of my sons, and although I feel assured that you would succeed, and soon become pleased with this country, yet it requires, on your part, mature consideration, unless you are disposed to sacrifice every thing for fame and fortune. For a few years, at least, you will experience much to dissatisfy you with your residence, until competence enables you to enjoy its pleasures. Should you decide to come you will receive a cordial welcome from our family, to whom you will not altogether be a stranger. I will furnish you with letters to my sons, which will be an introduction to every body else.'

"Mrs. Griffith has dwelt longer on the disadvantages of the country, not desiring me to be disappointed. But after all, her objections are nothing. Hot weather and musquitoes would not deter me even from a hunting expedition; and as to depravity, by which she means dissipation, I trust my morals and sense of propriety are sufficiently fixed. What a story it would be to tell a sailor brother, now buffeting with fortune on the angry waves, that such trivial obstacles influenced me! The climate itself is as healthy as this. Mistaken ideas of what constitutes pleasure lead many into dissipation, which, in warm countries, soon shuffles them off. Many young men who go South grow careless on account of the facility of making money, and plunge into every kind of excess. Young men born there to hereditary wealth, who have never felt what it is to want, set them the example. My ambition is of a more exalted nature. I am prepared to make sacrifices if I had any thing to sacrifice, but they shall be for fame and fortune, not for empty and evanescent pleasures. Society, literature, and love make life agreeable; but the true source of comfort and happiness is strict attention to the vocation we have selected for a career. While we are industrious, and have some noble object in view, time passes pleasantly and profitably, and we enjoy the sweets of life without feeling the sting that lies concealed under too many of them. I do not, however, like letter-moralizing, especially to an elder brother. I will only say that my eyes are fixed on the South. If I am fortunate, I entertain the hope of seeing you and other members of the family settled in Mississippi.

"Last year my percentage or fees in this office amounted to $81, which, with a little I made pettifogging, drawing conveyances, etc., has supported me handsomely. I have not much left. But, if I know Mr. Brush well, he will not suffer me to leave this place with a mean idea of him. We never made a contract, and I have rendered him essential service. He has always been generous and kind to me. I owe no man a cent. On the contrary, I have loaned money to several. For several weeks I have been breaking a wild young horse which Mr. Brush requested me to purchase for him. He has given me some severe falls, but is now a fine roadster. Nobody but myself has dared to back him. Perhaps I may get this nag for the journey. My spirits and health are good, though, like most of the Ohioans, I am tallow-faced."

To his Brother.

"Delaware, Sept. 2d, 1821.

"Since the receipt of your last, dear brother, I have been so harassed by the business of the office that I have had scarcely a moment's leisure to devote to my friends at home; and to-day, though it is Sunday, I have been for four hours making out our monthly returns to the General Land-office. I have never had two such busy months. In July, delving over my books from morning till night, preparing for my examination, and, in August, the land-sales occupied me day and night. You may form an idea of the business, when you learn that we offered at auction 45 townships, averaging 51,200 acres each, in 80-acre lots. Of these we have sold some 25,000 acres, and are still selling rapidly. The auction-sales close this week, and then the whole country, from this to the lake, will be subject to entry at $1 25 per acre, the finest opening for colossal fortunes in the world.

" Besides these engagements, I have to command a fine rifle company once a week (our captain being down with the eternal chills and fever), and occasionally have the godsend of a small case to plead before a justice of the peace. Thus time passes in an incessant routine of business; and then, instead of recreation, I have, as a duty, to visit my sick friends, and watch by and comfort them. My health and spirits were never better, but the village and country are severely scourged. Intermittent and bilious fevers are frequent and fatal. A third of our population is bedridden. Chill and fever and ague, daily, tertian, quotidian, and all the time, is a regular institution. I have not seen them shake the shingles off the roof, or the nuts off the hickories, or the toe-nails off the patient, but all these achievements are vouched for here.

" In the beginning of last month I was admitted to the bar. Thus far the only fruit has been to add esquire to my address. I am anxious to get rid of the necessity of clerking. To my profession I am resolved to adhere, whether I grow rich or starve. No melancholy notions for me. I have heretofore been prosperous in all my undertakings. Fortune has ever smiled upon me, nor am I now apprehensive of her frowns. I shall go South as winter approaches, if I can get money enough to carry me. My resources are at present very low. I have some books which I procured in the way of trade, and some other things, but none of them will command cash. My fees, from small law-cases, drawing deeds, etc., have enabled me to dress well and have pocket-money; but now the want of money to travel on and set me up, stares me in the face. If I can live but six months where I may locate, I shall have overcome every difficulty. Your transcript of Albert's letter is very gratifying. The dear fellow seems to be happy, and not a little amused at getting over the world so fast. I long knew he desired a sailor's life, and papa has done well in suffering him to go. Why should any human being be tortured by an occupation in which he can find no happiness? Of what account are honors and wealth, unless they promote our comfort? If we can be happy without either, why struggle for them?"

From his Father.

"Rhinebeck, September 15th, 1821.

"DEAR JOHN,—Inclosed I send you \$20, being the full amount due you by Mr. Hazelius for services at Hartwick, with some interest. I can add nothing to it from myself. Since you have resolved to settle at Natchez, I pray to God that He may be pleased to prosper your views, and this I do not doubt if you persevere in acting upon those correct and virtuous principles which you have always manifested, and do not push your expectations too far, or with too much eagerness. 'Unusquisque suæ fortunæ faber,' is an ancient and true saying, but it requires generally some time to see it realized. As I lived more than twelve years in a warm climate, I may give you some salutary hints with respect to your mode of life and diet. I found it prudent to pay attention to the manner of living of old and virtuous inhabitants of those regions, and to follow their example. I observed that those who preserved equanimity of mind and temper in the tropics lived commonly as long as the inhabitants of the temperate zones. Violent passions, too great exertion of mind or body, are particularly dangerous in countries where the blood is in almost continual agitation. Grief, discontent, and fretting are fatal. The evening air ought to be avoided, in particular at full moon. Your dress ought not to be too thin. Most of the sailors on board the Ceres, in the harbor of Curaçoa, escaped the yellow fever who wore woolen shirts. You ought not to consume much animal food, nor fruit, nor acids, nor punch, but rather drink a little Madeira diluted with water. Use the spices that grow in the country. The best preservative of all is a cheerful mind.

"Things change here. Since there is no opportunity of speculating in lands and money, we begin to speculate in religion. New sects spring up daily. We are surrounded with frantic Methodists, Erastians, or New Lights, Baptists, Universalists, etc. There is continually preaching (so called) in our neighborhood. The Methodists are at present in camp-meeting two miles beyond the Flats. This, and the sitting of the convention in democratic majesty, give us alternately sufficient reason for pity and laughter."

This was the last letter he received in Ohio. He had resided there long enough to establish a reputation for integrity and business habits, for good sense, courtesy, and every manly virtue, and now, with the good wishes of the whole community, he took his leave, once more to seek his living among strangers. With an income of less than one hundred and fifty dollars a year, laboriously earned in the land-office and by conveyancing, he had lived in the best society of the village, dressed neatly, read closely, and found time to study military tactics, masonry, and music.* So well had he husbanded his humble resources, we find him loaning money in Delaware; it is honorable to his debtors that, on the eve of his departure, they all paid their little dues, no doubt after many shifts and sacrifices. He received some aid from Colonel Brush, and, on the 5th of November, with a good horse and equipments, he bade adieu to the village, nearly the whole population assembling to say farewell. His own letters will tell the story of his journey and of his launch into life at the South.

* 1821, he was commissioned by Ethan A. Brown, Governor of Ohio, 1st lieutenant 2d rifle company, 3d regiment, 2d brigade, 7th division Ohio Militia.

Nov. 3d, he took the degree of master mason in Hiram Lodge, No. 8, Delaware, Ohio.

Oct. 22d, licensed to practice law by the Supreme Court of Ohio.

CHAPTER IV.

The Journey. — Jockeyed out of his Horse. — Feelings on the Road.
—Embarks at Louisville.—Arrives at Natchez.—His first Letter.
—Low State of his Finances.—Philosophy.—William B. Griffith.
—Natchez in 1822.— " Under the Hill."—Mississippi Planters.—
Mode of Life and Revenues.—New-year's Day in the South.—Ad-
mitted to the Bar.—Takes Charge of Mr. Griffith's Business.—
Southern Hospitality.—Letter from Mr. Griffith.—Northern No-
tions of the South.—Ohio Judges.—Dress.—His first Commission.
—Life at the South.—Slavery and Slave.—Life contrasted with
Life at the North.—Negro Habits and Characteristics.—Natchez
in an Epidemic.

To his Brother.

"Natchez, December 4th, 1821.

" HERE I am, dear brother, at last, in a temporary asylum such as the moneyed traveler can obtain in any quarter of the world; and as I have nothing else to do, like
other great men, I can issue bulletins of my campaign.
I left Delaware November 5th, with the blessings of numerous friends whom I shall never forget. The day was
pleasant and the roads good. I drew inspiration from
the prospect before me as I jogged on, yet I felt sad at
parting, perhaps forever, from those that loved me well.
Mr. Little, a merchant of the village, whom I have found
a generous friend, accompanied me to Columbus. On
the second day after parting with him it began to rain
and then to snow, and thus I traveled alone to Chilicothe, where I lay by several days, waiting for a change;
but there being no prospect, and having not the where-
withal to 'take mine ease in mine inn,' I pushed on
through rain, sleet, and mud, and literally fought my way
across the floating ice to Maysville. The roads were
frozen like glass, and my fine nag, Nancy Dawson, slipped, and so lamed herself I was compelled to put up at

a wayside tavern beyond the town of Washington. Next
morning she was wholly knocked up, and a gentlemanly
and friendly-disposed wayfarer at the same tavern declared that she would not be fit for the road for a month.
Seeing my distress, he invited me to 'peach and honey'
—something I had never tasted before—and, after a good
deal of chat, he offered to exchange his fine-looking
charger for my mare, and $25 to boot. The landlord
swore he was the best horse in the country, and that,
even if my mare had not been crippled, $50 premium for
such a swap was little enough. He alleged, likewise,
that Brigadier General Somebody, who came round once
a year to muster the brigade, would ride no other horse
on such occasions. The friendly Kentuckian said this
was true enough, but that here was a young fellow just
starting out in the world, not overburdened with cash;
he had taken a liking to me; he could afford to lose $25
in the trade, and would stick to his offer. The landlord
complimented him on his generosity, said it was just like
him, and insisted on a general treat. The peach and
honey was duly honored; I paid my $25, squared my
bill, and departed. I had not traveled ten miles next
day before I found I had been 'sold,' as they say in these
parts. My Bucephalus, as I had named him in my
pride, hung his ears, drooped his tail, dragged his hind
legs, stumbled every five minutes, and snorted like an
asthmatic steam-boat. With whip and spur, I could not
average over two miles per hour. Finding that, at this
rate, I would not have funds for the ride to Natchez, I
was compelled to steer for Louisville. I shall never forget how I felt when I found myself thus swindled, without redress, without a friend, and with no money to purchase another horse. Woe to the jockey if I could have
laid hands on him then!* Every body and every thing
strange and new to me, and once more I felt I alone in the
world. The very boys of the wayside villages sneered
at the sorry figure I cut. Every passer-by had his jest.

* This man removed to Mississippi, joked and fiddled himself into
the Legislature, and often told how he had diddled the young lawyer
as a capital jest. In after life Quitman not only forgave him, but
loaned him considerable sums of money at various times when he was
in distress.

At last I made a joke of it myself, and laughed as heartily as any body else. I sneaked into Louisville after
night, and sold horse, saddle, and bridle for $45, Kentucky
currency, thirty-five per cent. below par, little more than
the first cost of saddle and bridle. After a delay of three
days I got a berth in the first steamer that left (the ' Car
of Commerce'), for $37½, Kentucky currency. I arrived
here last night. I have $15 in my pocket, and the cheap-
est respectable board and lodging is $45 per month.
What of it? Was not Goldsmith's parson ' passing rich
on forty pounds a year?' Besides, he had a wife and
children, and the care of souls, and was altogether a man ·
of books and brains, unfitted to battle with the world.
I have strong arms and a resolute will, and if one thing
fails I can try another.

"Since writing this I have delivered my letter to
William B. Griffith, Esq., from his mother. He was
very kind, and encourages me much, and, from what I
observed this morning in court, I have no fears. High
fees, plenty of business, and not overstocked with eminent lawyers. There is room for a hard student and a
determined man, spurred on by necessity and pride. My
difficulty will be to live for a few months. I must appear as a gentleman, or I can not expect to be treated
as such. Mr. Griffith has offered me the use of his office
and books, and, except boarding, I shall have but few
wants. I shall cut them down to a narrow compass. I
begin my economy by writing on coarse and soiled paper
(a tavern waif), with the stump of a pen. Better station-
ery after a while, but now not a shilling for superfluities.
Tell papa and my sisters, that the farther I go from them
the nearer they are to my heart."

To his Father.

"Natchez, Jan. 16th, 1822.

"I write, dear father, because I know your solicitude
for me. From the cares that even I have had, I can estimate the feelings of a parent who has the happiness of
his children at heart, and to whom Providence has denied the means of setting them up in the world. You
have given your example, your instruction, and your
blessing, worth far more than money; and with these I

can fight my battle of life, and have no fears of the result. I had at first much anxiety as to how I could live here for the first few months, and until some business offered. My funds were very low, living high, and I could not bear the notion of running into debt. A few days after my arrival, however, conceive my joy when Mr. Griffith proposed to me to assist him in his office for a year, and, in the mean time, he would guarantee my support, hinting, likewise, that he would put other business in my hands to bring me some income. I am now, much to my satisfaction, located in his fine, large office, with an extensive library, and can reap the same instruction from his large practice as though it were my own. In short, my situation is as advantageous as you could wish. So much for my keel-boat expedition, and the happy accident that threw me into the society of Mrs. Griffith. Her son, who has been so kind, is a man of first-rate talents—a Princeton scholar—a few years older than myself, and has every quality to command respect. In the midst of the temptations which pleasure and dissipation hold out here, and with the means to enjoy them, and the temperament too, he pursues a steady and undeviating course in the true road to professional eminence. Politics he disdains. Even the florid eloquence that tickles the multitude he holds in contempt. Hard application and severe logic, thorough preparation of his cases, and astonishing energy of will are his characteristics. No part of the United States holds out better prospects for a young lawyer. Why did I not come here, instead of stopping in Ohio? Money is as plenty here as it is scarce there. You may have some notion of business here when I inform you that court has been in session twenty-eight days without disposing of the criminal business; there were 120 indictments. This would indicate a deplorable state of morals; but remember, the river brings here the floating population of the whole West, and the wealth of the country entices adventurers from many lands. Many of these are not novices in crime. Gambling and intemperance are carried to excess. 'Under the hill,' in this city (a straggling town at the base of the bluff, consisting of warehouses, low taverns, groggeries, dens of prostitution, and gaming-houses), vice and infamy are rampant and glaring, and the law almost powerless. Day and night the orgies of blackguardism and depravity are enacted without shame and restraint. The Sabbath is there particularly a day of profanation and debauchery. The gambler, the bully, and the harlot reign triumphant, and little jurisdiction is taken over their atrocities.

"In the city proper, and the surrounding country, there is genteel and well-regulated society. The religious classes are chiefly Presbyterians and Methodists—a few Episcopalians and Catholics. The planters are the prominent feature. They ride fine horses, are followed by well-dressed and very aristocratic servants, but affect great simplicity of costume themselves—straw hats and no neck-cloths in summer, and in winter coarse shoes and blanket overcoats. They live profusely: drink costly Port, Madeira, and sherry, after the English fashion, and are exceedingly hospitable. Cotton-planting is the most lucrative business that can be followed. Some of the planters net $50,000 from a single crop.*

"I suppose you are yet locked up in the grasp of winter. I spent New-year's Day at 'the Forest,' the residence of the late Sir William Dunbar, now owned by his son, Dr. Dunbar. The mansion, the stately oaks, the extensive park, and the vast, undulating sweep of cultivated fields, are really magnificent. On the table we had green peas, lettuce, radishes, artichokes, new potatoes, and spinach, grown in the open air, and roses, jessamines, jonquils, and pinks in profusion. What a delightful climate! I almost think of it as the retreat for your age. The peach and plum are in full bloom, and the birds sing merrily in the honeysuckes around my bedchamber.

"Natchez is a bustling place. The streets are lined with carriages, drays, and wagons. The rush to the river is incessant. Every hour we hear the roar of cannon, announcing the arrival and departure of steamers. Hundreds of arks, or flat-boats, loaded with the produce of the Western States, even from the interior of Pennsylvania, here line the landing for half a mile, often lying five tier deep!

---

* Many now have annual revenues of $100,000 and over.

"On the 8th I was examined before the Supreme Court, and am now a licensed attorney and counselor in the State of Mississippi.* Continue to give me your blessing, dear father, and your son Jack will never disgrace you."

To his Father.

"Natchez, August 12th, 1822.

"Separated from you so far, dear father, your health and prosperity, and my brothers and sisters, form the chief objects of solicitude, especially as I have no care as it regards my present and future prospects. My professional career commences with fair chances, and if I do not gain the highest pinnacle, my stand will be respectable. It shall be upright and honorable, whether I die rich or poor.

"Mr. Griffith, who has been like a brother to me, left for New Jersey last month by sea, and has promised to pay you a visit. The more I know him, the higher I esteem him. He is a noble fellow, and, as an orator and lawyer, is at the head of the Mississippi bar. He has left the business of his office entirely in my hands, and on his return will most probably offer me a partnership, especially since his recent appointment of United States District Attorney.

"Intermittent and bilious fevers are common now. I have not taken a dose of medicine; my health is perfect. If necessary, I can retreat to the country. I have made friends, and have several invitations. Dr. Dunbar, Mrs. Gen. Claiborne, and Judge Turner have all invited me to their delightful homes, more as an inmate of their families than as a guest. Cordial hospitality is one of the characteristics of the Southern people. Their very servants catch the feeling of their owners, and anticipate one's wants. Your coffee in the morning before sunrise; little stews and sudorifics at night, and warm foot-baths, if you have a cold; bouquets of fresh flowers and mint-juleps sent to your apartment; a horse and saddle at your disposal; every thing free and easy, and cheerful and cordial. It is really fascinating, and I seem to be lead-

---

* The judges were John P. Hampton and Powhatan Ellis. Examiners, Joseph E. Davis, Joshua Childs, Martin Whiting.

ing a charmed life compared with my pilgrimage elsewhere."

The visit of Mr. Griffith to the North, leaving Quitman
in charge of his office, brought him, every hour of the
day, in contact with the prominent business men of the
community and influential clients from all parts of the
state, whose confidence that distinguished lawyer enjoyed. It threw him in correspondence, likewise, with merchants and capitalists in other states and in Europe,
whose affairs had been confided to Mr. Griffith. It occasioned, too, more intimate relations between him and the
established members of the bar—a body of gentlemen distinguished then, as now, and at all times, for their integrity, patriotism, scrupulous honor, and high-toned courtesy. Quitman was not the man to throw away these
advantages; he put the proper value upon the opportunities thus providentially cast in his path, and exerted what
he himself considered a sort of magnetic faculty of at-
traction. When Mr. Griffith returned, he found not only
that his business had been conducted with admirable tact
and discretion, but the young attorney had become one
of the most popular men in the community. During his
absence he had written to Quitman thus—the sentiments
do honor to his memory and to the bar:

"I am afraid you have already had—and will have—
some difficulty in managing my business, arising from the
hurry of my departure, and want of time to prepare the
necessary instructions and explanations. I have, however, the fullest confidence in your abilities and industry;
and my regret at giving you so much trouble, when it
might perhaps have been avoided, is lessened by the reflection, that the greater your difficulties are, the greater
will be the eventual advantage you will gain in surmounting them. You must extend your acquaintance with the

people, and, without losing your dignity or descending to too much familiarity, acquire popularity and the esteem of the *profanum vulgus*.

"In relation to charges, when they are discretionary, and not fixed by the general consent of the bar, be moderate. You may, perhaps, smile to hear *me* say so. There are some persons who would not esteem the service if they were not required to pay heavily for it. There are many such about Natchez, whose whole idea is wealth and its importance. There are others who really can not afford heavy fees, though highly respectable men. These must be indulged. My rule has generally been, never to disagree with a respectable man on that score. *The poor*, I need scarcely say, *must be served freely, and with all our heart, when oppressed by the proud and powerful.* This is the glory and consolation of our profession."

Noble sentiments! Nor did they fall, like the barren seed of Scripture, on "stony ground," but on a heart full of natural equity and generous emotions.

The fame of his first success had now reached his distant friends, and he received numerous letters of congratulation and inquiry, some of them amusing enough. Natchez was at that period a sort of *ultima thule*, and queer notions of it prevailed among even educated men. The Rev. Dr. Mayer, of Philadelphia, wrote: "I have often heard Natchez described as seated on a high bluff, and, of course, likely to be as healthy as any other spot within 1000 miles of New Orleans. Still, I would advise you to make a frequent use of Lee's anti-bilious pills, two or three a day, as a preventive against the fall diseases of that climate. How shall I send you a dozen boxes? A pretty thick net is, I suppose, an indispensable defense against musquitoes. How do they differ from gallinippers? How do Yankees thrive with you? I have been told that girls of decent appearance and good education are sure to be snatched up as wives in three months after their first exhibition among you. Is this really so? If it be, I should wish to disseminate the information on your warrant among some friends of mine. Rumor has it, that ministers rarely fail to marry rich wives in that country, that they fall off gradually in their devotions, and become the most rigorous task-masters and cotton-makers. This, surely, must be scandal.

"Are you permanently fixed, or will you roll on? Is your ambitious eye fixed upon the mines of Mexico, or do you expect to go to the mouth of the Columbia? How does the capital of Mississippi please you as a resting-place? A resting-place only, I fear it will be, unless one of its fair sirens enchant you. Another foe, not a fair one, is to be guarded against. I suppose every body is down with high bilious fevers from July till December. Stick to your pills, and cheat the adversary. Some of your fellow-adventurers at Mount Airy have at length found places, and others are tossing about. Haslam has the Lutheran academy at Charleston. Goodman has gone to take charge of the churches near Troy. Backus has sailed for Pernambuco. Promotion is rapid, I hear, in your new country. When you shall have risen to the office of judge or member of Congress, let me know, that I may write you with becoming dignity.

"There is a colony of Germans near Natchez somewhere. Look after them, make them your clients, and keep them in the true church."

His old patron, Platt Brush, wrote as follows: "Give me a minute account of the country, contrasting it with ours; your own opinion as to the salubrity of various parts, and whether you can compare any particular section of it with Ohio; peculiarities of the people, law, religion, and politics, wealth and splendor, and the surest and speediest mode of acquiring the same. Mr. Pettibone will remove to your country in the fall, and it is very probable I may accompany him 'to spy out the nakedness of the land.' Mention the time of the fall meeting of your superior courts. I should like to take soundings there before I determine upon a move. I can fathom your bar in three days. Let us hear something of your judges. Are they deep or shallow, fast or slow? Are they fixtures for life? Much of our success depends on them. Here, you know, they are a sly set of old foxes, and very hard to head. With you, I take it, it is otherwise, and they die, if they don't resign. The practice is so profitable, your ablest men remain at the bar, and your stupid and pompous fellows go upon the bench. Is it not so? What about niggers? Are they really branded and cropped, and fed on salted cotton-seed? Does every master keep his mulatto concubine, and his harem of darkies? Do men from the land of steady habits fall into these practices? Are your creoles white? or white and Indian, or nigger and white, or all mixed together? And are these recognized conventionally, and allowed in society, or as jurors or witnesses?"

To his Brother.

"Natchez, Feb. 1st, 1823.

"You think my friend, Mr. Griffith, rather foppish in his dress. Why, brother, if you could see the extravagance in which most young men here indulge, you would consider him plain. Clothing is usually made to order in Philadelphia, of the most expensive materials and most fashionable cut. Our beaux here mostly patronize Watson, and his average charge is $100 per suit. Three or four suits are ordered for winter, double that number for summer. I have already caught the habit. We have few mechanics, except carpenters, masons, and ginwrights. There is not a shoemaker in Natchez. Our shoes come from the North, boots from Paris, and cost from $10 to $14. Extravagance and expense become familiar.

"Our Circuit Court has just adjourned. I had my share of business. I have recently visited what are called 'the Pearl River counties,' on a tour of duty, having been appointed brigade inspector, with the rank of major.* The place affords me some gratification, and occasions but little expense. Its duties are performed during vacation, and it will give me an extended acquaintance. So, you see, my winter evenings at Delaware, studying tactics and the art of war, are already available."

To his Brother.

"Natchez, March 11th, 1823.

"Your letters, dear brother, can not be too minute. My home feelings are intense. Could I but catch one glimpse of the old winter apple-tree in the yard, or the many faces that used to cluster under its branches, I should feel once more a boy. A thousand scenes of the past swim over my memory, like passing shadows, and I often find myself a dreamer when I should be a student. So tell me of home—my early home—the home of father, sisters, and brothers—the resting-place of our mother, humble though it be: all these lie very near my heart. But a truce to these vagabond fancies, that carry me away from the realities around me. You ask what are my prospects? If they continue three years I trust I shall be able to say, 'Come and see me,' and I will 'chalk your hat' for the journey. I think I shall become easy in my circumstances some day, if not rich. I must live genteelly, but, at the same time, when I know the gratification I should receive from being able to relieve those who are dear to me, and who deserve good fortune more, ephemeral pleasures have no charms, and I cast them away as unworthy of a reasonable man. What comparison can there be between the approving feelings of a heart conscious of doing good, and the mere sensual pleasures of feasting and drinking?

"As to marrying, I have not thought of it seriously. Money and splendor will never bias my choice, and, until my heart is thoroughly touched, I shall prefer the solitary yet snug elbow-chair of a bachelor."

* 1823, Jan. 10th, brigade inspector, 2d brigade, 1st division Mississippi Militia, commissioned by Walter Leake, Governor.

In the next letter, with a rapid pen, he sketches slave life in the South as it then existed. If modified since, it has been for the better. The condition of the Southern slave is not stationary,* but progressive. As the master's circumstances improve, the position of his slaves is ameliorated. Every comfort he gathers about him is enjoyed, more or less, by his dependents. They rough it, as he does, in the outset of life; but when he builds a comfortable house for himself the improvement of their quarters is certain to follow. As his stock increases, they get their share of milk and fresh meats, in addition to salted provisions. As his plantation expands, they are allowed more ground for the culture of esculents, from which, and their poultry, they derive no inconsiderable revenue; often more, for each family, than a hard-working New England yeoman realizes, by the labor of his household, at the end of the year. They enjoy, both at home and in the neighboring meeting-houses, the preaching of the Gospel. Convenient chapels are built on many plantations expressly for them. They do no compulsory labor on the Sabbath, and usually have most of the holidays kept by their owners, and participate in the festivities. They are clothed well, and often dress in the height of the *ton*. From the youngest members of the family they get the latest fashions. They dance polkas and mazourkas. They warble airs from the last opera. Their weddings are celebrated with the usual ceremonies, and their funerals with religious solemnity, the owner of his family often casting the first shovel of earth, and shedding tears over the tomb of the faithful servant. They occupy confidential positions, keep the stores of the plantation, collect dues, and are often intrusted with large sums to transmit from place to place,

* " Fix'd like a plant to a peculiar spot,
  To draw nutrition, vegetate, and rot."

and some of them are employed as overseers. By the will of the late Philip Hoggatt, of Adams County, Mississippi, one of his slaves, intrusted with the management of several plantations, receives $500 per annum. Many of them command a credit at the neighboring stores beyond the means of many Northern farmers, so well established is their reputation as punctual paymasters. They are attached to the whites; they imitate their manners and mode of dress; they are proud of an admixture of blood; their whole aim is to progress, and their strongest term of contempt, when a comrade incurs their displeasure, is to stigmatize him as a "·d—d black nigger." Compared with the original or recent importation of Africans, their progress has been wonderful. When first brought to this country they lived in hovels, got their peck of corn without meat, went almost naked, worked early and late, and were often severely whipped and otherwise punished. The whip is now rarely applied—on many plantations never. Besides meat and meal in abundance, and milk and vegetables, they get a reasonable allowance of sugar, coffee, and tobacco, flour and molasses; they have gardens, orchards, poultry-yards, and piggeries; corn, melon, and potato patches; they are never without money; their cabins are comfortable and neat, with an unlimited command of fuel; shoes, hats, blankets, mattresses, and winter and summer clothing are regularly apportioned to them; in sickness, the best nursing, the best medical advice, and nicely prepared diet; and the Sunday dinners of every thrifty family of slaves would be considered a sort of thanksgiving dinner in New England. In old age they are carefully sheltered and supported.

In the early stages of African slavery in the South, it was by many considered an *evil*, that had been inflicted upon the country by British and New England cupidity.

The Africans were regarded as barbarians, and were governed by the lash. The very hatred of the "evil" forced upon us was, in a measure, transferred to the unhappy victims. They were treated with severity, and no social relations subsisted between them and the whites. By degrees slavery began to be considered "a *necessary* evil," to be got rid of by gradual emancipation, or perhaps not at all, and the condition of the slave sensibly improved. The natural sense of justice in the human heart suggested that they had been brought here by compulsion, and that they should be regarded not as savages, but as captives, who were to be kindly treated while laboring for their ultimate redemption.

The progress of anti-slavery sentiment in the Northern States (once regarded by the South as a harmless fanaticism), the excesses it has occasioned, and the unconstitutional power it claims, at length prompted a general and searching inquiry into the true status of the negro. The moment that the Southern mind became convinced that slavery, as it exists among us, instead of being a moral, social, and political evil, *is a moral, social, and political good*, and is the natural condition of the negro, as ordained by Providence, and the only condition in which he can be civilized and instructed, the condition of the Southern slave underwent a thorough change. As a permanent fixture, as a hereditary heir-loom, as a human being with an immortal soul, intrusted to us by God for his own wise purposes, his value increased, and his relation to his owner approximated to the relation of guardian and ward. Interest taught us that it would be wise to cherish what was to be the permanent means of production and profit, and religion exacted the humane and judicious employment of the "talent" committed to our care. Thus the most powerful influences that sway the heart and the judgment are in operation for the benefit of the slave, and hence his present comfortable and constantly ameliorating condition. It is due, almost solely, to the moral convictions of the slaveholder. Our laws protect the slave in life and limb, and against cruel and inordinate punishment. Those laws are rigorously applied, though rarely necessary, for public opinion, more formidable than law, would condemn to execration and infamy the unjust and cruel master. Since these convictions in regard to slavery have been adopted almost unanimously in the South, the value of negroes has quadrupled. This, however, is in some measure an evil, because the tendency is to concentrate the slaves in the hands of the few, who are able to pay the extraordinary rates now demanded. It would be better for the commonwealth, and give additional solidity to our system of domestic servitude, if every family had an interest in it, secured, to a limited extent, against liability for debt. It should constitute in the South, if practicable, a part of every homestead, and then interest, and household tradition, and the friendly, confidential, and even affectionate relations that in the present state of public feeling prevail between master and slave, would unite all men in its defense. Neither land, nor slaves, which are here more valuable than land, should, by either direct or indirect legislation, be concentrated in few hands. Every citizen should have, if possible, that immediate interest in them which would make him feel that, in defending the commonwealth and its institutions, he is defending his own inheritance. Whether our laws, both federal and state, are not in this sense unfavorable to the permanence of an institution indispensable to the South, is a question now exercising the public attention, and it is not doubted that, ultimately, as was the case with the question of slavery itself, the Southern mind will arrive at a correct conclusion.

To Col. Brush.

"Soldier's Retreat, near Natchez, Aug. 23d, 1823.

" Since my last letter, my dear Col. Brush, I have been a refugee from Natchez, where the yellow fever is raging. Our bar is quartered at various country-seats—not boarding; a Mississippi planter would be insulted by such a proposal; but we are enjoying the hospitalities that are offered to us on all sides. The awful pestilence in the city brings out, in strong relief, the peculiar virtues of this people. The mansions of the planters are thrown open to all comers and goers free of charge. Whole families have free quarters during the epidemic, and country wagons are sent daily to the verge of the smitten city with fowls, vegetables, etc., for gratuitous distribution to the poor. I am now writing from one of those old mansions, and I can give you no better notion of life at the South than by describing the routine of a day. The owner is the widow of a Virginia gentleman of distinction, a brave officer, who died in the public service during the last war with Great Britain.* She herself is a native of this vicinity, of English parents settled here in Spanish times. She is an intimate friend of my first friend, Mrs. Griffith, and I have been in the habit of visiting her house ever since I came South. The whole aim of this excellent lady seems to be to make others happy. I do not believe she ever thinks of herself. She is growing old, but her parlor is constantly thronged with the young and gay, attracted by her cheerful and never-failing kindness. There are two large families from the city staying here, and every day some ten or a dozen transient guests. Mint-juleps in the morning are sent to our rooms, and then follows a delightful breakfast in the open veranda. We hunt, ride, fish, pay morning visits, play chess, read or lounge until dinner, which is served at two P.M. in great variety, and most delicately cooked in what is here called the Creole style—very rich, and many made or mixed dishes. In two hours afterward every body—white and black—has disappeared. The whole household is asleep—the *siesta*

---

* The late Gen. F. L. Claiborne.

of the Italians. The ladies retire to their apartments, and the gentlemen on sofas, settees, benches, hammocks, and often, gipsy fashion, on the grass under the spreading oaks. Here, too, in fine weather, the tea-table is always set before sunset, and then, until bedtime, we stroll, sing, play whist, or coquet. It is an indolent, yet charming life, and one quits thinking and takes to dreaming.

"This excellent lady is not rich, merely independent; but by thrifty housewifery, and a good dairy and garden, she contrives to dispense the most liberal hospitality. Her slaves appear to be, in a manner, free, yet are obedient and polite, and the farm is well worked. With all her gayety of disposition and fondness for the young, she is truly pious, and in her own apartment every night she has family prayer with her slaves, one or more of them being often called on to sing and pray. When a minister visits the house, which happens very frequently, prayers night and morning are always said, and on these occasions the whole household and the guests assemble in the parlor: chairs are provided for the servants. They are married by a clergyman of their own color, and a sumptuous supper is always prepared. On public holidays they have dinners equal to an Ohio barbecue, and Christmas, for a week or ten days, is a protracted festival for the blacks. They are a happy, careless, unreflecting, good-natured race, who, left to themselves, would degenerate into drones or brutes, but, subjected to wholesome restraint and stimulus, become the best and most contented of laborers. They are strongly attached to 'old massa' and 'old missus,' but their devotion to 'young massa' and 'young missus' amounts to enthusiasm. They have great family pride, and are the most arrant coxcombs and aristocrats in the world. At a wedding I witnessed here last Saturday evening, where some 150 negroes were assembled, many being invited guests, I heard a number of them addressed as governors, generals, judges, and doctors (the titles of their masters), and a spruce, tight-set darkey, who waits on me in town, was called 'Major Quitman.' The 'colored ladies' are invariably Miss Joneses, Miss Smiths, or some such title. They are exceedingly pompous and ceremonious, gloved and highly perfumed. The 'gentlemen' sport canes, ruffles, and jewelry, wear boots and spurs, affect crape on their hats, and carry huge cigars. The belles wear gaudy colors, 'tote' their fans with the air of Spanish señoritas, and never stir out, though black as the ace of spades, without their parasols. In short, these 'niggers,' as you call them, are the happiest people I have ever seen, and some of them, in form, features, and movement, are real sultanas. So far from being fed on 'salted cotton-seed,' as we used to believe in Ohio, they are oily, sleek, bountifully fed, well clothed, well taken care of, and one hears them at all times whistling and singing cheerily at their work.* They have an extraordinary facility for sleeping. A negro is a great night-walker. He will, after laboring all day in the burning sun, walk ten miles to a frolic, or to see his 'Dinah,' and be at home and at his work by daylight next morning. This would knock up a white man or an Indian. But a negro will sleep during the day—sleep at his work, sleep on the carriage-box, sleep standing up; and I have often seen them sitting bareheaded in the sun on a high rail-fence, sleeping as securely as though lying in bed. They never lose their equipoise, and will carry their cotton-baskets or their water-vessels, filled to the brim, poised on their heads, walking carelessly and at a rapid rate, without spilling a drop. The very weight of such burdens would crush a white man's brains into apoplexy. Compared with the ague-smitten and suffering settlers that you and I have seen in Ohio, or the sickly and starved operators we read of in factories and in mines, these Southern slaves are indeed to be envied. They are treated with

---

* Contrast this with *life at the North*, as recorded by his brother Henry in a letter dated Rhinebeck, Feb. 3d, 1823: "We have not had snow enough for sleighing, so every body has to stay at home. In the morning I feed the cows, take care of the horses, and cut wood until dinner-time. In the evening I take care of the cattle, and go to bed. I would willingly exchange my residence here for one where I might do for myself, were my earnings ever so small, and lay by a little for a rainy day. It is a hard place to get along in—cold winters and hot summers; snow, or slush, or dust, or drought. Work, work, work, and money always scarce. I wish I had been brought up a tailor, or shoemaker, as you say they have none at Natchez."

great humanity and kindness. I have only heard of one or two exceptions. And the only drawback to their happiness is that their owners, sometimes, from extravagance or other bad management, die insolvent, and then they must be sold to the highest bidder, must leave the old homestead and the old family, and pass into the hands of strangers. I have witnessed one of these scenes, and but one, though they occur often, and I never saw such profound grief as the poor creatures manifested. I am opposed, as you know, to all relief laws, but, I confess, I never hear of the sale of old family servants without wishing that there was some provision by which some of them, at least, might be retained as inalienable. It is a grave question for those interested in slavery to determine whether some protection of this nature is not a necessary adjunct of slavery itself."

To his Brother.

"Greenfields, near Natchez, Oct. 1st, 1823.
"I have been for a week or more at this charming abode, where Mr. Griffith and his family are likewise guests. We shall not return to town until December. Whole families there have been exterminated. I have lost several warm friends. Country air seems to be the antidote for this dreadful scourge. Outside the city—even a hundred yards beyond the corporation—it is as healthy as any part of the world. Sick persons, brought from the city, are received into crowded households, and nursed without fear of contagion, and I have heard of no instance of the fever being thus contracted.*

"Four weeks ago I left this county to ride the circuit of the first judicial district, about 150 miles. I returned three days since, and now enjoy, I assure you, the repose of country life. Hunting and angling constitute our amusements. The neighborhood is wealthy and populous. We meet in the morning, hunt or fish until dinner-time, and then turn in to the house of the nearest

---

* The disease, now to some extent localized, would be more terrible to an invading enemy than "an army with banners." Properly viewed, in some contingencies, it would be a source of strength to the South.

planter, and never fail to get a good dinner, with the choicest wines. The planters here are famous for their claret and Madeira. Many fine packs of hounds are kept, and they are always at our service."

To his Brother.

"Natchez, December 11th, 1823.

" I am writing, thank God, once more from our own office. Three weeks since a severe frost banished the epidemic, and we returned. It was painful to see the desolation of the streets. I looked in vain for faces with which I had been familiar. A gloom and sadness pervaded the whole place, and when friends met they pressed each other's hands in silence, or averted their faces and burst into tears. There was a chasm in every family, and ah! how many bleeding hearts!

" This, however, is disappearing under the rush and tumult of business and new-comers. Even the theatre has opened, parties announced, and an air of recklessness prevails. There is certainly more dissipation and extravagance than we had this time last year. This is, perhaps, one effect of epidemics. It was observed when London was plague-stricken. It is seen in cities during a siege, and I hear curious details of the *saturnalia*, the debauchery and excesses, that occurred here when the fever was at its worst—wine-parties after funerals, card-playing on coffins, shrouded figures whirling in the waltz!

" I am incessantly occupied bringing up our business. It shall never be said of me that business placed in my hands has been neglected. Perseverance and punctuality are indispensable in our arduous profession."

CHAPTER V.

ON the 24th of December, 1824, he married Eliza, only daughter of the late Henry Turner, a native of Virginia, whose parents removed to Kentucky, whence he came, when a young man, to New Orleans and Natchez, and, by his enterprise and sagacity, accumulated a large estate. He died at Woodlands, near Natchez, many years since, leaving a name and reputation greatly respected. By this marriage Quitman came into possession of a large estate, but continued to devote himself sedulously and successfully to his profession.

To his Brother.

"Natchez, December 6th, 1827.

"I have met with a heavy and unexpected calamity. I have lost my best friend and partner, William B. Griffith. He died on the 28th of October from apoplectic convulsions. He had been slightly ill for several weeks of bilious fever, which resulted in jaundice, and the day before his death he was seized violently with convulsions, which succeeded each other rapidly until he expired. I heard his last words, and closed his dying eyes. Poor fellow! with him I have lost my first benefactor in this country, the bar its brightest ornament, society one of its most valuable members. Long will it be before his place can be filled. He has left behind him an amiable wife (daughter of Judge Turner) and two children. I am almost worn down with this sad dispensation, and the accumulation of business it has thrown upon me. I have received as a partner John T. M'Murran, a native of Ohio, who has been a year in our office, and bids fair to be an eminent lawyer."

This partnership proved fortunate and profitable. Mr. M'Murran, who was then a very young man, a native of Pennsylvania, but more recently from Ohio, of singularly modest and prepossessing address, rose rapidly in the profession, and soon attained its highest rank. He was strongly attached to Quitman, and remained through life his devoted friend and counselor.

During this period, as in after life, he contributed liberally to the education of some of his relatives. To one of them he thus wrote—let the young student carefully peruse it:

To his Nephew.

"Natchez, June 20th, 1825.

"I am much pleased to hear of your arrival at Hartwick, and that you are determined to employ your opportunities to the best advantage. Write freely and often, and tell me what profession you wish to adopt. Treat me with the utmost candor, and without reserve. Upon the profession must depend your line of studies. I wish you to be thorough in all you undertake. I have not offered you my assistance to leave you on the threshold. Be industrious, be economical, be virtuous and honorable, and I will stand by you always. I have been led to believe that you prefer the law. My partialities are in its favor. In our country it opens the road to distinction and wealth. Remember, however, it is laborious, and requires unremitted industry. There is no position in society so abject and mean as that of a mere pettifogger, and none more elevated and noble than that of the honest and distinguished lawyer. Persevere; few men of good intellect have ever failed of success in any pursuit to which they have given their whole mind and heart. There is a very seductive kind of mental dissipation, to which young men too often give way; it consists in changing their aims and objects too often—a kind of waiting upon Providence. They make as little real progress as the mariner who sails about the ocean without a chart, driven by the shifting winds; they pursue every shadow that flits across their path. Such persons always fail, because they have no ultimate aim. The young man who sets out upon the journey of life should fix his eye upon some great object, and then resolutely and perseveringly exert all his energies to accomplish it. If the tide of adversity sets against his progress, he should row the harder; if difficulties intervene, grapple with and overcome them. Keep this in view, and you may commence your career with many advantages. In the mean time, consult your venerable instructor in all things; determine to be first among your fellow-students; write me once a month; choose your topics; do not try to be stiff and learned; any thing that amuses and interests you will be pleasing to me; above all things, be unreserved. I would not have you an imitator or a parasite, but it is a good plan for a student to select some model from the great men of the past, or from those that figure in contemporary history, and resolve to be equal to him. Epaminondas used to engross my affections, but of all the great republicans that history has handed down to us, I now most admire Cato; he was willing to sacrifice not only his person but his reputation and character in the cause of liberty.*

* In 1856, while in Congress, he thus wrote to James M. Kennard, of Natchez:

"My young Friend,—I have to-day nominated you to the President for a cadetship at West Point. I will soon forward your commission, and now inclose some of the rules that govern the appointment. The delay in notifying you of this result has been occasioned by my sense of duty, to give ample time for the coming in of similar applications before making my selection. My choice has fallen on you because, from your appearance and high recommendations, I believed you would do credit to the district, to the state, and to the service, as well as to my own judgment in selecting you out of so many worthy

In 1827 Capt. Quitman became a candidate to represent the city of Natchez and county of Adams in the Legislature, his principal competitor being Col. Adam L. Bingaman, a native of the county, and a man of talents, fortune, controlling family influence, and great personal popularity. It was necessary to canvass with energy against so formidable an opponent, and our young lawyer entered with spirit into the contest. He traversed every section of the county, and just before the election attended a large gathering at Hering's store, the extreme precinct, near the Franklin County line. He went in his usual neat dress, but soon threw off his coat, and astonished the crowd by his feats in wrestling, leaping, and boxing. A foot-race was got up, a sweepstake for six, a hundred and fifty yards, and he beat the fastest. The heavy weights from Hoggatt's cotton-gin were on the ground, and he lifted more, at arm's length, than the strongest man present. His strength of arm was remarkable. By this time a fat ox—the prize of the day—was driven up, the target fixed at sixty yards, and the shooting commenced. There were several expert riflemen on the ground, among whom was the noted John Hawkins, the crack shot of the whole country round. No one would shoot against him and "Brown Bess" (as he called his favorite rifle) without the odds. To the astonishment of the crowd, Quitman refused the odds and took an even chance. The contest was left to them. Hawkins's pride was aroused, and he shot more deliberately than usual. Three times they tried their skill, and three times the veteran was beaten. He seemed thunder-struck and grief-smitten, angry and churlish. At

applicants. I shall look to your conduct and career with an almost paternal interest. I will be proud to hear that you achieve a high position. I feel authorized to require of you every effort of which you are capable to meet my expectations. Let me hear from you, and do not fail to visit me here on your way to West Point."

length, however, admiration at what he considered something almost supernatural, got the better of him, and he stepped up to Quitman, and, taking off his hat, said, "Sir, you have done what no other man has been able to do. The beef is yours, and John Hawkins is yours, too." Quitman took his hand, praised his shooting, caressed Brown Bess, presented him the beef, and proposed a general treat. The crowd pitched in with three cheers for Quitman, and from that moment the contest was decided. He was chosen by a large majority. He ran altogether independent of politics, and upon his personal popularity, as he always preferred to do. He never was a partisan; he despised the arts of the politician, and had no taste for the intrigues and machinery of party.

He was placed on the Judiciary Committee, which consisted of Wm. L. Sharkey, P. R. R. Pray, and other able jurists, and took, it would appear from the journals, an active part in the House. Among other things, he advocated a memorial to Congress for the extinction of the Indian title within the state. It was likewise proposed to extend civil process, by statute, over the Indian territory, abolishing the jurisdictions of their chiefs, and thus paving the way for their voluntary removal to the fine domain assigned to their tribe on the waters of the Arkansas and Red Rivers. There was, however, a strong opposition to this measure, especially among the religious classes, prompted, chiefly, by missionaries quartered (and very comfortably quartered) among the Indians by societies located in Boston and New York. These men, aliens to our section in birth and feeling, secretly opposed to our domestic institutions, and having no pride in our progress, operated on the influential bodies with whom they were associated, whose conscientious scruples and sympathies were aroused by *ex parte* statements, and thus a formidable opposition was organized, even in Mississippi, to what was called the Indian policy of Jackson's administration. The proposed measure was at that session defeated, but in 1830 it was again brought forward by the Hon. Wm. Haile, of Hancock,* and passed with but one dissenting voice. In 1830 the Choctaws accepted a liberal proposition from the United States for their lands, which were soon organized into counties, and shortly afterward the Chickasaws followed their example. Those counties now comprise a large portion of the population and agricultural wealth of the state. It is satisfactory to reflect that our red brethren have profited, as it was intended they should, by the exchange, and have become well-organized nationalities, governed by humane and enlightened laws, and will soon enter, it is hoped, on terms of perfect equality, our family of united and sovereign states. The states of Mississippi and Alabama should never lose their interest in these fraternal tribes. Natives of our soil—born under the same stars and skies—having shed their blood, in critical times, freely in our defense—and having laws and institutions identical with our own—it is our duty to maintain friendly relations, and their political integrity as sovereign states.

Mr. Quitman, while in the Legislature, effected many reforms in the practice in chancery and courts of law, in the various branches of the state government, the law of administrators and guardians, and many other useful measures.

Just before the close of the session, he was invited by joint resolution to prepare a militia system for the state. A vacancy soon after happening in the office of chan-

* Previously a representative in Congress from Mississippi. He was a man of genius and of noble impulses, devoted to his native South. He died soon after in Wilkinson County.

cellor, he was appointed by the governor, and when the Legislature assembled, he was unanimously elected by that body.

He was a warm friend of the chancery system, and it was retained by the convention called to revise the Constitution solely through his influence, and by the confidence reposed in him as chancellor. Jan. 12th, 1829, he thus wrote Hon. Franklin E. Plummer, then a leading member of the Legislature: "I regret the inclination of your mind in relation to the Chancery Court. I will not now discuss the matter, lest I expose myself to the imputation of improper interference in which I am personally interested. I may, however, say that, in the infancy of our state, we should set the example of sober and well-considered legislation to our successors. We have much to answer for to posterity, and it will perhaps bless us for acts which short-sighted contemporaries condemn. Of all the Republican characters which history has handed down to us, I most admire Cato, who was willing to sacrifice not only his person, but his reputation for the sake of liberty. I have just read the report of the Secretary of War, and cordially approve of his plan for removing the Indians from the limits of the states. Our Legislature should act upon the suggestion, and extend process into the Indian territory, and impose taxes on white persons residing therein. Drive off the Northern missionaries and the lawless whites in the Indian nation, and we shall have no trouble in removing them. We have nothing new here, except that the members of Congress from Georgia and South Carolina have appeared at the Capitol in homespun. This is my plan for resisting the tariff."

His militia code, a work of great labor, was adopted, and, as he refused compensation, the Legislature, on motion of Mr. J. F. H. Claiborne, member from Adams County, presented him with a splendid copy of the writings of Jefferson, thus recognizing him as a disciple of that illustrious statesman.

In 1830 the Hon. Thomas B. Reed, a U. S. senator from the state of Mississippi, died. He had come to this state at an early age from Kentucky, with his family, in very limited circumstances. He was a fine-looking, commanding personage, of florid complexion, but never enjoying good health. He was irritable and somewhat haughty in his manners, and never personally popular; but, by his great ability, he placed himself at the head of the bar, and rose to be attorney general. He had violent enemies, as most men of superior talents have; but, after a struggle characterized by unusual bitterness, he had been elected to the Senate of the United States. In that body his first speech, on the extension of the U. S. Circuit Court system, gave him a high reputation, and he was advancing to the first class, when his health rapidly declined.

To fill his vacancy, George Poindexter, Joshua Childs, James C. Wilkins, Charles B. Green, David Dickson, William Haile, and Chancellor Quitman, all of them distinguished citizens, had been proposed. The following letter was addressed to Judge Quitman by one of the representatives from Natchez and the county of Adams.

From J. F. H. Claiborne.

"Soldier's Retreat, Oct. 20th, 1830.

"MY DEAR SIR,—Your name is mentioned in connection with the senatorial election. I have mentioned it myself in correspondence with members of the Legislature. Do you desire to be a candidate? If so, it will be expedient and proper to take bold ground on the leading questions of the day. You are not regarded strictly as a party man, but your sentiments are believed to be in harmony with the great body of the people.

As chancellor, I admire your course in standing aloof from politics; but if you become a candidate, not pledges, but *avowals* become necessary. My intention is to vote for George Poindexter. He desires the place, and it is due to his services and great abilities. In your general views I think you harmonize; I know you do as to the relative powers of the state and federal governments, and the dangerous propensity of the latter to usurp power. This is the last opportunity we shall have to recognize the services of Poindexter. He is old and infirm, but his intellect shines as brilliantly as ever, and his name will give strength to our section. I know he has bitter and powerful enemies in this county, and that my support of him will stimulate my opponents and alienate many of my friends; but he was the schoolmate, and, in after life and in troublesome times, the friend of my father. I know, too, that he is a Republican of the school of Jefferson, and I will vote for him to the last, if I sacrifice myself by so doing. I have already heard of menaces, but how little they know me who fancy that threats or opposition ever changed my purpose! From the past, and from the rebellious blood I inherit, they should know me better. You are my second choice. If Poindexter can not be elected, and you authorize your name to be brought forward, I will gladly support you. I do not believe our friend Colonel Wilkins desires the place. I *know* he can not be elected as interests now stand, and I have so informed him in the presence of Colonel Campbell, and given him names and reasons.

Judge Quitman replied as follows:

To J. F. H. Claiborne.

"Monmouth, Oct. 25th, 1830.

"In answering your last, I will commence at home. Your friendly feelings have associated my name, in a certain contingency, with the senatorial election. A number of partial friends from other counties, and among them some of your fellow-members of the Legislature, have hinted the same thing, and I believe, if my political sentiments upon the great national questions which are now discussed were better understood, I should stand a respectable poll. I have, however, thus far succeeded by adhering to a rule, from which I must not now depart—to establish my reputation in the office conferred upon me before I seek another. The people expect that I will faithfully perform the responsible duties now confided to me, not only the duties of chancellor, but reporting my own decisions, and their expectations shall be fulfilled if in my power. Besides, much of my future reputation will depend upon these official opinions, and I am content to abide by the judgment which shall be pronounced upon them, not for the evidences of superior talent they are to exhibit, but for the marks of industry and a conscientious regard for the rights of suitors which they shall manifest. Under these circumstances, I would not, I assure you, become a candidate, even though my election was certain. I am induced by your frankness thus to give you my notions, the loud thoughts of a constituent and friend, who will ever counsel with and advise you, and never quarrel, although you may differ from him. I note what you say about Mr. Poindexter. I respect the feeling that makes you prefer your father's friend. I marked this as one of your characteristics when you were in my office, and it first attracted me to you. I, too, would prefer Poindexter if he had health and his former vigor. Our friends M'Niel and Merrick both saw him at Louisville, and they assure me that he is unable to stand or move. What are we to do? We must have an intellectual man. R. J. Walker tells me he will not be a candidate. What is to be done but to take Wilkins? You are wrong in thinking that he does not desire the place. I am sure he does. Whether all his doctrines square with your and my views, is proper subject for inquiry."

Before the Legislature assembled the opposition to Mr. Poindexter had concentrated on Robert H. Adams, Esq., a distinguished member of the Natchez bar, who, at the general election a few months previous, had been elected, with Mr. Claiborne, to represent the county of Adams and city of Natchez in the Legislature. He did not take his seat as representative, but appeared there as a candidate for the Senate of the United States. He was what was then called "'a Jackson man" in his politics; but the influence of the Natchez bar, of the banks, the commercial interest, then chiefly concentrated at Natchez, and of the combined opposition, were brought into action in his favor. They had never before been exerted for "a Jackson man." Besides this, the deplorable condition of Mr. Poindexter's health was urged as an argument for the election of Mr. Adams. When the Legislature assembled, several of Mr. Poindexter's friends, finding they were to be hard pressed, urged him to visit Jackson, the seat of government. His reply was characteristic:

"Ashwood Place, Wilkinson Co., Dec. 25th, 1829.

"MY DEAR SIR,—I had written you, before I received yours of the 22d, on the subject to which it relates. I differ with you entirely as to the effect of a visit to Jackson. It would be degrading to both parties. On my part, it would manifest a mean solicitude for office which, thank God, I do not feel; and, on the part of the electors, it would imply that they might be led from one man to another, with perfect ease, if one would only take the proper pains. Show yourself in person, flatter their vanity, and convince them by actual inspection of your physical powers, and you will find them the most docile creatures on earth. If I had no public character to rest my claims on, if I had rendered no service to the state, if I were entirely unknown as a politician and a jurist, I would eagerly substitute for merit personal attentions, urgent solicitations, and disgusting professions and protestations. The line of conduct which I have marked out for myself is founded on moral virtue, and supports the dignity of the senatorial character. The other course is sycophantic and demoralizing in all its tendencies. You will find that no gentleman who intended to vote for me will decline doing so because I do not choose to approach him with personal importunities. Those who do not mean to vote for me may make my remaining at home a convenient excuse. There can be no mistake about the state of my health. If I am worthy of the high trust of senator in Congress, I certainly may be trusted to tell the truth as to the state of my health. On former occasions I have rejected important offices, because my health would not justify my accepting them. This very office of senator was offered to me in 1825, but I could not fulfill the duties, and it was declined. But if other evidence is wanted concerning my health, my friends and neighbors, who will be at Jackson, and my physicians will testify to it. If I had the strength of my overseer (a very stout man) I would not make my personal appearance at Jackson until after the vote is taken. I should then take great pleasure in paying my respects to the members. Candidates without merit, who are willing to rely on management, will honor the members with their company and conversation on all occasions, and will be 'all things to all men,' that they may gain favor with a few. If, then, my friends think that my presence is a *sine qua non*, they may drop my name as a candidate. You seem to doubt whether the senator from —— will vote against me. I can assure you I should as soon expect to see a white crow as to obtain the vote of any man in this state of the name of ——. Huston and others are laboring in their vocation. They expect to get a share of Mr. Adams's practice—all pure patriotism and love of country! A Clay man supporting a Jackson man, and the Jackson men of Adams County electing a Clay man to the Legislature. 'Heads I win, tails *you* lose.' The good people of Mississippi have been duped and ridden for many years past, and I suppose they are not yet sufficiently gulled.

"Your friend, most truly,   GEO. POINDEXTER. ·
"Hon. J. F. H. Claiborne, Jackson."

The Legislature did not take this high-toned view of the case, and Mr. Robert H. Adams was elected. He was, it is believed, a native of Tennessee. At all events, he came from that state to Mississippi, and took at once a high position at the bar. He was in the vigor of life, and, though not a man of liberal education, had been endowed by nature with extraordinary powers. He was both argumentative and eloquent, and as an advocate has, perhaps, never had an equal at the bar of that state. He served but one session, and died soon after his return home from Washington. At the ensuing session of the Legislature, George Poindexter was elected to fill his place.

Chancellor Quitman, though properly taking no active part in politics, and occupied almost daily with the responsibilities of his office, nevertheless found time to think a good deal on public concerns.

To J. F. H. Claiborne.

"Monmouth, Oct. 18th, 1830.

"DEAR CLAIBORNE,—I have put off a further reply to your letter of the 25th August with a view to minute the amendments of which our code is susceptible, as they might occur to me from time to time; but I have found myself so engrossed by the preparation of my decrees and opinions for publication, and by other official business, that I am still, in a measure, unprepared, and must answer you now only in part.

"It will be certain that an amendment to the Constitution will be necessary in a few years. The acquisition of the Indian territory will make this imperative, and the only question is, whether the present is a more suitable time than the period when the actual necessity shall occur. It seems to me that the absence of political excitement, and the serenity of our horizon, point out the present as the most suitable moment to careen the ship of state. Talent will be called to the performance of this duty without regard to party. We know not how long this quiet atmosphere will continue. Storms may arise in a few years, by which the scum and dregs of society may be agitated to the surface, and disturb and destroy the pure element we now enjoy. Let us do, then, what may be necessary, while we may do it in peace.

"The 2d and 3d articles of the compact limiting the number of judges, and the 9th section of the 3d article limiting the number of representatives to 36 until our white population amounts to 80,000, and yet requiring that each county shall have a representative, are incompatible with the acquisition and organization of new and extensive territory. Even setting aside the necessity of the matter, policy requires some amendments to the charter. Our judicial system is exceptionable. The trial of questions in the last resort should be vested in an independent, impartial, and unprejudiced tribunal, composed of judges in number sufficient to avoid as well the frailty or errors of one individual, as the great division of responsibility where there are too many judges. Three is, in my opinion, the golden number. When a set of men are called on to decide upon their own errors, we must expect to find some bias toward former impressions, or a disposition to question the accuracy of one who has detected a flaw.

"I likewise am in favor of biennial sessions of the Legislature, and some change made to prevent important questions of legislation from being made subsidiary to the election of a senator or a judge. Our whole bloody criminal code calls for radical revision. I see no cure for it but amputation. The limb should be cut off from the body politic, and a scion of less barbarous growth engrafted thereon. For the many grades of moral turpitude which are considered proper subjects for the denunciation of the laws, many and various grades of punishment are required, and the punishment of all crimes, except, perhaps, those of the deepest dye, should be so inflicted as to leave room for amendment. It were better to punish with death in all cases than to brand the culprit with an indelible stigma and turn him loose upon society. Yet for all the various classes of crime known to our laws, we have but four kinds of punishment—the whipping-post, the pillory, the hot iron, and halter. Imprisonment in the common jail is seldom resorted to. When the courts have the alternative they rarely order imprisonment, owing to its expense to the state. The prisoner must be supported at considerable cost, while his labor, which, under a better system, might be profitably employed, is wholly lost. The penitentiary is the remedy. This would enable us to graduate punishments, and would be followed by more certainty in the conviction of offenders. Many crimes of dangerous character— negro stealing and forgery, for example—which are now capital, go unpunished, in consequence of the disinclination of juries to find a verdict of guilty. In my opinion, the man who shall succeed in introducing the penitentiary system in this state will deserve the highest honor. Were I in search of popularity, I would feel certain of success with such a subject. It is not a mere experiment. Good management will enable the system to more than support itself.

"Let me urge upon you, by all means, the necessity of a law to prevent and punish the circulation of incendiary pamphlets, etc., in this state."

At the session of the Legislature of 1830, the great question of interest was the extension of the laws of Mississippi over the Indian tribes within their limits. The constitutionality and justice of the measure were boldly denied, very generally, by the opponents of the national administration. Chancellor Quitman was consulted on the subject, and replied in the following characteristic letter:

To J. F. H. Claiborne.

"Monmouth, Jan. 8th, 1830.

"DEAR CLAIBORNE,—I regret that we did not meet before your departure for Jackson. I had much to confer with you about, and could have done so more satisfactorily than in writing. You ask my opinion upon the constitutional power of the General Assembly to tax and otherwise legislate for the Indians within our limits. I take this view, briefly, of the question. By the laws of nature, no portion of the human race have a right to appropriate to themselves a greater part of the surface of the earth than is necessary, with the aid of agriculture, for their comfortable maintenance. This is the fundamental principle of the right, claimed and exercised by European nations upon the discovery of this continent, to appropriate portions of it to their own use, and a denial of the right would invalidate their and our title. The United States claims federal jurisdiction over the whole territory within its boundaries. The states severally claim municipal jurisdiction over their respective limits, and over all persons within the same, without exception or distinction. By what principle, then, are the Indians exempt from this authority? The Constitution of the United States is silent upon the subject. It only provides that Congress may regulate commerce with the Indian tribes. All other powers are reserved to the states. When not restricted by the federal Constitution, they have absolute powers. Mississippi could only be admitted into the Union upon an equal footing with the other states. The power of Massachusetts and New York to tax their Indians is not questioned. Our state has made no treaty with the Indians, by which she is trammeled in this respect. Where, then, are the restraints upon our sovereign right to tax and legislate for all persons within our limits? Because the United States has treated with the Choctaws for cessions of their soil, are we to consider them independent nations? The federal government may treat with an individual or a company within the limits of a state, but that does not release them from their allegiance to the state, nor from their responsibility to its jurisdiction, nor their obligation to contribute to its support. Good faith and Christian charity require that we should exact nothing more from the Indians than we impose on ourselves. The idea of two municipal authorities in the same territory is absurd and irrational. The truth is, some of our Northern *friends* appear to have taken our Indians and negroes under their special care, and, if we submit to their assumptions, we shall next find them claiming to regulate all our domestic legislation, and even the guardianship of our wives and children. .

"The governor has probably laid my militia system before your honorable body. I bestowed much labor upon it. Impress upon the members the necessity of compromising individual opinions a little. We must have an efficient militia. Keep the Supreme Court at Natchez a while longer. I presume you are all absorbed with the elections. I hope you have made Joseph Dunbar speaker. Your declining the written invitation from the Eastern members in his favor, so much your senior and your relative, was right. We regard the election of Robert H. Adams to the U. S. Senate as certain. Are you still resolved to vote for Poindexter? Adams is certainly the choice of this county. I can not be mistaken in this. He is a man of very superior talents, and of many noble qualities. He esteems you highly, and feels mortified that he is not to get your vote. Your friends are anxious about your course, and it would be unkind to conceal from you that, should you vote against a constituent who is so popular and deserving as Adams, for a citizen of another county, who never has been popular here, and whose physical inability is not doubted, there will be a great clamor, and your next election will be bitterly opposed. Construe these remarks as I mean them. They are not intended to dictate to you. Your vote for Poindexter will not change *my* feelings, though I am warmly for Adams. But, as your friend, it is my duty to apprise you of the state of feeling in Natchez on this subject. In the county you are very strong, and may, probably, sustain yourself, but the city is devoted to Adams, and expects much from him in the Senate.

"Let me advise you, likewise, not to appear too often on the floor."

In 1831, after the spring term of his court was over, he went North with his family on a visit to his venerable father at Rhinebeck. He had left there eleven years before, with only a few dollars in his pocket, with no connections in the Western country to which he was bound, with only one human being there whom he had ever met with, and he had made his way successfully, established friendships that endured through life, studied a profession, and secured the means to go to the far South. Once more among strangers, but again to succeed by the same qualities that had distinguished him at Hartwick, at Mount Airy, and in Ohio — modest and decorous habits, scrupulous integrity, and close attention to business. He now returned, identified by marriage with one of the oldest and wealthiest families of Mississippi, in possession of an ample income from his own lucrative practice, and chancellor of a sovereign state. His relations, his neighbors, and schoolmates clustered about him, rejoicing at the prosperity of their old favorite, and proud to see that it had not rendered him arrogant or vain. His simple tastes, his rural habits, the kindness of his nature, and his affability of manners were unchanged. The dogs, the guns, the boats of the village were put in requisition for his amusement, and even his old musk-rat traps were not forgotten. Nor did the happiness he experienced from re-entering once more the paternal circle and renewing the associations of youth, direct his thoughts from public concerns and the interests of his adopted state. He wrote the following characteristic letter, which foreshadows the views that marked his future career :

To J. F. H. Claiborne.

"Rhinebeck, July 31st, 1831.

"DEAR CLAIBORNE,—On my return yesterday from a fortnight's tour through the New England States, I had the pleasure to receive your favor. It was a great treat. You must either know my taste in familiar correspondence, or, from some parity of disposition, you have served up a series of dishes that suit my palate. I have but one objection to your letter, that is, to 'burn it.' I will execute your injunction with regret. When you

E 2

understand my method and care in filing letters received
in an off-hand, friendly correspondence, you will be under
no apprehension that even an accident will ever expose
your sensibility or your criticisms to the curiosity or remarks of others. I have the same delicacy myself.
There are flowers that bloom in the shade of personal
confidence that the storms of vulgar life would convert
into worthless weeds.

"You fancy that the short respite I am now enjoying
from the vexatious cares of my office will destroy my
taste for active pursuits. Not so. In 1826 I determined
to devote the vigor and strength of my life to honorable
and useful ambition. Sweet as the repose and retirement of philosophy may be—and a charming picture you
have drawn of it—I will not shrink from the labor and
the struggle which that determination will cost. To
raise the standard of independence, and boldly fling it in
the face of any party; sink or swim, to stand by the
best interests of our country; to brave the shock of public opinion when required, shall be to me a pleasure. In
pursuing such a course, how happy I shall be to find myself side by side with the virtuous, intelligent, and generous young men of our state. A phalanx of bold, independent, and honest men may be, for a long time, in the
minority, but even then their influence upon public affairs will be felt and respected, and an intelligent and
high-toned people will, sooner or later, appreciate their
merits.

"Aug. 6th. Since writing the above I have been in
motion about the country, and will now gallop over a
few of the many political observations collected during
my long journey from Natchez, reserving particulars until my return. A very fierce struggle is going on in
Kentucky. In no part of the Union have I seen so much
excitement. In Virginia, which I traversed from west
to east, there is evidently an important change working
in sectional politics. They are growing lukewarm in
support of the (Jackson's) administration, and I have no
doubt the dissensions in the cabinet, and the develop-
ments that have been made, will ferment the leaven now
generally diffused. My opinion is that Virginia is in favor of Calhoun, and, if so, Jackson can only be support-

ed upon the principle of being the least of two evils. At Charlottesville I had the pleasure of an hour's interview with our senator, Mr. Poindexter. I found his political opinions so nearly my own, you may conceive I enjoyed a great treat in his conversation. He is more pungent and tart than ever, and his tone is something like a sneer. He is awfully severe on Jackson and his advisers, and no less bitter against some of our folks at home. He tells me he has written you at length upon the politics of the day. I found him walking among the people in the court-yard, without assistance and without crutches. He is a man of extraordinary intellectual powers. You knew him from your childhood, and I do not now wonder at your risking your popularity to support him. He has fascinated me. How is it that his private character is so bad? Why do we hear so much said against him in Adams County? His intemperance, his gambling, his libertinism, and his dishonesty. He gives no indications of these defects, and he is here, where he once resided, taken by the hand by the first people and followed by the crowd. By the way, have you ever met with the pamphlet published by Dr. Brown against Poindexter? I met with it in Kentucky. It charges him with base cowardice in several personal difficulties in Mississippi and at the battle of New Orleans. Can so bold a politician be deficient in personal courage? Can a public speaker who so fiercely arraigns so many influential citizens be himself a knave? The testimony in this pamphlet is very strong. The witnesses are Dr. Brown, Colonel Percy, Dr. Hogg, Dr. Stephen Duncan, Elisha Smith, and others whom we well know. I send the pamphlet to you.* Mr. P. is quite decided in his opposition to the administration, and thinks our congressional delegation will act with him. Will his opposition to General Jackson affect your relations to him? He is for Calhoun.

"Here in New York I can plainly perceive among the Jackson party an alienation of feeling. The Democratic anti-tariff men, the free-trade and state-rights men, who

---

* All this will be explained in a biography of the Hon. George Poindexter, based on his own correspondence and manuscripts, which I am now writing.—J. F. H. C.

were all under the banner of Jackson, begin to feel uneasy, but, as yet, have not determined on their course. The anti-masons, the no-Sunday-mail party, the manufacturers, the working interest, and the latitudinarians and so-called philanthropists all incline to Clay. The free-trade and state-rights portion of the Jackson party may well open their eyes when leading papers like the New York Courier and Enquirer are evidently shifting over to the tariff side, to prepare the way for Mr. Van Buren. I lately dined with a large party of intelligent men, who all along had supported the administration. Being asked about the impression which the late cabinet explosion had made in Mississippi, I ventured the opinion that a great majority of our politicians were disposed to side with Mr. Calhoun. One of them replied, 'We have the same feeling. The President is abandoning the principles which raised him to office.'

"For my part, I hope Mr. Calhoun, or some decided anti-tariff man, will become a candidate. We must know the opinion of presidential candidates on this tariff question. An idea has frequently occurred to me of proposing to the Southern Republicans to run an independent or unpledged ticket for electors. How would this do? I wish you would reflect upon it, and give me your advice. In the mean time mention it to no one. If Mr. Van Buren is a decided tariff and internal-improvement man, I have no notion of smoothing his road to the presidency by a compromising course of policy.

"Among the masses in the Northern States, every other feeling is now swallowed up by a religious enthusiasm which is pervading the country. Wherever I have traveled in the free states, I have found preachers holding three, four, six, and eight days' meeting, provoking revivals, and begging contributions for the Indians, the negroes, the Sunday-schools, foreign missions, home missions, the Colonization Society, temperance societies, societies for the education of pious young men, distressed sisters, superannuated ministers, reclaimed penitents, church edifices, church debts, religious libraries, etc., etc.: clamorously exacting the last penny from the poor enthusiast, demanding the widow's mite, the orphan's pittance, and denouncing the vengeance of Heaven on those who feel unable to give, or who question the propriety of these contributions, whether wholesale or specific. They are not only extortionate, but absolutely insulting in their demands; and my observations lead me to believe that there is a vast deal of robbery and roguery under this stupendous organization of religious societies. That there is misapplication of funds, and extravagance, and a purse-proud and arrogant priesthood supported by these eleemosynary appeals, there can be no doubt. When in the city of New York, I lodged at the Clinton Hotel. From my window I saw several splendid edifices, which could not be valued at less than $100,000, belonging to the American Tract and other societies! Thus is the industry of remote parts of the Union taxed to build palaces in the Northern cities, and to support herds of lazy cattle. Here are clerks by the hundred, salaried liberally out of contributions wrung from pious and frugal persons in the South; and these officials, like the majority of their theologians and divines, are inimical to our institutions, and use our own money to defame and damage us! Respect for the proposed object of these societies, and the fear of their power, have deterred even the bold from exposing their abuses. But such thraldom must not be submitted to.* I am heartily tired of the North, and, except

* I find these opinions, uttered near thirty years ago, singularly confirmed by the Rev. Dr. Thornwell, of South Carolina, in a speech delivered by him in the General Assembly of the Old School Presbyterian Church, May, 1860. The subject was the policy of the Church in regard to mission and other boards. The quotation is from the Cincinnati Commercial:

"Dr. Thornwell, of South Carolina, who addressed the Assembly at Nashville, in 1855, on the same subject, most certainly made an able effort to convince the Assembly that the Church has no power to delegate authority committed to her by her Master; that she should do her own work, and not appoint boards or other organizations to do it. He argued, too, that it is a sin and a shame to have boards where the membership is complimentary, and the privilege of consulting in which can be purchased with money. The principle is money. The seed of the serpent may be harmless, but the seed contains the poison. We need unity, simplicity, and completeness of action; and he closed by rejoicing that, when the millennium comes, we will not find it necessary to change our principles. But I can not say, as the brethren

parting from my relations, shall feel happy when I set my face homeward.

have, 'We have done well enough.' Look at 800,000,000 of heathen without the Gospel! Look at the resources, the riches of our Church, and dare we say we have done well enough? I believe these boards have stood in the way of free action of the Church.

"He referred, likewise, to Dr. B. M. Smith's history of those boards, as full of startling disclosures."

In the New Orleans Christian Advocate of May 30th, 1860, edited by Rev. C. C. Gillespie, one of the strongest writers in the Methodist Episcopal Church, South, I find an able article, prompted by the anniversary meetings of the societies referred to in Quitman's letter. The article, which furnishes thoughts enough for a book, and a very interesting book, thus concludes:

"We confess we are sick of societies. We may be wrong; if so, we hope for pardon and more light. There is a cold, heartless, mechanical utilitarianism about this exclusive associational way of doing good that crushes out all individuality of reason, affection, and progress. Societies grow fat and strong, and individual Christian character remains stationary, or, rather, assumes dwarfish proportions. It is a sort of concentration of all the surplus energy of the artificial, cantish Yankeeism there is in American character. It is true, there must be associated effort. We do not deny that. But it should be harmonious with those individual aptitudes and social relations and sympathies which God has ordained. Such association we find in the Church. God made our individual constitutions, He established our social relations and sympathies, and He ordained the Church. They are all harmonious. It may be said that, condemning High Churchism, we are High Churchmen ourselves. In the sense of giving the Church the place, and the importance, and the allegiance intended by its Divine Founder, and set forth in the Scriptures, we are High Churchmen. We have almost as little sympathy with Low Churchmen, of any school, as for societarians. They both undervalue the Church in theory, or are unfaithful to their own Church ideal. High Churchism, in the sense of giving the Church a character and power not taught in the Scriptures, is the other extreme. Societarianism and Low Churchism lead to indifferentism and infidelity. Devotion to the Church of Christ, as set forth in the Bible, as 'the purchase of Christ's blood'—as 'the body of Christ,' as 'the pillar and ground of the truth,' as the 'kingdom' of Christ, against which the gates of hell shall not prevail—is simple Christianity, as far as it goes."

These are striking illustrations of the forecast and sagacity of Quitman. He saw, thirty years ago, what no one else saw at that day, but what is now viewed as a serious social and religious evil.

"Your elections are now over. I look forward to hear that you and Bingaman are elected representatives, and Gridley sheriff. Write me again at Lexington, Ky. Your description of Plummer's visit to Natchez, and of the intrigues it occasioned, amused me much. I know he has the ready talent and tact to carry him through, if he has prudence. What is the editor of the 'Clarion' about, in his severe strictures on Ingham, and Branch, and Berrien, who very properly retired in disgust from Jackson's cabinet?"

On his return to Mississippi, Chancellor Quitman took ground against the administration, advised earnest opposition to Mr. Van Buren, chiefly on account of his alleged tariff proclivities, and declared himself for Mr. Calhoun. He organized a State Rights association in Adams County, and others were formed in Amite, Hinds, Wilkinson, and two or three other counties, through his instrumentality. Little headway, however, was made by those bodies. The State Rights movement had little sympathy then, even in the South. Mr. Calhoun, outside of his own state, had no general popularity. In Mississippi his supporters were "few and far between." In Natchez and Adams County, where Quitman resided, the Jackson party had discarded Calhoun, and the friends of Mr. Clay were even more hostile to him, many of them construing his doctrines as dangerous and treasonable. Yet Quitman never hesitated a moment to hoist his standard and publicly hold his monthly State Rights meetings, with seldom more than fifteen or twenty supporters.

In 1832 he presented himself as a candidate to represent the county of Adams in the convention called to frame a new Constitution for the state. The county had great interests at stake, and highly appreciated his influence and talents, and the general conservative character of his opinions. There would have been no serious

opposition to his election but for the real or affected
fears of a few persons, Whigs and Democrats, who
perceived, or pretended to perceive, that his views as
to federal and state relations, like Mr. Calhoun's, were
mischievous and revolutionary.   The following hand-bill
made its appearance:

"Public Meeting.

"The citizens of Adams County, adverse to the election
of judges by the people, and opposed to *Nullification*,
are requested to meet at the court-house, in the city
of Natchez, on Thursday next, the 10th instant, at 11
o'clock.

"The necessity for calling this meeting is deeply regretted; not the more so, that it has occurred at a period
so close upon the election, than as affecting the political
standing of a gentleman who has been placed before the
people of Adams, by the spontaneous act of a large portion of its citizens, as a candidate for one of their highest
gifts.   It is believed by a large body of those of Judge
Quitman's friends who sustained his nomination, and who
intended by their votes to have contributed to his election, that he is a *Nullifier in principle!*   That his opinions, frequently of late expressed upon the subject of
nullification, are the same as Mr. Calhoun's and Mr.
Hayne's; the one its author, the other its first public
propagator.   Judge Quitman's friends in this county believe that nullification is unsound in theory, and contrary
to the Constitution; that its tendency is anarchy, and
that the effect of its practical application to any given
case *is disunion!*   They look to the indications in South
Carolina, and despair of its permanency, while she asserts
her right and intention to nullify a law of the United
States.   They look to the threats of her governor that,
before the year is out, her citizens will be in arms; to the
declarations of a portion of her delegation in Congress,
who wish to go home and prepare for war.   They are
also well aware of the disposition of the leaders of the
party to form a great Southern league to crusade against
the Union.   Under these circumstances, and at such a
crisis, a large portion of Judge Quitman's friends can not

sustain him, without sustaining nullification, and putting at issue in this state the question of union or disunion.

"It is therefore thought proper that this meeting be called, with the view of endeavoring to produce such reconciliation as will prevent any serious division in the ranks of those opposed to the election of judges by the people, or, if that is found to be impracticable, to bring out another candidate in place of Judge Quitman. It is expected and desired that Judge Quitman will attend; and, if his opinions have been misrepresented, that his friends may be undeceived and again united.

"MANY CITIZENS."

To this he responded as follows:

"To the Citizens of Adams County.

"I have just learned that there has been industriously circulated a notice, anonymously signed 'Many Citizens,' calling a public meeting of the citizens of Adams County adverse to the election of judges by the people, and opposed to nullification, for the purpose 'of bringing out, if reconciliation should be found impracticable, another candidate in my place, and desiring me to attend.' Such a desire coming from friends I would cheerfully comply with, but I can not recognize the authors of such a course as '*friends*,' nor can I permit myself to be made the football of political opponents. I have protested, and do again solemnly protest, against making my private political or religious opinions the test of my qualification for the convention. The former have been brought before the public without my consent or agency. They are now branded by terms odious and unmeaning to the public ear, and party excitement is brought to bear upon me. To the calm and deliberate expression of the public will I will most cheerfully submit. I can not, in justice to my friends, accept the invitation of those whom I must consider political opponents, and the time is too short to give this notice full circulation before the contemplated meeting. I therefore respectfully request that those of my fellow-citizens who feel interested in this matter will assemble at the court-house in Natchez on Friday next, at 11 o'clock, when I will candidly express my views of the relation which the states and general government bear to each other, and endeavor to show that the doctrines which I entertain were not 'invented by Mr. Calhoun and first propagated by Mr. Hayne,' but were propagated by Mr. Jefferson in 1798, and have ever since been the true test of Republican and ultra Federal doctrines, and continue to be the grand landmarks of distinction between the advocates of a constitutional government and the arbitrary despotism of an oligarchy.   JOHN A. QUITMAN.

" Monmouth, July 17th, 1832."

Finding, however, that the meeting called by the first hand-bill for the 19th instant was a large one, the excitement having assembled the people from all parts of the county, he appeared, and defended himself with vigor and skill. The result was thus announced:

"A meeting of a portion of the citizens of Adams County was held at the court-house in Natchez on the 19th inst., pursuant to public notice in a hand-bill signed 'Many Citizens,' calling a meeting of citizens adverse to the election of judges by the people and opposed to nullification, for the purpose of bringing out, if reconciliation should be found impracticable, another candidate for the convention in the place of Chancellor Quitman. Fountain Winston, Esq., was called to the chair, and R. M. Gaines appointed secretary.

"Judge Quitman explained his reason for appearing at the meeting, after having declined to do so in his hand-bill of the 17th inst., by stating that he had been since requested to attend by many of his known friends. He then addressed the meeting at considerable length on the subject of the respective rights of the general and state governments, after which Dr. Duncan, in a spirit of conciliation, submitted a resolution which, being modified on the motion of John T. M'Murran, Esq., was unanimously adopted by the meeting in the following form, to wit:

"*Resolved*, As the sense of this meeting, that we are opposed to the doctrine of nullification, and believe that its propagation would endanger our dearest and best interests; that John A. Quitman having at this meeting

made a distinct exposition of his views upon the subject
of the relation which the state and federal governments
bear to each other, said views do not amount to nullification, according to the usual acceptation of the term,
and that said John A. Quitman ought to be supported
for the convention on the ticket as originally selected at
a general meeting of the citizens of this county, in this
place, in May last.

"FOUNTAIN WINSTON, Chairman.
"R. M. GAINES, Secretary."

In his speech he neither renounced nor qualified a principle, but he traced his whole code to Mr. Jefferson; and
the Democrats dared not vote a resolution of censure
(and the opposition were not strong enough to do so)
upon the illustrious founder of their party. In the course
of the speech he expressed, with regard to the state Constitution, opinions so acceptable to his audience, and
there were such evidences of his personal popularity, especially among the young men of all parties, threatening
to override any and every organization, that it was deemed prudent to find nothing to condemn.

Quitman had no notion of evading the issue. He met
it at the threshold. He proclaimed the doctrines of Calhoun to be the doctrines of Jefferson, and he appeared
in the court-house, in the face of his opponents, and
proved it. After his luminous defense, there was nothing to censure. This was the first time that his state-
rights opinions had been publicly arraigned. He had
adopted them when studying the Constitution and history of his country. He brought them with him when
he came to Mississippi. He knew they were unpopular
in his immediate vicinity, where the opposite school of
politics prevailed, and throughout the state, where enthusiasm for President Jackson diverted the public from
abstract discussions. He adhered to these opinions
through life with a constancy that neither opposition nor

temptation could shake, and his faith in them as the only true interpretation of constitutional power, and the only guarantee for pacific relations between the federal and state governments, grew stronger at every stage of his career.

A few days after this meeting he issued an address on the mooted questions of state policy of that day, which even now may be profitably read.

"*To the Electors of Adams County.*

"FELLOW-CITIZENS,—It is known to you generally that I have been nominated, by a public meeting of citizens of this county, one of the candidates to represent you in the convention. I believed that a long residence among you, together with the public stations I have held, had made my character and political principles so well known to most of you, as to render a public communication of this kind unnecessary. I was anxious that the people should be left to the quiet exercise of their own good sense and judgment in the selection of members of the convention, and had determined to confine my agency to verbal discussions and arguments.

"Some recent occurrences, the example of most of the candidates, and misrepresentations of my opinions, have induced me to change my course, and to appear, at this late period, before the public in a circular, for the imperfection of which I must ask all the indulgence to which great haste and limited time may entitle me.

"A most important crisis is near at hand. We are about to remodel our organic law. The people of this state are called upon to appoint representatives to alter, revise, and amend their frame of government. This work will require the wisest and most experienced heads, for upon it will depend mainly, not only the character of our state, both political and moral, but the happiness and prosperity of our citizens.

"The slightest defect in this work will create discontent, and may produce incalculable misery. Upon its provisions must rest our most sacred rights, the free enjoyment of our lives, our personal security and private property. It is not, therefore, surprising that the objects of the proposed convention should be matters of the deepest interest to every citizen.

"The organization of the judiciary, and the mode of appointing judges, are prominent subjects of inquiry. There are those among us who are disposed to try a new experiment in this department. Believing as I do, that this experiment would be dangerous in the extreme, would tend to corruption, and strike a fatal blow at the independence of the judiciary, I will stop and examine it briefly.

"Every argument that I have seen or heard, in favor of the election of judges by the people, has been commenced with old and stale maxims, such as, 'The people are the source of all political power;' 'We should not delegate any power which we can conveniently exercise ourselves.' Maxims which nobody now denies, which are so generally acknowledged that the repetition of them can only be intended to create the impression that others dispute them. A disposition is, also, evinced by some aspiring men to flatter and tickle our ears with praises of our virtue and intelligence. We are represented as the most perfect people on earth—all of us saints and philosophers! Do you suppose our flatterers believe what they assert? If they did, fellow-citizens, they would not dare to utter such fulsome adulations in our ears. When a man flatters us *we should* take it for granted he has an indifferent opinion of our sense and judgment. We are treated like spoiled children, who must be bribed by sweetmeats to love the giver. I have too good an opinion of those among whom my lot is cast to court your favor by flattery and praise. I will address myself to you as men—full grown—sensible men, who will act from judgment and principle, and will approbate candor though it may appear in a rough dress.

"We all agree that we have the *right* and are *capable* of electing our judges if we think fit. The question is solely one of policy, whether it will be to our interest that we should choose them by popular suffrage; if not, it would be madness to exercise the *right*. We have a right to burn down our houses, but surely, before we do so, we will reckon the advantage to be derived from such an act. If we direct any of our public servants to appoint judges, we exercise as much power as if we chose them ourselves. Be not deceived, then, with the idea that a right which you possess is in danger. Allow your reason and your judgment, with the aid of your experience, coolly and calmly to investigate the subject. If you then find that popular elections would not be so likely to place upon the bench upright, talented, and independent judges, do not permit the false idea of a contest for rights to prejudice your interests. A constitution is intended not merely to establish a frame of government, but also principally to define and limit the powers of the several departments, and to protect the private citizen in his reserved rights. It is thus intended for the benefit of the minority, to protect them against the action of the majority; to protect the weak against the strong, the poor and infirm against the rich and powerful. The judicial department is to apply these restraints. Is it not therefore improper, in the very threshold, to place this department strictly and immediately under the influence and control of those who are to be restrained? If the judicial department is to be completely under the influence and control of the mere majority, that majority might as well govern without any restrictions, and a limitation of powers would be absurd. Let it not be said that the majority will never do wrong. I admit that in times of quiet, when men's minds are left to the influence of sober reflection, it is not probable that the many will unjustly oppress the few. I grant farther, that, when this does occur, they will eventually correct their errors. But the history of nations, of our sister states, of our own infant state, shows that, in times of violent excitement, the many have abused their powers, and attempted to oppress and tyrannize over the minority. I refer you to the excitements in Kentucky, which produced the occupying claimant-laws and the relief projects. Look to the intense feeling produced in Georgia by the Yazoo claims, to the agitation which pervaded Alabama on the subject of usurious interest. Majorities were, in all these cases, ready to break down all constitutional restrictions, and invade the sacred rights of their fellow-citizens. A firm, intelligent, and independent judiciary was found to check the mad career of grasping interest and ambition. Suppose, in these cases, that the judicial departments had been placed directly under the influence and control of the interested majority, constitutional restrictions would have been but ropes of sand, and the judges would have lent their aid to trample under foot the lives, liberties, and property of the weak and defenseless. But not so. A well-organized judiciary has always been found the friend of the poor and the ark of safety to the oppressed. We should, then, as we regard our liberties as citizens, sustain and support an independent judiciary. By *independent*, I do not mean *irresponsible*. No. I would make them most rigidly amenable to some impartial tribunal for a proper and virtuous discharge of their important duties. I know, too, that the constitutional expression of the will of the majority is, and must be, the rule of action. Constitutional restrictions are not intended to defeat that will, but to restrain it until it can be ascertained to be the result of solemn and mature reflection. Every man of observation must have perceived that all our public officers, however appointed, feel their dependence upon public sentiment. Most men, from a principle of timidity, are actuated more by that feeling than by their own judgment. I am, therefore, inclined to think that there is no necessity for increasing this sense of dependence. A greater portion of it would not make our public servants more honest, but might have a tendency to render them, like the courtiers of a despot, more subservient and sycophantic.

"My time admonishes me to pass rapidly over the many strong arguments against popular elections. I will briefly touch upon some, and leave the good sense and experience of my readers to supply what is wanting. We all admit that no human tribunal and no mode of appointment can be perfect. If we could call down from heaven superior intelligences to apply the laws, and to decide controversies between man and man, we might expect perfection. We are compelled to place upon the bench human nature with all its infirmities. It is all-important, then, that we should remove it, as far as practicable, from all influences that can operate upon the weakness to which all men are liable. Partiality is not necessarily the result of a corrupt heart. It may arise from weakness or timidity. Its possessor may be ignorant of its existence. Impartiality rarely exists where the feelings are excited. Can we, then, expect this quality in a man who has just come from a hot electioneering canvass, in which he has succeeded, after a hard-fought battle, who sees before him, on the one side, friends who have risked every thing for his promotion, and, on the other hand, opponents who have waged a war against his public and private character, propagated calumnies against his reputation, and now sullenly mutter threats of revenge? These friends and opponents have controversies before this judge involving their fortunes or their characters. I leave the answer to every man's breast, whether strict impartiality can be expected from a judge under such circumstances. But, suppose the judge should rise superior to frail human nature and should even decide impartially, will the suitors be satisfied? If the decision be in favor of his friend, will no voice be raised to impugn his motives? I fear that the whispers of suspicion would drive every honest man, jealous of his reputation, from a station of such difficulty and danger.

"The advocates of popular elections of judges have reversed the rules of logic, and attempted to place the burden of proof upon us. Firmly convinced of the truth of our cause, we have made no opposition to this course, though unfair in principle. They propose a new experiment. Let them prove its advantages. Have they shown that one benefit would result from it? Have they shown that objections to the present mode may not be remedied without resorting to untried theories?

"I appeal to the candor of every man to justify me, when I say that their addresses have been more directed to the feelings and prejudices than to the judgment. We are accused of holding doctrines absurd in the extreme. You have been told that we, who are opposed to popular elections of judges, assert that the people are not to be '*trusted*' with the election of their judges; that 'guardians should be appointed over them; that they are *incapable* of forming a correct opinion of the qualifications of a judge;' that the community in which we live ' is *weak* or *dishonest* enough to vote for a partial judge.' I need scarcely say that such nonsense has never dropped from my lips, nor have I ever heard such arguments from a sensible man. Is it, then, fair—is it candid for our opponents to attempt to prejudice the public mind by such misrepresentations of our opinions? The weakness of a position is always displayed when its friends attempt to warp the judgment by appeals to the passions. We have no objections to fair arguments. Though we honestly believe that our principles are best calculated to promote the happiness and prosperity of the people, we may be wrong, and our opponents may be right. We are disposed to submit to the discrimination and good sense of our fellow-citizens, without exciting their prejudices or their partialities.

"An argument has been used in favor of popular elections, which, I am free to confess, appears plausible, but will not bear the test of close scrutiny. It is this, that as public sentiment will be likely to fix upon the individual best qualified for the station, popular elections will afford the best indications of that public sentiment. I am perfectly aware that some of the arguments which I may make use of may be said to be equally applicable to elections for political stations. This would only show that there is perfection in no system. The action of a judge is private, and not general; his duties are essentially and radically different from those of political officers who act upon the community as a mass. Upon this distinction are, in fact, founded the principal reasons for appointing them differently from most other officers. I may, therefore, be permitted to apply an argument to this case which might not be justified in the case of other public servants. Besides, the reasoning of our opponents is calculated to mislead, unless we apply the practical test of experience. Admitting that, where there was a unanimity, or even a majority of votes in the selection of a judge, it would be the strongest evidence of public sentiment and of his fitness for the station, I say, without the fear of contradiction, that, in nine cases out of ten, the opinion of the people of the qualifications of a candidate for judge can not be obtained by any mode of popular election which is practicable. If a majority of the whole number of votes be required, we would be for long periods of time without a judge. Such a provision has not, I believe, even been suggested by any advocate of popular elections. I therefore discard it, and take for granted that a plurality of votes must decide. Minorities, small minorities, will, in most cases, be enabled to elect their judges, who may be perhaps the last choice of the great majority of the people. It must be recollected that, should the judges be elected by popular suffrage, our state and every district of it will swarm with candidates. There is now no office more eagerly sought for than that of sheriff; and why? Because it is lucrative. The prize of $2000 a year will attract to our country the pettifoggers of every state in the Union—men having no pretensions to professional eminence—who would starve if left to their own talents and industry—who yet possess sufficient shrewdness and cunning to prepare a flattering tale for our ears, to open our hearts with hollow professions of friendship. They will approach us as the lover does his mistress, full of vows and protestations, and leave us to discover their faults when it shall be too late. By intrigue and electioneering, by raising our sympathies, by slandering their competitors, they may deceive us for a time. They may not succeed. But my object is to show that such men will be here, attracted by the prize held up for successful competition in the contest for popular favor. In case of a great number of candidates, a small minority may elect the judge, and thus the great object of the friends of popular elections would be defeated. I will endeavor to illustrate this argument practically. Should a separate court of appeals be established, the judicial circuits will be enlarged. Each circuit will consist of at least six counties. This judicial district will, perhaps, consist of the counties of Adams, Franklin, Lawrence, Simpson, Covington, and Jones. There is nothing more certain than that each county will present before the people at least one candidate, this county probably two. The district contains about 2800 votes. Each of the candidates will receive a respectable support, and the probability is that their number of votes will be nearly equal. With seven candidates in the field, it may happen that 401 votes will elect. This is a contingency; but the probability is that less than 700 votes will in all cases elect. Will this result show the voice of the people ? The voice of the majority only is the voice of the people, and in this case the voice of the majority is shown to be against the successful candidate. But let us go farther back to show conclusively that the opinions of the majority of the qualifications of a candidate will not be obtained. I will venture to say that hundreds of you—of the voters—will prefer men who are not candidates. If left to your own choice, you would select a man whose modesty and sensibility had induced him to avoid a warm electioneering contest. This man whom you would select, if you had the power of appointment, you can not vote for because he is not before the people. You are forced to make a choice between the candidates, neither of whom, perhaps, you like. Here, then, is one restraint upon your choice. Next, out of the number of those who are candidates, your favorite may, perhaps, stand no chance of an election ; you are compelled to drop him and take up a third. Here is another restraint upon you. At last, reduced almost to Hobson's choice, you give your vote, yet your candidate may not be elected. Here is a third restraint upon your choice. Numbers of your fellow-citizens, yes, even a majority, may be, and will probably be in the same predicament. But this is not all ; our peculiar local situation deserves some consideration. Men who aspire to be elected judge of this district will not settle in Adams County. A residence here is not a good stepping-stone to public office. They will locate themselves in Simpson or Jones, and you may rest assured that Eastern candidates will always succeed. But few of your lawyers practice even in Franklin County, whereas members of the bar who reside in the East are in the habit of attending courts through an extensive district of country, and have an opportunity of becoming extensively known: I do not advocate our right to give a judge to the district, but in the spirit of prophecy warn you of what will assuredly take place in case popular elections prevail. The voice of the majority will seldom, your voice will never be heard. It seems to me, then, that the wishes of the majority will be more nearly approached by an executive appointment, subject to the check of the Senate. The governor will seek to comply with the wishes of the people. It is his interest so to do. He is responsible to them for the propriety of the appointment, whereas the voter is responsible to no human power. I have never known an executive appointment of a judge in this state which was not acceptable to the people over whom he was to act. An obnoxious appointment will never be made. The powerful principle of self-interest, and the elevated station of the executive forbid such an idea.

"Now, fellow-citizens, one word more upon this subject. We are a new state; most of our citizens are recent immigrants. We have many men of talents, but few who, from their capacity, age, and experience, stand preeminent and distinguished. Let us not be the first, upon slight grounds, to try a rash experiment. There is no state in the Union, no country upon earth, in which the judges are elected by votes of the people. The southern sun, that warms the blood and quickens the pulse, while it produces the most generous emotions of the heart, has the same tendency to excite the fancy and to stimulate the passions, and renders us less fit to make an experiment of this new-fangled political theory. Prudence dictates that we should leave it to be tried by others first. If it should succeed well, we will follow the example. The moment I am persuaded that it is for the good of the country, for the protection and happiness of the private and humble citizen, I too will become one of its warmest advocates and supporters. An anxious desire to preserve the judicial department in its purity, to protect the equal rights of all, has brought my mind to the conclusion that the appointment of judges by the governor, by and with the consent of the Senate, for a limited period of time, is the best and most democratic mode. This is not an experiment, it has been practiced upon and approved by some of the oldest of our sister states, and has given birth to the most distinguished judges. The tenure of office should be such as to avoid too great a sense of dependence on the part of the judge, and at the same time to protect the public from the possible effects of weakness, imbecility, and decay of mind. When nominating a judge for the Supreme Court, the governor represents the whole state. When acting for a district, he is the representative of that district alone. Biennial elections of that officer will insure the most rigid responsibility on his part. To secure the integrity of the judge, having full confidence in the trial by jury, I am quite willing that for corruption in office he should also be liable to presentment, trial, and conviction, before the regular courts of the country.

" A misrepresentation of my sentiments upon some subjects appears to require from me a formal contradiction. It has been said, ignorantly or designedly I know not, that I am opposed to universal suffrage, that I favor a representation of property, and that I had declared, in a speech at Washington, that mechanics had no concern with politics. The last is so absurd as scarcely to deserve serious notice. Many of those who heard my remarks at Washington were of that respectable class of citizens, and I know will do me the justice to give this ridiculous report a flat contradiction. I have ever considered entire indifference to the political concerns of the country blamable in any man, whatever his situation and circumstances might be.

" The right of universal suffrage is inseparably connected with our republican institutions. Restrictions of this right must eventually end in discontent and revolution. I consider it the sheet-anchor of a free government, and would be the last man to surrender it. Its abandonment would be a virtual recognition of the principle that we can not govern ourselves. Positive political power should be distributed as equally as possible throughout the state. An attempt on our part to obtain an undue advantage, by taking more than we ought to possess, would certainly be visited upon us at some future period. Principles and policy both demand that we should be content with our just proportion. *Men* should be represented, and not *property* or *territory*. I am, therefore, in favor of that basis which will secure equal rights and equal representation throughout the state. While, however, we admit the right of equal representation, it is no less important that we should protect ourselves against partial and unequal taxation. Because we live within twenty miles of the Mississippi River, we should not be required to pay more taxes in proportion to the clear value of our property than our fellow-citizens in other sections of the state. One district of country or one set of men should not be compelled to bear a greater portion of the public burdens than another quite as wealthy. It is, therefore, all important that the rights of the minority should be protected, and that some constitutional provisions should be adopted to prevent partial and unjust taxation. This, in my opinion, may be readily effected by placing some restrictions on the taxing power, or by requiring that all revenue bills should be based upon the ad valorem principle of taxing every citizen according to the value of his property. The tax upon sales of merchandise is, in my opinion, partial and unjust, and the exercise of such a power should be restrained.

"The leading principle of my political creed is, that a state should not control its citizens in their opinions, their conduct, their labor, their property, any farther than is necessary to preserve the social tie, to punish offenses against society, and to sustain the powers of government.

"I am opposed to all property qualifications whatever for members of either house of the General Assembly. Experience has shown that they are entirely useless.

"A recent attempt has been made to affect my public standing by the charge of entertaining obnoxious political principles. I have met these charges publicly, and in the spirit of candor. The result is known to the public. I desire of those who would judge me but a candid investigation. Believing that I have as much confidence in the virtue and intelligence of my fellow-citizens as those who flatter them more, I will cheerfully submit to their verdict.   JOHN A. QUITMAN."

He was elected by a handsome majority. In the convention he was placed at the head of the committee on the judiciary, from which he made an able report against the popular election of judges. The report, however, was overruled by a large majority, and the State of Mississippi was the first community in the world that adopted the principle. Other states followed the example; and in some of them, especially where large cities exist, with a numerous class of irresponsible, ignorant, or freshly-naturalized voters, the experiment has worked badly; nor is the system, even in agricultural Mississippi, as popular as when it was first introduced.

On this subject the following correspondence subsequently took place between a late distinguished citizen of Louisiana and Gen. Quitman:

From Hon. J. Fenwick Brent.

"New Orleans, March 19th, 1845.

"DEAR SIR,—As the question of an elective judiciary will shortly engage the attention of the Louisiana Convention, now in session in this city, and as it is important that correct information should be obtained relative to the operation of that system in Mississippi, the only state in the Union where the experiment has been fairly tried, I trust that you will pardon the liberty I take in requesting that you will furnish your views, in writing, upon that subject, based upon your experience and observation as a practicing attorney in the courts of that state. The chief objection urged against the system here is, that if the election of judges be intrusted to the people their choice will be generally, if not universally, determined by mere party and political considerations; and I beg leave to call your attention particularly to this point, as connected with the working of that system in Mississippi."

To J. Fenwick Brent.

"New Orleans, March 22d, 1845.

"DEAR SIR,—I have received your letter of the 19th instant, requesting my views upon the operation in the State of Mississippi of the system adopted there of electing judges by the direct votes of the people, and asking my attention particularly to the objections urged against the system, that such elections would generally, if not always, turn upon party or political questions.

"Having no objections to the public avowal of either my former opinions or present views upon this interesting subject, I will cheerfully comply with your request.

"At the time of the adoption of this system in Missis-

sippi, in 1832, I opposed it as a new and hazardous experiment; not that I doubted the capacity or intelligence
of the people, but that I feared that the judiciary would
be too much influenced by sudden popular excitement.
As a member of the convention that revised the Constitution I used my best influence against it, or, rather, to
confine the experiment to the selection of the judges of
the inferior courts by a direct vote of the people.   The
experience and observation of twelve years have, however, convinced me and many others who were opposed
to the experiment, that our fears were not well founded;
and, so far, our system has not been attended with any
of the serious evils which were apprehended.   I have
looked upon its operation in our state for twelve years
with peculiar interest, and, from my former opposition to
the measure, without any bias; and candor compels me to
say that I now regard it as the best mode of selecting
judicial officers."

Judge Quitman took a prominent part in the deliberations of the Convention, but chiefly distinguished himself
by introducing a proposition to prohibit the Legislature
from borrowing money, or pledging the faith of the state
for the purpose of banking—a provision which, though
slightly modified, he succeeded in ingrafting upon the
Constitution.   He deserves great credit for this salutary
provision, and for his boldness in pressing it when the
banking system was in successful operation, and when
all parties were zealously in favor of multiplying those
seductive but mischievous institutions.   This great principle, initiated by Quitman, has since been adopted by
many other states, and is regarded on all sides as conservative and salutary.

Several ineffectual attempts at impeaching judges for
high misdemeanors having occurred in the state, Gen.
Quitman, although chancellor at the time, desirous of
holding all public officers to strict accountability, introduced a proposition to make all judicial officers, for will-

ful neglect of duty or other misdemeanor, liable to indictment or presentment by a grand jury, and to trial by a jury. When told that such a proposition would degrade the ermine, he replied that the great tribunal which could determine the life of a citizen was dignified enough to decide upon the removal of a judge from office. In the convention he moved:

"*Resolved*, That all judges, clerks, sheriffs, and other officers of court, for willful neglect of duty or misdemeanor in office, shall be liable to presentment or indictment, and upon conviction shall be removed from office."

The failure of this resolution left the people with the remedy by impeachment before the Legislature, costing enormous expense, and, as all experience has shown, without any prospect of success, however criminal a judge may be.

He voted in convention steadily against all monopolies or exclusive privileges, whether for banking or other purposes.

He also voted against attainders and forfeitures, those relics of feudal barbarism.

He finally voted to submit the Constitution to the people, but it was rejected by a majority of the Convention, and the present Constitution of Mississippi never was directly submitted to the people.

F 2

CHAPTER VI.

Elected Chancellor. — Death of his Father. — Family Afflictions. — Resigns his Office. — Elected Senator. — Railroad Enterprises. — Union and Brandon Banks.—His busy Life.—Domestic Slavery an Element of Strength.—War in Texas.—Public Meetings in Natchez. — The Fencibles. — Banner Song. — Departure. — Letters. —Extracts from his Journal. — The Gamblers. — Adventure with Robbers. — Returns home. — His Services and Humanity. — His early Faith in Volunteers.—Quitman and Stephen Girard.—Runs for Congress.—State of Parties.—Clay, Webster, Calhoun, Harrison, Van Buren, and White.—Coalitions demoralizing.—Grandeur of Van Buren's Position.—Quitman's Mistake.—His Defeat.—Appointed Brigadier General.

.At the first election after the adoption of the new Constitution he was elected, without opposition, Chancellor of the State of Mississippi—an evidence alike of the satisfaction he had already given in that office, and of the liberality of the people in voting unanimously for a man who had so recently denied the expediency of confiding to them the election of their judges. He consented to accept the office at the urgent demand of the bar throughout the state.

In 1832, the recharter of the Bank of the United States agitated the country, and the friends of the bank in Mississippi proposed to waive all other issues, and nominate an electoral ticket solely with reference to that question. With this view they announced the names of several gentlemen who, as to other leading questions, held conflicting opinions. The nomination of Chancellor Quitman drew from him the following letter:

To James K. Cook.

"Monmouth, August 28th, 1832.

"On my return from the eastern section of the state, I read in your paper of the 10th inst. an editorial suggestion of the names of several citizens ' as electors for President and Vice-president of the United States, who are known to be in favor of a renewal of the charter of the Bank of the United States,' with a request that the individuals named should signify to you their acceptance or rejection of the proposed nomination. My name having been suggested, I conceive it a duty to state that, although I have long considered the Bank of the United States a valuable institution, well calculated to promote the general good by its tendency to lessen the price of exchange, and to produce and preserve a uniform and sound paper currency throughout the Union, and would be pleased to see its charter renewed for a limited period, with such modifications as would prevent an abuse of its powers, yet, without wishing to underrate its consequence, I do not consider the question of rechartering it the *only* or *most important one* which is likely to be involved in the election of the first and second officers of the government.

"In the present important crisis there are, in my opinion, several great questions of constitutional construction and national policy, much more vitally interesting to the people of the United States, and particularly to the citizens of the South, than any which can arise out of the bank question. I can not, therefore, consistently with these views, agree to become a candidate for elector for President and Vice-president, solely with reference to their opinion on the renewal of the charter of the Bank of the United States."

On the 26th of June, 1832, the Rev. Dr. Quitman died, at an advanced age, at Rhinebeck. Chancellor Quitman addressed the following letter to his brother:

To his Brother.

"Monmouth, July 23d, 1832.

"By the last mail I received the truly afflicting intelligence of the death of our poor old father. Your last letter had prepared me, and I expected to hear of it by every mail. We should not grieve. He had long since been deprived of every enjoyment which a participation in the affairs of this world can give. Death to him must have been a relief from the burden of existence. His very useful career had long since terminated. When we have performed the part which Providence has assigned us, and when the faculty of enjoying even the few pleasures of old age has ceased, it can not be considered a misfortune to die. I have felt a melancholy gratification in learning from Dr. Wackerhagen's letter that the last hours of our venerable father were free from pain. There will be many in another world to bear witness to the good he has done in this. The time of each of us is to come, but while we are here let us act well our part."

In a few months after writing this letter, affliction fell heavily on the household at Monmouth. Its peaceful and salubrious shades were invaded by that mysterious scourge, the cholera. The following affecting letter, a heart-cry from his broken spirit, was written to his sister:

To his Sister.

"Monmouth, May 21st, 1833.

"But a few days ago, my beloved sister, your now wretched brother was the happy father of four blooming children. The hand of Providence has fallen heavily upon me in these last three days. Our beloved little Edward, who had never before had a moment's illness, was for about a week affected with derangement of the bowels, which at length resulted in cholera, and his pure spirit left this world for a better on the morning of the 18th. Oh! this was a severe blow to his fond parents, but a heavier yet was in store. On the night before last, my beloved, my beautiful, noble, and affectionate little John was seized with the fatal scourge, without any premonitory symptoms, and in six hours the little angel left this world for a better one. He had no pain, and was resigned, fond, and affectionate to the last expiring sigh. His poor mother is almost inconsolable at the loss of her two darlings. His sister, the constant, inseparable companion of his studies and his sports, looks as if she was deserted by all the world. His father's hopes, his high expectations, where are they? Oh! there is a void in my heart, a burden on my breast; yet I have strength, and will resign myself to this hard, hard dispensation; but Eliza, my dearest Eliza, with all her firmness, is nearly broken-hearted. Who shall describe a mother's sorrow? Two sweet children, upon whom her soul doted —around whom were twined the very tendrils of her heart—torn from her bosom so suddenly! The pestilence fell upon our house with unexampled fury. My German gardener died the day poor little Edward was buried. A servant-maid was attacked the same day, and still lies very low. We are now at Woodlands. A storm passed over last night, and physicians say the pestilence will cease. Its peculiarity has been to fall upon the most healthy localities and avoid others. Its sweep was short, but, merciful Heaven, what a blow! Eliza and I have determined to be resigned to our hard lot. Our poor little son appeared uncommonly beautiful and intelligent the day before his death. He breathed affection for all, and, though perfectly well, he seemed to have some presentiment of his fate. I saw its shadow along my path for weeks. Two hours after the first symptom of his disease, he said, 'Father, I will never get well.' He was at the grave when his infant brother was buried, observed every thing with attention, and gave his mother an account of all. Their little graves are side by side, under a beautiful tree, below the garden. We had two of the best physicians, but no human skill could save them. Their heavenly Father had selected their pure spirits to surround His throne."*

* The following touching letter from a very remarkable man will be read with interest:

"June 16th, 1833.

"MY DEAR FRIEND,—I have heard with feelings of great sorrow the severe visitation of Providence which you have suffered in the loss of your dear children. When I reflect what they were when I saw them, how much of promise they evidenced, how healthy, intelligent, and beautiful they were—all that could warm with hope the breast of a parent—I think, with tears in my eyes, of my own dear Joseph, and that he, like them, was, by untimely fate, taken from the arms of those

This sad dispensation affected him long and deeply. He often recurred to it, and years afterward, in the midst of his preparations for the campaign in Mexico, we shall find him recurring to it at midnight, when alone at Monmouth, and almost fancying himself in spiritual communication with his lost children.

In 1834 he resigned the chancellorship, carrying with him from the bench the confidence and respect of the community. He had displayed great capacity for labor, cheerfulness, patience, method, and a clear perception of the difference between the technical application of law and the comprehensive principles of equity. He was polite in his demeanor to all, above the suspicion of influence or partiality, and even those who disputed his decisions never doubted his conscientiousness and integrity.

In his politics he was what was, at that day, termed a Nullifier, in a small minority in the state, the people being generally Jackson men and Clay men, or Whigs; hostile to each other, but uniting in their opposition to nullification. The Nullifiers met in convention at Jackson,

who had too much of their happiness, too much of their hopes dependent on him. Oh, my friend, how much of all our fondest anticipations, of our warmest affections and dearest hopes, may be buried in these little tombs! I have suffered more while thinking and deploring the loss of my boy, who was so promising, so much intertwined with all my plans, all my hopes, and with my very heart-strings—more than I thought my stubborn nature would submit to. Often have I shed tears on the midnight pillow, and my heart would swell as though it would suffocate me. Such was the shock, that I felt as though it would madden me; and even now I sometimes lose that self-control and equanimity which I had fancied I possessed. These are afflictions to which stoicism must yield, for nature is stronger than all the consolations of philosophy.

"Accept, my friend, my sincere sympathy with you; consolation I can not offer; but the tears which I have shed over the grave of my child have again flowed over the remembrance of yours, who are fresh to my mind as beautiful flowers that have been crushed by the ravages of a dreadful tornado. Assure Mrs. Quitman of my regret for her bereavement, and may Heaven preserve you and her.

"Your friend,   FELIX HUSTON."

May 21st, 1834, and adopted an address written by Quitman, which embodies the opinions he held through life.

His sentiments were unpopular in Adams County, where he had but a corporal's guard of followers, yet, such was his personal popularity, and the value set upon his practical abilities by that enlightened community, he was chosen senator in 1835, and was then elected president of the Senate. He steadily opposed the whole brood of banking institutions, and the charter of the celebrated and infamous Union Bank. An interregnum occurred by the expiration of the term of Gov. Runnels, who had been elected under the old Constitution; and the period fixed by the new Constitution for the installation of Charles Lynch, governor elect, not having arrived, the executive functions devolved on President Quitman, and he delivered an able message to the Legislature, that may even at this day be studied with advantage. He predicted at that early period, when the cloud on the horizon was a mere speck, the channels that anti-slavery feeling would flow in, and the momentum it would gradually acquire. He saw then what we see now, that anti-slavery at the North is but another name for fanaticism; that fanatics never reason, and are never satisfied; and that compromises with them, like the contributions we formerly paid to the pirates of the Mediterranean, are but acknowledgments of their power, and only provoke extortion and outrage.

Judge Pray, of the High Court of Errors and Appeals, dying about this time, the commission was offered to Quitman, but he declined it.

He consented, however, to serve as president of a company for building a railroad from Natchez to Jackson, connecting the Mississippi with Pearl River. The embarrassments of the times, and the doubtful policy of the state, in sanctioning lines of railway through her territory terminating beyond her jurisdiction, defeated the enterprise, after the expenditure and loss of a good deal of capital.

At that day two railroad enterprises were proposed. The capitalists of New Orleans, then and now, by the course of trade and the necessities of the planting interest, exercising great influence in Mississippi, proposed a grand line from New Orleans, along the western shore of Pearl River and through the fertile interior, then rapidly filling up, to Nashville.

The city of Natchez, and the river counties generally, opposed this, and urged the line from Natchez to Jackson, and then eastward.

Quitman embraced the latter proposition with enthusiasm. He was desirous of building up a direct trade between Natchez, the then commercial metropolis of the state, and Europe, to emancipate Mississippi from her dependence on New Orleans. He apprehended, too, the influence which a great corporation, with its army of agents and employés, controlled in another state, might exercise over legislation and internal affairs, and like a true state-rights man as he was, he opposed the New Orleans company. It would have been defeated, and at this moment the state would have been enjoying the fruits of a home policy and of direct intercourse with Europe; but, unfortunately, the question was thrown into the caldron of national politics. The Jackson party of Mississippi, then supporting Mr. Van Buren, who was unjustly accused of being an abolitionist in disguise, finding themselves hard pressed by the unnatural coalition between the friends of Clay and Calhoun in favor of Hugh L. White, adopted the New Orleans scheme, with the view of securing the votes of the central and interior counties. Thus, when the Legislature met, the Louisiana company obtained a charter, with the privilege of choos-

ing their own location for a road. The other charter
was likewise granted, but it had not the capital to com-
pete with the foreign company, which, after all, exploded,
after perpetrating enormous frauds.

Very injudiciously, though it was the error of the era,
the Legislature conferred banking privileges on the
Natchez and other railway companies, most of which,
losing sight of the design of their charters, became monstrous swindling concerns, and robbed whenever they
had the opportunity.

It has been satisfactorily established, however, that,
during Quitman's connection with the Natchez company,
not a single accommodation note was discounted, and no
notes were issued but to pay for work done upon the
road.

But for this unfortunate and indiscriminate grant of
banking privileges—the mania of the times—and the
temptation it held out to speculate and swindle, not only
would Natchez and the capital of the state have been
connected, but the grand scheme of connecting the interi-
or with the sea-shore, and the building up of an export-
ing and importing city at a harbor unrivaled on the Atlantic, would long since have been accomplished. The
Legislature of that day saw at once the grandeur and
practicability of the enterprise. A marine, and very
thorough and satisfactory, survey was made. A line of
route, admirably adapted for railroads, was marked out,
when, in an evil hour, they were persuaded that banking
privileges would enable the company to build the road.
This was the death-knell of that magnificent measure.
It was secretly strangled and interred by the unprinci-
pled managers in charge, and from its rotting members
there sprung up the notorious Brandon Bank—the most
audacious and infamous of all the swindling corporations
of those times—and whose record should, even now, be

burned with fire drawn from the skies, to fix upon it the
condemnation of God and man, that it may be a warning
to future Legislatures—a lurid and ghastly light, shining
from "whited sepulchres and dead men's bones."

To his Brother.

"Monmouth, Oct. 17th, 1835.

"To show you that I am not wasting the prime of life
in ignoble case, I may mention that I am a senator in the
Legislature, President of the State Rights Association,
President of the Anti-abolition Society, of the Anti-gam-
bling Society, of the Anti-ducling Society, of the Mississippi Cotton Company, of the Railroad Company, Direct-
or of the Planters' Bank, Grand Master Mason, Captain
of the Natchez Fencibles, Trustee of Jefferson College
and of the Natchez Academy, besides having charge of
a cotton and a sugar plantation, and 150 negroes. You
may readily imagine I am not much troubled with *ennui*,
and that time seldom lags upon my hands. I have a
higher ambition to be a useful member of society than
to bear a more conspicuous and sounding title.

"The excitement that existed in the upper part of this
state last summer, like most other excitements about negro insurrections, was more that of indignation than
fear.* Indeed, every day's experience and observation
convince me that our domestic institutions are based
upon a more solid foundation than those of the non-

* In allusion to what was called the Murrell excitement, growing
out of the revelations of one Virgil A. Stuart, a notorious scamp.
An organized band, very much like John Brown's, was said to have
been formed, and a general insurrection was to occur on a certain day.
In the central counties martial law was declared; committees of safety and armed patrols were established; many suspected persons were
arrested and hung. Stuart was made the guest of the state, and
received every where with manifestations of public gratitude. Large
sums of money and costly presents were given to him. He is now
known to have been an impostor. The whole story was a fabrication.
Murrell was simply a thief and counterfeiter, and Stuart was his
subordinate, who, having quarreled with him, devised this plan to
avenge and enrich himself. The whole "plot," and its tragical consequences, may now be regarded as one of the most extraordinary and
lamentable hallucinations of our times.

slaveholding states. Admitting the remote chance of partial insurrectionary movements here, which the moment they are known would be suppressed, yet you are in more real danger from the gradual and sapping tendency of agrarian and fanatical doctrines which, it is evident, are rapidly making way at the North. Should we ever live to see the proud institutions of our country overthrown, you may be assured the last retreat of freedom will be in the South. I may be an enthusiast on this subject, and I will not undertake, in a letter, to advance arguments upon a topic on which I have reflected much, but I think I can demonstrate that our institution of domestic slavery is in harmony with, and almost indispensable to a constitutional republic.

"You refer to the politics of Mississippi. We have in the new sections of the state a recent population whose political complexion has not yet been ascertained, but, so far as I can judge, the people of this state are one third for Van Buren, one third Nullifiers, and one third Whigs. The two latter parties will vote for Judge White for President. No man believes that Van Buren has the least chance of getting the vote of Mississippi. His party is losing ground daily. Our elections come on in a fortnight.

"There is war in Texas. Were I without family, I would repair there immediately. Freemen who are struggling for their violated rights should not be left to struggle unaided."*

* *Gen. Sam. Houston to Gen. Quitman.*

"Nacogdoches, Texas, Feb. 12th, 1836.

"DEAR SIR,—It affords me peculiar pleasure to acknowledge the receipt of your letter by Mr. H. C. M'Neill, and the present of a Polish yager which has once been employed in the cause of liberty.

"By this personal compliment I feel flattered. But the generous, liberal, and manly sentiments which you have expressed in behalf of Texas and the glorious struggle in which she is engaged, command my gratitude, and awaken in me the associations of other days connected with the land of my birth, when her sons were battling against their invaders in defense of the rights of freemen. We will peril all for freedom, and I trust that the next Convention will declare Texas 'free, sovereign, and independent.'

"Could your situation enable you to render to Texas and her cause an auxiliary aid so useful and important to her prosperity as your presence and the force of your character and example, I can assure you

A noble sentiment! and he pondered over it day and night. It was his table talk. His restlessness and anxiety were remarked by his friends. The conflict was strong between his duty to his young family and devoted wife, whose heart yet bled over the loss of her children, and what he conceived to be his duty to his fellow-men, Americans by birth, then threatened with a war of extermination. At length, about the last of March, 1836, tidings reached Natchez that Santa Anna was advancing into Texas with 10,000 men. Soon followed news of the fall of the Alamo.

> "From the Far West,
> From Bexar's silvery tide,
> That Travis, Bowie, and the rest
> Of warriors bold, in battle press'd,
> On glory's bed had died."

Upon receipt of this intelligence at Natchez, the public excitement was intense. A public meeting was called, John A. Quitman in the chair, Gen. Felix Huston secretary. Judge Jesse Bledsoe, long distinguished in Kentucky as an orator, and Col. Childress, of Texas, addressed the meeting. On motion of Judge Wm. Vannerson the following significant resolution was adopted:

" *Resolved*, That the proud dictator, Santa Anna, must fall like the Alamo, and the blood there shed for liberty and glory must be avenged."

Messrs. John M. Ross, Wm. Parker, Wm. Vannerson, R. W. Abbey, R. Stockman, Wm. P. Mellen, G. R. Girault, Wm. B. Duke, A. J. Coffin, and A. L. Gaines were appointed a committee to collect subscriptions and supplies.

The meeting closed with an impassioned speech from

that no circumstance would be hailed with more pleasure by every patriot whose plans of government and policy have assigned to Texas the proud station of an independent people governed by a liberal Constitution and just laws."

the chairman, in which he declared his intention of repairing forthwith to the scene of action.

At a called meeting of the Fencibles,* the following resolution was adopted:

"*Resolved*, That Captain Quitman be excused from duty so long as he may deem his presence necessary to the glorious cause he has espoused, and may the God of battles speed and protect him."

Quitman, with characteristic promptitude, gave notice that in five days he would set out for Texas. Apprehending some interference on the part of the United States district attorney to enforce the neutrality laws, which for the remainder of his life he was destined to contend with, the following notice was issued:

"Some misunderstanding existing in relation to the character of our contemplated visit to Texas, we think it proper to state to the public that Captain Quitman will embark up the Red River in the beginning of the next week, and General Huston will follow with those who wish to travel with him in about two weeks afterward. Those who may desire to accompany us will furnish themselves with a good horse, rifle or musket, and pistols, with the understanding that each man who accompanies the expedition embarks on his own responsibility, at his own expense, and subject to no other rules than may be adopted for the convenience of traveling.

"Understanding that the sum subscribed by the citizens of Natchez in aid of the cause of Texas has been placed at our disposal, we shall appropriate it solely to procuring provisions, supplies, etc. Those who arrive from time to time from other parts of the state will communicate with General Huston.

"FELIX HUSTON,
"JOHN A. QUITMAN.

"Natchez, April 2d, 1836."

* He had organized this fine company, April 21st, 1824, and was its first captain. He retained his membership in it during his life, and often, when high in civil and military station, mustered in its

On the morning of the 5th, the people of Natchez and of the surrounding country assembled to witness the farewell of the Fencibles to their beloved captain. The late John M. Ross, a young advocate and a member of the company, pronounced a thrilling address. Quitman was much affected, and could only reply in a few broken sentences. But the example of such a man—late chancellor and acting governor of the state—relinquishing his business, his family, his luxuries, and the refined society in which he lived, for a rough and perilous campaign, from no incentive but humanity, was more electrical than eloquence.

The beautiful banner song of the Fencibles was chanted by the whole company:

"Our maiden banner courts the wind,
    Its stars are beaming o'er us;
Each radiant fold, now unconfin'd,
    Is floating free before us.
It bears a motto proud and high,
    For those who dare defy us;
And loud shall peal our slogan cry
    Whene'er they come to 'Try us.'

"The hallow'd ray that freedom gave,
    To cheer the gloom that bound us,
And shone in beauty o'er the brave,
    Still brightly beams around us.
The day our fathers bravely won
    Shall long be greeted by us;
And loudly through our ranks shall run
    The gallant war-cry, 'Try us.'

"Now fill the wine-cup to the brim,
    Fill, fill the ruby treasure;
Pour one libation forth to Him,
    Nor stint the burning measure.
And o'er the board, or in the field,
    His spirit shall be nigh us;
The patriot's hope—the soldier's shield,
    Whene'er they come to 'Try us.'

---

ranks. It was composed for years of the flower of the young men of Natchez, most of whom preceded their captain to the tomb.

"Then give our banner to the wind,
  Its stars are beaming o'er us;
Its maiden folds now unconfin'd
  Are floating free before us.
It bears a motto proud and high
  For those who dare defy us;
And loud shall be our slogan cry,
  Whene'er they come to ' *Try us.* ' "*

And then, amid the acclamations of the whole city and the roar of "Old Saratoga," Captain Quitman and his

* Written by Francis Baker, a native of New Jersey, but then a member of the Natchez bar, a man of genius, and the life and soul of the convivial circle.

In 1824, Francis Baker was traveling through Kentucky with a considerable amount of money on his person. He spent the night with Mr. Desha, son of Governor Desha, and next morning was found murdered on the road not far from Desha's house. Many circumstances pointed to Desha as the murderer, and he was arrested. Public opinion ran strongly against him, and he applied to the Legislature for a change of venue. The application was refused, chiefly through the instrumentality of the late Robert Wickliffe, then a representative from the county of Fayette, a personal and political enemy of Governor Desha, and one of the ablest lawyers in Kentucky. Young Desha was convicted of murder; the father held the pardoning power, and believed him innocent. There were some circumstances to justify this belief. After the son had been a second time convicted, and a new trial had been a second time granted, the second jury unanimously and a portion of the first jury petitioned for his pardon. The prisoner sent for his father, protested his innocence, and declared his unalterable purpose not to live unless he were acquitted by a jury, and vowed that, should a pardon be sent to him, he would forthwith put an end to his life. It was found impossible to obtain a third unbiased jury, and the wretched man remained in jail from term to term. Finally, on that day of horrors when Beauchamp was executed for the murder of Colonel Sharpe, after the suicide of his wife and his own unsuccessful attempt, young Desha cut his throat, severing the windpipe quite in two. He then beckoned for pen and ink, and wrote a solemn protest of his innocence. The tragedy did not here stop. Mr. Benning, editor of the Lexington Gazette, a warm friend of Governor Desha, animadverted on the course of Mr. Wickliffe, and was shot down by his son in his own office. He stood his trial and was acquitted, but soon after fell in a duel with the successor of Benning.

comrades embarked in the steamer Swiss Boy for Natchitoches, where they arrived on the night of the 7th.*

He wrote his friend, General Felix Huston, an ardent
friend of Texas, who expected to follow with re-enforcements:

To General Felix Huston.

"Natchitoches, April 8th.

" We shall proceed this morning toward Nacogdoches,

---

* The following letter was addressed to him by a lady then well
known in literary circles. It was written in the agony of "hope de-
fered," but the sentiments are worthy of the granddaughter of General
Warren. Her son, an only child, perished at the Alamo. She tried
to bear it with Christian resignation, but smiled no more, and at last
died of a broken heart. Many of the daughters of Mississippi and
Louisiana were educated by her, and will read this memorial of her
affliction with melancholy interest:

Mrs. Caroline Matilda Thayer to Gen. Quitman.

"Clinton, Miss., April 5th, 1836.

"DEAR SIR,—Having learned that you have embarked in the cause
of suffering Texas, I take the liberty of addressing you a line, with the
hope that you may be able to relieve the anxiety of a mother whose
last earthly hope has been devoted to the same cause. You may have
known that my son was among the volunteers who left this place in
October last. I have heard from him occasionally by individuals who
have returned, but have received only one letter, and that was dated
immediately after his arrival.

"The late distressing intelligence from San Antonio has filled me
with irrepressible apprehension, and I beg you, my dear sir, to endeavor
to aid me, if possible, in ascertaining whether he was at that place. I
can never suffer more than I do at present if my worst fears are confirmed, and any information will be preferable to the suspense which
now corrodes my life.

"There certainly must be somewhere a record of the names of those
who fell, but situated as I am, so remote from any source of information except the newspapers, I know not how to apply to obtain access
to that record.

"If you will have the goodness to advise me how to proceed, or aid
me in any way in obtaining information, you will confer a favor that
will never be forgotten.

"I feel a degree of enthusiasm in the cause in which you are embarked which even my worst apprehensions are not sufficient to repress; and if I am a childless widow, it shall solace the residue of my
days to reflect that I have lost my all in so glorious a cause.

"Accept my fervent aspirations for your complete success in an enterprise worthy of a La Fayette."

making a slight *detour* to avoid the United States garrison at Fort Jessup. There is no necessity for 'bearding the lion in his den,' and incurring risk of detention, though I doubt not the officers sympathize with us.

"I have paid the passages of our party and of two gentlemen from Warren County, and have given five dollars each to some stragglers who are on foot and have rifles, but no powder and lead. At Alexandria there was great enthusiasm. Here there are conflicting opinions as to the issue. Kaufman, my old law student, represents the state of affairs as gloomy, owing to dissensions among the chiefs, many of whom are speculating in lands. I am also informed that the Texan convention has confiscated all claims held by citizens of the United States—a very false step, if it be true. This much for the gloomy side of affairs. I must judge for myself. Others say that a cordial union now exists among the leaders. General Houston is said to be on this side of the Colorado, with 500 men. He lies in the post oak woods, to protect himself from the Mexican horse. Santa Anna is said to have 6000 troops, of which 2000 are mounted, armed with lances, pistols, and sabres."

In the face of this intelligence they pushed forward, and on the 9th crossed the Sabine at Gaines's Ferry, where the band halted, and elected John A. Quitman their captain, and subscribed an instrument to be governed by the regulations of the army and the articles of war. Each man had a good horse, and carried a rifle, holster and belt pistols, and bowie-knife. Two mules, carrying a few blankets and tin cups, sugar and coffee, constituted the whole commissariat.

Their subsequent adventures are related briefly in a pencil memorandum made by their captain from day to day.

Extracts from Diary.

"April 10th. Entered San Augustine late at night. A gang of gamblers, recently driven from Vicksburg, Natchez, and other places on the Mississippi, had col-

lected, overawing the inhabitants. They were little better than brigands. My party quartered for the night in
a large unfinished building, six men having been detailed
to watch our horses. The gamblers, it appears, recognized me as captain of the Fencibles who had aided in
their expulsion from Natchez (although really we had
restrained the fury of the people, and thus prevented a
tragedy like that at Vicksburg), and resolved to have revenge. About 12 at night, I was about to lie down in a
small tenement, near where my men were sleeping, and
had just taken off my coat, when the door was thrown
open, and a tall, well-dressed, and fierce-looking man stood
before me. A bowie-knife was belted to his side, and
he held in his hand a large dueling-pistol. Fortunately,
I had on my belt-pistols, and, instantly drawing one, I
confronted him, and said, 'Sir, I know you, and you know
who I am. I am here on other business, and desire no
quarrel with you; but I fear you not.' I kept my eye
steadily fixed upon him. We stood five feet apart, and
my intention was to shoot him down upon the slightest
motion of his pistol. He glared at me for a few moments, when, to my surprise and great relief, his features
relaxed into a smile, and he said, 'Captain, you are a
brave man, and I will be your friend.' Saying this, he
retired.*

"11th. Great alarm here; people moving toward the
Sabine. Rode to-day through fine red lands, interspersed
with prairie, and camped at Martin's, eight miles west
of Nacogdoches. Here we overhauled Mr. Archer and
several Virginians.

"12th. News arrived during the night that a large
detachment of the Mexican army had reached the Forks
of Trinity, and that the Cherokees and other Indians in
the vicinity would attack Nacogdoches in a few days.
The Virginia gentlemen, who had come to look at the

* It appears that the gamblers then at San Augustine, who considered themselves very ill treated at Natchez, and were in desperate circumstances, had determined to revenge themselves on Quitman and
his party, most of whom were Fencibles. They meditated a night
assault, and their leader, a man of desperate courage, went to reconnoitre, when he encountered Quitman. After this interview, he exerted his influence, and prevented an attack.

country, turned back ; we rode on, and halted a half mile from town. Sent Parker with a note to the commandant, or alcalde, advising him, if the news was confirmed and he was not strong enough to fight, to retreat, offering my services to cover his rear. He sent this answer :

" 'Nacogdoches, April 12th, 1836.
" 'CAPTAIN,—We have received your communication on the subject of the retreat from this place. With great satisfaction we acknowledge your proffered kindness to protect the women and children, and we accept the same. The retreat will commence immediately, and your co-operation will be relied on.
" 'R. A. IRION, *Acting Com. of Municipality.*'

"On receipt of this, we rode into town, and found it deserted. About 70 armed men had crossed the bayou and camped. In the afternoon we returned to Martin's. Parker and M'Neill, who had been left in the Texan camp, came dashing up, with the report that 3000 Mexicans and Indians were marching upon the town. Immediately after, Maj. Gaines brought a request from Col. Irion that we would join him and defend the town. Called up my boys and submitted the question to them. They answered that the odds were fearful, but that where I led they would follow. In five minutes we saddled up and galloped into Nacogdoches. We there learned that the panic had been occasioned by some spies coming in and reporting that they had been fired on by the Mexican advance. We took post, with Irion's men, at Simm's, about 120 men, and resolved to abide the issue. If we perish, we shall, at all events, gain time for the women and children to reach the Sabine and escape the enemy. Each of my Natchez boys swears he is good for ten Mexicans ; the Texans say they will not be outdone. If I must die early, let me die with these brave fellows and for such a cause. Several alarms during the night ; every man at his post, but no enemy appeared.

"13th. Learned that some 300 Mexicans of the vicinity (rancheros) were in arms near by, under Col. Cordova.

"14th. Accompanied several Texan officers to Cordova's camp. He declared that he intended no attack ; that he had embodied his men to resist the anticipated attacks and depredations of the Indians, who were greatly disaffected and talked of taking Nacogdoches. I distrusted his statement, but did not disclose my suspicions to him, and we all parted apparently good friends."

The next day Capt. Quitman wrote to Gen. Felix Huston as follows:

"Nacogdoches, August 15th, 1836.

"At length, a little repose in this warlike village gives me an opportunity of writing a line. From Natchitoches we traveled to the Sabine. At Gaines's Ferry we found many families coming over into Louisiana. As we advanced, the refugees rapidly multiplied. At San Augustine we first heard a rumor that several thousand Mexican cavalry had crossed the Brazos above, and were lying near the forks of Trinity, 120 miles N.W. from this place, and that 1500 Indians had joined them there. Many fled from San Augustine. Advancing into the country, we found the roads literally lined with flying families, and, instead of the men turning their faces to the enemy, we met at least 300 men, with arms in their hands, going east. Perhaps they considered the contest hopeless, and did not care to throw away their lives. The reports of the enemy's overwhelming numbers and bloody intentions were indeed alarming. We must have met, at least, 1000 women and children, and every where along the road were wagons, furniture, and provisions abandoned. Almost every house was deserted, and its contents left open to depredation. On the 11th we reached Martin's, eight miles east of this place. Here we found Mr. Archer and a party of five or six Virginians, who had been a little in advance of us, and learned from them, and from persons flying from the west, what seemed to confirm previous reports of the strength and advance of the Mexicans; and, in addition, that the Cherokees and Caddos would join them at the Sabine, 70 miles from this place. The two latter are warlike tribes, well-equipped and mounted, and are hostile to the Americans. The conduct of the former, a part of whom reside only twenty-five miles north of this, has been for some time suspicious and domineering, and Bowles, their chief, is known to be unfriendly.

"During the night of the 11th at Martin's, alarming news came in, and I really supposed we were proceeding upon a forlorn hope, when we resolved in the morning to proceed hither and, at least, try to cover the retreat of the flying families. I thought it prudent to halt on an eminence half a mile out. I sent a dispatch in, offering my services. They were accepted. We rode into town, and found but about seventy men under arms, who spoke of camping near us. I preferred, however, to return to Martin's, keeping a communication by express with the town during the night. At half past 2 a scout, who had been sent to reconnoitre the road west of the town, returned at full speed, without his arms or hat, and reported that a band of Mexicans had attacked him, and he had barely escaped with his life. His flight through town produced universal consternation. A few brave men rallied, and Major Gaines was sent to request our immediate advance. At this moment Parker and Henry M'Neill came riding into camp with foaming horses, and confirmed the report. When about three miles from town, northeast, on an elevated ridge, we discovered a long line of smoke, which we did not doubt was the encampment of the enemy. On reaching Nacogdoches we found a company of about eighty men, who had marched to join Houston, but fell back to this place on hearing of the proximity of the Mexicans. At my instance Colonel Irion sent out a strong party of spies to ascertain facts, for there are new rumors every hour. Fifty men from San Augustine have joined us, and we are now, in all, about 250. There is not a woman or child in the town or neighborhood. Some days ago the commandant issued an order that the resident Mexicans should surrender their arms. This they refused to do, and at night disappeared. They immediately embodied under Col. Cordova to the number of 250 or 300. It was their camp-fires that had attracted my attention as I advanced. We have had an interview with them, and matters seem now to be amicably settled. The Cherokees have likewise disclaimed hostilities, declaring that they had assembled to prevent the incursions of predatory tribes, and to protect their stock.

"The facts seem to be that a body of Mexican cavalry were sent early last month to co-operate with the Indians on the upper frontier, and make a descent upon this unprotected country, and that the Cherokees had given them assurances of support; that owing to incessant rains, the unprecedented floods, and the rottenness of the soil in the woods and prairies, the cavalry have not been able to operate this side of Trinity River, and that the Indians, finding themselves unsupported, and learning that the 4th and 6th regiments U. S. Infantry had arrived at Fort Jessup, and that Gen. Gaines had resolved to keep them in check, have dissembled their intentions, and now profess friendship. I conclude, therefore, that the Mexicans on Trinity will endeavor to operate on Houston's rear, and that there is no immediate danger to this section. The panic, however, has done its work. The houses are all deserted. There are several thousands of women and children in the woods on both sides of the Sabine, without supplies or money. Every thing was left in the flight—the corn in the crib, the meat in the smoke-house, their poultry, cattle, and furniture.

" We shall probably set out for the Brazos to-morrow. An express has just arrived from Gen. Houston. He is at Gross's Ferry, 20 miles above San Felipe. A corps of 900 Mexicans are attempting to cross the swollen river 40 miles below him. He has no enemy in front; if you intend to come, do so immediately. The advance of our little party, in the face of the rumors and the fugitives, inspired confidence, and prevented the citizens from burning the town and retreating to the Sabine. On our way we met Gen. ——, Col. ——, Col. ——, and several other leading men, taking 'the *Sabine chute*,' or, as they say here, 'putting.' A detachment of my Fencibles, sent yesterday to bring in our baggage from Martin's, fell in with 100 Mexican rancheros, armed and mounted. My men faced them boldly, determined to sell their lives dearly, but they made friendly demonstrations. You may be sure I am proud of my pets."*

* *From the New Orleans Bulletin, April 20th.*

"Dear Sir,—Nacogdoches has been abandoned, and probably by this hour is in ruins. A detachment of the Mexican army has, by an extraordinary movement, been united with the Indians of the north, who, it is reported, are 1500 strong; and unless timely succor is obtained the country will be overrun, and the depredations and horrors

"17th. Quiet being restored, we left Nacogdoches for the west. Crossed the Trinity at Robins's Ferry. Here we found 100 families, or more, flying eastwardly, in charge of Major Montgomery. We aided them to cross the river, which was then nearly three miles over, owing to floods of rain. We were here informed that Gen. Houston had fallen back before the Mexicans, and would probably make a stand at Fort Bend, to resist their passage across the Brazos. Thither we proceeded with all possible dispatch, and then learned that Houston had dropped down the Brazos, and was marching to Harrisburg. We pushed forward by forced marches, and arrived at head-quarters, unfortunately, two days after the battle of San Jacinto. Santa Anna had just been captured. The commander-in-chief has not determined what to do with him. He tells me he is much pressed to bring him before a court-martial, in which event he desires me to be judge advocate.

"Arrangements have been made with Santa Anna, and there will be no trial. He is unquestionably a man of genius, fertile in resources, and of great energy. Gen. Houston exhibits much nerve in resisting the popular clamor for vengeance on the Mexican.

"I am treated here with great kindness and distinction. Among other testimonials, I have just received the following from Lieut. Col. Millard.

"'CAPTAIN QUITMAN,—Sergeant Major Smith will deliver to you a lance and stand of colors, taken from the enemy on the memorable 21st of April by the troops under my command, which do me the favor to accept, in testimony of your own gallantry, and of my respect for the State of Mississippi, of which, for ten years, I had the honor of being a citizen.'

which were lately enacted in Florida will now be removed to the western border of our happy land. Hundreds of families are rapidly fleeing before the ruthless savages, who are hastening down upon them, and all is confusion between here and San Augustine. Gov. Quitman, the noble and brave Quitman, who merely went to explore the country and lay out the promised land, has heedlessly found himself and his handful of devoted adherents hemmed in by the Mexicans on one side and the cruel Indians on the other, and he is now rallying the scattered inhabitants, and forming a rear-guard to protect the unfortunate women and children, who are hurrying with all possible speed to the Sabine."

"Gen. Rusk, who succeeded to the command of the Texan army, invited me to accompany him in his march west, which I did for some days; but, having ascertained confidentially from him the provisions of the secret treaty with Santa Anna, and that he was ordered merely to observe Filasola's retreat, and knowing that the presence of Gen. Gaines on the Sabine would restrain the Indians, I considered the war virtually at an end, and, therefore, determined to return home. Such of my young men as chose to remain I provided for. Those who wished to return were shipped from Galveston. I prepared to travel by land, with my servants, on the lower, or Opelousas trail.

"When near the Sabine, after crossing a small stream, and rising a bank which had a dense underwood on both sides, I found that two trees had been felled, forming an effectual barricade. In our rear, three men with guns were seen coming up. We could neither advance nor retreat. I sprung from my horse, drawing a pistol from my holsters, the horse being between me and the banditti. This was done in an instant; but, at the same moment, I was startled by the sharp crack of a rifle behind me, and the rush of the ball over my head. A horseman came up at full speed. It was ——, the gambler, whom I had encountered at San Augustine. For a moment I resigned myself to die, but determined to shoot him first. He dropped his gun to signify that he was no enemy. He informed me that he had retreated from San Augustine with the crowd of fugitives to Fort Jessup, had gone to Opelousas, and hearing of the battle of San Jacinto, was then on his way, with three or four comrades, to try his luck at the Texas head-quarters. Being a few yards in advance of his companions, on turning an angle of the path, he perceived my situation, and thus, in all probability, saved my life. When he recognized me, he said, 'Well, Captain, I am glad I have had the chance to serve you.' I thanked him most cordially. We found traces of blood, showing the effect of his shot, but the robbers had disappeared, and we had no time to pursue them.*

* This man was of respectable parentage, and was well educated.

"Without further adventure I arrived at Natchez on the 27th of May, regretting that I had not been able to do more, but grateful to Providence for permitting me to do as much as I did for a suffering people, and for vouchsafing me health, and safety, and a cheerful spirit meanwhile."

This gallant officer had no opportunity, during the campaign, to appear on the field of battle. But there is no doubt that his march into Nacogdoches, and the support he gave to the few determined men there assembled, deterred the rancheros and the Indians from the hostilities they meditated, and thus prevented the massacre of hundreds of defenseless families, flying before Santa Anna. It is appalling to dwell on the horrors that would have ensued had those unhappy fugitives been attacked while seeking to cross the angry flood of the Trinity, or on the long march thence to the Sabine. Between those retreating families and their foes—then believed to be in ambush at no great distance—in the face of a thousand alarming rumors, each enough to try the firmest nerves, he placed himself and his devoted band, and, one and all, resolved to die, not for fame, but in an obscure and hopeless struggle, to gain time for the fugitives. He lived to serve in stricken fields—to be foremost in the desperate charge—to be remarked for his calm, cool courage, when whole platoons were mowed down by his side—to be the first to hoist the flag of his country on the capitol of a conquered empire. But, in his whole heroic career, there is nothing grander than the humanity and determ-

A number of years afterward, he was convicted of dealing faro in a neighboring state, and sentenced to six months' imprisonment and $1000 dollars fine. At the intercession of the writer, the governor remitted the imprisonment, and the fine was paid, one half by his own friends, and the other $500 by Quitman, who never forgot him. He is now a minister of the Gospel.

ined purpose exhibited, at this critical period, on the bleeding frontier of Texas.

Not only did he thus jeopard his life for the defenseless, but he contributed liberally to their support. Several thousand dollars he bestowed upon the indigent, who were without the means of purchasing food. Many families, too, in independent circumstances, had been compelled, by their precipitate flight, to go unprovided with means to defray their expenses. Of the relief he extended to them there are numerous instances similar to that referred to in the following touching letter, from a highly respectable gentleman.

From ——.

"Washington, Texas, Oct. 30th, 1836.

"Hon. John A. Quitman,—I avail myself of the first opportunity to acknowledge your great kindness to my family while I was absent with the army. The fifty dollars you so generously handed my wife will be returned to you, with interest, out of the first earnings of my profession. The length of time I have been in the service, my family expenses on the retreat, the destruction of our property, and our government not yet able to pay a dollar, leaves me unable to pay you now. It shall be faithfully remitted to you, but we can never repay the obligation but with thankful hearts. May God bless you, sir!

"I returned with my family to this place last month. Our friends met us with cheerful countenances, but our once cozy home was desolate. We have all been very sick, but, thanks to Providence, are now up. May Heaven's smile and sunshine attend you, sir, and be assured that your name will ever be pronounced in Texas with emotions of gratitude and pride."

The campaign, in benefactions to the needy and assistance and advances to his men, cost Capt. Quitman over ten thousand dollars; but he never regretted the expenditure, and never reclaimed a cent that he had loaned. Those who accompanied him to Texas enjoyed his friendship, and, when they desired it, his aid during their lives, and their attachment to him remained unbroken to the last.*

* Many years afterward this Texas expedition occasioned the following correspondence :

From the Washington Union of February 8th, 1851.

"We have no recollection of having published the 'false report' to which Gen. Quitman alludes in the following card and correspondence. But, as we take it for granted he is right in speaking of its circulation in our paper, we most cheerfully give place to the explanation which he has transmitted to us :

"'Jackson, Miss., January 18th, 1851.

"'Sir,—As you have thought fit, through the columns of your paper, to give circulation to the false report alluded to in my letter to Gen. Rusk, herewith inclosed, I now request that you will aid in correcting the calumny by publishing the correspondence which I inclose, as well as this note.

"'With due respect, your obedient servant,
"'J. A. QUITMAN.

"'Thomas Ritchie, Esq., Editor of the Union.

"' *Gen. Quitman to Gen. Rusk.*

"'Jackson, Miss., December 4th, 1850.

"'Sir,—I inclose an extract from the "Sea-shore Sentinel"—a paper published in this state—which has just met my eye.

"'I am informed that similar statements are made in other papers. Aware that but little reliance is to be placed upon newspaper reports of speeches, and unwilling to believe that you could have uttered such language in regard to me, I still deem the circulation of these reports as entitling me to call upon you to say whether you have made the statement attributed to you, or used any other language in connection with my name to warrant such a report ; and if I was alluded to in your speech at San Augustine, what were your remarks about me. I feel quite assured, from your candor and sense of justice, as well as from the kind relations which have existed between us, that you will appreciate the motives which prompt these inquiries, and will reply to them promptly and frankly.

"'I remain, very respectfully, your obedient servant,
"'J. A. QUITMAN.

"'Hon. Thomas J. Rusk, Washington City.

[Extract.]

"'General Rusk made a speech at San Augustine, on his arrival there, in which he defended the Ten Million Bill and the Union, and bore down pretty sharply upon the Southern ultras, not even sparing Gov. Quitman, of whom he is represented to have stated that he (the governor) had once failed to redeem the pledges of assistance to Texas

On the 6th of June the Fencibles gave Capt. Quitman a formal reception. His narrative of the expedition and of the glorious achievements of the Texan volunteers at San Jacinto was warmly received, and the day closed with a resolution authorizing their captain to tender the services of the company to the President of the United States, the Creeks and Seminoles holding, at that time, a threatening attitude on the frontiers of Alabama and Georgia.

The ensuing anniversary of our national independence

at a time more fraught with difficulty and danger than the present, and that they were not to be desired now.

" ' *Gen. Rusk to Gen. Quitman.*

" 'Washington, December 26th, 1850.

" ' Sir,—Having been detained by sickness on my journey to this city, I did not receive until last night your letter of the 4th instant, inclosing an extract from the "Sea-shore Sentinel," in relation to a speech lately made by me in San Augustine.

" ' I take the earliest occasion to answer the inquiries made by you in the frank and friendly spirit in which they are presented.

" 'On my way home I addressed the people of San Augustine in defense of my course in the Senate upon the Ten Million Bill, and urged them to accept the proposition, as the best way of settling the boundary question with honor and advantage to the state. In the course of my remarks I alluded to you, but in a style the reverse of the one described by the correspondent of the " Sentinel." It is impossible for me to recollect the precise language used; but the idea intended to be conveyed was that, in a contest with a government as powerful as that of the United States, it would be the duty of Texas to rely upon means which she could command more than upon the sympathies of other sections of the country, which she would doubtless have had, but had no right to demand. In this connection, I mentioned the fact that you had, in 1836, come to the aid of Texas, and stated my belief that the expression of your readiness to do so again, contained in your letter of last summer, had probably been of service, inasmuch as it showed the country that, in the event of a collision with the general government, Texas would possess the good wishes of her sister states; but I added that, under such trying circumstances, her chief reliance should be placed upon the resources which she could command promptly. I believe that if you had heard the remarks in question, you would have been convinced that they were dictated by a spirit of kindness rather than a disposition to censure. Very respectfully, your obedient servant,

" 'Thos. J. Rusk.

" ' His Excellency John A. Quitman.' "

was celebrated in Natchez with much enthusiasm. Capt.
Quitman, in full uniform, read the Declaration of Independence, and an eloquent oration was pronounced by
the Hon. J. S. B. Thacher, himself sprung from a family distinguished in the Revolution. At the dinner that
followed, Capt. Quitman offered a sentiment showing
the confidence he entertained then, and maintained to
the end of his life, in the volunteer soldiery :

"The battle of San Jacinto—like Bunker Hill, Eutaw,
and the Cowpens—proves that volunteers, in the cause
of freedom, are invincible."

Nor did Quitman, amid the congratulations of friends
and the enjoyments of home, forget his comrades whom
he had left in Texas. On the 13th of August, when six of
them* arrived, he called out the Fencibles, received them
at the landing with a salute, and escorted them to West's
Hotel, where, by his orders, an elegant entertainment had
been provided.

* Wm. Strickland, T. J. Golightly, M. M. Railey, J. S. Munce,
A. G. Coffin, J. Steen.

One of his comrades, Maj. Golightly, had previously written him
as follows:

"Camp, 5 m. E. of La Bahia, June 8th, 1836.

"DEAR CAPTAIN,—We have had hard times since you left us. For
13 days we lived on beef alone. Our company never halted till within 20 miles of the Guadalupe, where we lost our horses, and, after
hunting them five days, recovered them and went to Victoria, where
we arrived six days after the Mexican army had left. When the Texan forces came up we moved to La Bahia, where we saw a force of
1000 Mexicans retiring from Bexar, but in consequence of the armistice there was no fighting, very much against the will of some of us.
Capt. Strickland, 'of ours,' with 10 men, set out this morning to escort
Gen. Woll beyond our outposts on his way to Mexico. On our march
to Goliad we passed Fanning's battle-ground. There is no particular
military advantage in the place he selected. The bones of those who
were burned, and of those that were shot at Goliad, were buried on the
4th inst. with the proper rites. We found the place so intolerable on
account of the stench, and provisions and forage so scarce, it was resolved to return to Victoria, to which place the main army moved on
the 6th, leaving our company to protect General Woll."

I know of but one survivor of this gallant band—Capt. Francis
Duffau, now a much respected citizen of Austin, Texas.

This episode in the life of Quitman suggests a parallel between him and Stephen Girard, a man of proverbial shrewdness and good sense, yet there was a time when he was considered a lunatic by his most intimate friends. A fearful epidemic yellow fever prevailed in Philadelphia in 1793. Dismay and consternation were visible in every countenance. All who could fly, fled. Friends avoided each other in the streets. A person in crape was shunned like a viper. Husbands and wives, parents and children, abandoned each other. All the horrors of the plague in London, as described by Defoe in his narrative of that terrible visitation, were realized in Philadelphia. The poor, when stricken, were dragged off to the Bush Hill Hospital, whence, under the panic and malpractice that prevailed, few ever returned. Massachusetts, whose sympathies are only for the negro, passed a legislative act to arrest, turn back, or imprison any one, of any age or sex, sick or well, coming from Philadelphia, or suspected of so coming. New York passed a similar law. In the midst of this panic and universal fear of contagion, great was the public amazement when it was announced that Girard, the wealthiest merchant of the city, had taken charge of Bush Hill, whence no one had ever returned, waiting on the sick, shrouding the dying, and interring the dead. The most of his acquaintances declared that he had become insane. His death was considered certain. In a few days great was the astonishment to learn that Girard was neither sick, or dead, or crazy. He had brought order out of chaos, had substituted a better treatment, had largely diminished the mortality, and put a stop to the silly dread of contagion so fatal to the sick. He had built a new house and rented a barn in the vicinity, to accommodate the patients who now crowded to Bush Hill as the place where they could hope to be cured. One day this brave

man disappeared from the hospital, and the report re-
vived that he was dead. But he was found in a large
house on Fifth Street, in which he had installed sixty
little orphan children whom he had found in the deserted streets. This was the foundation of the Philadelphia
Orphan Asylum.

The history of Girard in '93 is the history of Quitman
in '36. Let Texas be substituted for Philadelphia, and
Santa Anna's devastating army for the epidemic, and the
analogy is complete. Santa Anna had entered Texas,
spreading every where conflagration and massacre. Universal panic prevailed. Fanning and his detachment
had been treacherously slain. The Alamo had fallen.
Houston, for a period, had no force to arrest the headway of the enemy. The Indians held a menacing attitude. The people were terror-stricken.

At that dreadful crisis, the young, wealthy, and distinguished Quitman, with the probability of certain death
staring him in the face, determined to go to their relief.
His friends pronounced the undertaking quixotic and insane. But there was a divinity within him, which buoyed
him up against remonstrances and sneers. He was constantly asked "what he could expect to do with his handful of boys against that powerful and glittering host?
what but to die?" "We will die, then," he calmly answered, "for I feel it is *my duty* to go." They declared
him a doomed and demented man. His wife implored
him, but his moral convictions were stronger even than
his affection for her. His example was felt every where.
The panic subsided. The star of Texas soon burned
brightly in the horizon. The prodigy of San Jacinto
was achieved, and her independence secured.

On the death of General Dickson, a representative from
Mississippi, in 1836, Judge Quitman resigned his seat in
the state Senate and became a candidate for Congress.

The election for President was then pending. General Jackson, who was about to retire from office, had maintained, against all opposition, his popularity in Mississippi. The opposition, confined chiefly to the western or river counties, had long concentrated on Mr. Clay, whose national doctrines they admired and approved. For Mr. Calhoun they had no admiration. In Wilkinson, and in a few counties on the Tombigbee, where many South Carolinians had settled, Mr. Calhoun had very warm friends. But neither his friends, nor the friends of Mr. Clay, separately or combined, could contend successfully, in Mississippi, with the popularity of Jackson. The nomination of Mr. Van Buren for the presidency was objectionable to the friends of both Clay and Calhoun. His political creed was considered by Mr. Clay as radical and unsound, and his imputed connection with the cabinet explosion, and proclamation policy of General Jackson, and his old partiality for William H. Crawford, of Georgia, made him particularly obnoxious to Mr. Calhoun. The friends of those gentlemen, therefore, combined to defeat him, but with singular inconsistency concentrated, in the South, on Hugh L. White, of Tennessee, who had advised and supported all the prominent measures of the Jackson administration, the war upon the bank, the veto power, removals from office, and the Proclamation and Force Bill. Inferior to Mr. Van Buren in abilities and position, his rupture with the Democratic party, so sudden that it looked like desertion for the sake of office, should never have recommended him to an opposition embracing so much of the talent and character of the nation, especially when one of the purest and most illustrious of their number was a candidate for their suffrages —the late General Harrison—a man of enlightened understanding and of moderate opinions, not likely to adopt the ultra policy of either of the great leaders of the national parties. Had the opposition concentrated on him, as they might have done without undue concessions of principle on their part, or the suspicion of treachery on his, he would undoubtedly have been elected in 1835. Without any concert among his friends, without the agency of a national convention, he had received 73 electoral votes, Massachusetts throwing away her vote for Webster, South Carolina for Mangum, Tennessee and other states for White, Pennsylvania, Connecticut, and Rhode Island giving very slim majorities to Van Buren. This demonstration of popularity with the masses secured the nomination of Harrison, four years afterward, against the claims of Webster, and the almost imperative demand of Clay. The only plea for the adoption of White in Mississippi and other Southern States was the unsound plea of necessity and availability—the improbability of securing a majority for either a Whig or a Nullifier—having to choose between Mr. Van Buren and some other statesman of the same party, in whose political integrity they had more confidence. Quitman took this view of the case, ran for Congress on the White ticket, and was defeated with it. In after life his judgment did not approve the course he then pursued. Such coalitions can be considered only as political errors, or as derelictions from principle. They are either based on the corruption of a few leaders, or on speculations as desperate as the chances of a gambler. They rarely do any good, generally much evil, and are altogether demoralizing.

The conservative doctrines announced by President Van Buren in his inaugural address, and the enlightened financial measures he had the moral courage to recommend at that period of " pressure" and " panic," when his co-operation would have converted the republic into a government of corporations, gradually brought Mr. Calhoun, Quitman, and the state-rights men generally, to his support. They perceived the error they had fallen into in supporting Judge White, whose subsequent course and associations leave little room to doubt that his election to the presidency would have been followed by the revival of the bank, the distribution of the public funds, and other federal schemes. Mr. Van Buren, on the contrary, disdained an alliance with the banking power, and, though he clearly foresaw that to' separate the government from the banks must be the work of time, and that he would be a victim to the "madness of the hour," he boldly exposed the mischievous tendencies of those institutions, their corrupt management and ambitious designs, and recommended, in their stead, the INDEPENDENT TREASURY.

In doing this, he virtually surrendered office; he placed himself upon the principles of the Constitution, and doomed himself to popular clamor, to the hostility of the combined capital of the country, and to defeat, when, by pursuing the opposite course, he might have tranquilized his administration, secured his re-election, and nominated his successor. His administration refuted all the calumnies of the canvass, and, instead of seeking to perpetuate his power by mercenary combinations, he presented the grand spectacle of a chief magistrate daring to be right, when the people, the fountain of all honor, were determined to be wrong. The State Rights party promptly gave him their support, until a difference of opinion in relation to the annexation of Texas compelled them again to separate.

The election in Mississippi figured up as follows: Van Buren, 9899; White, 9666: Gholson, 9676; Quitman, 8897. This defeat, however, manifested the great personal popularity of Gen. Quitman. Party spirit, of course, ran high. The Democratic candidate for Congress was an able man, commanding the confidence of his party, with strong local influences in his favor, and popular legislative antecedents to recommend him. Quitman's reputation was chiefly judicial; he had opposed, in the convention, the popular demand for the election of judges; from constitutional scruples, he had opposed the admission of members from the lately organized counties; the Whig party, and many of the Democrats, regarded his state-rights doctrines as disorganizing and destructive, and there were certain absurd sectional prejudices in his way. Nor had he canvassed the state.

There was no humiliation in this defeat. On the contrary, like Antæus, he sprung up from it refreshed, and confident in himself and of his strength. From that contest until the moment of his death he was, personally, the most popular man in the state, and throughout the South he became a representative man, thoroughly individualized and identified with a peculiar set of principles. Instead of cherishing resentment and chagrin, as men of inferior minds would have done under similar circumstances, he drew nearer to the Democratic party, and supported such of its measures as he could reconcile with his severe principles.

In 1837 a terrible epidemic ravaged the city of Natchez. A number of the Fencibles sickened and died. Quitman left his secure retreat in the vicinity to attend them in their illness, and made it a point to inter them with military honors. There was a general flight of the citizens, but duty carried him every day into the midst of the epidemic, and at night to guard the property of the fugitives from the burglar and incendiary. His venerable relative, the late Judge Edward Turner, one of the most humane and benevolent of men, thus remonstrated with him on his imprudence:

From Judge Turner.

"Franklin Place, October 18th, 1837.

"My hastily but firmly expressed opinion the other day is the result of much experience and reflection, and is the judgment of discreet medical men, given years ago, during epidemics such as is now afflicting the city. I have been a large participator in those trials and scenes of distress and sorrow, and have felt and suffered deeply, and without flinching; but I never felt that a friend was 'buried like a dog,' as you please to express yourself, because he was not buried with military pomp; nor that those who think as I do are to be considered *timid*, as you hint in your note, because they deem it prudent, at such times, to avoid large gatherings, and the sun and dust in a pestilential atmosphere. If you will consult our best physicians, you will find I am not alone in the opinion which so shocks your notions of duty and humanity. If I have wounded your sensibility, impute it to the affectionate regard I have for you and yours."

In 1837 he was commissioned by Gov. Lynch brigadier general of Mississippi militia, an appointment in which he took peculiar pride, encouraging the formation of volunteer companies, attending the semi-annual reviews, and bringing his command into a high state of discipline.*

* In those "flush" times it required a long purse to hold office in Mississippi. A canvass for Congress cost from $5000 to $10,000. Candidates were expected to indorse for their "friends," to loan indiscriminately, to pay any price asked for entertainments, and to establish and support newspapers, besides sundry other outlays. One canvass cost Mr. Prentiss $40,000. When Gov. Lynch and Col. J. C. Wilkins were candidates on the White ticket, and Franklin E. Plummer was the financial manager of the canvass, he drew from each of them $10,000, besides borrowing as much on their responsibility from the various banks. I subjoin a copy of one of Gen. Quitman's military bills.

1838.	To City Hotel,	Dr.	
Nov. 1. Sundries for friends from Clinton..................		$60	00
" " " six		12	50
" 21. Governor and suite.....................................		499	62
" 19. Treat to company......................................		100	00
Received payment.		$672	12

In 1838, finding that many of his friends of the Calhoun school of politics, having no organization in Mississippi, were co-operating with the Whig party, and thus losing sight of the old landmarks of their faith, he took the opportunity thus to define his sentiments:

To T. Bole and S. Shackelford.

"Natchez, Dec. 13th, 1838.

"GENTLEMEN,—On my return from Vicksburg a few days since, I received your communication, requesting my opinions upon some of the leading political questions of the day, and desiring permission to give them publicity. Believing that the free interchange of political sentiments tends to promote inquiry, elicit truth, and expose error, I have made it a rule never to disguise my own. Having no political aspirations to gratify, I am not interested farther than the patriotic and honest of all parties are concerned for the welfare of their country. I will therefore cheerfully comply with your request by communicating my views frankly upon the several subjects to which your letter refers, regretting that the pressure of important engagements will not permit me even to sum up the reasons or arguments which have irresistibly led me to cherish them as sound and orthodox Republican principles. I am, on questions of constitutional law, a strict disciple of the political school in which Jefferson, and more recently Calhoun, were able expounders and teachers; in favor of a strict construction of the federal compact, and of a vigilant and jealous protection of the reserved rights of the states. Believing that the latter retain also the remedy adequate to that protection, I thus claim to be a true Loco and Nullifier. I consider the system of internal improvement by the federal government not only without the pale of its delegated powers, but in general unjust, partial, and corrupting in its influence; tending to promote combinations and log-rolling schemes; tending to gratify private and sectional avarice at the expense of the public good; causing wasteful and useless expenditures of the public funds, raised from the industry of the country for the necessary support of government alone. The federal government was not constituted to do that which the state or the people can do without its agency.

"A 'tariff for protection' is against the spirit, if not the letter of the Constitution, and, in my opinion, is opposed to all the great principles of free trade, that constitute so important a part of the new and noble science of political economy. As it operated in the United States under the name of the American System, it was in truth a system of legal robbery.

"I am opposed to a national bank, because I consider its constitutionality at least doubtful in any shape, but still more, because I believe its establishment would tend to perpetuate the heavy commercial tribute which the states now pay to a limited number of Northern monopolists for credit based upon their own exports, would destroy forever the bright prospects now dawning upon us of a direct trade, and would, I fear, soon create a colossal money power, which, by the concentration of capital and credit, would possess the despotic control of all branches of industry, oppress the productive classes, and either wage a war with the government, or, what is still worse, would succeed in corrupting it by attaching itself to it for corrupt purposes.

"I am decidedly favorable to an unqualified separation of the government from the banks, and to the collection of the federal revenue in the constitutional currency; in other words, to the Independent, or Sub-treasury Bill, as introduced by Mr. Wright, specie clause and all. It is my sincere conviction that the connection of the treasury with the banks would soon corrupt both; a separation, entire and eternal, is the more necessary in the present condition of the country, when stock-jobbing and wild and visionary schemes of creating capital, misleading the public mind from labor, industry, and sound enterprise, the real source of national wealth, prevail to such an alarming extent. I see no other means of effectually checking the desolating effects which must result from ill-digested banking schemes, at times pampered and stimulated, and then again depleted to exhaustion.

"The receipt and expenditures of the public moneys, without permitting them to be mingled with the banking capital of private moneyed corporations, would, in my opinion, keep up a moderate and healthy demand for specie, and thus operate as a sure check to excessive issue of paper currency, limiting them to an amount always convertible.

"It would, by throwing the influence of the money power in opposition to an increase of revenue, tend to check extravagant expenditures and useless appropriations, and thus reduce the revenue and expenses of the government to an economical standard, enforce reform, and remove all temptation to dishonesty. Nor have I a doubt, notwithstanding the senseless clamor of some of the opponents of this measure, that in its operation, instead of increasing, it would diminish the executive patronage, in precisely the same ratio that the influence of money, the use of which for private purposes is forbidden under severe penalties, is less than if permitted to be made the basis of bank credit, discount, loans, and issues. The custody of a million of dollars, locked up in an iron chest, certainly confers less powers than the control of the same amount used frequently as the basis of banking operations, which, it is supposed, may be extended to three times the amount of the capital.

"In every point of view in which I have been enabled to examine the subject, I am led to the conclusion that the country would be benefited, and even the sound banks, disposed to be content with moderate profits, would be rendered more independent by the proposed divorce. I am at a loss to perceive how a genuine state-rights man, unprejudiced and impartial, can oppose measures so evidently tending to promote his principles.

"Differing entirely and radically from Messrs. Clay, Harrison, and Webster in every essential political tenet, I certainly shall not support either of them for the presidency. Believing that the elevation of either of these candidates would result in the establishment of the most dangerous principles, I shall, as a citizen, do all I can to prevent it. I consider the *Nationals*, composing a great part of the Whig party, as Federalists of the old school, with whom I have no elementary feeling in common. I shall co-operate freely and boldly with all genuine Republicans, be they Democrats or Nullifiers, in asserting the principles to which I have alluded.

"It is a matter of sincere regret to me to perceive many state-rights men, whom I know to be sound and orthodox in the abstract, and with whom I have long co-operated, disposed to rally under the broad banner of a candidate for President whose creed is the very opposite of that which they profess. I fear they permit prejudice against men to warp their judgments upon the practical political questions of the day. They seem to be aiding and cheering on a party whose success will overwhelm their cherished principles and all the great bulwarks of the Constitution in one common ruin.

"I have thus, gentlemen, briefly touched upon the interesting subjects presented by your letter. I have written this reply hastily, without time for revision or correction. It, however, contains my honest opinions. If you should consider them of any interest, you are at liberty to use them."

CHAPTER VII.

Sails for Europe. — Theatricals in Cork. — Irish Beggars.— Grand
Review in Dublin.—London.—An American Lady.—Wellington
and Lord Brougham,—The Tomb of André.—The Tower.—The
Old Bailey.—London at Midnight.—The great Bell of St. Paul's.
—The Queen.—The Royal Chapel.—Sabbath in Rotterdam.—A
Yankee Tar. — Gin-drinking among the Dutch. — Meets an old
Townsman.—The Dinner-table.—Coblentz.—Waterloo.—Fails to
sell the Bonds.—Letter from Thomas S. Munce.—Return to the
United States.

On the 25th of May, 1839, Gen. Quitman sailed from
New York for Liverpool, with the view of negotiating
the bonds of the Planters' Bank and the Mississippi
Railroad Company, to accomplish the completion of the
road. His *compagnon de voyage* was the Hon. J. S. B.
Thacher, of the Natchez bar. They embarked in the
Sheridan, Captain De Peyster, a crack ship of a famous
line. She made the run from land to land in thirteen
days, but when off Cape Clear encountered a head-wind,
which the captain thought would baffle her for eight or
ten days. Quitman and his friend got on a "hooker"
alongside, and reached Kinsale at night. A ride of
eighteen miles, through a pretty country, brought them
to Cork. Here they attended the theatre, and were
more entertained by the audience than by the performance. Loud conversation was going on across the house,
from one gallery to the other jokes and repartee, while
the dress-circle flashed with the bright eyes and jewels
of beautiful women. Presently there was a cry, "Three
cheers for Daniel O'Connell!" which were given as only

Irishmen can give them. After a while, three groans for "Sir Robert Pale" (Peel). This was the first time our countrymen had heard such a demonstration. The English cheer and the wild hurra of the Germans are fixed institutions on our side of the Atlantic, but the Irish groan has not yet been naturalized. Before the groans had well subsided there was a call, in a very shrill treble, "*Three cheers for the Amirikin jintlemen in the boxes!*" This was startling. They were strangers to every body. Their confusion drew upon them every eye. The cheers were given obstreperously, with three times three, which brought Quitman to his legs. He looked as though he was about to make a fourth of July speech, but, on reflection, merely bowed his acknowledgments, and the performance went on. How this incident happened, or how it had been got up, they never ascertained.

By the Lakes of Killarney and Limerick they proceeded to Dublin. The most contented class of people they met with were the beggars. They rival the lazaroni of Naples in idleness and the enjoyment of mere animal existence. Half a dozen were frequently seen basking in the sun half asleep, holding their hands toward the coach. If a sixpence was held up, too lazy to move, they would motion to the passenger to pitch it to them.

On the 18th of June, the anniversary of the battle of Waterloo, they witnessed in Phœnix Park, Dublin, a grand review. Twelve thousand regulars, under the command of the Marquis of Anglesey (who had lost a leg in the battle), exhibited the various evolutions of that terrible day. The manœuvres were concluded by a general charge of infantry, cavalry, and artillery, the clash of martial music and the roar of a hundred cannon. Quitman was electrified. He cried out, " Oh, let me see a field like this, and let me die!" For months he recurred to this magnificent spectacle. It set his military enthusiasm in a blaze.* The grand reviews he afterward saw in Paris did not impress him so much. They were dramatic and showy, but not so martial and imposing. The display of cavalry at Dublin and the riding far surpassed any he saw on the Continent. The average weight of a British light dragoon, fully accoutred, is 250 pounds; a heavy dragoon 280 pounds; a cuirassier, 308. Great power is required to carry these ponderous masses, and great speed; and only bloods, and half-bloods well crossed, are accepted for the service. In the Crimea the light brigade of Lord Cardigan, which made the celebrated charge and retreat, each of a mile and a half, were mounted on horses either pure or three parts blood. Had they been mounted on ordinary horses they would have been annihilated before they reached the Russian batteries. The heavy brigade of General Scarlett, which rode down the Russian troopers and trampled them under foot, were mounted on chargers having two crosses of pure blood.

From Dublin they went to Liverpool, thence to Birmingham, Kenilworth, Stratford-upon-Avon, and fair Woodstock, paying double tolls at all the turnpike gates for traveling on Sunday.†

* Maj. Gen. Wm. O. Butler, writing to the author, April 9th, 1860, says: "When talking on military matters, it was manifest that Quitman was something of an enthusiast; but his was an enthusiasm that served to stimulate without misleading his judgment. He was a military man by nature."

† Old John of Gaunt, "time-honored Lancaster," who once resided at Kenilworth, had in one of our travelers a lineal descendant. Judge Thacher is the 17th on his father's side, and the 18th on his mother's side, in direct descent from Edward III., King of England. Nor is his genealogy on this side of the water less distinguished. John Adams, second President of the United States, wrote of his great-grandfather, Oxenbridge Thacher, who died 1765, that "he was the second who gave the first impulse to the ball of independence." His grandfather, the Rev. Dr. Thacher, was present at the battle of Bunker's Hill, and wrote the best account of it ever published. In an ora-

In London, through their introductions, and the kindness of the American minister, Mr. Stevenson, they saw much society and received many attentions. They met a very distinguished circle at the house of an eminent American merchant, the architect of his own fortunes, whose wife, once a barefooted lass on the beach of Cape Cod, entertained the hereditary nobility of England with a grace surpassed by none of them, and with the air and mien of an empress, proud of her origin and equal to her fortunes. Through the courtesy of the Marquis of Lansdowne and Lord Brougham, they were admitted into the House of Lords. They had the satisfaction of hearing the Iron Duke. It did not take Wellington, on that occasion, more than ten minutes to express his sentiments, but he said a great deal in that time, and not a word amiss. There was neither effort nor excitement about him. He negligently tapped his boot with his riding-whip while he was speaking, and seemed perfectly indifferent as to the reception of his discourse. The Education Bill was before the Lords. Lord Brougham delivered a powerful and elaborate speech. In reply to some statement in disparagement of the intellectual capacity of the working classes, he said that on that very morning he had been called on by a deputation of people, dressed in paper hats and leather aprons, who complained that a work he had himself compiled on some scientific subject, for public instruction, did not go deep enough into the matter, and was altogether imperfect and superficial. "And now, my lords," said he, with a nasal sneer long drawn out, "I doubt if any of *you* would ever make such an objection." The members of the House of Lords,

tion which he delivered to the American troops under Washington, during the siege of Boston, March 5th, 1776, he first used the expression, afterward incorporated into the Declaration of Independence, "free and independent states." The Natchez descendant of this proud line of patriots and of kings is a thorough-going Democrat.

and the great majority of the Commons, and indeed the bulk of the people, are a finely-developed race. They have the good sense to cultivate the physical powers by manly exercises and out-door sports, and the females enjoy, to a great extent, a similar training.

In Westminster Abbey, among the tombs of the mighty dead, our travelers were attracted by a memorial closely. interwoven with the history of their own country. On a moulded paneled base and plinth stands a sarcophagus, on which is inscribed, "*Sacred to the memory of Major John André, who, raised by his merit, at an early period of life, to the rank of adjutant general of the British forces in America, and employed in an important but hazardous enterprise, fell a sacrifice to his zeal for his king and country, on the 2d October, 1780, aged 29, universally beloved and esteemed by the army in which he served, and lamented even by his foes. His gracious sovereign, King George III., has caused this monument to be erected.*"

On the plinth is inscribed, "*The remains of Major André were deposited, on the 28th November, 1821, near this monument.*" The sarcophagus is adorned with emblematic figures; one of them holds a flag of truce, and is in the act of presenting to Gen. Washington the letter which André addressed to him the night previous to his execution.*

Washington, it is well known, was deeply moved by

* "SIR,—Buoyed above the terror of death by the consciousness of a life devoted to honorable purposes, and stained with no action that can give me remorse, I trust that the request which I make your excellency at this serious period, and which is to soften my last moments, will not be rejected. Sympathy toward a soldier will certainly induce your excellency and a military tribunal to adapt the mode of my death to the feelings of a man of honor. Let me hope, sir, that if aught in my character impresses you with esteem toward me; if aught in my misfortune marks me as the victim of policy and not of resentment, I shall experience the operation of those feelings in your breast by being informed that I am not to die on a gibbet."

this letter, and so was the tribunal that adjudged the case. But the request could not be granted, and the unfortunate soldier was executed as a spy, manifesting the utmost fortitude and composure to the last. Many writers have contended that the prayer of André for military execution should have been granted; that, as men of undoubted honor and of high rank often accept the same risk for their country and penetrate the enemy's lines in disguise, there can be nothing so disgraceful in it as to demand a felon's death; that the service is strictly military, and the penalty should be in accordance with military law.

Gen. Quitman considered—notwithstanding the British government, by placing the ashes of André in this national mausoleum, had classed him among its heroes, and virtually reproached Washington with cruelty—that the proceedings against André were right, and that his prayer had been justly rejected. Such missions, insidious and unmanly in their very nature, so inconsistent with honorable warfare, so fatal, if successful, to an army, should be discouraged by inflicting the most ignominious punishment. Besides, the hanging of Capt. Hale, of the Connecticut line, only a short time previous, under circumstances of aggravated cruelty, rendered the death of André on the gibbet imperative.

What most interested Quitman in London was the Tower and the Inns of Court. His mind was essentially military and judicial, and here it was fully occupied. At once a fortress, a palace, a prison, and a tomb, there is not in this old Tower a turret, hall, chapel, gateway, court, stair-case, or chamber that does not tell its story of vicissitude, suffering, crime, and blood. In the celebrated "Hall of Arms" are deposited the weapons of war from the earliest periods of British history to the present day. We speak with admiration of the won-

derful imprόvement in agricultural implements, but it is
clear, after an inspection of this great repository, that
much more genius and skill have been lavished in de-
vising ways and means to "shuffle off this mortal coil."
Death, with his old-fashioned sickle, is too slow for this
"fast" age, and the ingenuity of man has come to his
assistance.

The famous criminal court, the "Old Bailey," being
in session, Quitman visited it to see how justice was ad-
ministered.   The contracted space set apart for-specta-
tors was crowded with the friends of the accused parties,
not the most savory neighbors, but a shilling fee introduced them very near the be-gowned and be-wigged
lawyers in the bar.   Justice was dealt out in double-
quick time.   One or two witnesses were sharply examined; very brief speeches made; a briefer charge delivered; a putting of heads together by the jury without
leaving the box; the word "Guilty" uttered by the fore-
man, and the "sentence" instantaneously pronounced.
Among the rest, a small boy was sent on his travels to
a penal colony, after a trial of only twelve minutes, for
having stolen a mason's trowel!

The judges here bustled from the bench, as the bailiff
said, "for 'alf han 'our to heat sandwiches hand drink
sherry," and Quitman and his friend took occasion to
withdraw, deeply impressed with the folly of drum-head
court-martials in halls of justice, and with the wisdom
of the old fogy maxim, "*Festina lente*" — deliberate
speed.

Quitman used to say that he never had an adequate
notion of the population of London until he undertook
a midnight walk through "the city" to his hotel in the
"West End."   When he reached St. Paul's it was just
12 P.M.; but the streets were filled with vehicles of
every description, and the pavements as densely packed

with foot-passengers as when he had passed at midday.
The gaslights from the street lamps and the illuminated
windows of the shops lit up the moving panorama as
with the light of day, while the great bell of St. Paul's,
more than four hundred feet above their heads,

> "Swinging slow, with sullen roar,"

tolled "the witching hour of night." High above the
crashing tumult of the streets, this numerical thunder
made itself counted. The great bell is heard at Wind-
sor Castle, twenty miles from London. A sentry on
duty in the castle was once accused of sleeping on his
post, but defended himself by alleging that on that particular night he heard St. Paul's strike *thirteen* times for
midnight. This was found to have been so, and he was
acquitted. It is usually two at night before the moving
column on the street dwarfs down to a straggling line
of wayfarers, the houseless unfortunate or the prowling
vagabond, having no place wherein to lay their heads;
and at all hours there is a hoarse murmur, as of a heavy
surf rolling upon some distant shore.

While walking in St. James's Park one fine Sabbath
morning, near Buckingham Palace, General Quitman and
Judge Thacher had the honor to salute her majesty on
her way to the Royal Chapel. She returned it with a
smile, and so pleasantly they resolved to attend divine
worship at the same shrine. But when they arrived,
they found that the sacred promise, "Knock, and it shall
be opened unto you," was no passport to their admission. Thacher argued with the sanctimonious and be-
dizened janitor that they were strangers from the Southern States of America; but the official remarked, "That
can not be so, for you are both as *white* as I am." While
Thacher was smothering his wrath at this insinuation
and swearing that he was a sovereign at home, and had

older blood and better blood than Queen Victoria in his veins, Quitman quietly stepped up and slipped half a guinea in his hand. The door flew open, and, with low bows, they were ushered to a convenient seat.

On the 15th of July they left London for Rotterdam, where they arrived next day. While pulling about the various canals to see the town, they came under the stern of a small brig which displayed the stars and stripes. On the rail aft a young fellow was leaning, staring into the town. " What brig—where from ?" said Quitman. In true Yankee style the answer came,

" Who hails ?"

" Countryman. Who commands that brig ?"

" Sarah Ann, of Salem, Capt. Job Pratt, who's jist gone ashore to meetin'."

As they pulled off, he cried out, " Come aboard. Do come, and take some rum and 'lasses." ·

It was the Sabbath, but the great bulk of the Rotterdam people were in the fields and public gardens, with their children around them, indulging in recreation and chit-chat—a cheerful scene, in pleasant contrast with the stillness and dullness of the same day in the large cities of England and the United States.

In early times in New England, and now, it is presumed, in some parts of it, the Sabbath commenced at sundown on Saturday evening, and continued until the same hour next day. The children, their features sharpened by abstinence and constraint, grouped themselves at the window looking to the west, and, as soon as the sun sank, would sing out, " Hurra ! boys, Sunday's out !"

The Sabbath should, unquestionably, be a day of worship and of rest ; but worship may spring from the grateful emotions of the heart, as well as from the grand anthems of the choir ; and rest may be found in the social circle, as well as in a hired seat, in the glare of worldly

II 2

splendor, under the drowsy and formal accents of a pensioned preacher.

> "Religion never was designed
> To make our pleasures less."

At any rate, this seemed to be the opinion of the Rotterdamese, and of the people of the Continent generally.

The next day the general and his party visited the town of Bommel, on the Rhine, in search of his relatives, the descendants of Admiral de Verien. In the evening, when it was ascertained that they were Americans, they were waited on by the most substantial burghers, and invited to the Casino, where citizens of standing usually resorted. The general spoke the language fluently, and became the centre of the crowd. He answered a thousand questions about our sources of prosperity, our reception of immigrants, and our institutions, and was deep in state rights, when a little boy entered the circle with a salver filled with liqueur glasses. It proved to be pure Hollands, of exquisite flavor. Every ten minutes, while the general was discoursing, the little fellow came round. After this had been repeated fifteen or twenty times, the American guests contented themselves with merely putting the glasses to their lips, but the cry was universal, "*Drinken out*"—thus hinting very plainly that the Bommel aristocracy tolerated no "heel taps." There was no evading the etiquette, and the drinking was honest and accurate. It was fearful odds—gin-drinking Dutchmen against Yankees, and under their own juniper-tree! They saw with a shudder, through the tobacco-smoke, the yellow curls and violet blue eyes, set in porcelain, of the little white-aproned boy, with his tray suspended by a leather strap around his neck, and as he reached them in his incessant rounds, crying, "Schnapps!" our friends were strongly tempted to fly. At last, however, there was a general movement. Some dozen gentlemen es-

corted the strangers to their inn. On reaching it, they
found the landlord at the door, evidently anticipating
the visit. Instead of retiring then, as they expected, the
escort followed them in, where the landlord had pipes
and tobacco in waiting, and, before they were fairly seated, another little boy, as like the other as two peas, with
his apron and tray, and yellow curls and blue eyes and
china face, was circulating the liqueur glasses! When
a Dutchman sits down, he is not going to get up in a
hurry. Finding they were in for it, the American reputation at stake, and an escort in their own hotel, they resigned themselves to what Sir Walter Scott calls "serious drinking." They soon saw, or fancied they saw,
two little boys, two trays, and two sets of liqueur glasses, and the company seemed to multiply amazingly.

The social bout, however, came to an end, and at a certain hour next day they rose perfectly sound. What a
pity the great Udolpho Wolfe can not get a recipe from
the burghers of Bommel!

After visiting some relatives of his mother at Rossum,
Quitman proceeded to Dusseldorf, and traveled post into
Westphalia, the country of his forefathers. The roads
are excellent. There are no wayside cottages or fences.
The necessity that anciently compelled people to congre-
gate in villages and fortified towns has become the cus-
tom of the country. Agricultural laborers walk five or
ten miles every morning to their daily toil. Cattle are
stabled, or closely watched when on pasture, and hence
there is no necessity for inclosures. The road is lined
on either side with stately Lombardy poplars, here called
the "King of Prussia's grenadiers." Post-horses on this
route were strong and serviceable. The postillion every
now and then dismounts, and baits them with a few
slices of coarse brown bread, which he carries in the
boot.

He visited Iserlohn, where the Quitmans resided in remote times. It lies in the spurs of the Hartz Mountains, and is famous for its mines and zinc manufactories. Over the entrance to several of these artificial caverns the name of QUITMAN was engraved in iron in Gothic capitals, thus indicating the original proprietor of the mines. At Loest, enjoying a baronial castle and its honors, he was entertained with great hospitality by his old friend, William Brune, who, after having made a large fortune in the hardware business at Natchez, had returned to his native country and purchased a barony. The general met at his table a number of distinguished military men, who were found well versed in the history of our country. Dinner commenced with the pudding and ended with soup, interspersed alternately with substantials and delicacies. After dinner every one was expected to contribute a song. Baron Brune led off with "Yankee Doodle," the words a *jeu d'esprit* of the late Francis Baker, in which Captain James K. Cook, an old editor of Natchez, was the hero.

> " Captain Cook went on the bluff
> A firing off his cannon,
> And every time he fired it off
> He used a yard of flannel," etc.

The Prussian officers heartily joined in the refrain, and roared off,

> "Yankee doodle, doodle doo, Yankee doodle dandy,"

in true German style. Quitman gave the "Banner Song" of the Natchez Fencibles, which he considered the best piece of music extant, and Thacher followed with "Old Rosin the Bow," which quite electrified the company, who joined lustily in the chorus. Next morning a German translation of these songs appeared, and they are now sung in many parts of the father-land.

At Cologne, famous for its perfumed waters and its

concentrated stinks, they crossed the Rhine on a bridge of boats, such as was introduced by Julius Cæsar in his conquest of the country, whose footsteps may be said to be still visible wherever he carried the Roman eagles. At Coblentz, at the *table d'hote*, the *carte des vins* had on it a wine entitled *Pis-porta*. The explanation was, that it was made at a vineyard near the ruins of a Roman gate, or portal, which still bore the inscription, *Pisonis Porta*, or the gate of Pisa.

After calling on the Rothschilds at Frankfort-on-the-Maine, to arrange his business, the general and his friend paid a visit to the field of Waterloo. A cicerone, as usual, was accepted, who commenced his description of the details of the battle, pointing out the position of the different corps of the two armies, and the sacred places where distinguished officers had fallen. The enthusiasm of Quitman became intense, and, interrupting the guide, he took up the narrative, and entered into a minute and critical account of the operations of that eventful day. The guide listened in silent admiration for a while, as did a trio of British officers who had joined them. At length, lifting his cap and bowing to the ground, he said, "I have the honor of standing in the presence of a general of Waterloo!" Quitman laughed, and said to his party, "I have had a chart of this ground in my head for years; it seems to have been specially designed for a great battle. It is but the surface of the earth, but to me it appears higher than the Pyramids."

Having failed, in consequence of the pressure of the times, the prostration of American securities, and the mismanagement of the Natchez Railroad corporation in his absence, to dispose of their bonds, he embarked at London on the "British Queen" for New York.* The voy-

* The late Thomas S. Munce, who held a confidential position in the bank, addressed him while in Europe as follows:

age was unpleasant, the weather stormy, and the ship and her officers were not to be bragged of. A protract-

---

"Natchez, July 23d, 1839.

"My gratitude and affection for you will not let me lie down and see engagements entered into (without your knowledge, and the burden of which you will have to bear), and the credit of the company jeopardized, and you thrown forward to meet the storm. I may not have penetration enough to perceive the wisdom of the policy of our board, yet I can not believe that we have any right to extend our engagements one dollar until the receipt of satisfactory intelligence from you. If I understood arrangements rightly, not one additional contract should have been let, and the farther prosecution of the road depended upon your success in Europe. You had scarcely left the United States before 'to let contracts' were published. Of course, they were taken, and perhaps low enough, as they are to be paid in our *currency*. Our own circulation now consists of 12 months postnotes, bearing 5 per cent. interest; they are *only* 25 per cent. discount. Our *currency* (made up of all sorts of notes and shin-plasters) is, of course, a grade lower. Thirteen sections, running to Torry's store, have been let. We are building a splendid dépôt, and putting a brick wall around the same; likewise a machine-shop, and are about to make a contract for a road to the river. There are other smaller engagements. This may be all right, and in consonance with the true interests of the company, but it seems to me vastly imprudent. To be sure, it is easy to make and sign post-notes at 12 months and 5 per cent., but they will come due some day; and it seems to me that we are saddling ourselves with a debt that will cripple us for years, even if you succeed in disposing of the bonds. To let you see what new engagements you will have to provide for, let me specify:

"13 sections of road $325,000
Dépôt 35,000
Shop... 20,000
River road, probably...................................... 80,000
                                                        ─────────
                                                        $460,000

Our circulation—
On demand 8,000
6 months post-notes, due in September.......... 66,000
8   do.   do.   27,000
12 do.   do.   due May, June, July...... 394,000
                                                        ─────────
                                                        $495,000

I fear this showing will discourage you, but it is my duty to advise you of it, if nobody else will."

No wonder that this concern soon afterward blew up with a crash that shook every pane of glass in Natchez, and took the meat out of the pot of many a poor family. The other kindred institutions throughout the state followed the same road; and as all men and all parties had supported and confided in them, so all alike shared the general distress, save the few who were in the secret all the time, who, by borrowing large amounts from the banks, and investing in lands and need tempest, and a fire, providentially discovered just in time to save the ship, and a proposition at one time entertained to depose the captain and put her in the hands of a more competent or vigilant officer, for the common safety, were the only incidents of the voyage.

To his Brother.

"London, August 11th, 1839.

"Since I wrote last I have been to the Continent, traveling up the Rhine to Frankfort, and thence to Paris. My principal object was to make an effort with the capitalists of Holland, Germany, and France to negotiate some of my bonds. I could not succeed. Money is also scarce at every point, and interest high. They, of course, prefer investments in their own country, and can not be induced to touch others. On my way up the Rhine I stopped at Bommel, and made inquiries for the family of Admiral De Verien, the husband of our mother's sister. He is dead. I, however, met with his brother and nephew, by whom I was received very kindly. They told me that two of our cousins resided at the small town of Rossum. There I accordingly went, and met with Mrs. Du Fee, wife of Captain Du Fee, of the Dutch navy, and her sister, Matthia Henriette De Verien, being full cousins of ours. They received me very affectionately, and spoke most feelingly of the affection and love of their mother to ours, which they had often heard of. The other children I did not see, to wit, Jan Casper, Carl Cornelius, and Anna Elizabeth, married to a public officer named Kinschat, all of whom live at Rotterdam. This family is among the best of Holland, and they appear to live comfortably. At Iserlohn, in Westphalia, I called on two ladies, named Shirriffe, who were daughters of a Mr. Quitman, their brother, a young man of our name, not being at home. All I could learn was that their father's grandfather and ours were brothers. I went to see an old gentleman at the zinc factory who

groes, amassed colossal fortunes, often going, six months or a year thereafter, to the very men from whom they had purchased their estates, buying up the worthless bank issues at 30, 20, and even 10 cents in the dollar, to repay their original debt to the banks.

was descended from Quitmans on both sides. He informed me that one branch of the family had gone to
Cleves several generations past, but that he had not the
' stamff baum' (genealogical tree) ; that it, however, was
still in existence. He took me to an old zinc factory, on
which was inscribed, 'Joh: Fred: Quitman, medecin doctor und prac. 1752, and Joh: Flem: Quitman Kauf Rath-
man, und hospitals prov. 1752,' as the founders of the
factory. This family is one of the richest and most respectable in that country. I saw also the tombs of some
of the family, and the church-pew which they had occupied for more than a century. When I saw the hills
about Cleves and the prune orchards, I could not but
think of the time when our father, a beautiful and healthy
boy, was bounding among them. Along through this
region of country is the finest race of people I have seen
in Europe. I traveled from Frankfort to Paris, spent a
few days there, and returned to this place to make another effort here to raise some money. I will probably
sail for home about the beginning of September. I shall
be very happy to return. I have stored away much information, and have learned much, but I prefer, in every
respect, our own country, and shall be more contented
than I have ever been with the oaks of Monmouth and
its tranquil retirement."

CHAPTER VIII.

On his return to Natchez, Gen. Quitman, never content with inaction, renewed his partnership with John T. M'Murran, Esq., who had read law in his office, and had become one of the most distinguished lawyers in the state. At this period the General was somewhat embarrassed, owing to the depreciation of securities of every kind and the heavy liabilities he had incurred for friends. To pay these liabilities, after exhausting the proceeds of his crops, he borrowed money at 10 and 12 per cent., and now relied on his profession to meet his engagements. It is in allusion to this embarrassment that the following letter was written to one who was indebted to him. It is inserted to show the strong attachment he had for his faithful slaves, the best friends of our race, placed by Providence in our hands in the condition of perpetual wardship, and whom we are bound, by the strongest moral obligation, to care for and protect.

To J. F. H. Claiborne.

"Monmouth, Jan. 27th, 1840.

"DEAR CLAIBORNE,—It is now nearly twelve at night. After completing the harassing toils of the day (and my days now run far into the nights) I have just read, for the second time, your touching letter. As self is ever first in the reflections of the strongest as well as the weakest of us, I will commence with that portion of yours relating to myself. Your fancy presents me as surrounded by all that can make life happy. I know you have the benevolence to delight in the scene which your fancy has drawn, and I regret to dispel the illusion by stern realities. I·assure you that I too am compelled to drink to the very dregs of what is worse than poverty, the care, the anxious, corroding care arising from pecuniary embarrassment—to toil and struggle to sustain my credit—to make humiliating appeals to traders and purse-proud money-lenders for *time*—to forego every recreation and even physical exercise—and to adopt the most rigid economy in my household. This I have done ever since my return from Europe, and must do for some years to come. I owe $95,000, over $40,000 of which I have had to assume for others. I am likewise indorser for our unfortunate friend —— for $24,000, and for various others whose circumstances are very doubtful, for over $20,000. All this, it is probable, will fall on me. I have 160 slaves. My other property is worth, perhaps, $200,000. The former, however, are all that would be available in an emergency, and they are my chief source of revenue. I am strongly attached to them. They are faithful, obedient, and affectionate. I would rather be reduced to abject penury than sell one of them. My debt is nearly all due now. It requires the last dollar of my plantation revenue to preserve my credit. Were suits instituted against me, should any calamity happen, nearly all that we have might be swept away. These are unpleasant reflections. I have three households to provide for besides my own, and several private charities that I·have long been committed to, and must not neglect—the wives and orphans of departed friends. So you see I am suffering not the pleasures but the cares of splendid poverty. With a revenue of $45,000, I can not

build a green-house for my wife or buy a new piano for
my daughter; and when I meet ——, the trader, or ——,
the Christian Shylock, I am compelled to acknowledge
the superiority which the look of '*you owe me, and can't
pay,*' gives them.   I never have avoided a friend or an
enemy, but I confess, when I see these men approaching
on the street, and the supercilious smirk on their faces,
and know that my pockets are empty, if I can conveniently dodge them I do.   I am not, however, subdued.
I resume my profession with M'Murran in February, and
even his characteristic industry shall not exceed mine.   I
will never quit it until I discharge my debts, and, when
once free, will never be a slave again.   If you were with
me now, we would take a glass together and give three
cheers for the very dream of freedom.   I have, very
lately, paid $6000 for our poor friend ——, who started
in life with you——both my earliest friends.   He is utterly broken down, and his once high spirit succumbs to
ruined fortunes and a shattered constitution.   Alas! he
will only find freedom in the grave.   As for yourself, do
not despond.   If you have lost your fortune, you have a
better capital, which neither false friends nor your own
over-confidence can deprive you of.   Employ it boldly,
and you may place your banner where you will."

To J. F. H. Claiborne.

"Monmouth, Feb. 26th, 1840.

"DEAR CLAIBORNE,—There was no poetry, I assure
you, in my late letter to you.   It was naked fact, and
I am not gifted with your imagination to plant a flower
in the arid desert of pecuniary troubles.   The skeleton
DEBT stands rigidly in my path, and stares me in the face
as though to wither and terrify me; but I return my de-
fiance, and will struggle boldly for victory.   I am now
insensible even to the allurements of ambition, and would
reject a crown but for the gold and jewels it might contain.   Not that I am avaricious; do not suspect me of
that.   With one third of my present income, and free, I
should be happy, and eagerly court distinction and fame.
I confess myself anxious for a popularity founded on
what you have happily termed 'integrity of principle.'
I know that ——, and ——, and ——, and men of that

school, though apparently friendly, are hostile to me. My principles and habits are too republican for them.

"I feel the force of your quotation from the Greek poet. I know I have arrived at the period of life when the effort for fame should be made, if made at all. It will soon be too late. But first, I must disengage myself from creditors whose very looks stir my blood to rebellion.

"You speak of taking charge of a newspaper. It would please me much to see you in the editorial chair. Your views of politics and of political economy are, in the main, right. You have a thorough knowledge of men and of state politics, or rather intrigues, for Mississippi politics have been, for a long time, only a series of selfish plots and counterplots for the benefit of men; and what inferior men! Were I to consult my personal wishes, or the cause of genuine democracy, I would urge you to become an editor. It would give you power and distinction, but would it pay? I have never known a poet or an editor to get rich. Your politics and your pride cut you off from the means that some resort to for wealth; editorial life, I fear, would shut the doors of legitimate accumulation. But more of this when we meet.

"I concur with you that, after the re-election of Van Buren, the Democratic party will divide between Calhoun and Benton, and that the friends of the former should begin to organize. This consideration almost tempts me to say to you, go at once into the editorial chair. Benton is electioneering already. Have you read his speech in favor of striking out portions of the 19th and 20th sections of the Sub-treasury Bill? It is a piece of disgusting charlatanry and demagogism. I do not like that man, yet I fear he will succeed. The gigantic and lofty mind of Calhoun scorns to descend to the vulgar occupation of dealing out gingerbread and beer to the people for popularity. He is too intellectual, too philosophical, and too pure for the age we live in. His name will shine brighter a century hence. I hope sincerely that Van Buren may be re-elected. Yet I begin to doubt it. I have never seen such enthusiasm as the opposition now display. In the North and West the 'log-cabin and hard-cider' candidate is sweeping all before him. We are, in fact, it appears to me, on the threshold of a revolution. State credit has exploded. The paper bubble has burst. Ruin and consternation every where prevail. We can not foresee what direction the tempest will take, or where it will stop, or what effects it will produce. It may re-establish sound Democratic principles. *It may result in the triumph of money and the establishment of monarchy.* It is useless now to speculate. The time for *action* will come.

"I am now in full practice—forced to it to save my property, though my own debts do not exceed $10,000. I am zealous as a boy, and sanguine of success. I shall have to decline the nomination for presidential elector; I am too busy to do justice to such an appointment."*

His expectations of a lucrative practice were fully realized. In a few years he relieved himself of debt, and again retired to the family circle, his oaks, and his library, which he loved so well. No man was happier in private life; his temper was bland and amiable; his flow of spirits was equable and lively; he was fond of the society of his friends, and took part even in the pastimes of children; he had a taste for horticulture, and a passion for flowers. His literary habits found ample scope in his well-stocked library, and a portion of his time was devoted to those duties that devolve on every good citizen. At this period, and until the 19th of May, 1847, he was President of the Board of Trustees of Jefferson College, and took a great interest in the fortunes of that venerable institution, maintaining the inviolability of its charter, and resisting the insidious and narrow-minded attempt to undermine it.† About this time the degree

---

* He did resign this position, and the author was appointed to succeed him, but, for similar reasons, could not accept.

† He was one of the founders of our noble State University—one of its original trustees; took a decided part in giving it its present broad organization and high caste, and favored the most liberal policy in relation to it.

of A.B. was conferred on him by Princeton College, and · .
LL.D. by the College of La Grange, Tenn.

His brother Albert and himself had opened a sugar-
plantation on Grund Carllon, La., which the former chiefly managed. From their correspondence I extract a few
paragraphs, showing the humanity of the slaveholder,
and his attention to the comfort of his negroes:

"Monmouth, May 9th, 1839.

"I am very sorry to hear of poor Kitty's death; she
was faithful, honest, and industrious. Encourage the negroes to report their complaints to you early. They
have a great aversion to lying-up in hospital, and to diet-
ing, and often conceal their complaints until it is too late.
The stoutest and most sensible and trustworthy of them
must be watched like children. They seldom reflect, and
have bad memories. Clothe them well, make them be
clean and neat in their persons and dwellings, encourage
them to have gardens and fruit-trees and vines, regulate
their little domestic dissensions, and grant them every
indulgence consistent with discipline. Harshness makes
the negro stubborn; praise, and even flattery, and, more
than all, kindness, make them pliable and obedient. Keep
them cheerful. I love to hear a gang of hands singing
at their work, whistling on their way home, and fiddling
and dancing at night. This manifests a contented heart."

To his Brother.

"November 22d, 1839.

"I was very sorry to hear of our bad luck in the loss
of so many negroes. This is indeed serious; but we
should not sit down and lament what we can not prevent.
Take misfortune coolly. In the business of life, reverses
will come. We must oppose them with patience, prudence, and courage, and struggle on. The tide will
change; and, if we still continue unfortunate, we may
console ourselves with the reflection that we have deserved a better fate, and that better men than we are
have suffered more, and suffered without complaining.
Pray attend to the sick, and let them have every possible comfort."

To his Brother.

"January 16th, 1842.

"I have spent several long years past in constant and severe exertions, and harassing and painful anxiety—enough to break down any but a resolute mind and vigorous constitution. I have been crippled by every sort of pecuniary embarrassment, and have had nothing but the bright hope to cheer and support me, that a few years more of toil and anxiety will rid me of the burden I have borne so long. Why, however, should I afflict you with my cares? With a good conscience, a resolute heart, and a strong arm, I hope to conquer every difficulty. It would be better for my interests, all things considered, to sell negroes to pay my debts. Cotton is now too low to be profitable, and I am paying 10 per cent. and upward for money—much more than the labor of my negroes brings me in. But I can not bear to part with those who are so faithful and so attached to me; they are of my household, and I never will barter them away. So I must endure the toil and anxiety, and the impertinent smirk of money-dealers, and the ostentatious pretension of the rich parvenu, a few years longer. If there be any set that I heartily despise, it is those who plume themselves upon their riches, and regard a man who happens to get in debt as a criminal. Their supercilious sneer is offensive, and their patronizing pity is little less so. Every day I see two or three whose noses I am tempted to wring. I confess to you that wealth for me has no attractions. I love neither its pomp, its luxury, nor its responsibilities. Give me independence and tranquillity, and I ask no more.

> "'Seek'st thou for happiness?
> Go, stranger, sojourn in the woodland cot
> Of innocence, and thou shall find it there!
>   Ah! that thus my lot
> Might be with peace and solitude assigned,
> Where I might, in some little quiet spot,
> Sigh for the crimes and miseries of mankind.'"

The following extract from a letter to an early friend, who was in difficulties at the time, will show the generous features of his character.

"Monmouth, October 19th.

" I will make every effort to do what you desire. You have not reminded me of our early friendship, but I shall ever bear in grateful remembrance the kindness I received from your family years ago, and many proofs of friendship I have received from you. I am reminded of this at this moment, when I see in my library the splendid testimonial presented to me by the Legislature at your instance, at the outset of my and of your career. Rely on me always."

The Mexicans, under the perfidious Santa Anna, having again invaded Texas, General Quitman thus wrote to a friend at Galveston. It glows with the fire of his ardent and chivalrous nature.

"Natchez, March 19th, 1842.

" DEAR SIR,—I read with pleasure your letter of the 11th. I rejoice that the Mexicans have invaded Texas, because it will end in what I have ever believed to ·be the true policy of Texas, the invasion of Mexico. You have now no alternative. You must conquer the invaders, or be exterminated. The Lone Star of the West will be extinguished forever, or it will blaze over the towers of Mexico. I am too well acquainted with the character of your people and that of your enemy to doubt the issue, were the latter twice as numerous. The enthusiasm you describe must lead you to victory. All that you want is a head. Your ablest men should be selected to command, and, for a time, should be vested with dictatorial powers. The Santa Fé expedition failed for want of a leader. If well-commanded, our Southern militia are invincible. In personal courage, and skill in the use of weapons, you have the very best material. In fighting Mexicans, as in fighting Indians, mere military tactics are of no importance. In such a warfare I would not have a mere martinet to command even a company. The general should have the entire confidence of his men and command their implicit obedience. If you have such a man, place him at once at the head of your army. Send the fiery cross throughout the land. Summon every man between the ages of sixteen and forty-five. Muster them on the Colorado as quietly and secretly as possible. Encourage the invaders to advance by some show of timid resistance. When half the numbers shall have confidently crossed that barrier, suddenly concentrate your forces, let your deadly rifles do their part, and then rush to the attack sword in hand, firmly resolved to conquer or die. No Mexican army can stand the shock of your charge. Let your battle-cry be San Jacinto. Your victory will be easy and complete. Follow it up without delay. Carry the war at once into the heart of Mexico, and, before the end of summer, the banner of the single star will float proudly over the walls of the city of Montezuma. If you succeed you will gain the admiration of the world. If you suffer yourselves to be defeated you will have its contempt, and need scarce expect its sympathy.

"The *government* of the United States will be cautious in the matter. The *people* of the South will cheer you on and aid you. We are too much absorbed in our pecuniary distresses to exhibit much public enthusiasm, but we will never permit an Indian and negro colony to be planted on the frontier. Come what will, that must not happen."

To General Sam. Houston.

"Natchez, April 7th, 1842.

"My DEAR SIR,—I have seen your comments upon the extraordinary letters of Santa Anna to Mr. Bee and General Hamilton. Independently of the evidence you bring forward to prove that the dictator had pledged himself not to attempt another invasion of Texas, I well recollect a long conversation which took place between you and the President Santa Anna, in which I also participated, on our way up the Buffalo, at the time of the change of your encampment from San Jacinto. By your invitation I had a seat in the boat which conveyed you and the dictator to the new camp. After some compliments upon you and your brave men, he remarked that he was now persuaded that Texas, if reconquered by the power of Mexico, could never be retained; that the cost of such an attempt to Mexico would greatly exceed the value of the acquisition; that it would be policy in

VOL. I.—I

Mexico to suffer an independent nation to grow up between her and the great and grasping power of the
United States, and that, should his influence ever prevail
in Mexico, he would urge the recognition of the independence of Texas ; that all must be sensible that such
was the true policy of Mexico, and that no obstacle could
be thrown in the way but what might grow out of national pride.

"This is the substance of his remarks on that occasion.
If my certificate should be of any service to you, I will be
happy to furnish it in more form. I heartily wish you
success in your glorious enterprise to force the recognition of the independence of your country from Mexico at
the point of the bayonet."

In 1843 the people of Mississippi were distracted by a
great question growing out of the bonds issued by the
state for the celebrated Union Bank. Old political issues
were wholly laid aside, and parties were classed as Bond-
payers and Anti-bonders. General Quitman took position with the former, though he by no means indorsed
the platform as laid down by the Hon. C. P. Smith,
chairman of the Bond-paying Committee in 1843, nor did
he acquiesce in the views which the same gentleman, as
chief-justice, announced subsequently from the bench.
This distinguished jurist has a mind remarkable for its
acuteness and capacity for analysis; it is logical, compact, and severely disciplined, but strictly technical, and,
from his habitual line of reading, too contracted for enlarged and popular conceptions of statesmanship. His
view of the great question of 1843, in which he endeavored to demonstrate that the Union Bank bonds had
been issued in pursuance of the original act creating
that bank, and not under the supplemental act, and were
therefore legal, constitutional, and binding on the state,
was a view strictly in conformity with the subtle and
plausible structure of his mind. Quitman, on the other
hand, more slow and much less brilliant than the chief-

justice, seemed to grasp and comprehend, intuitively, as it were, the great principles of natural justice which lie at the bottom of equity and jurisprudence. Sophistry was no part of his nature. Discarding technicalities, he applied those great principles to the question, and thence deduced the obligation of the state to pay. He thought that the question of the liability of the state for the redemption of those bonds, being purely judicial, should not be submitted to the popular vote. The principle that, when a government, through its lawful agents, enters into a contract with another government, or with an individual or company, and a dispute arises between them, it should be decided not by tribunals lawfully established, but by popular suffrage, and that too under circumstances unfavorable to impartial judgment, he condemned as unsound and dangerous. He was ambitious of popularity, but he would not flatter the people by professing to believe that, in their tumultuous meetings at the polls, under the excitement of inflammatory harangues, they were as competent to construe the fundamental law and conflicting statutes as judges who had devoted many years to the study of such matters. He saw no equity in the proposition that the debtor should assume to be the final and authoritative arbiter as to the fact and the sum of his indebtedness.

The Anti-bonders resisted payment of the bonds, chiefly on the plea of *non est factum*—that the instruments purporting to be the bonds of the State of Mississippi, although signed by the governor, countersigned by the treasurer, and bearing on their face the broad seal of the state, were not in fact, and did not in law constitute a valid or binding obligation, because they had been executed, issued, and sold in fraud of the Constitution, and in contempt of the terms and conditions on which the alleged obligees had consented to be bound. They

planted themselves on the 9th section of the 7th article
of the Constitution of the State, which declares that
"No law shall ever be passed to raise a loan of money
upon the credit of the state, or to pledge the faith of the
state for the payment or redemption of any loan or debt,
unless such law be proposed in the Senate or House of
Representatives, and be agreed to by a majority of the
members of each house, and entered on their journals,
with the yeas and nays taken thereon, and be referred
to the next succeeding Legislature, and published for
three months previous to the next regular election in
three newspapers of this state; and unless a majority of
each branch of the Legislature, elected after such publication, shall agree to and pass such laws; and in such
case the yeas and nays shall be taken, and entered on
the journals of each house."

They admitted that the original act of the Legislature,
passed February 5th, 1838, chartering the Union Bank,
with a capital of $15\frac{1}{2}$ millions of dollars, and authorizing
the issuing of state bonds to net that amount, had been
passed in conformity with the aforesaid 9th section of
the Constitution, and had the bonds been issued in pursuance of the Act of February 5th, no constitutional
objection could have been urged. But those bonds,
they contended, instead of being issued by authority of
said act, were issued by virtue of an act of the Legislature, entitled, "An Act *supplemental* to an act to incor-
porate the subscribers to the Mississippi Union Bank,"
approved February 15th, 1838, ten days after the passage and approval of the original act.

It was argued that, by the first, or original act, in order to facilitate the bank in obtaining the requisite capital, the faith of the state was pledged for the sum of fifteen and a half millions, as *security* for the capital and
interest, evidenced by the bonds of the state. The cap-

ital and interest were to be paid by the bank when due.
In order to *secure* the capital and interest of the bonds,
the subscribers for stock in the bank were bound to give
mortgages on productive property, at a reduced valuation, to be in all cases equal to the amount of their individual stock. When the stock had been secured, as required by the charter, the governor was directed to issue
bonds in amount equal to the stock *thus secured*. The
bank bonds and mortgages were required to be deposited in the institution, as a reimbursement of the capital
and interest of the state bonds.

Had these requirements been complied with, no difficulty, it was alleged, would have ensued. But instead
of allowing the bank to go into operation under its charter, which had received the sanction demanded by the
Constitution, the Legislature was induced, upon its own
responsibility, to improve the original, and passed the
" *Supplemental Act*," introducing new and incompatible features—changing the relations between the state
and the bank—and materially modifying, in essential
particulars, some of the leading conditions on which
the people of the state had assented to the original
act.

By this famous supplement, instead of merely loaning
her credit to the bank, the state was made a stockholder
to the amount of five millions of dollars. This, of course,
would make her debtor to the bank in that amount; and
as the 9th section of the 7th article of the Constitution
forbids the passage of any law pledging the faith of the
state for the payment of any debts (except in the mode
therein specified), this *Supplemental Act*, which required
the governor to subscribe for five millions of the capital
stock of the Union Bank, and execute bonds therefor,
should have been submitted to the people for approval
according to the formalities of the Constitution. Had

this "supplement" received the same sanction as the original act, there would have been no controversy as to the validity of the bonds. But undertaking, as it unquestionably did, to dispense with the vital conditions on which the people had agreed, in the original act, to loan their credit to the bank, causing the bonds of the state to be issued before the mortgage security (solemnly stipulated in the original act) was provided to indemnify the state against loss, in the contingency of the failure of the bank, making the state a debtor to the bank, as principal, without security, when the people had only consented that she should stand in the relation of indorser, with ample security against loss, based upon productive real and personal estate, mortgaged at a reduced valuation. The "Supplemental Act" was therefore rejected and denounced by a large portion of the press and the people as no law, and, as a consequence, the bonds issued in pursuance of it were held not to be binding or obligatory upon the state.

The "Supplemental Act" was the result of pressure upon the Legislature. No peculiar party or individual is responsible for it. It was the era of speculation. Legitimate trade had been swallowed up by the passion for gambling and adventure. Men every where bought and sold without having any real capital, upon fictitious securities, and the rage for banking perceived no obstacle in the 9th section of the Constitution, which had been devised by QUITMAN eleven years before, to prevent the very evils that were now about to occur. Men hitherto prudent had become reckless. The public conscience had grown unscrupulous. Barefaced swindling was considered clever financiering, and the most desperate became the most influential. Society in private life, and in every department of government, lost sight of the old landmarks of right and wrong, and rapidly deteriorated, and, in the general corruption that infected all parties, the Supplemental Act had its origin.

Many of the so-called bond-payers, with General Quitman at their head, concurred in the arguments against the validity of the bonds. As a strictly legal proposition, they held it to be incontrovertible that the Supplemental Act violated both the letter and spirit of the Constitution, that the Legislature had transcended their power of attorney, which is the Constitution, and, according to technical rules of law, their principals, the people, were not bound by their acts.

But, while these were his sentiments on the abstract question, he did not acquiesce in the propriety of referring the decision of the question to the people, a party interested, and, from the nature of things, not capable in this instance of rendering an impartial or enlightened judgment. Admitting the force of the maxim *caveat emptor*, it was known that most of the bonds had passed, for a valuable consideration, into the hands of innocent third parties, whose inducement to purchase had been their confidence in the resources and good faith of the State of Mississippi, and her failure to redeem them would ruin many, and give a fatal blow to her credit and character. Quitman therefore held that the bondholders should be invited to come with their claims, as other litigants, and have a full and fair adjudication of them before the tribunals of the state. He believed that, although the strict letter of the law would be found adverse to their claim, and be so determined, nevertheless, that the investigation of all the facts by a high and important tribunal would determine the people of the state, upon those generous principles of equity that influence civilized communities, to provide a suitable indemnity for the holders of the bonds. He insisted that the community knew or believed the Supplemental

Act, when it was proposed, to be of doubtful validity.
Its objectionable features were pointed out at the time
by a few clear-sighted individuals; a few members of the
Legislature protested against it; a portion of the public
press exhorted and warned the governor not to put the
seal of the state to the five millions of bonds called for
by that act.   But the governor, the Legislature, and the
people were captivated and demented by the splendid
vision of a colossal corporation which was to realize the
fable of Midas, and convert every thing it touched into
gold.   If the monster bank, yearned after by so many
for relief against impending bankruptcy, and for the
means of farther speculation, should have to await the
tardy progress of the prescribed preliminaries enumerated in the original act, the governor, Legislature, and
their sovereigns would be ruined by delay, for all were
alike deep in debt and speculation.   Circumstances would
not wait.   There was no time for discussion.   Constitutional questions must be waived for the present and settled afterward.   The day of judgment was at hand, and
nothing but the bank could save them, and nothing but
the state credit and the five millions of state bonds
could put the bank in operation.   Such was the pressure
—such the common delirium—the "madness of the
hour."   Birds of prey, from all quarters of the country,
allured by the scent of carrion; rapacious creditors, with
appetites whetted by frequent disappointment; ambitious politicians, who looked to the bank as a means of
controlling public sentiment and of furthering their personal designs; and gambling speculators, who thirst-
ed for millions, but would have sold their Savior for
less than thirty pieces of silver—all flocked to the seat
of government.   The giddy and unreflecting populace
united with them, and the howl was absolutely terrific.
Those were the days of summary justice—if that sacred

name may be so profaned—the day of drum-head court-martials, cross-road executions, Lynch law, the pistol, and the bowie-knife! High public functionaries sanctioned deliberate violations of the law and fellowshiped with criminals; executive officers reeled across the public squares from one coffee-house to another, and judges spent the Sabbath at the gambling-table, and adjourned court next day to finish their game! No wonder, then, that the "still, small voice" of the Constitution was unheard. The multitude roared. The members of the Legislature would have been mobbed if they had not passed the "Supplemental Act," to hasten the borrowing operation; the governor would have been mobbed had he refused to issue the bonds, and the commissioners appointed to dispose of them would hardly have escaped if they had not hurried away to find a market and a purchaser.

The commissioners soon disposed of them to a party deeply infected with the gambling infirmity of the period, who was fully apprised of the constitutional difficulties in the way of the transaction, but who passed them over, fraudulently, to third parties ignorant of this drawback. The original law prohibited any sale of state bonds issued or to be issued for the capital stock or interest of the Union Bank at less than par value; but, in point of fact, they were negotiated and sold in violation of this provision of the law. Nevertheless, such was the general exultation, the commissioners, on their return with the means of putting the "monster" in operation, were received with bonfires, illuminations, public festivals, and other demonstrations of popular approval. The proceeds were soon squandered, and the bank, after having stimulated the evil spirit of gambling to the utmost extent of its means, after a vain attempt on the part of its imbecile managers to control the politics of the state,

and to substitute low trickery and swindling for legitimate financiering, closed its profligate career in hopeless
insolvency, and sunk, like some huge ship upon the
ocean—

Rari nantes in gurgite vasto—

leaving behind it, in every quarter, the evidences of the
ruin and demoralization it had wrought.

And now was heard, for the first time, the alarum of
repudiation. The governor, who had signed the unconstitutional "Supplemental Act" and executed the bonds,
joined in the cry.* Those who, from the first, had op-

---

* *Correspondence of the Governor of Mississippi with Hope & Co., of
Amsterdam, Holland, in relation to the payment of the interest on the
Union Bank Bonds.*

"*To the Governor of the State of Mississippi:*
"The undersigned, as trustees for the holders of debentures of the
Bank of the United States at Philadelphia on deposit of American
state stocks, and, among others, of a considerable amount of bonds of
the State of Mississippi bearing five per cent. interest, issued through
the Union Bank of Mississippi, and made payable at the agency of
the United States Bank of Pennsylvania in London, the principal in
1850 and 1858, and the dividends semi-annually in May and November, having been refused payment of the interest due the first of this
month on said bonds, are compelled to address themselves to the government of the State of Mississippi; and from their confidence in the
faith of that government, they feel convinced that the simple mention-
ing the fact of the nonpayment will be a sufficient stimulus for the
government of the State of Mississippi to take immediate measures for
the payment of the interest now due and which will further successively become due on those bonds, and to prevent irregularities or demur
so prejudicial to the interest of American credit in general and to that
of the State of Mississippi in particular.   HOPE & Co.
"Amsterdam, 22d May, 1841."

"Executive Department, City of Jackson, July 13th, 1841.
"GENTLEMEN,—I have received your letter, dated Amsterdam, 22d
May, 1841, postmarked Washington City, June 21st, 1841, and bearing the official frank of the Hon. Daniel Webster, Secretary of State
of the United States. I have duly considered the contents thereof.
Those bonds were not sold in accordance with the Constitution and
laws of this state. They were delivered by me as *escrows*, to be sold
at not less than their *par value*, and for cash, as the statute of this
state required. The charter of the Mississippi Union Bank prescribes
not only the substance, but the form of the bonds, and provides that
they shall be in the sum of two thousand dollars each, 'which sum

posed that act as illegal and inexpedient, or the majority
of them, took the same view. Thousands, for various

the said State of Mississippi promises to pay *in current money* of the
United States' to the order of the bank, with interest at the rate of five
per cent. per annum, payable half yearly at the place named in the
indorsement of the bonds. The act farther provides that 'said bonds
shall not be sold under their par value.' The bonds having been
delivered to the managers of the bank to be sold on certain conditions,
the state can not be bound for their redemption unless the terms prescribed were complied with in the sale. The Constitution of this state
expressly provides that 'no law shall ever be passed to raise a loan
of money upon the credit of the state, or to pledge the faith of the
state for the payment or redemption of any loan or debt, unless such
law be proposed in the Senate or House of Representatives, and be
agreed to by a majority of the members of each house and entered on
their journals, with the yeas and nays taken thereon, and be referred
to the next succeeding Legislature, and published for three months
previous to the next regular election in three newspapers of this state;
and unless a majority of each branch of the Legislature so elected,
after such publication, shall agree to and pass such law; and in such
case the yeas and nays shall be taken and entered on the journals of
each house; *Provided* that nothing in this section shall be so construed as to prevent the Legislature from negotiating a farther loan
of one and a half millions of dollars, and vesting the same in stocks
reserved to the state by the charter of the Planters' Bank of the State
of Mississippi.'

"Five millions of state bonds, dated the 5th, 6th, 7th, 8th, and 9th
days of June, 1838, were sold by the commissioners appointed by the
Mississippi Union Bank to Nicholas Biddle, Esq., on the 18th day of
August, 1838, for 'five millions of dollars, lawful money of the United
States, payable in five equal installments of one million of dollars each,
on the first day of November, one thousand eight hundred and thirty-
eight, and on the first days of January, March, May, and July, in the
year one thousand eight hundred and thirty-nine,' and 'made payable at the agency of the Bank of the United States in London *in
sterling* money of *Great Britain* at the rate of four shillings and sixpence to the dollar, with interest payable semi-annually at the same
place and rate.' No authority was ever given by any act of the Legislature of this state to change the currency in which said bonds were
made payable. By selling the bonds on a credit, and changing them
from dollars current money of the United States to pounds sterling of
Great Britain, the following sums were lost:

Interest on five millions state bonds from 7th of June, 1838, to 1st of
    November, 1838 ....$100,000 00
Interest on four millions two months........ 33,338 38
Interest on three millions two months...... 24,999 96
Interest on two millions two months........ 16,666 64
Interest on one million two months......... 8,333 32
                       ——————— $183,338 30

reasons, joined in the clamor, and slowly that thunder-voice rolled across the Atlantic, and the startled bond-

Difference between five millions of dollars, principal of state bonds, in current money of the United States and sterling of Great Britain at four shillings and six-pence to the dollar...	478,750 00
Difference of interest on $1,250,000 of state bonds pay-able in twelve years between current money of the United States and pounds sterling of Great Britain at four shillings and sixpence to the dollar.............	69,625 00
Difference of interest on $3,750,000 of state bonds payable in twenty years between current money of the United States and pounds sterling of Great Brit-ain at four shillings and sixpence to the dollar.........	353,068 00
	$1,084,781 30

"From the above statement it will be perceived that one hundred and eighty-three thousand three hundred and thirty-eight dollars and thirty cents were lost by selling the five million dollars of bonds on a credit, and paying interest thereon from their respective dates, and the farther sum of nine hundred and one thousand three hundred and forty-three dollars was lost by changing the bonds from dollars current money of the United States to pounds sterling of Great Britain. These two items amount to the enormous sum of one million eighty-four thousand seven hundred and eighty-one dollars and thirty cents. Surely such a sale can not be binding on the State of Mississippi. The faith of this state was pledged for the payment of those bonds only upon the condition that they were sold at not less than their par value. The state expected the full amount of those bonds to be paid into the vaults of the Mississippi Union Bank. If the full amount had been received, and the currency in which they were made pay-able not have been changed, the bank would have been better enabled to indemnify the state.

"It appears that the bonds were indorsed in blank by the officers of the bank and delivered to the commissioners charged with their sale. Neither their power of attorney nor letter of instructions authorized those gentlemen to fill up said indorsement by making the bonds and coupons payable in pounds sterling of Great Britain at the rate of four shillings and sixpence to the dollar. If such a change had been made on the face of the bonds after their execution and de-livery to the bank, the parties making the alteration would have been guilty of forgery, and could have been immured in the Penitentiary for the offense. It will be no answer to the argument to allege that the indorsement could only bind the Mississippi Union Bank. That institution has undertaken to pay both the principal and interest of the bonds. If the bank is compelled to pay the one million eighty-four thousand seven hundred and eighty-four dollars and thirty cents for the loss sustained by the credit sale of the bonds and the change in the currency in which they were made payable, her means will be reduced that amount, and the risk of the state thus greatly increased.

holders for the first time learned the uncertain and doubtful nature of the obligations in which they had intrusted their means—many of them their all.

The state was willing to intrust her credit to the bank on the conditions prescribed in the charter. The faith of this government has never been pledged for the illegal and fraudulent sale of those bonds.

"This is a constitutional government, and all its officers take an oath to support the Constitution of the State, and faithfully to discharge the duties of their respective offices. Her chief magistrate is required to take care that the laws be faithfully executed. He would be recreant to his trust and violate his official oath were he to suffer the laws of the land to be trampled upon and the Constitution disregarded.

"The contract for the sale of the state bonds shows that the statutes of the state in relation to the bonds were made a part of the contract. The purchaser was well aware of the conditions on which they were issued, and *knew* that the purchase was neither sanctioned by the Constitution and laws of this state nor of Pennsylvania. The contract was guaranteed by the Bank of the United States. The whole of the purchase-money was paid by that institution. The name of Mr. Biddle was merely used in the contract as a *device* to get round that clause in the charter of the Bank of the United States which prohibits her from dealing in state stocks. The currency in which the bonds were made payable was changed from dollars to pounds sterling to give a false coloring to the transaction, and make it appear that the bonds were sold at par value. The principle is universal that fraud vitiates all contracts. The commercial law of this state relative to negotiable paper is different from that of most other countries. The transfer of bonds and notes does not prevent the drawer from setting up any defense against an innocent purchaser which could be made available against the original payee.

"The state therefore denies all obligation to pay the bonds held in trust by you for the following reasons:

"1st. The bonds were sold on a credit.

"2d. The currency in which the bonds were made payable was changed from current money of the United States to pounds sterling of Great Britain at the rate of four shillings and sixpence to the dollar.

"3d. The contract of sale was fraudulent.

"4th. The Bank of the United States was not authorized to make the purchase.

"5th. The bonds were sold at less than their par value, in violation of the charter of the bank.

"The money paid for those bonds did not come into the state treasury. The officers of this government had no control over its disbursement. The bonds were disposed of in August, 1838, by collusion and fraud, in violation of the Constitution and laws of this state. The Mississippi Union Bank and the Bank of the United States were parties to this unlawful transaction. You have the indorsement of both of these institutions, and to them you must look for payment. *This*

An influential portion of our citizens, of both the old political parties, believed that the bonds had been legally issued, and they insisted upon a tax being levied by the Legislature to redeem them. And this party, General Quitman among them, contended that, legally, the state was not liable, but that the moral obligation to pay was equally binding on a just and high-toned people of vast resources and expanding energies. This obligation, they maintained, was created by the almost universal recognition by the people of the acts of their agents—the negotiation of the bonds—accepting and using the proceeds within the state, and only complaining of unconstitutionality after the money had been received and squandered. Applying to it the principles of honor and equity, which should govern in private transactions, they contended

state never will pay the five millions of dollars of state bonds issued in June, 1838, or any portion of the interest due, or to become due thereon.

"When I ascertained in January, 1839, the terms on which the bonds had been sold, I communicated the same by message to the Legislature, and denounced the sale as illegal. At that time only two millions of dollars had been paid on the bonds by the Bank of the United States. By a proclamation I subsequently issued, the sale of the second five millions of dollars of state bonds delivered to the Mississippi Union Bank was prevented. I absolutely refused to execute the last five and a half millions of dollars of state bonds demanded by that institution. These decisive measures prevented the illegal disposal of ten and a half millions of dollars of state bonds, and will convince you that the government of this state never has countenanced, and can not be made responsible for the fraudulent acts of the Mississippi Union Bank.

"I have forwarded to your address the Journals of the Legislature of this state for the years 1840 and 1841. It will afford me much pleasure to forward you such other documents as you may desire. I am anxious that the bond-holders should be possessed of all the facts in relation to the issuance and disposal of the bonds held by them. Your great experience in commercial affairs no doubt has made you familiar with the principle that parties contract with reference to the law, and that in a constitutional and free government every act of a public functionary is merely an exercise of delegated power intrusted to him by the people for a specific purpose, and that his acts are the acts of the people only while within the powers conferred upon him.

"I am, gentlemen, very respectfully, your obedient servant,

"A. G. M'NUTT.

"Messrs. Hope & Co., Amsterdam, Holland."

that, if an individual should authorize an agent to go into the market and borrow money for him on certain conditions, and that agent should return and tell his principal that he had got the money, but not on the conditions specified, it being optional with him to receive the money or not, if the principal receive it, he thereby waives the change of conditions, and ratifies and confirms the act of his agent, and can not afterward honestly plead a violation of conditions. So Quitman argued that, after the state had accepted and used the proceeds of the bonds, no matter how illegally they had been issued, no matter how improvidently they had been negotiated, no matter how recklessly the money had been squandered, she was morally bound to redeem them.

Upon these conflicting issues a furious contest ensued, which called forth a vast amount of talent and energy. It resulted in the triumph of the anti-bonders, who, during the contest, besides the argument already referred to, took the high ground that, in resisting the payment of the bonds, they were defending the Constitution ; and that, though they sympathized with the innocent and unfortunate parties now holding said bonds, no sympathy and no misfortune would authorize a deliberate sanction to an unconstitutional act.*

* The celebrated Gouverneur Morris, one of the leaders of the old Federal party, and one of the most distinguished lawyers of his times, expressed the following opinions applicable to this question: "The debt, you say, is contracted according to the forms of the Constitution. This I doubt; but let it be admitted that public faith is pledged according to the constitutional forms: suppose a majority of the House should contract a debt of 30 or 300,000,000, and divide the stock among themselves, would their successors be bound to provide for the payment ? This, you will say, is an extreme case, but I must have a plain answer, yea or nay. If it be yea, I shall insist that forms so absurd be instantly abolished. If nay, the inference is that cases may exist in which the pledge given according to constitutional forms is not to be redeemed. * * * You insist that we are bound to pay public debts by the same moral principle which binds us to pay our private debts. Agreed. But we are bound to pay only just debts ; or, to speak

Had the bond-payers generally exhibited the moderation of Quitman, and taken the middle ground he recommended, the result, in all probability, would have been different. But many leading men on that side of the question, for ambitious objects, involved it with national politics, and provoked by their violence when the obvious policy was conciliation. Threats of retaliation on the part of foreign governments—of reprisals on our commerce—of excluding us from the comity of nations, and even of seizing our cotton *in transitu* and after it reached a foreign market, were proclaimed. They ventured to arraign the state in Congress and in the British Parliament, and the Continental press. This roused the pride of our people. Millions they might have been prevailed upon to concede, liberally they would have given had the application been put in some other form than a peremptory demand for payment, but not a dime would be yielded to insult and menace. It was on one of these occasions, in a public meeting, after Quitman had pronounced a warm appeal for the payment of the bonds, that the speaker who followed him spoke of English cruisers in the Gulf, and their right to seize our cotton. The patriot orator immediately rose, and, with a voice of indignation, and his whole frame trembling with emotion, said: " Sir, in that event I join my countrymen who oppose the payment of the bonds. My sword—ay, sir, the last drop of my blood, shall be spent in resisting the demand. My *state*, sir—may she be always right; but, right or wrong, the STATE, sacred, intangible, and unprofaned, forever !"*

more accurately, that is no debt which is not justly contracted. * * *
An agent, though he comply with legal forms, can not bind his principal to a matter which is illegal or immoral; and a third person can not ground a claim on such transaction if he was privy to the wrong."—Sparks's Life of Morris, vol. iii., p. 287.

* John Marshall, Esq., the able editor of the Austin (Texas) State Gazette, and long the confidential friend of Quitman, says:

It was this high-toned, fervid patriotism, this intense love of country, this sensitiveness to any attack upon it

"It is true, General Quitman was among those who advocated the payment of the Union Bank bonds, but he always regarded the Constitution as having been violated in their emission. He was only willing to pay the debt in the event of the people waiving their constitutional right to repudiate the unwarrantable acts of their servants. The people sternly and wisely disavowed these acts, and made an example of unbridled power which subsequent legislators have never forgotten. General Quitman afterward held that the question had been finally decided upon, and we have before us, from his own pen, the declaration that he was *firmly opposed, whether as a private citizen or in an official capacity, to a resuscitation of the question. Without a new assumption by the people, he would regard a law for the payment of the rejected bonds as a fraud on their rights.* He had opposed the charter of the Union Bank at the time of its incorporation, and had also opposed the issue of the bonds at the time of the discussion of the question as a matter of state policy."

The following extract from a letter written by him in 1849 is the latest that I find on the Union Bank bond question. He stood upon this position in his first canvass for governor, his opponent being the Hon. Luke Lea.

"Upon all questions of practical state policy it is my duty to express my opinion, if honestly desired. The Union Bank bond question is of that character. If we are to judge from the proceedings of the Whig convention, they will make the payment of the bonds one of the issues of the present canvass. Upon this subject I have no disguise. When, in two successive elections, the question of the validity of these bonds was before the people, I, as a citizen, advocated their payment, and used all arguments which suggested themselves to my mind to induce others to concur in my opinions. While I supposed that, in the opinion of the world, some discredit would be attached to our state for the rejection of these bonds, I have never attributed to those who differed from me any but pure and patriotic motives in opposing their payment. It is unnecessary to refer to the arguments used by those who favored, or those who opposed the payment of these bonds as unconstitutional and void. The issue was twice made before the people at the general elections, and, after a full and elaborate discussion, the people of this state, by large majorities, deliberately, and I think honestly, pronounced against the constitutionality and validity of the bonds given for stock in the Union Bank. In this solemn and deliberate decision upon that subject I acquiesce. Unless set aside by a reassumption of these bonds by a vote of the people, this decision is and must continue to be binding upon the public authorities of the state. Under our Constitution, all questions involving the appropriations of money out of the treasury belong exclusively to the Legislature, and, consequently, to the people, whose will the Legislature should represent. Questions, therefore, concerning the appropriation of money, whether or not they involve validity of bonds

from any quarter, that gave him his strong hold on the public confidence, and enabled him to pursue the truth, whether in a majority or minority, without any diminution of personal popularity.

In 1845, a vacancy having occurred in the Senate of the United States, Gen. Quitman was prominently mentioned in connection therewith. The suggestion of his name in the public papers brought a flood of letters from every section of the state, encouraging to his hopes. They were so flattering, and from such influential men, that he fixed his heart upon the matter, and, in private letters to his brothers, expressed little doubt of his success. A strongly written and very plausible communication appeared in the Vicksburg Sentinel, over the signature of " Hume," charging him with many political errors, and impeaching his claim to be considered a Democrat. It bore the earmarks of A. G. M'Nutt, late governor of the state, and then a candidate for the vacant seat in the Senate. He was a man of vigorous intellect—an original thinker—satirical and sardonic, with a memory of astonishing tenacity—one of those provoking memories whose exactitude is so often inconvenient to aspiring politicians. His

or contracts under which such payment is claimed, belong not to the executive or the judicial power, but to the people, through their representatives in the Legislature. In my opinion, therefore, this important question of the validity of the Union Bank bonds, and their payment, has been deliberately and authoritatively settled by the tribunal that possesses supreme power over this and similar subjects. It can not be disturbed except by a proposition laid before the people to assume this debt. It would be a political fraud upon their rights for any department of the government, without such assumption—or reassumption, if the term be preferred—to apply moneys or effects of the state directly or indirectly to the payment of these rejected bonds. Any other view of the subject, whether by bond-payer or anti-bonder, would, in my opinion, be opposed to the principles of our government. Admitting not only the constitutional right of the people of this state to determine for themselves the validity or nullity of these bonds, but also convinced that their decision has been deliberately made, and in good faith, to protect their Constitution from infraction even by the Legislature, I am opposed to the resuscitation of the question."

own career had been marked by inconsistencies, growing, perhaps, out of the fact that he entered public life in the service of a constituency strongly Whig, and when banking corporations had not, by their abuses and enormities, provoked public scrutiny. As chief magistrate, he had committed grave errors in regard to the Union Bank which were never satisfactorily vindicated. But he now stood the acknowledged head of the opposition to banks, and the radical feeling of the state was embodied in and directed by him. He was, on this point, inflexible and uncompromising, and was surrounded by devoted followers, but had made bitter enemies by the harshness of his manners and the vituperative style of his oratory. The Whigs detested him, but his most violent opponents were inside of the Democratic organization. He was the most formidable candidate for the Senate, and while actively canvassing, the article in question, intended to drive Quitman from the arena, appeared in a journal well understood to be the organ of M'Nutt.

The following reply, which seems to have been addressed as a sort of circular to his political friends, was found among the papers of Quitman, in his hand-writing. It covers his whole political course, and gives his own reasons:

"I came to Mississippi at the age of twenty-one. Devoted to my profession, and in straitened circumstances, I had given little attention to national politics. My predilections, however, were for William H. Crawford, of Georgia, for President, against either Adams, Jackson, or Calhoun. I early imbibed, from the writings and speeches of Virginia statesmen, the state-rights and free-trade doctrines, and have adhered to them ever since. I made no opposition to the election of John Quincy Adams—the contest in Mississippi being between him and Jackson—when he was first a candidate, because he had been acting against the Federalists since 1803, and his orthodoxy was not impeached until his first message in 1825.   In 1828, while absent from Natchez, my name was placed, without my authority, on a committee of his friends, but on my return I refused to act on it.   In 1827, during Mr. Adams's administration, I was elected to the Legislature chiefly by the Jackson men of Natchez and Adams County.   Adam L. Bingaman, the leader of the Adams party, was my opponent.   Duncan S. Walker, a Jackson man, succeeded me, and John F. H. Claiborne, a very ultra Jackson man, succeeded him, and was elected three times successively, by decided majorities, over Bingaman and other Whigs.   So my election *from the county of Adams* is no proof that I was for John Quincy Adams.

"In September, 1828, I was appointed chancellor by a Democratic governor, and unanimously confirmed by a Democratic Legislature.   I was no advocate of the United States Bank, nor did I exert any influence to bring a branch of it to Natchez.   With other Democrats I acted for a time as a director, and as a director of the Planters' Bank, in which the state had a large interest, and which General Jackson had selected to hold the government deposits.   In both instances, as my friends well know, I was induced to serve to protect the planters from the too great influence of the commission merchants.

In 1832 I was a member of the Convention.   I refer to the record for my course.   I was the author of the section restraining the use and abuse of the public faith and credit.   This clause has preserved the state from hopeless insolvency.   Without it, such was the mania for borrowing and banking, there would have been no limits to its misuse.   Had Governor M'Nutt adhered to the spirit of this clause of the Constitution, and refused to sign the Supplemental Act and the bonds for the Union Bank, the distracting questions which have since been made would never have disturbed the state.   The people of this Democratic state, after the convention, elected me chancellor without opposition.   In 1832 I voted for Jackson and Barbour, because I did not consider Mr. Van Buren sound on the tariff question.   I did not "*become*" a Nullifier in 1832.   I was *always* a Jeffersonian state-rights man.   I admired the character of General Jackson and his message of 1832, but I opposed and de-

nounced his proclamation, and do it now. In politics I
hold much the same position as Calhoun and Troup. Of
the Northern politicians, Woodbury, of New Hampshire,
is my favorite. I wrote, in 1832, some political essays,
which certain mousing politicians condemned, but they
were complimented by such men as Calhoun, Rowan, and
Hayne. In 1834 I was elected senator from Adams
County, where a Whig majority existed, but they knew
my opinions, and I was known to be President of the
State Rights Association. It is true that, at the adjourned session of the Legislature of 1835, with General
P. Briscoe and other stanch Democrats, I opposed, on
strictly constitutional grounds, the admission of some
members from new counties, which had been created
by the same Legislature. We thought their admission
would violate the constitutional provision as to appor-
tionment and that regulating the proportion between
the two branches of the Legislature. The inference attempted to be drawn that I acted in a spirit of hostility
to that section of the state is false. As far back as 1827
I advocated the extension of civil process over the Indian
territory with a view to its acquisition. In 1834, when
acting governor, I took, for the first time it had been
broached here, strong grounds in favor of the claim on
the federal government for the school lands and the five
per cent. fund in the Chickasaw cession, as my message
will show. It is false that in 1834 I strenuously urged
an increase of banking capital. Considering the mania
that raged, my message should be construed as intended
to restrain its extension. In 1836 I was re-elected President of the Senate, Governor M'Nutt voting for me on
every ballot. I was opposed to the Union Bank.

"In 1836 I voted for Judge White, whom I believed
to be as good a Democrat as Van Buren, and sounder on
the tariff question. I ran for Congress on the White
ticket. I believe the Whigs, to some extent, voted for
him and for me; but this did not make Judge White
and myself Whigs. It is not true that in 1837 I was in
league with Prentiss in opposing the right of the Chickasaw members to places in the Legislature. I was not
in the Legislature, but I condemned the opposition. I
voted for Claiborne and Wilkins for Congress, the first

being one of the Van Buren and the other one of the White candidates for Congress. I supported Claiborne and Gholson's vote for the Independent Treasury. . I had been one of its earliest advocates.* I sustained Prentiss and Word in the contested election on state-rights ground alone. In 1840 I was compelled by the pressure of my private affairs, which had become embarrassed, to decline the appointment of Van Buren elector, but, by letters every where to my state-rights friends, I urged his election.

"It is not true that I denounced Gov. M'Nutt's proclamation in regard to the Union Bank bonds, so far as it was intended to arrest the farther negotiation of these bonds. I denounced his act in signing the unconstitutional Supplemental Act of 1835, and fixing his signature to ten millions of bonds. I did not in 1841 vote for Shattuck, the Whig candidate for governor. Afterward I used every effort to produce harmony between the bond-payers and anti-bonders, but failing in this, at the next election for governor I voted for the bond-paying candidate, that excellent Democrat, Thomas H. Williams. I had, at the same time, most friendly relations with, and kindest feelings for, the anti-bond candidate, Hon. A. G. Brown. I did not vote for the Whig state officers. In 1844 I preferred, as I had before and do now, Mr. Calhoun to any other man for the presidency, but I acquiesced in the nomination of Van Buren, and, until the appearance of his anti-Texas letter, gave him my zealous support.

"My connection with the Mississippi Railroad Company is made a charge against me. When this great enterprise was set on foot, I was earnestly requested to take charge of it. I consented at a heavy sacrifice to do so. The Legislature gave it banking privileges, but during my connection with it not a single note was dis-

---

* It is not improbable that the idea originated with him. The earliest articles I can recall in print, hinting at a total separation of bank and state, are from the pens of John A. Quitman and his friend James S. Johnston, Esq., of Jefferson County, a gentleman of rare talent and extensive learning. Bred in the strictest school of Virginia strict constructionists, of a family distinguished for ability, he early formed a close intimacy with Quitman, and they wrote and acted together.

counted, and no notes issued but to pay for work. I admit that I exerted my influence in favor of what is called the "Transfer Act," and the state has never lost a dollar by that act. It was my object, in drafting the bill, to protect the state from loss in every contingency, and so it has resulted. The bill was supported by many leading Democrats, and Gov. M'Nutt approved it. I was, after its passage, induced to consent to go to Europe for the purpose of making sale of the state stock in the Planters' Bank, but, owing to its depreciation, a negotiation was impossible. This was no fault of mine."

This, it must be confessed, is a plausible defense against the charge, so often urged against him, of political vacillation. "Every man," says Gouverneur Morris, in a letter to Timothy Pickering, "has a right, and is in duty bound to change opinions when good reason occurs for the change, and every man has a right to pursue a course different from what he intended, when, in the lapse of time and of events, the existing circumstances shall be different from what he anticipated."

Among the charges most used against Quitman was that he had been instrumental in the passage of an act transferring certain stocks and securities of the state to the insolvent corporation with which he was associated. To this charge he most triumphantly replied, interesting even now as a part of the history of the times, and as showing the fallacy of calculations based on paper securities, charters, and corporations.

Gen. Quitman to Hon. R. H. Boone.

"Monmouth, October 29th, 1845.

"DEAR SIR,—Some months since I saw a communication over your signature in the Mississippian, in which you invite me to communicate my views in relation to the effects of an act commonly called the '*Transfer Act.*' At the time I laid the paper aside with the intention of addressing you on the subject through the same channel, but frequent indisposition throughout the spring and summer, and the consequent pressure of important business, prevented it. I regret this, because since that time our relations are somewhat changed. I am now a candidate for the Senate, and you may be entitled to a vote for that office. I may appear on that account solicitous of your favorable opinion. However desirous I may be on that score, I assure you, in this communication, I am alone influenced by the desire of justifying my course in the eyes of a fellow-citizen whose opinion I respect. I believe that a very brief examination of the 'Transfer Act' will show that, so far from having been injurious to the state, it has resulted in a decided advantage to her. I frankly admit that I used my exertions as a citizen to procure the passage of that bill. I then believed the state might gain much by the passage of the bill, and that it could not possibly result in loss to her. Subsequent facts have proven that these opinions were not erroneous. The state held stock in the Planters' Bank to the amount, estimated at the par value, of two millions of dollars. In other words, she held twenty thousand shares of the capital stock of that bank. The remainder, about twenty-five thousand shares, was held by private individuals and corporations. This stock did not consist in money which could at any time be withdrawn, but in mere script or certificates of stock. The money itself, which had been invested in stock, formed the basis of the banking operations, and was scattered in loans over the whole state. Under the charter of the Planters' Bank the state stood precisely in the condition of a private stockholder. She had no lien, no mortgage, no security. In the case of the failure of the bank her stock would be lost. Should the bank have been wound up, the assets must first have gone to the payment of the debts and liabilities of the bank before one dollar could have been paid to the state. Such is the well-settled law of corporations. In this condition stood the state stock in 1839 prior to the passage of the 'Transfer Act;' a time when all prudent men began to fear the explosion of our inflated bank system. My arguments, not made in secret, but publicly through the columns of the Mississippian, will show that I then believed that our bank stocks would depreciate in value, and probably become

valueless. Such was the state of things when it was proposed that the state should exchange her stock in the Planters' Bank for an equal amount of stock in the Mississippi Railroad Company, established to effect a scheme of internal improvement in which the people of a large portion of the state were interested. The company agreed, in consideration of such transfer of stock, to give the state all the security in their power by mortgaging all the private stock and all the effects of the company, to protect the state from loss, and also assumed absolutely the payment of the principal and interest of the bonds of the state as they should fall due, by guaranteeing that the dividends on the state stock should meet these payments. These terms, so much more favorable to the state than those contained in the charter of the Planters' Bank, were ingrafted on the bill, and in this form passed the Legislature. It was provided in the bill that the stock transferred by the state should not be sold below its par value. Before the sale could be effected the stock began to decline. At length the Planters' Bank failed, and the stock became utterly worthless. The inability of the railroad company to dispose of this stock, and the wide-spread ruin which the explosion of the banking system produced, rendered the private stockholders of the company unable to meet the installments on their stock, caused the failure of the railroad company, and consequently her stock also became worthless. Now the question is, Has the state gained or lost by the 'Transfer Act?' To ascertain this, let us consider what she would have had if the Transfer Act had not been enacted. In that case the state would now be the holder of twenty thousand shares of Planters' Bank stock, at this time utterly and hopelessly worthless. I venture to say that no sensible man can now be found who would give one tenth of a dollar a share for that stock. But suppose we estimate this stock as worth one dollar per share. Then, if the Transfer Bill had never passed, the state would have held stock in the Planters' Bank worth........ $2,000
But by that act she has gained—

    1st. The payment made by the railroad company for interest on the state bonds, say..   20,000
    2d. The state holds a mortgage on the prop-

Vol. I.—K

erty of the railroad company, now in process of foreclosure, which the committee of the Legislature estimate as worth more than 150,000

$170,000

Deduct value of stock transferred........... 2,000

Gain by transfer bill....................... $168,000

But, in addition to this, I am advised that the greater portion of the Planters' Bank stock transferred by the state to the railroad company is still in their hands, and ready to be delivered up to the state. Thus the state will get back her stock, and, in addition to this, nearly one hundred and seventy thousand dollars. This shows that the Transfer Act was cautiously guarded, and that the draftsman of that honestly intended, under all contingencies, to secure the state from loss. We are all liable to be led into error, but had not the Planters' Bank failed and her stock depreciated, it could have been made use of by the railroad company to complete their great work. Had this been done, it is probable that the income of the road would have enabled the company to pay the interest and eventually the bonds of the state. Experience has shown that most of the railroads in the state have yielded good profits. The gross income of the Vicksburg and Jackson road now amounts to $300,000 per annum, and is increasing, while banking operations have of late years yielded little profit and promise less. While I have endeavored to show that the advocates of the Transfer Act were honest in their intentions to guard the rights of the state, I am well aware that many of those who opposed it were equally honest, and were influenced by a zealous regard for the interests of the state, which prompted them to resist what they deemed a hazardous experiment. So far as I was concerned, and I frankly admit that I used my best exertions to procure the passage of the bill, I can with sincerity say that my first and leading desire was to protect the state, and it is a source of great consolation to me to believe that I have not, even innocently, been instrumental in doing any injury to the public."

Gov. M'Nutt opened the canvass with great energy.

He always appeared on the hustings with a budget of old documents to prove the delinquency of his opponents. His system was the aggressive; he never waited to be attacked, and rarely defended himself. Quitman and Dr. Wm. M. Gwin (who was likewise a candidate) do not appear to have canvassed to any extent; but, at their instance, Gen. H. Stuart Foote took the field, not, as he alleged, as an aspirant, but "to expose the enormities of M'Nutt." Of all the public men in the state, he was best fitted for the encounter. He knew the inconsistencies of M'Nutt, and was utterly indifferent to his own. What he lacked in logic he made up in dexterity. His fluency and fancy were inexhaustible. M'Nutt was a man of facts and figures, thoroughly posted in state history and statute law; Foote had a limited knowledge of these, but a vast stock of miscellaneous information, and the facility of appropriating to his own use the facts supplied by his adversary. M'Nutt was a master of broad humor and smutty anecdote, which he freely retailed; Foote revolted from a vulgar epithet, but, as a harlequin, was irresistibly droll. M'Nutt told jokes; Foote recited epigrams. M'Nutt presented himself to the people as a patriot assailed by a triumvirate of ambitious aspirants for favor without regard to principle; Foote appealed to them as a disinterested guardian of the public purity, and the generous champion of his absent friends:

> "Absentem qui rodit amicum,
> Qui non defendit, alio culpante,
> Hic niger est: hunc tu Romane caveto."

M'Nutt was a formidable man any where, and under any circumstances. He was said to be deficient in personal courage, but of this there is no proof, and the imputation is wholly irreconcilable with the firmness and inflexible will he exhibited in many emergencies; Foote was impetuous and fearless, often, through caprice or for imaginary injuries, deserting his friends, but never turning his back to an enemy. Two years before, in the memorable contest for the Senate between Geo. Poindexter and Robert J. Walker, he had been put up by the Jackson party to worry the former, and actually teased him from the field; and in this contest of 1845, though M'Nutt had little sensibility and great power of endurance, he was terribly badgered by Foote.

From Gen. Foote.

"Panola, August 9th, 1849.

"My dear Sir,—According to my agreement with you, I have every where presented your claims to a seat in the United States Senate in terms of respectful and cordial commendation, and defended you with zeal and such energy as I possessed against all that Gov. M'Nutt has either directly charged or darkly insinuated. Our mutual friends in all the country through which I have yet passed will bear full testimony on this point; among whom, Col. Bainbridge Howard, who has attended all the meetings in Carroll, Tallahatchie, and Yalobusha, I would mention specially.

"You requested, when I saw you last, that I should inform you, if you should be assailed so seriously as to render your personal presence necessary. I will give you *facts*, and let you judge for yourself. In every speech M'Nutt has made, he has alluded to your course as a bond-paying champion in 1843. Generally he has contented himself with that. I have defended you on each occasion as I best might on this point, and presented you as a gentleman, a scholar, an old and approved public servant, and a stanch, fearless, and unexceptionable State-rights Democrat, of the true Jeffersonian and Calhoun school. I carried the war into Africa in all cases. Col. Moore, of Canton, having given me a statement in writing averring his capability of proving the ex-governor to be the author of 'Hume,' I charged the authorship upon him, and challenged denial. This was done first at Grenada, his organ at Carrolton having then republished the article, evidently at M'Nutt's instance. At Grenada, Mr. Balfour having denied before the meeting, as M'Nutt's friend, the authorship of 'Hume,' I read Moore's certificate, and announced my determination to *prove the authorship.* So soon as Balfour could see M'Nutt, he came to me and withdrew the denial. So matters stood up to the day before yesterday. At Charleston, the Carrolton paper being in general circulation, and being likely to do you serious injury, I denounced it, and especially 'Hume,' reviewing the article particularly, and charging authorship on the 'great repudiator' anew. On yesterday, at Pharsalia, in the most begging speech I ever listened to, so far as I was concerned, he endeavored to meet the charge of authorship. He said his friend Balfour had denied it, and he was a most respectable man. I rose up, and announced that Balfour had afterward withdrawn his denial; and farther declared that, if M'Nutt would then deny authorship, I would have it proved on him. This embarrassed him much. He declined denying it, and went on to say that *circumstances* did not apparently prove him to be the author; that it seemed to him at least as probable that his friend, Mr. Plummer, quite as familiar with your political history as he was, might have written it. He then proceeded to defend 'Hume,' repeating and urging strenuously all the material charges contained in that article against you, and devoting some half an hour to a most unfriendly review of your pretensions, warmly remonstrating against any attempt on my part to defend you, suggesting that he and I stood on the same ground politically, as you did not, and that our friends corresponded more nearly in sentiment than yours and mine. All this I replied to as I deemed discreet and proper. Among the *new* matters that he urged against you, he accused you of being the instigator of the charge against him of having, while in the Legislature, given his sanction to the Choctaw fraud.

"Having thus, my dear sir, in a hurried and imperfect manner, given you some account of his proceedings, so far as you are affected by them, need I add that it is highly important, in my judgment, that you should meet him face to face, and put him down at once? I am doing all I can for your vindication; but your not having supplied me with full *materials* for your defense, I am by no means satisfied as to my own capacity to effect the desired purpose. I think you could meet us by the time we get round to Columbus, at any rate. The *facts* contained in this letter you may rely on and use as you please. I stand prepared to substantiate all that is herein contained."

This contest terminated, as every body except the parties immediately interested foresaw, in the election of Gen. Foote himself to the Senate of the United States.

Quitman subsided, after this contest, into private life. He was deeply stung with what he considered ingratitude, and had good reason to consider treachery, and for a period he expressed himself with bitterness. It is impossible to read the numerous letters addressed to him during the canvass, many of them prompted by mercenary motives, without sharing his disgust. Incapable of a dishonest or mean action himself, he was entirely too credulous, and never suspected the adventurers whose plausible professions were almost invariably accompanied with applications for money or indorsements. He had numerous devoted friends, in many instances without distinction of party, but his correspondence reveals how much he suffered, especially in this senatorial contest, from dissimulation and fraud. Men the most profligate, and wholly without merit, contrived to inspire him with an exaggerated opinion of their worth and influence, and wormed their way into his pockets. One can not review the correspondence he has left without being astonished that a man of his sagacity and experience could be so readily deceived, and by persons, in the main, so little entitled to confidence. His ambition was stronger than he supposed; he was easily flattered; he was credulous to a fault; and he was too proud and too honorable to stoop to the arts of professional politicians. Hence he was often tricked and disappointed, and his money lavished on unworthy men.

The letters he has left, illustrating personal character and political intrigues, in Mississippi and elsewhere, the mercenary nature of parties now extinct, and the duplicity of politicians, many of whom are now living in and out of the state, reduce one's estimate of human nature, and would, of themselves, make an instructive volume.

The military movements on the Rio Grande, and the belligerent attitude of Mexico, which had denied redress, and shut the door to reconciliation by refusing to receive the distinguished plenipotentiary (Mr. Slidell) sent out by the United States, now attracted the attention of the country. It occasioned the following correspondence between General Quitman and the Governor of Mississippi. Quitman had been elected major general, Mississippi Militia, in 1841.

To Governor Brown.

"Monmouth, Sept. 6th, 1845.

"DEAR SIR,—Some months since, in personal conversation, I expressed to you my desire to be remembered, in case a military requisition should be made upon this state. I now perceive by the Washington papers that it is the determination of the President to keep in readiness a sufficient military force to protect from invasion our boundary on the Rio del Norte from every contingency. Anticipating that a requisition may possibly be made upon this state, in case the Mexicans should display any considerable force upon the frontiers of Texas, I take this opportunity to say that I have no doubt that any requisition upon this state would be met at once, without a draft, by a call for volunteers.

"I feel quite confident that my division alone would be ready to furnish any probable quota, not doubting that the other military divisions of the state would display equal patriotism.

"In case your excellency should be called on, and should think fit to adopt the plan suggested of inviting volunteers, I take the liberty of requesting that I, as the oldest major general of the state, may be charged with the duty of collecting, organizing, mustering, and commanding when in service, any volunteers that may be called for. I respectfully suggest that my long service in the militia, my rank, and some little experience, present some claims to the consideration of the commander-in-chief.

"The volunteers might be called from the several divisions in proportion to their strength. I am using every exertion to cause my division to be completely organized."

From Governor Brown.

"Jackson, Sept. 17th, 1845.

"DEAR SIR,—Anticipating the probable wishes of the militia of this state in the event of open hostilities between Mexico and this country, I wrote to the secretary of war some weeks since, asking that our people might be allowed to take part in any fight that might be going on. His answer has been received. But little expectation is entertained at Washington of any serious difficulty, and the secretary does not encourage the hope that Mississippi will get any part of the glory of the struggle if it occurs. The honor is first reserved for Texas, and then for Louisiana and Alabama. We are informed that it is possible our aid may be needed in a very remote contingency. The secretary, nevertheless, expresses his pleasure in knowing that we are always ready.

"It will be your right to have the first command in case of a call, and that right will be respected so far as I have any thing to do with the matter. The secretary speaks of the possibility of a call in this state for one regiment of volunteers, and furnishes me with a list of officers, etc., etc., required in such an emergency. But the prospect of a war in which our services will be needed is so remote that it is scarcely necessary to speculate about it.

"By reference to the register in the adjutant general's office, I find that your commission will expire on the 15th of November. I have, therefore, ordered an election 3d and 4th November. This precaution was deemed by me necessary. In the present state of the country no vacancy should exist, if it can be avoided, in any military office. I take it for granted, if you desire a re-election, you will get it, and most likely without opposition."

General Quitman had, previous to this correspondence, written as follows to our delegation in Congress:

" *To Messrs. Davis, Adams, Thompson, and Roberts, senators and representatives in Congress.*

"Natchez, May 22d, 1846.

" GENTLEMEN,—We have just received the late act of Congress providing for the Mexican war. Our people are in a state of the highest excitement. Old and young, rich and poor, Democrats and Whigs, are ready to volunteer. They fear Mississippi will not have a fair chance. Already Louisiana has been permitted to send 4000 men to the Rio Grande, and General Gaines has granted numerous commissions to persons around him in New Orleans to organize regiments. We are dissatisfied. We have been ready from the commencement to raise 5000 men—men who have at heart the good of Mississippi, and who wish to serve, as Mississippians, under the flag of their own state, under the direct command of their own officers—brave men, who desire to serve their country, confer honor on their much-abused state, and win laurels for themselves. But the door is closed to them. They are chafing at this neglect. We were foremost in the measure of annexation. We regard the present as our own quarrel. We feel strong enough to fight it out; ay, if need be, to carry our eagle to the Pacific. We desire no aid from the Abolitionists. The Northern States question our strength in war. Then let this war be the test. England is looking on to witness the weakness of the slaveholding states. Let President Polk give us an opportunity of showing our spirit, muscle, and resources, and of repelling the slanders upon our institutions. If he refuses, he is not the man we took him for. We are near the theatre of war. We are inured to the summer sun. We have no dread of chapparals or yellow fever. Far from the seat of government, should the call for volunteers be made general, the requisition will be filled before we even hear of the call. We ask, therefore, that to Mississippi be assigned the privilege of fur-

K 2

nishing a quota of volunteers equal at least to Louisiana. She is entitled to it from her propinquity, from the spirit she has ever displayed, from the blood and treasure she gave to Texas when-danger and death, not laurels or riches, were the harvest. Our people are proud and spirited. They will not volunteer while subject to the mortification of having their services rejected. They are too much attached to the free spirit of their state Constitution, which gives them the selection of those who are to command them in peace and in war, to submit to be enlisted as mercenaries. They look to you, as their ministers at the seat of government, to protect their honor and their interests. The present mode of appointing or commissioning individuals is odious. It will destroy the moral effect of the system of volunteering. It will repress their ardor, and withhold from the ranks the best material of the country.

"I am happy to hear our patriotic governor (Brown) has appealed to the President in behalf of this state. If we are not allowed to participate in the perils and glory of this war, woe to those who prevent it.

"I have been an active officer in the militia more than twenty years, and I feel a deep interest in preserving the military reputation Mississippi acquired in former wars."

CHAPTER IX.

War with Mexico.—Quitman offers his Services.—Coldness of the President.—Parallel between Quitman and Polk.—The Cabinet.— Exertions for Quitman.—His Appointment.—Diary.—The Army at Camargo.—Character of Gen. Taylor.—Neglect of the War Department.—The March.—Monterey.—The Battle.—The Capitulation.—Gen. Taylor's Letter to Gen. Gaines.—Political Jealousy.— Col. Jefferson Davis.—Moral Effect of the Capitulation.—Quitman's View of it.—Letter to Robert J. Walker.

WAR with Mexico had now commenced, and Congress, by an act passed May 13th 1846, had authorized the President to call for 50,000 volunteers, and to appoint a number of general officers. On the 20th of May, Gen. Quitman wrote to a friend who had urged him to enter the army as follows:

To J. F. H. Claiborne.

"DEAR CLAIBORNE,—I received your letter at a time when we were plunged in the deepest grief for the loss of our second daughter. The stirring events on the Rio Grande have roused me from my lethargy. I feel anxious to take part in the conflict, and some of my friends think me entitled to the command of such troops as may volunteer from this state. I have been so often disappointed that I am prepared now to believe that my few ardent friends overrate my pretensions and popularity. I make no claim whatever. I have served actively in the militia over twenty years, and have some knowledge of tactics and discipline, and a turn for military life. It would be a proud day for me to lead the gallant sons of Mississippi to victory. Without any assurances that I shall be selected, I wish to say to you that, should the event occur, and your health will allow you to go, it

would gratify me much to have you with me.   I shall
address the President to-morrow, and on the 28th I shall
leave for Washington.   If the President does not give
me an equal chance with Louisiana, I shall not be silent.
Should I be appointed, all is ready, and I will be promptly in the saddle."

On the 21st, Gen. Quitman made a formal tender of his
services to President Polk.   No notice was taken of his
letter.   He was not a favorite with the President.   They
were constitutionally dissimilar.   Quitman cared little
for party forms or names, but adhered inflexibly, and at
any sacrifice, and in scorn of all compromises, to a certain set of principles.   Polk was a political martinet, a
rigid disciplinarian, and regarded the decision of a cau-
cus as sacred and binding as the decree of a court.   He
was a man of ability, but a man of expediency, and found
in compromises, which are, in fact, concessions of rights,
the easiest solution for political difficulties.   Quitman
was genial, ardent, and impulsive.   Polk was grave almost to sadness, self-restrained, and chilling.   One had
the frankness and sincerity of a soldier; the other the reserve and tact of a diplomatist.   The popularity of one
was owing to his engaging qualities, and the general confidence reposed in his integrity and firmness; the other
was indebted for his elevation to his energy, his circum-
spection, his capacity for labor, his fidelity to party, and,
more than all, to the influence of Gen. Jackson, who, for
the sake of Texas, reluctantly abandoned Mr. Van Buren,
the most loyal of his friends, and gave the weight of his
great name in favor of Mr. Polk.   Quitman never deserted a friend, or forgot a favor.   Years after he became
rich and influential, he had a grateful recollection of kindness and hospitality when he was a poor young man; he
never forgot his early comrades in the Texas expedition,
and to the last hour of his life was mindful of their inter-

ests. Mr. Polk, once seated in the presidency, even forgot his obligations to Gen. Jackson. Quitman was a man prompt to decide, and acted upon his decisions with energy and fearlessness, as confident when proceeding singly, on his own judgment, as though he had the approval of all the world. Polk was constitutionally timid, and only bold when supported by others bolder than himself. He had a vigorous and able cabinet*—one of

* *Written for the New Orleans Sunday Delta.*

THE CABINET—PAST AND PRESENT.—The speculation in relation to the incoming cabinet may be unprofitable, but is not unpleasant. It gives every one an opportunity to have "his say," or his fling at this or that man.

The importance attached to the cabinet is very much exaggerated. Those who are curious as to the origin of the departments may refer to Laws of the U. S., vol. i., Bioren and Duane's edition. In England the cabinet is every thing, and the crown a symbol, an effigy. In this country, with a great man for chief magistrate, cabinets are mere conveniences for administration.

Gen. Washington was a firm, safe, and prudent man, and with Jefferson, Hamilton, Pickering, Wolcott, and Knox in his cabinet—in spite of the jealousy and counter-intrigues of the two first—the early and trying stages of a new government were passed in safety.

John Adams was a self-willed, crotchety, suspicious, impulsive, egotistical, and ambitious man, but full of the stuff of which patriots are made. He was "never," as he said of himself in 1778, "much of a John Bull. I was John Yankee, and as such I shall live and die." This bold, high-spirited, but pig-headed man got on badly with his cabinet. His jealousy of Hamilton made him distrustful of every one about him.

Thomas Jefferson threw his cabinet into deep shadow. There were very able men in it, but his views, not theirs, were stamped upon the administration.

James Madison was a closet statesman, a philosopher—pure, but timid to infirmity—ignorant of men, unsuspicious and confiding. He required bold, energetic advisers to counteract his idiosyncratic tendency to hesitate. For the most part his ministers were, in this respect, as deficient as himself, and hence the blunders that occurred during his administration, both in our financial policy and in the war with Great Britain.

President Monroe was a dull, weak man—singularly so; a man of phraseology and ceremonial; elevated by the traditional ascendency of Virginia, and a combination of factions comprising the highest talent of the nation, all jealous of each other, but willing to put him in power as one easily moulded to their own personal views and aspirations. The consequence of this state of things was a cabinet of match-

the ablest ever assembled around any executive—and
the achievements of our armies gave éclat to his admin-

less ability. John Quincy Adams, Wm. H. Crawford, John C. Calhoun, William Wirt, were members of it—all struggling for the presidency. There was but one point in which those distinguished men
resembled each other—insatiable ambition. In every thing else—figure, countenance, manners, temperament, opinions, tastes—they differed.

The first was low, swart, cold, and repulsive, irritable and eccentric;
more deeply read than his father, yet knowing even less of mankind.
A splendid writer, a master of rhetoric, defiant in his opinions, easily
inflamed, brave to martyrdom, yet so frigid, formal, and saturnine that
few could approach, and none could love him. His political opinions
were erratic and variable, and were, all his life, controlled more or less
by personal resentments. His first great apostasy may be traced to
this source, and to the same feeling may be justly attributed the war
that he waged against domestic servitude in his latter days—a war utterly at variance with his recorded and deliberate opinions when secretary of state.

Mr. Crawford was a man of colossal stature, and of massive intellect. In astronomy or mathematics he would have been pre-eminent.
No man in this or any other country had a more thorough knowledge
of political economy, and especially of finance. He spoke with great
cogency, and wielded a luminous pen. A Virginian by birth and education, he carried the political opinions of the renowned commonwealth
into Georgia, and, until he was stricken down by paralysis on the threshold of the presidency, she never wavered from the true Jeffersonian
faith. Her subsequent career has been one of inconsistency and error,
until lately she has taken her stand as the empire state of democracy—
great in her resources, great in her moral and physical development,
great in the ability and reputation of her sons.

The third on this list—the proud and sensitive Carolinian—was tall,
but not stately; rather with the slight stoop of a student than the presence of a soldier; with strongly-lined, intellectual features, and manners simple and winning as a child's. The young loved him most,
for his noble heart and generous affections were fenced in by no con-
ventionalities, but were freely, and often injudiciously bestowed. Few
public men have suffered more from ill-timed confidences, or paid,
without flinching, heavier penalties for the indiscretions of others.
A man of purer sentiments, of simpler habits, or more irreproachable
morals, never lived. The atmosphere of the metropolis, its sirens and
seductions, had for him no taint. Calumny itself never imputed to
him, during a lifetime of temptation, a single lapse from virtue. Yet
he viewed with no ascetic eye the infirmities of others, and never pursued error as a crime. His most intimate friend, the late Warren
R. Davis, one of the most gifted men of his day, was proverbial for
his frailties and indiscretions. Mr. Calhoun was fixed, rigid, and immovable in his notions of right and wrong. He early adopted certain great principles for the regulation of his political conduct, but,
with singular blindness, he constantly wandered from them. His in-

istration; but he can only be regarded as a man of mediocrity, who rose to power in the train of Gen. Jackson,

tellectual vision, miraculously acute in all other respects, was notoriously obtuse when studying himself. To the last hour of his life he was persuaded that his political career had been uniform and inflexible, when to every one else his inconsistencies were transparent. He was less deeply read than Mr. Adams; he knew less of mankind than Mr. Crawford; nothing of the management or discipline of party. But he had more intellect, more individuality, more concentrativeness, more enthusiasm, a higher and purer appreciation of truth than either of them, or any other statesman our country has produced.

Mr. Wirt, the attorney general, was of large stature and heavy cast of features, with little, at that period, to indicate the vivid imagination that colored and exaggerated his early productions. He was either too florid or too jejune; always too elaborate. He was an excellent man; a little too saintly, perhaps, in after life, in atonement for early indiscretions, as the feudal barons founded monasteries in compensation for their crimes; a delightful companion, very susceptible of flattery, very didactic, very credulous, and very ambitious, as his acceptance of the Anti-masonic nomination for the presidency at an advanced period of his life demonstrates—a nomination a truly great man would have scorned to accept, even though certain of success; and which ended, as it deserved to do, in disgraceful abortion, a complete eclipse of Mr. Wirt's political sun, and he soon after died of vexation and disappointment.

This cabinet, it may readily be inferred, was *the* government. They made of Mr. Monroe a mere pageant. He traveled from city to city, and from state to state, while his ministers conducted affairs. In this respect they Anglicized our government for the time being. The splendid diplomatic correspondence of Mr. Adams, elaborate, highly finished, and full of national spirit; the luminous treasury reports of Mr. Crawford; and the powerful impetus given to fortifications, internal improvements, and manufactures by Mr. Calhoun, withdrew public attention entirely from President Monroe. The cabinet was every thing. The game was for the presidency, and each of the triumvirate played a bold hand for it—Mr. Calhoun the boldest and most hazardous, full of promise for himself, but prolific of evil to the republic. His policy favored centralism. He pushed the constructive powers of the government to the farthest boundary, but lived to atone for this fundamental error by consecrating his intellect, in its meridian glory, and his untiring energies, even to the closing scene, to the defense of states' rights.

The cabinet of John Quincy Adams was only remarkable because Mr. Clay conducted the department of state. Mr. Adams, avowing from the first his intention to stand for a second term, of course shaped the policy of the administration, sometimes, no doubt, against the advice of his illustrious premier; and shaped it to his own defeat and the exclusion of Mr. Clay. Had their positions been reversed—had Mr. Clay been the chief magistrate and Mr. Adams the minister, Gen. Jackson, in all probability, would not have been elected. Our coun-

exempt from positive vices, remarkable for his prudence, and a thorough master of the strategy of politics. With

try, at this moment, might occupy a very different attitude. What was called the "American System"—the rapid development of home manufactures by a schedule of exorbitant and, in some instances, prohibiting duties, concentrating vast capital in few hands; national banking in close connection with the federal treasury; the federal government penetrating the states, and controlling their Legislatures and popular suffrage by internal improvements involving large outlays of public money; and a close-fisted policy in relation to the public lands, holding them at fixed prices, refusing the right of pre-emption, and impeding, as much as possible, the flow of immigration from the manufacturing to the agricultural states — this vast machinery would, doubtless, have been ingrafted upon the national policy, had the chief magistrate been a really great man, of popular attributes, like Mr. Clay, instead of a political enthusiast who, obstinate as his distinguished sire, never knew when to retreat, and regarded Fabius as an historical coward. Under this policy we should have grown compact, formidable, very aristocratic, very English. The four great events most memorable in our annals since the Revolution—the separation of bank and state, the metallic currency, the annexation of Texas, and the conquest of California—would yet have been in the womb of time. A scholar and not a statesman—a creature of passion, not of purpose —a man of intense and unquenchable ambition, who nevertheless lived in an atmosphere of ice—consumed by his own fire, but chilling and repelling sympathy and confidence—was chief, and the government, by popular forms, but by what was, morally, a revolution, passed into the hands of the democracy. A democracy not contingent upon the mere triumph of its leader, or the duration of his official term, but, to all intents and purposes, a democracy under every administration, and by whatever name the prevailing party happens to be called.

Andrew Jackson, though he knew little of books, still less of national law, and nothing of diplomacy, had less need for a cabinet than any of his predecessors. Chiefs of bureau, or a few competent clerks, would have been enough for him. Nature stamped him GREAT, and the most sagacious in his councils, to pass current, had to be recoined from the same die. A transfusion of ideas flowed from him to them. He astounded experienced politicians and jurists by his intuitive perception and masculine grasp of the most complicated subjects. He converted men to his views as much by this great faculty as by an indomitable will; the timid felt his inspiration, and the powerful and factious were subdued by a sublime constancy very different from the insane obstinacy of the Adamses, or the dogged courage of Gen. Taylor. He, however, surrounded himself with able men, but he moved them about like figures on a chess-board, transferring them to other spheres of duty, or kicking them, unceremoniously, overboard, to rise no more. Van Buren, Forsyth, Cass, Livingston, Berrien, M'Lane, Taney, Barry, Duane, Woodbury, Eaton, Dickerson, Ingham, Branch, and Butler, were in his cabinet at different periods.

all the power and patronage of the government (greatly augmented by the war), and with the lustre of victory

Mr. Van Buren had played a masterly *rôle* in the political drama. Regarding politics as a game, his great *forte* was in stocking the cards. His peculiar trait was caution, improperly termed non-committalism. It was something more comprehensive—forecast and sagacity. Under the mask of great moderation, and with something of the air of a *petit maitre*, there lurked a vaulting ambition. His faculty for governing men, his untiring energy and imperturbable coolness, enabled him to achieve great results without apparent effort. Thus this accomplished tactician, while Adonizing before his looking-glass,[1] and toying with the square-rigged belles of Albany, or the more voluptuous beauties of Washington, was dethroning De Witt Clinton, checkmating Clay, Webster, and Calhoun, and scattering roses in his pathway to the presidency. When news of the advance of Napoleon upon Waterloo reached the Duke of Wellington, he was in the ball-room of the Duchess of Richmond, at Brussels, and, with undisturbed composure, escorted her grace to supper. Thus, while the great tribune of the Senate was hurling his thunderbolts at Vice-president Van Buren, threatening his political fortunes with every blow, that gentleman sat with a quiet smile upon his face, and, with inimitable *sang froid*, sent his snuff-box to Mr. Clay the moment he resumed his seat! The good-humor of the Senate was restored, and the great orator himself perceived that his mighty effort had been fruitless. The little magician was "up to snuff."

The late John Forsyth was one of the most accomplished men of his times. As an impromptu debater, to bring on an action, or to cover a retreat, he never had his superior. He was acute, witty, full of resources, and ever prompt—impetuous as Murat in a charge, adroit as Soult when outflanked and outnumbered; he was haughty in the presence of enemies, affable and winning among friends; his manners were courtly and diplomatic. In the times of Louis XIV., he would have rivaled the most celebrated courtiers; under the dynasty of Napoleon he would have won the baton of France. He never failed to command the confidence of his party; he never feared any odds arrayed against it, and at one crisis was almost its sole support in the Senate against the most brilliant and formidable opposition ever organized against an administration. With the ladies he was irresistible. During his diplomatic residence in Spain the demand for duennas could scarcely be supplied, and even royalty smiled more indulgently than he wished. This gallant and high-spirited gentleman died suddenly, in the enjoyment of great popularity.

Gen. Cass I have, on a former occasion, elaborately sketched. His massive intellect, his highly cultivated tastes, his consistent political career, the landmarks he has left on our foreign and domestic policy, are all matters of history. He was a prominent feature of the Jack-

[1] When Mr. Van Buren was elected president he sold the lease and furniture of his house in the "Thirteen Buildings" to a distinguished senator. With him I inspected the premises. Every thing was found in perfect order, and nearly new, except the carpet before a French mirror in his dressing-room; that was worn *threadbare*.

and vast territorial acquisitions reflected on him, he, nevertheless, in four years, witnessed the decay of his popu-

son administration, and, by a single but masterly article in the North American Review, brought to a satisfactory conclusion the Indian question, the great party and moral excitement of that period—an excitement which, up to the appearance of that article, had marshaled the press and pulpit of the North, and much of the conscience of the South, against the administration. Subsequently he went to France, and the influence he exerted there upon momentous issues has never been exceeded in the history of diplomacy. His career thenceforth is a household word to the nation.

Mr. Berrien and Mr. Livingston were both very eminent at the bar. The one was an able lawyer merely; the latter a great jurist. The one had the sharpness, the plausibility, and the acute but contracted grasp of the technical attorney; the other was comprehensive, eloquent, and learned. Mr. Berrien could split hairs like Mr. Tazewell; Livingston grappled with generalities like Lord Brougham. The mind of one resembled a dictionary; the other a code. Berrien was a conscientious man, who always meant to do right, but by an unfortunate process of ratiocination usually got wrong. Livingston was unscrupulous, but from policy generally did what his discriminating judgment decided would be right. He was courtly and insincere, prone to intrigue, with no fixed principles, political or moral; and the stain of official defalcation will ever shadow the lustre of his fame.

Both Mr. M'Lane and Mr. Taney had belonged to the ancient Federal party, but since its extinction had acted with the Democracy. In one respect their fortunes were not the same. The former, at every period of his career, has been singularly exempt from political vituperation, while the latter, before he became chief-justice, literally walked through the fiery furnace—an ordeal that he sustained with unshaken equanimity.

Mr. Woodbury shared the opprobrium that was cast upon Mr. Taney. Every form of detraction was exhausted upon him. He was a man of strong sense and clear perceptions, but an awkward and involved style by no means expressed the impressions of his mind. He thus, while in the treasury, had the reputation of being obtuse; but when he resumed his place in the Senate, and had the opportunity of explaining his reports and vindicating the financial policy inaugurated by Gen. Jackson, his reputation rose to its proper level. Unhappily, in the full vigor of a well-preserved life, he died with his hand upon the presidency. His mansion at Washington was noted for its liberal and elegant hospitality—always crowded by the young and gifted, and adorned by a household of incomparable grace and beauty.

Of the other members of this cabinet, Mr. Dickerson was a sensible and amiable man, but too infirm for his place. Mr. Barry was a man of talent—an orator cultured in the great controversy of the old and new court parties of Kentucky. His voice, his manner, and his declamation were of the school of Patrick Henry, but he was utterly unfit for the Post-office Department. Mr. Duane was fantastic and feeble, though he fancied himself profound. Mr. Ingham was stolid

larity, and no one but himself dreamed of his re-election.

Mr. Polk regarded many of the leading men of the state-rights school with a jaundiced eye ; but, as that wing of the party had assisted him to defeat Mr. Van Buren, and occupied a strong position in the South by their resolute attitude on the Texas question, he could not venture, in this instance, to disoblige them. Mr. Calhoun, who, like Mr. Clay, had never from any administration asked a favor for a relative,* applied in person to the President for the appointment of Quitman. The South Carolina delegation united in the application.

and treacherous; Mr. Branch honest, but impracticable ; and Major Eaton—lately dead—could not be classed above mediocrity.

Benjamin F. Butler, attorney general and secretary of war—a political saint—studied finance, I believe, under Jacob Barker, at Sandy Hill, and psalmody and the prayer-book with Henry Ward Beecher. He never took a questionable step in politics or peculation without first finding a precedent or a text to justify it, precisely as Beecher pretends to find, in the New Testament, a warrant for Sharpe's rifles, insurrection, and massacre.

Of succeeding cabinets, of the policy likely to be pursued by the President elect, and of the duty of the country, and especially of the South, without distinction of party, in the crisis before us, I may treat in my next number.

Bay of St. Louis, January 1st, 1857.

* When Mr. Polk went into the presidency, Mr. Clay had a son-in-law—a most estimable man, who had lost a large fortune without the slightest stain on his character—in an office connected with the customs, but carrying with it little or no patronage. He was a Whig, but had never taken any part in politics, except to advocate very warmly the annexation of Texas, a favorite measure with the Democratic party. Mr. Clay made no effort in his behalf. But a distinguished Southern senator, acting with the administration on the Texas question, and who had placed Mr. Polk under peculiar personal obligations (warmly expressed) by his course in another matter, and the author of this biography, urged the retention of this gentleman both on account of his personal merits, as an act of policy and conciliation, and as a graceful compliment to Mr. Clay. Mr. Polk acquiesced in the points urged with great apparent cordiality ; assured the parties that their friend should be retained, and authorized the senator so to inform him. He was shortly thereafter superseded, without any charge, complaint, or explanation. I am not aware that Mr. Clay ever had any other relative in office. He several times expressed in writing a grateful recollection of the efforts made at the time, without his knowledge, in behalf of his son-in-law and friend.

The senators and representatives from Mississippi, aided by Messrs. La Sere and Harmanson, of Louisiana, and Messrs. Rusk and Kaufman, of Texas, and Westcott, of Florida, strongly urged the appointment. Many early and constant friends in Mississippi, with the Hon. A. G. Brown, then governor of the state, at their head, claimed it for him in the strongest terms.

This pressure from so many influential quarters was not to be resisted, and his commission as brigadier general was duly made out. He addressed the secretary of war as follows:

"Barnum's Hotel, Baltimore, July 2d, 1846.

"Sir,—My friend, Mr. Chalmers, of the U. S. Senate, has just informed me that I have been appointed a brigadier general of volunteers, under the late act of Congress. Not doubting that it is the wish of the department that the volunteers shall be, as early as possible, under the immediate command of responsible general officers, I desire to repair to my post immediately. To make arrangements for my family during my absence, and to equip myself for the service, it will be necessary for me to spend one day in New York. Unless, therefore, I receive orders to the contrary, I shall proceed there to-morrow morning, and in three days thereafter will present myself for orders. In the mean time, should it be important to the service that I should receive orders while in New York, I will be happy to receive them by express, at my own cost. These arrangements have been made for the comfort of my family, who are with me, and to prevent some pecuniary sacrifice on my part, which might result from failure to see my agent in New York. If, however, they are not compatible with the service, I will forego them, and with promptness conform to the views of the department."

Among his papers is a sort of diary, in pencil, of his movements about this period.

"1846, July 6th. Bid adieu to my family in Philadelphia and reached Washington at night.

"7th. Called on the adjutant general and received my commission. Took the oath of office. Waited on the secretary of war and General Scott. Both agreeable and pleasant. In the afternoon called on the President. Has a haggard and careworn look. Polite and chilly. Was informed that the relative rank of brigadiers had been decided by lot, and that I had drawn No. 5.

"8th. Devoted to preparations for my journey and letters to my family.

"9th. Took the cars for Cumberland; at the dépôt Col. Sevier, of Arkansas, and Hon. Jacob Thompson, placed under my charge Miss W., of Rodney, a charming young Mississippian, who had just completed her education and wished to return home. At the Relay House I had the pleasure to find in the cars from Baltimore my young friends Griffith,* Dunbar, and Buhler, on their way to Natchez—an agreeable addition to our party. They assisted me in attending to my young ward. They were lively and entertaining, and diverted my mind from dwelling constantly on the separation from my family.

"12th. At Pittsburg, thermometer 102° in the shade; a foretaste of Mexico. Twenty-seven years ago I arrived here, a foot-worn traveler, with a few shillings in my pocket, and all my worldly goods in a single trunk. My comrade† and myself spent two days chaffering for a cheap passage in a keel-boat. To-day I can draw on my merchants in New Orleans, New York, and Liverpool, and the attentive landlord at the noble hotel where I put up secures for me a state-room in a splendid steamer. I hope time and fortune have dealt lightly by my friend. He had a small adventure of goods, and was bound toward the Upper Mississippi. I had an engagement to teach school in Ohio, and the privilege of reading law. My past has been fortunate, but what of the future? I have sometimes thought I had a forecast of coming

* The only child of his early partner and benefactor, a young man who inherited his father's talents, and died on the threshold of a brilliant career. He had been carefully educated for the bar under the eye of his distinguished grandfather, the Hon. Edward Turner, of Natchez.

† Jason Whiting. The last trace I find of him is in a letter dated Litchfield, Connecticut, in 1835, where he had resided for sixteen years, merchandising and manufacturing paper.

events. But now every thing is strangely dim. In this
uncertainty let *duty* be the watchword, and forward!
ever forward!

"13th. Embarked for Cincinnati, where we arrived on
the 15th.

"16th. At Louisville. Had the pleasure of meeting
General Butler, and to learn that he would descend the
river with us.

"18th. Left in the Peytona, heavily loaded; ground-
ing continually; fast on Cumberland bar.

"22d. Got in the very slow steamer C. Conner and
crept ahead. A pleasant little party. General Butler
and his aid, Captain Lay, exceedingly agreeable. Miss
W. played the guitar and sung sweetly, and my young
comrades serenaded her at night. At Memphis General
Butler and aid left us. Here I met General Pillow.

"28th. Arrived at Natchez, having left Miss W. at
Rodney. Got to Monmouth late at night. My servants
all well, but ah! how solitary was my home in the absence of wife and children. I was saddened and de-
pressed, and should have felt alone in the world, but the
mild spirits of my lost children came to fill my heart.
The little group of angels, John, Edward, Mary, and
Sarah, seemed to gather visibly about me, and my mind
was soothed with gentle and tranquil visions.

"30th. With my faithful servant Harry, a free boy
named Albert whom I had hired at Louisville, my good
horse Messenger,* and another purchased from Doctor
Ford, I set out in the Cora for New Orleans, where we
arrived next evening. My old friend and pupil, Claiborne, came to meet me on the boat, delighted at my
appointment. Took lodgings at the St. Charles, where
I found General Butler and aid, General Wool, General

---

*   *From Hon. Joseph Dunbar.*

"Arundo, May 27th, 1845.

"MY DEAR GENERAL,—I sent my favorite bay, 'Messenger,' to Mr.
Murray, of the Mansion House, yesterday. He is in fine spirits, and
will speak for himself. He will carry you, where I know you desire
to go, into the trenches of the enemy, or, if need be, you can overtake
with him their flying hosts. He is not 'without price,' but you are
welcome to him 'without money.' If I was a little younger, or, old
as I am, if I were not so infirm, I would go with you to the post of
honor and of duty. Your friend,   Jo. DUNBAR."

Shields, General Pillow, and many other officers. Lieut. Colonel Hunt, United States quarter-master, promised to provide me transportation as soon as possible. This officer was, like President Polk, imperturbably civil, but not disposed to accommodate the volunteer arm of the service more than he could help.

"Purchased from Peterson and Stewart a man cook, Cæsar, to carry to Mexico.

"Had some daguerreotypes taken. Left with Mr. John G. Gaines, Canal Street, one for my wife, one for my sisters, and one for my friend M'Murran. M'Murran and his son came from Pass Christian and spent a day with me.

" Aug. 4th. Embarked in the Steamer New York, with Gens. Butler, Marshall, Shields, Pillow, and several other officers. At the Battle-ground received two companies Illinois Volunteers.

" 8th. Brazos St. Jago. Was surprised to find upward of twenty vessels in port. Anchored off the bar, and went over in a small steamer. In the afternoon I rode down the beach to the mouth of the Rio del Norte, where I found Col. Jeff. Davis, with the Mississippi regiment. Was well received by him. A great deal of sickness, chiefly diarrhea, among the troops. One poor fellow expired while I was there; several others very low.

" The inspector general of the army, Col. Belknap, is very obliging. He advises me to take as my aid Lieut. Chase, of Duncan's battery, or Lieut. Peck, of the infantry.

" 10th. Embarked in the Aid for Matamoras with my servants and horse. Arrived on the 11th. Met at the restaurant Gens. Henderson and Hamer.

" 11th. Left in the Eagle for Camargo. The river very high; current some five miles per hour; very muddy, but palatable and healthy. Lands on the banks low and subject to overflow; soil very rich. Farms or settlements occasionally, but poorly cultivated.

" 13th. River and country much the same; timber a little larger. Navigation difficult; channel narrow and rapid, and exceedingly crooked. Most of the land under water. The steamer purchases muskeet-wood at $2 50 per cord for dry, $2 25 green. At one of the landings the Tennessee Volunteers foraged a cotton-field for melons; on returning to the boat they were required by their officers to pay for them.

" 14th. Passed Reynosa, a rather pretty town, built on a limestone ledge. A number of Mexicans of both sexes bathing in the lagoon. They resemble Indians.

" 17th. Arrived at Camargo, on the right bank of the San Juan, three miles above its junction with the Rio Grande. The town is now in ruins, owing to a great spring freshet which undermined many of the houses, built of unburnt brick.

" Found Gen. Taylor's quarters just above the town, and pitched my tent in his vicinity. First division of regulars are encamped half a mile below; the Kentucky Legion and several companies from Tennessee near by.

" 18th. Dined with Gen. Taylor; farmer-like, frank, and friendly; not at all *à la mode* Polk.

" 20th. Ordered to take command of the 3d brigade, second division, volunteers, consisting of the regiments from Mississippi, Alabama, and Georgia, and the battalion from Maryland and the District of Columbia.

" Appointed First Lieut. W. A. Nicholls, 2d artillery, a clever, intelligent, and active young officer, my aid.

" 25th. Maj. Gen. Butler and staff arrived.

" 20th. Gen. Worth, with his division, crossed the river *en route* for Seralvo. Gen. Twiggs is to march next. Gen. Taylor informs me that he will follow with 4000 volunteers. It is hinted that Gen. Patterson, should he arrive in time, will be left in command here, and Butler, with two brigades, accompany Gen. Taylor.

" Any arrangement which garrisons a considerable number of volunteers on the left bank will produce discontent. We came for action, and must have it."

Gen. Taylor decided to move toward Monterey with only 2000 volunteers, and selected the 1st Kentucky, Ohio, Tennessee, and Mississippi regiments. They were formed into a field division under Maj. Gen. Butler; one brigade, the two first-named regiments, under Gen. Hamer, the other two led by Gen. Quitman.

To J. F. H. Claiborne.

"Camargo, September 5th, 1846.

"DEAR CLAIBORNE,—I am now, where you know I have long wished to be, at the head of a brigade, and with the prospect of active service. I wish you were here. The Mississippians and Tennesseans constitute my command. Maj. Gen. Butler heads the division. Pillow will garrison this place. It is a hard fate when there is a fight ahead, and I thank God it did not fall on me. My health is excellent and my spirits light. I know what my friends expect of me, and, if opportunities offer, they shall not be disappointed. A major general's baton, fairly won on the field of battle, or a Mexican grave! Our men are chafing to be off, and murmur at 'Old Zach.' He seems to me to be slow, and we all know he *will* fight."

General Taylor was *not* slow; on the contrary, he was a man of extraordinary energy, as his operations on the northwestern frontier, in Florida, and on the Rio Grande had demonstrated to the satisfaction of his countrymen. His embarrassments were not known to the volunteers, who, for the most part, eager for battle and for fame, censured him for delay. He had not transportation to move his army in mass from Camargo, nor was there sufficient forage in the country to subsist his teams.*

* "The administration did not appreciate the difficulty of moving troops in an enemy's country, and amid a sparse and impoverished population. * * * It was the duty of the authorities to see that the usual supplies and means of transportation were sent with the troops, leaving it simply to the general in the field to make requisitions for unusual supplies and means of transportation. Thus, while some 20,000 volunteers were sent to the theatre of war, not a wagon reached the advance of General Taylor till after the capture of Monterey."—*Campaigns of the Rio Grande and Mexico*, p. 21, by *Brevet Major Isaac L. Stevens, since Governor of Washington Territory, and now its delegate in Congress.*

From General Quitman to General F. Huston.

"Camargo, August 24th, 1846.

"I am entirely out of patience with the tardiness of every movement. The quarter-master's department is wretchedly managed.

The movement on Monterey commenced on the 19th of August. The regulars, under Generals Worth and Twiggs, took possession of Seralvo. Six thousand volunteers, whom he would gladly have employed in the field, were left at Camargo and other places, for want of transportation, and with Butler's division, consisting of four regiments of Ohio, Tennessee, and Mississippi volunteers, divided into two brigades led by General Hamer and General Quitman, he moved forward on the 6th of September. On the 13th the army left Seralvo for Monterey. The march was trying, especially to volunteers. A sultry sun, no shade, dusty roads, and great scarcity of water.

The different columns united on the Rio San Juan, twenty-four miles northeast of Monterey, and on the 18th resumed the march. Our army consisted of Twiggs' and Worth's divisions of regulars, Butler's division of volunteers, a battalion of regular cavalry, and two regiments of volunteer cavalry, in all 6220 men and 240 officers. Of artillery we had only four light batteries, one battery of two 24-pound howitzers, one 10-inch mortar, and a hundred shells.

Monterey, the capital of New Leon, lies at the base of the Sierra Madre, in a beautiful valley fertilized by the Rio San Juan. It stretches along this stream a mile and a quarter, and has an average population of about fifteen thousand. The houses are of stone, of solid Spanish masonry, square, with a court in the centre, flat tiled roofs with parapets, iron-grated windows, and heavy-barred doors. Each building is, in fact, a fortress, capable of resisting small-arms. To defend the city on the Saltillo

The medical department worse. There are here no horse-shoes or nails, no iron to make them ; and, though we have 6000 men, there are no medicines. The twelve-months troops are armed with refuse muskets, and their knapsacks, canteens, haversacks, and cartridge-boxes are unfit for service."

road, four strong works had been erected, Fort Independence, the Obispado, Fort Soldado, and Fort Federation. On its opposite front had been constructed a series of works so arranged as to rake the approaches to any one of the series, and to concentrate the fire of the whole upon any one that might be assailed. In the rear of this line of lunettes and redoubts stood the citadel, a fortified square, with bastions, embrasures, and ditches, mounting twelve guns, chiefly 18-pounders, and capable of throwing their metal into the redoubts, so as to render them untenable if taken. In this square stands a spacious church, inclosed by high and strong walls, affording secure shelter for musketry. On the southeast the steep banks of the San Juan, and gardens, hedges, vineyards, and ditches rendered approach difficult, and it was covered likewise by a heavy battery at the bridge of La Purissima. Behind these formidable defenses, the streets of the city were barricaded and defended by artillery, and at every angle a cannon was mounted for flank firing. The parapets running round and above the houses had been loopholed for musketry, affording protection to the inhabitants while they poured a destructive fire on the assailants. The defenses, generally, were so masked by chapparal, vineyards, and innumerable ditches cut for irrigation, as to render thorough reconnoissances, under the circumstances, impracticable.

The force assembled by Gen. Ampudia to defend the city consisted of 7000 regulars, embracing some of the veteran troops of Mexico, and 1500 rancheros, besides many citizens armed with muskets, and who knew how to fight behind barricades and castellated roofs. He had with him five or six generals of distinction.

Gen. Taylor pitched his camp at the Walnut Spring, in the wood of San Domingo, three miles from Monterey. On the morning of the 18th he approached with his advanced guard within 1500 yards, but was compelled to fall back by a heavy fire of cannon. The report of these guns was received with cheers by the volunteers. They believed that the hour of battle had come, and in a few moments the column was in close order, and ready for the assault. Even the invalids of Quitman's brigade sprung from the wagons, seized their arms, and filed in with their comrades. Such was the ardor of men who had never been in battle, and who only served for honor and the glory of their country!

Gen. Quitman, sharing the enthusiasm of his troops, addressed them as follows:

" Volunteers, we are now in the vicinity of the enemy, and may, in an hour, be called to encounter them in battle. Your spirit inspires me. I know your metal, your impetuosity, and your recklessness of danger. There is no coward in my command. I shall never have to urge you on, but I must impress on you the necessity of preserving your ranks under all circumstances. Repress your personal impetuosity. Confide in your officers, and preserve your discipline in the excitement of the conflict. The eyes of the veteran officers of the army and the whole of the regulars will be fixed upon you. They know your gallantry, but they doubt your coolness. Prove to them, to your country, and to the world, that American volunteers are as admirable for their discipline and self-restraint as for their courage."

On the 20th, Worth, with his division and Hay's Texas regiment of mounted rifles, took position before the strong fortifications southwest of the town. On the 21st, Henderson's regiment of eastern Texans and May's battalion of dragoons were directed to re-enforce him. To divert the attention of the enemy from that quarter, Lt. Col. Garland, with the 3d infantry, and the 1st infantry, Lt. Col. Watson, making 600 bayonets, were ordered to make a demonstration on the eastern approach to the town. Major Mansfield, the chief engineer, supported by Lieut. Hazlett and a company of infantry, was making a bold reconnoissance in advance. Capt. Field, of the 3d, was soon after pushed forward to his assistance. Mansfield perceived the exigencies of his situation, and requested Garland to advance with his whole command within supporting distance. As he was moving forward, he received a message from the same source to advance in line of battle. He encountered a terrible fire in front from the masked batteries, and an enfilading fire from the citadel. Moving rapidly to pass this ordeal, he came within the deadly range of their musketry. At this juncture Major Mansfield indicated a movement to the right, to enable Garland to obtain a footing within the town, and in rear of the redoubts. The movement was unfortunate. He found himself entangled in short and narrow streets, where he was exposed to a triangular and destructive fire, without being able to manœuvre to advantage, or to charge the enemy. At this moment Capt. Bragg galloped up with his light battery and asked for orders. He placed a gun forthwith in position to rake the street, but it being perceived, after several discharges, that his fire was ineffectual against the barricades and the heavier metal of the Mexicans, and his men and horses being severely cut up, he was directed to retire. By this time Lt. Col. Watson, Major Mansfield, Major Lear, Major Barbour, Major Abercrombie, and many other officers had fallen, and Garland sullenly fell back, in good order, but pursued by the lancers, who cut off a few stragglers.

While this slaughter was going on General Taylor ordered the 4th infantry to the support of Garland. Three companies of the 4th assailed Fort Teneria, but nearly all the officers and a third of the men were mowed down by the first discharge from its batteries. Captains Backus and Lamotte, however, had fortunately, just before, secured a sheltered position in a tan-yard, which enabled them to ply their musketry with some effect behind the works of the fort. This was the only advantage thus far that we had gained. Garland, being joined by the remnant of the 4th, was ordered to storm the second redoubt. In attempting to execute this order, with not more than half his original force, he penetrated the town, forced several barricades, and moved forward, raked by artillery and small-arms, until he considered himself sufficiently advanced to enter the rear of the redoubt. Here he suddenly encountered a masked battery, and the guns of La Purissima, and on the opposite side two heavy guns were opened upon him. Here Captain Morris, in command of the 3d infantry, fell. Lieutenant Hazlett sprang forward to place him under shelter, and was shot down, mortally wounded. Thus exposed to a murderous fire from masked batteries and barricades—from garden walls and terraces—with no knowledge whatever of the localities or of his position, most of the officers down, his brave men lying in masses around, dead or wounded, this heroic leader and his Spartan band were compelled once more to fall back.

During this desperate and disastrous affair—the result of a formidable and well-served artillery on one side, and imperfect knowledge of localities on the other—Butler's division had been drawn up about a mile from the city, partially screened from the guns of the citadel by a slight elevation of the intervening plain. Leaving the Kentucky regiment to guard the camp, General Butler was ordered to advance with the Ohio troops to support Garland. Quitman's brigade, which had been chafing in the line, was put in motion at the same moment.

The defenses on the eastern side of Monterey, it will be remembered, consisted of a series of lunettes, on the extreme right of which, flanked by the River San Juan, was Fort TENERIA, mounting six heavy pieces, and on the extreme left, commanding the plain, was the citadel, or Black Fort. Between these, on a concave line, were Forts Diablo and Rincon, and a *tête du pont* of great strength at the bridge La Purissima. These works were so constructed as to support each other by flank and angular firing, and from them, as we have seen, Garland had suffered severely. Butler, pursuing the instructions of the commander-in-chief, felt his way gradually, with little knowledge of the ground, into the suburbs, near the lines of batteries. He encountered a heavy fire in front and flank. While struggling forward he fell in with Major Mansfield, who informed him of Garland's failure, and that an onward movement in that direction would be impracticable. This was communicated to General Taylor, who directed him to fall back. About the same time he learned that Quitman's brigade had stormed Fort Teneria and the contiguous redoubt. This determined Butler to make an effort to storm Fort Diablo. Advancing boldly through a terrible fire, a severe wound compelled him to withdraw. Almost at the same moment Colonel Mitchell, who succeeded him, his adjutant, and other officers, were struck down. The men were falling fast under the converging fire of three batteries and the incessant discharge of musketry, and reluctantly this gallant regiment followed their wounded officers from the field.

QUITMAN'S MARCH.

Sept. 21st, 1846. Gen. Quitman, avoiding the track of Garland and Butler, inclined his command to the left, moving by a flank upon Fort Teneria.* They were exposed to a terrific fire of grape and round shot. The

* So written in most of the official reports. The proper name is El Tortin de la Tanniere.

dense smoke clouded the light of day, and only the dark outline of the city was visible by the flash of musketry and the bright line of flame, like the red lips of a volcano, that denoted the different batteries. They faced the infernal storm with the steadiness of veterans. A round shot, raking the Tennessee regiment, cut down seven men, but did not check their advance an instant. The firing of small-arms had ceased, and when the brigade halted before the fort and fronted it, a small party, in the undress of United States regulars, was seen standing in a position that masked the right companies of the Mississippi regiment. A movement of the Tennesseans having created an interval on the left of the Mississippi regiment, Col. Davis promptly occupied it, thus executing a movement which gained to the front and left, and gave him precedence in the attack. When his regiment was re-formed into line the party of regulars had disappeared. The attacking force now consisted exclusively of the Tennessee and Mississippi regiments, the latter on the right and directly in front of the fort. A deep and wide embrasure, which seems to have been intended as a sally-port, stood immediately before the fifth Mississippi company, numbering from the right. The gun belonging to this embrasure had been run behind the parapet. The Mississippians commenced firing as they advanced, the men having been directed specially to select their objects and fire as sharp-shooters. In ten minutes, so fatal was their aim, most of the Mexican gunners had fallen by their pieces, and the order to charge was given. Lieut. Col. M'Clung, placing himself at the head of the company in front of the embrasure, led it at full speed, the flank companies converging to this central point of approach, which was a smooth field from which the corn had been recently cut. The martial form of M'Clung, swinging his sword above his head and hoarsely shout-

ing to his men, towered upon the parapet.   Col. Davis
and Lieut. Patterson, closely followed by other gallant
spirits, leaped into the embrasure, while the flash of the
last Mexican gun enveloped them in its lurid light.
Near them, in the clash and clangor of the charge, Gen.
Quitman and Maj. Bradford were seen cheering on their
men.   Bradford had but one word, and it was heard
above the tumult of the battle: " *Charge! charge!*" and
he suited " the action to the word."   Quitman's horse
was shot under him; but the gallant Lieut. Nicholls
promptly furnished him with his own, and, dashing up
to the ditch, he dismounted and rushed with his men
into the works.   The Mexicans, who had stood manfully
to their guns until most of the artillerists had been cut
down, appalled by this headlong charge, and seeing the
Tennesseans breaking over on their left, now fled through
the sally-port at the other extremity of the works.   The
impetuous Mississippians pursued them to a fortified stone
structure in rear of Teneria, and drove them thence across
the stream, under the shelter of Fort El Diablo.

While this desperate charge was being made, the Tennessee regiment, on the left, by a flank movement, had
advanced upon the fort with the characteristic valor
of their race.   The sons of those who fought at King's
Mountain, Emuckfau, Talladega, and the plains of Chal-
mette, proved worthy of their sires, and won new laurels in this desperate enterprise.   With this brilliant
event closed the operations of the day.   All had fought
gallantly.   The regulars had stood immovable as statues
under a galling fire, and faced death without emotion
when ordered to advance; but the only advantage thus
far, on the eastern approach, had been won by Quitman's
brigade.

On the 22d, Quitman, with Ridgeley's battery, was ordered to hold the works he had stormed on the preced-

L 2

ing day. The position was uncomfortable: they were exposed to an incessant cannonade, and the corpses of the slaughtered Mexicans had become offensive; the weather was wet and cold; they had neither blankets nor fire. The general shared the fare of his troops, and established his quarters on one of Ridgeley's guns. It was here his faithful servant Harry, who had followed the assaulting column, was heard remonstrating with his master, and imploring him, "for the sake of mistress and the children," not to expose himself so much. "Take care of yourself, Harry," said the general. "Help the wounded; keep as near me as you can. I must push on with the foremost and trust to Providence."

Before day, on the morning of the 23d, the conflict was renewed. Gen. Quitman, availing himself of discretionary orders, boldly advanced into the city. Col. Davis led the way. From every dwelling a heavy fire was directed against them. These houses were filled with musketeers. The streets were strongly barricaded, and the garden walls, parapets, and barricades were all crenelled for small-arms. Ditches and canals added to the difficulties of the advance. Yet from house to house, from barricade to barricade, the volunteers fought their way into the plaza. It was a succession of assaults obstinately resisted and bravely carried with clubbed rifles and at the point of the bayonet. The bloody conflict lasted from 8 A.M. until 4 P.M. It may justly be regarded as one of the boldest movements in the history of war, and quite as brilliant as the famous attack on Seringapatam, which gained for Cornwallis great military fame, a marquisate, and a splendid pension. There are some striking analogies in these great engagements. Seringapatam was defended by bridges, and ditches, and two lines of redoubts, by the renowned Tippoo, with a numerous army and an enormous amount of cannon.

Without artillery, and with only 9000 men, Cornwallis, wisely deciding on a night attack—one of the few instances where they are to be commended—assailed his lines and stormed them at the point of the bayonet. With less than 500 men—without artillery—the largest portion of his command without bayonets—with young and inexperienced troops—with the discomfiture of the regulars on the previous day to repress their ardor—without even being sure of the approbation of the commander-in-chief, Quitman entered a strongly-fortified city, defended by 6000 troops, and an infuriated populace firing from their roofs and windows, and fought his way, inch by inch, to the central square of the city. During the engagement, he was re-enforced by the 2d Texan regiment and Bragg's light battery, who share the glory of the achievement. Many brave men fell. Gen. Quitman narrowly escaped. His horse was wounded. The rim of his hat was torn off. The roof that he occupied temporarily was riddled with balls, and he received a contusion from the fragment of a shell.*

On the western suburb Gen. Worth had carried, by a series of masterly operations, the fortifications of the enemy. He had penetrated the city, and was advancing to co-operate with Quitman, when he received an order from head-quarters to halt. Gen. Taylor, it appears, contemplated a combined attack with his whole force next day, but early on the morning of the 24th he received a flag, with proposals for an interview, from the Mexican general.

Thus terminated three days' hard fighting, against great odds, and under many disadvantages. The fortifications of the enemy, constructed with much skill, mounted forty-two guns served by practiced artillerists. Six thousand regulars, and two thousand irregular

* For further details of the battle of Monterey, see Appendix.

troops, commanded by experienced officers, defended the
city.   Every dwelling and street had been converted into
a fortress or a battery.

Our force consisted of 6220 men and 425 officers, many
of them volunteers only partially drilled, and who had
never been under fire.   Our guns were merely light field-
pieces, incapable of silencing the heavy metal of the enemy, or of making any impression on their defenses.   The
only mortar in our hands, from some gross neglect, was
almost unavailable.   To attack the city, the American
troops had to advance, a mile or more, across an open
plain, exposed to a destructive fire in front and flank,
from the whole series of redoubts and masked batteries.
The most serious disadvantage, however, was the want
of exact information of the defenses of the enemy, and
the location of his works, and therefore it seems to have
been more an impromptu fight, arising from contingencies, than a concerted plan of battle.   Gen. Worth appears to have exercised a quasi-independent command
from the afternoon of the 21st until the reception of the
flag of truce.   The main portion of the army remained
supine, until Worth recommended a demonstration on
the eastern works of the city.   Then commenced Garland's unfortunate enterprise, in which, without any positive orders what to do or where to go, and knowing
nothing of the localities, he followed the extemporaneous
signals of Major Mansfield, who was making an abortive
reconnoissance at the hazard of his life.   Henderson, with
his mounted regiment of Texans, and May, with his dragoons, had been dispatched to re-enforce Worth, but,
finding it impracticable, had returned.   Nothing was
known at head-quarters of what Worth was doing,
though they were only five miles apart.   The operations
on the east seem to have been experimental, and, to
some degree, spontaneous.   It is yet a question whether

Quitman had orders to assault Fort Teneria; and it is still more doubtful whether he was ordered to advance into the city on the 23d. The truth seems to be, that he had a discretionary order from Gen. Taylor, to act and fight according to the exigencies of the moment. He assumed the responsibility, and won the victory.*

Some military writers condemn the arrangements of General Taylor. These criticisms are stated with force and precision in Ripley's "War with Mexico," a work of much ability, from the pen of an eye-witness and actor in the war, but certainly tinctured with partiality and prejudice.

The American general was a man of iron nerve. He was headstrong and obstinate. He knew little of fear, and was not easily discouraged. Against the opinion of a large majority of his oldest and most distinguished officers, after the battle of Palo Alto, he advanced and won the brilliant victory of Resaca de la Palma against odds so great that, if it had been lost, he would have been recalled, if not degraded, as too rash for command. Not disheartened by the inefficiency of the quarter-master's department or the cool civility of the secretary of war, he had advanced upon Monterey with an inadequate force, and without transportation, hospital stores, artillery, or intrenching implements. He confided more in the bayonet and in his rifles, and in his own capacity for desperate expedients in cases of emergency, than on

---

* It would be an amusing study to trace the ambiguities and uncertainties that hang over grave military events that have decided battles, campaigns, and even the fate of empires. All wars furnish some of these examples. An error of this nature led to the quarrel on the field between Washington and Lee. And notwithstanding months of Parliamentary discussion, and the scrutiny of a court of inquiry, it was never determined whether Burgoyne was responsible for the advance upon Albany which resulted in his defeat and surrender at Saratoga. A similar doubt hangs over the expedition to Bennington. The war with Mexico supplies a number of instances, by no means settled by the court of inquiry at Frederick.

the support of the government or the rules and axioms of war. Of these he had only a limited knowledge, having been trained exclusively on the frontier. But he had a military eye and brain, perfect composure in moments of peril, a knowledge of men, and the faculty of commanding obedience and confidence. He was known to be as firm as brave, and his presence never failed to inspire his troops. Indiana, Florida, and Mexico bear monuments of his genius which defy criticism, and are independent of praise. His military instincts have the stamp of intuition. The Duke of Wellington closely studied and applauded his campaign, and impartial history will class the conqueror of the Rio Grande as one of the most successful soldiers of the age. No city in Europe, in the wars of Napoleon or Wellington, or at any other period, so strongly fortified by nature and art, so well defended, with such a preponderance of men and of artillery, was ever carried in so short a time. It was a battle of force and not of strategy, and as such may challenge comparison and criticism. Wellington's sieges in India and in the Peninsula, from the time they consumed, are considered as failures; the great Hannibal lay eight months before Saguntum; Monterey fell, literally by the sword, the bayonet, and the axe, in three days. Its defenders fought, as men of the Spanish race always fight, obstinately behind their solid defenses; and a less determined general, and troops less enthusiastic and impetuous, must have been defeated. But the composition of our army—the spirit of emulation between the regulars and volunteers, the presentiment of promotion in the line and of political distinctions at home, and the prevalent belief that the war was for the glory and *the extension* of the republic—rendered our arms irresistible.

Early on the morning of the 24th, as has been stated,

General Ampudia proposed to evacuate the city upon conditions. In an interview with General Taylor, he declared that he had official information that the two governments were about to conclude peace, and that to prolong hostilities would be inhuman. A joint commission to arrange the terms of the capitulation was appointed, and on the morning of the 25th the Mexican army marched from the citadel, and on the 28th Worth's division took possession.

The propriety and terms of this capitulation have been quite as much canvassed as the famous convention of Cintra. Junot, a marshal of France, trained by Napoleon, and representing the imperial power in Portugal (who, only six months before, in contempt of a British fleet, of 14,000 Portuguese troops, and a hostile population of 300,000, had seized Lisbon with a few hundred grenadiers, the vanguard of his army), after the battle of Vimiero demanded an armistice (although he had 25,000 veteran troops, and abundant armaments, and numerous fortresses) from a British army inferior to his own, and almost destitute of transportation! The emperor was about to send him before a council of war, which probably would have ordered him to be shot, when he learned that the British generals, Sir Hew Dalrymple, Sir Harry Burrard, and Sir Arthur Wellesley (Wellington), had already been arraigned for consenting to the convention. Two of these never recovered the confidence of the British people, and the latter was with difficulty sustained by the influence of his aristocratic connections, until, invested with the sole command, he immortalized himself in the subsequent campaign.

The administration did not approve the capitulation of Monterey, although it had been consented to by Gen. Taylor in consonance with the views and policy of the President, who pertinaciously and prudishly disclaimed the imputation of "a war for conquest." Negotiation was by no means the weakness of the American general. On the contrary, he was impatient of delay, knew little of policy, and preferred the arbitrament of the bayonet. This propensity for "fight" was one of his characteristics. He had exhibited it in every exigency of his career, and, if Mr. Webster is correct, it was with difficulty restrained during his brief occupancy of the executive chair, when he was disposed to exert the military power of the United States to sustain the federal jurisdiction over New Mexico, upon territory claimed by the sovereign State of Texas, and upon a title easily maintained, and which her sister states of the South would have joined her in maintaining, had she not ignobly, and to the surprise of all parties, surrendered her rights.

The capitulation was consented to, on the part of the victorious general, to support the views and policy of his government. But he found himself attacked in many quarters, and chiefly by the organs of the administration, whose policy with regard to Mexico he had endeavored to subserve. Ours is, emphatically, a military nation. We have the Norman thirst for territory. The victories of Taylor had aroused the appetite for glory and for acquisition. "Onward" was the word. The armistice of Monterey was, therefore, repugnant to the million, and the hero of the battle found himself about to be made, by jealous politicians who dreaded his rising popularity, the victim of the capitulation. Stung by this ingratitude, the veteran soldier addressed a letter to Maj. Gen. Gaines. It first appeared in the New York Express. In justice to the illustrious dead, and for its historical interest, a portion of it is here inserted.

"Monterey, Nov. 9th, 1846.

"I do not believe the authorities at Washington are at all satisfied with my conduct in regard to the terms of the capitulation entered into with the Mexican commander, which you no doubt have seen, as they have been made public through the official organ, and copied into various other newspapers. I have this moment received an answer (to my dispatch announcing the surrender of Monterey, and the circumstances attending the same) from the secretary of war, stating that 'it was regretted by the President that it was not deemed advisable to insist on the terms I had proposed in my first communication to the Mexican commander in regard to giving up the city,' adding that 'the circumstances which dictated, no doubt justified, the change.' Although the terms of capitulation may be considered too liberal on our part by the President and his advisers, as well as by many others at a distance, particularly by those who do not understand the position which we occupied (otherwise they might come to a different conclusion in regard to the matter), yet, on due reflection, I see nothing to induce me to regret the course I pursued. The proposition on the part of General Ampudia, which had much to do in determining my course in the matter, was based on the ground that our government had proposed to his to settle the existing difficulties by negotiation (which I knew was the case without knowing the result), which was then under consideration by the proper authorities, and which he (General Ampudia) had no doubt would result favorably, as the whole of his people were in favor of peace. If so, I considered the further effusion of blood not only unnecessary but improper. Their force was also considerably larger than ours, and, from the size and position of the place, we could not completely invest it; so that the greater portion of their troops, if not the whole, had they been disposed to do so, could any night have abandoned the city, at once entered the mountain passes, and effected their retreat, do what we could. Had we been put to the alternative of taking the place by storm (which there is no doubt we should have succeeded in doing), we should in all probability have lost fifty or a hundred men in killed, besides the wounded, which I wished to avoid, as there appeared to be a prospect of peace, even if a distant one. I also wished to avoid the destruction of women and children, which must have been very great had the storming process been resorted to. Besides, they had a very large and strong fortification a short distance from the city, which, if carried with the bayonet, must have been taken at great sacrifice of life, and, with our limited train of heavy or battering artillery, it would have required twenty or twenty-five days to take it by regular approaches.

That they should have surrendered a place nearly as strong as Quebec, well fortified under the direction of skillful engineers—their works garnished with forty-two pieces of artillery, abundantly supplied with ammunition, garrisoned by 7000 regular and 2000 irregular troops, in addition to some thousand citizens capable of (and no doubt actually) bearing arms, and aiding in its defense— to an opposing force of half their number, scantily supplied with provisions, and with a light train of artillery, is among the unaccountable occurrences of the times.

I am decidedly opposed to carrying the war beyond Saltillo in this direction, which place has been entirely abandoned by the Mexican forces, all of whom have been concentrated at San Luis Potosi; and I shall lose no time in taking possession of the former as soon as the cessation of hostilities referred to expires, which I have notified the Mexican authorities will be the case on the 13th instant, by direction of the President of the United States.

"If we are (in the language of Mr. Polk and General Scott) under the necessity of 'conquering a peace,' and that by taking the capital of the country, we must go to Vera Cruz, take that place, and then march on to the city of Mexico. To do so in any other direction I consider out of the question. But, admitting that we conquer a peace by doing so—say at the end of the next twelve months—will the amount of blood and treasure which must be expended in doing so be compensated by the same? I think not, especially if the country we subdue is to be given up; and I imagine there are but few individuals in our country who think of annexing Mexico to the United States.

"I do not intend to carry on my operations (as previously stated) beyond Saltillo, deeming it next to impracticable to do so. It then becomes a question as to what is best to be done. It seems to me that the most judicious course to be pursued on our part would be to take possession at once of the line we would accept by negotiation, extending from the Gulf of Mexico to the Pacific, and occupy the same, or keep what we already have possession of; and that, with Tampico (which I hope to take in the course of the next month, or as soon as I can get the means of transportation), will give us all on this side of the Sierra Madre, and as soon as I occupy Saltillo, will include six or seven states, or provinces; thus holding Tampico, Victoria, Monterey, Saltillo, Monclova, Chihuahua (which I presume General Wool has possession of by this time), Santa Fé, and the Californias, and say to Mexico, ' Drive us from the country'—throwing on her the responsibility and expense of carrying on offensive war; at the same time closely blockading all her ports on the Pacific and the Gulf. A course of this kind, if persevered in for a short time, would soon bring her to her proper senses, and compel her to sue for peace, provided there is a government in the country sufficiently stable for us to treat with, which I fear will hardly be the case for many years to come. Without large reenforcements of volunteers from the United States, say ten or fifteen thousand (those previously sent out having already been greatly reduced by sickness and other casualties), I do not believe it would be advisable to march beyond Saltillo, which is more than two hundred miles beyond our dépôts on the Rio Grande—a very long line on which to keep up supplies (over a land route, in a country like this) for a large force, and certain to be attended with an expense which will be frightful to contemplate when closely looked into.

" From Saltillo to San Luis Potosi, the next place of importance on the road to the city of Mexico, is three hundred miles; one hundred and forty badly watered, where no supplies of any kind could be procured for man or horses. I have informed the War Department that 20,000 efficient men would be necessary to insure success if we move on that place (a city containing a population of 60,000, where the enemy could bring together and sustain, besides the citizens, an army of 50,000), a force

which, I apprehend, will hardly be collected by us, with
the train necessary to feed it, as well as to transport various other supplies, particularly ordnance and munitions
of war.

"In regard to the armistice, which would have expired by limitation in a few days, we lost nothing by it,
as we could not move even now, had the enemy continued to occupy Saltillo; for, strange to say, the first
wagon which has reached me since the declaration of war
was on the 2d instant, the same day on which I received
from Washington an acknowledgment of my dispatch
announcing the taking of Monterey; and then I received
only one hundred and thirty-five; so that I have been
since May last completely crippled, and am still so, for
want of transportation. After raking and scraping the
country for miles around Camargo, collecting every pack-
mule and other means of transportation, I could bring
here only 80,000 rations (fifteen days' supply), with a
moderate supply of ordnance, ammunition, etc., to do
which all the corps had to leave behind a portion of
their camp equipage necessary for their comfort; and,
in some instances among the volunteers, their personal
baggage. I moved in such a way, and with such limited
means, that, had I not succeeded, I should no doubt have
been severely reprimanded, if nothing worse. I did so
to sustain the administration.   *   *   *   *

"Of the two regiments of mounted men from Tennessee and Kentucky, who left their respective states to join
me in June, the latter has just reached Camargo; the
former had not got to Matamoras at the latest dates
from there. Admitting that they will be as long in returning as in getting here (to say nothing of the time
necessary to recruit their horses), and were to be discharged in time to reach their homes, they could serve
in Mexico but a very short time.

"The foregoing remarks are not made with the view
of finding fault with any one, but to point out the difficulties with which I have had to contend.

"Monterey, the capital of New Leon, is situated on the
San Juan River, where it comes out of the mountains—
the city, which contains a population of about 12,000, being in part surrounded by them—at the head of a large

and beautiful valley. The houses are of stone, in the Moorish style, with flat roofs, which, with their strongly-inclosed yards and gardens in high stone walls, all looped for musketry, make them each a fortress within itself. It is the most important place in Northern Mexico, or on the east side of Sierra Madre, commanding the only pass, or road, for carriages from this side, between it and the Gulf of Mexico, to the table-lands of the Sierra, by or through which the city of Mexico can be reached."

This letter produced much sensation. Distinguished politicians already began to feel the pangs of jealousy, and the central organ of the administration strongly condemned the publication. The following bulletin soon after appeared. It had an awful squinting at Taylor and Gaines:

" *General Orders—No.* 3.

"WAR DEPARTMENT, Washington, Jan. 28th, 1847.

"The President of the United States directs that paragraph 650 of the General Regulations for the Army established on the 1st of March, 1825, and not included among those published January 25th, 1841, be now republished, and that its observance as a part of the general regulations be strictly enjoined upon the army.

"By order of the President.

" WM. L. MARCY, Secretary of War.

"650. Private letters or reports, relative to military marches and operations, are frequently mischievous in design, and always disgraceful to the army. They are, therefore, strictly forbidden; and any officer found guilty of making such report for publication, without special permission, or of placing the writing beyond his control, so that it finds its way to the press, within one month after the termination of the campaign to which it relates, shall be dismissed from the service."

The capitulation had now become the subject of general discussion. The President and secretary of war were known to disapprove it. Facts were perverted. The motives of Gen. Taylor were misrepresented. Dissension and distrust were propagated in the army. Under these circumstances, Col. Jefferson Davis, of the Mississippi Riflemen, one of the commissioners, a man educated with the most fastidious notions of military punctilio and honor, deemed it his duty to defend the transaction. This able paper, and the accompanying documents, demand a place in history.

"Victoria, Mexico, January 6th, 1847.

" DEAR SIR,—After much speculation and no little misrepresentation about the capitulation of Monterey, I perceive by our recent newspapers that a discussion has arisen as to who is responsible for that transaction. As one of the commissioners who were intrusted by Gen. Taylor with the arrangement of the terms upon which the city of Monterey and its fortifications should be delivered to our forces, I have had frequent occasion to recur to the course then adopted, and the considerations which led to it. My judgment after the fact has fully sustained my decisions at the date of the occurrence; and feeling myself responsible for the instrument as we prepared and presented it to our commanding general, I have the satisfaction, after all subsequent events, to believe that the terms we offered were expedient, and honorable, and wise. A distinguished gentleman, with whom I acted on that commission, Governor Henderson, says, in a recently published letter, ' I did not at the time, nor do I still, like the terms, but acted as one of the commissioners, together with Gen. Worth and Col. Davis, to carry out Gen. Taylor's instructions. We ought, and could have made them surrender at discretion,' etc., etc.

" From each position in the above paragraph I dissent. The instructions given by Gen. Taylor only presented his object, and fixed a limit to the powers of his commissioners; hence, when points were raised which exceeded our discretion, they were referred to the commander; but minor points were acted on, and finally submitted as a part of our negotiation. We fixed the time within which the Mexican forces should retire from Monterey. We agreed upon the time we would wait for the decision of the respective governments, which I recollect was less by thirty-four days than the Mexican commissioners asked, the period adopted being that which, according to our estimate, was required to bring up the rear of our army with the ordnance and supplies necessary for farther operations.

"I did not then, nor do I now, believe we could have made the enemy surrender at discretion. Had I entertained the opinion, it would have been given to the commission and to the commanding general, and it would have precluded me from signing an agreement which permitted the garrison to retire with the honors of war. It is demonstrable, from the position and known prowess of the two armies, that we could drive the enemy from the town, but the town was untenable while the main fort (called the new citadel) remained in the hands of the enemy. Being without siege artillery or intrenching tools, we could only hope to carry this fort by storm, after a heavy loss from our army, which, isolated in a hostile country, now numbered less than half the forces of the enemy. When all this had been achieved, what more would we have gained than by the capitulation?

"General Taylor's force was too small to invest the town. It was, therefore, always in the power of the enemy to retreat, bearing his light arms. Our army—poorly provided, and with very insufficient transportation—could not have overtaken if they had pursued the flying enemy. Hence the conclusion that, as it was not in our power to capture the main body of the Mexican army, it is unreasonable to suppose their general would have surrendered at discretion. The moral effect of retiring under the capitulation was certainly greater than if the enemy had retreated without our consent. By this course we secured the large supply of ammunition we had collected in Monterey, which, had the assault been continued, must have been exploded by our shells, as it was principally stored in 'the cathedral,' which, being supposed to be filled with troops, was the especial aim of our pieces. The destruction which this explosion would have produced must have involved the advance of both divisions of our troops; and I commend this to the contemplation of those whose arguments have been drawn from facts learned since the commissioners closed their negotiations. With these introductory remarks, I send a copy of a manuscript in my possession, which was prepared to meet such necessity as now exists for an explanation of the views which governed the commissioners in arranging the terms of capitulation, to justify the commanding general, should misrepresentation and calumny attempt to tarnish his well-earned reputation, and, for all time to come, to fix the truth of the transaction.

"JEFFERSON DAVIS."

"*Memoranda of the Transactions in connection with the Capitulation of Monterey, capital of Nueva Leon, Mexico.*

"By invitation of General Ampudia, commanding the Mexican army, General Taylor, accompanied by a number of his officers, proceeded, on the 24th of September, 1846, to a house designated as the place at which General Ampudia requested an interview. The parties being convened, General Ampudia announced, as official information, that commissioners from the United States had been received by the government of Mexico, and that the orders under which he had prepared to defend the city of Monterey had lost their force by the subsequent change of his own government, therefore he asked the conference. A brief conversation between the commanding generals showed their views to be so opposite as to leave little reason to expect an amicable arrangement between them.

"General Taylor said he would not delay to receive such propositions as General Ampudia indicated. One of General Ampudia's party, I think the governor of the city, suggested the appointment of a mixed commission: this was acceded to, and General W. S. Worth, of the United States Army, General J. Pinckney Henderson, of the Texan Volunteers, and Colonel Jefferson Davis, of the Mississippi Riflemen, on the part of General Taylor; and General J. Ma. Ortega, General P. Requeña, and señor the governor M. Ma. Llano, on the part of General Ampudia, were appointed.

"General Taylor gave instructions to his commissioners which, as understood, for they were brief and verbal, will be best shown by the copy of the demand which the United States commissioners prepared in the conference-room, here incorporated:

"Copy of Demand by United States Commissioners.

" I. As the legitimate result of the operations before this place, and the present position of the contending armies, we demand the surrender of the town, the arms and munitions of war, and all other public property within the place.

" II. That the Mexican armed force retire beyond the Rinconada, Linares, and San Fernando on the coast.

" III. The commanding general of the army of the United States agrees that the Mexican officers reserve their side-arms and private baggage, and the troops be allowed to retire under their officers without parole, a reasonable time being allowed to withdraw the forces.

" IV. The immediate delivery of the main works now occupied to the army of the United States.

" V. To avoid collisions, and for mutual convenience, that the troops of the United States shall not occupy the town until the Mexican forces have been withdrawn, except for hospital purposes, store-houses, etc.

" VI. The commanding general of the United States agrees not to advance beyond the line specified in the second section before the expiration of eight weeks, or until the respective governments can be heard from.

"The terms of the demand were refused by the Mexican commissioners, who drew up a counter-proposition, of which I only recollect that it contained a permission to the Mexican forces to retire with their arms. This was urged as a matter of soldierly pride, and as an ordinary courtesy. We had reached the limit of our instructions, and the commission rose to report the disagreement.

"Upon returning to the reception-room after the fact had been announced that the commissioners could not agree upon terms, General Ampudia entered at length upon the question, treating the point of disagreement as one which involved the honor of his country, spoke of his desire for a settlement without farther bloodshed, and said he did not care about the pieces of artillery

Vol. I.—M

which he had at the place. General Taylor responded to the wish to avoid unnecessary bloodshed. It was agreed the commission should reassemble, and we were instructed to concede the small-arms, and I supposed there would be no question about the artillery. The Mexican commissioners now urged that, as all other arms had been recognized, it would be discreditable to the artillery if required to march out without any thing to represent their arm, and stated, in answer to an inquiry, that they had a battery of light artillery manœuvred and equipped as such. The commission again rose and reported the disagreement on the point of artillery.

"Gen. Taylor, hearing that more was demanded than the middle ground upon which, in a spirit of generosity, he had agreed to place the capitulation, announced the conference at an end, and rose in a manner which showed his determination to talk no more. As he crossed the room to leave it, one of the Mexican commissioners addressed him, and some conversation, which I did not hear, ensued. Gen. Worth asked permission of Gen. Taylor, and addressed some remarks to Gen. Ampudia, the spirit of which was that which he manifested throughout the negotiation, viz., generosity and leniency, and a desire to spare the farther effusion of blood. The commission reassembled, and the points of capitulation were agreed upon. After a short recess, we again repaired to the room in which we had parted from the Mexican commissioners; they were tardy in joining us, and slow in executing the instrument of capitulation. The 7th, 8th, and 9th articles were added during the session. At a late hour the English original was handed to Gen. Taylor for his examination, the Spanish original having been sent to Gen. Ampudia. Gen. Taylor signed and delivered to me the instrument as it was submitted to him, and I returned to receive the Spanish copy with the signature of Gen. Ampudia, and send that having Gen. Taylor's signature, that each general might countersign the original to be retained by the other. Gen. Ampudia did not sign the instrument, as was expected, but came himself to meet the commissioners. He raised many points which had been settled, and evinced a disposition to make the Spanish differ in essential points from the English instrument. Gen. Worth was absent. Finally, he was required to sign the instrument prepared by his own commissioners, and the English original was left with him that he might have it translated (which he promised to do that night) and be ready next morning with a Spanish duplicate of the English instrument left with him. By this means the two instruments would be made to correspond, and he be compelled to admit his knowledge of the contents of the English original before he signed it.

"The next morning the commission again met; again the attempt was made, as had been often done before by solicitation, to gain some grant in addition to the compact. Thus we had, at their request, adopted the word 'capitulation' in lieu of surrender; they now wished to substitute 'stipulation' for capitulation. It finally became necessary to make a peremptory demand for the immediate signing of the English instrument by Gen. Ampudia, and the literal translation (now perfected) by the commissioners and their general. The Spanish instrument first signed by Gen. Ampudia was destroyed in presence of his commissioners; the translation of our own instrument was countersigned by Gen. Taylor and delivered; the agreement was complete, and it only remained to execute the terms.

"Much has been said about the construction of Article II. of the capitulation, a copy of which is hereto appended. Whatever ambiguity there may be in the language used, there was a perfect understanding by the commissioners on both sides as to the intent of the parties. The distinction we made between light artillery, equipped and manœuvred as such, designed for and used in the field, and pieces being the armament of the fort, was clearly stated on our side, and that it was comprehended on theirs appeared in the fact, that repeatedly they asserted their possession of light artillery, and said that they had one battery of light pieces. Such conformity of opinion existed among our commissioners upon every measure which was finally adopted, that I consider them, in their sphere, jointly and severally responsible for each and every article of the capitulation. If, as originally viewed by Gen. Worth, our conduct has been in accordance with the peaceful policy of our government, and shall in any degree tend to consummate that policy, we may congratulate ourselves upon the part we have taken. If otherwise, it will remain to me a deliberate opinion that the terms of the capitulation gave all which could have followed of desirable result from a farther assault. It was in the power of the enemy to retreat and to bear with him his small-arms and such a battery as was contemplated in the capitulation. The other grants were such as it was honorable in a conquering army to bestow, and which it cost magnanimity nothing to give.

"The above recollections are submitted to Generals Henderson and Worth for correction and addition, that the misrepresentation of the transaction may be prevented by a statement made while the events are recent and the memory fresh.   JEFFERSON DAVIS,
"Colonel Mississippi Riflemen."

"Camp near Monterey, October 7th, 1846.
"The above is a correct statement of the leading facts connected with the transactions referred to, according to my recollection. It is, however, proper that I should farther state that my first impression was that no better terms than those first proposed, on the part of General Taylor, when I found him disposed to yield to the request of General Ampudia, and at the same time gave it as my opinion that they would be accepted by him before we left the town. General Taylor replied that he would run no risk when it could be avoided; that he wished to avoid the farther shedding of blood, and that he was satisfied that our government would be pleased with the terms given by the capitulation; and being myself persuaded of the fact, I yielded my individual views and wishes; and, under that conviction, I shall ever be ready to defend the terms of the capitulation.
"J. PINCKNEY HENDERSON,
"Maj. Gen. commanding the Texan Volunteers."

"I not only counseled and advised, the opportunity being offered by the general-in-chief, the first proposition, but cordially assented and approved the decision taken by General Taylor in respect to the latter, as did every member of the commission, and for good and sufficient military and national reasons, and stand ready at all times and proper places to defend and sustain the action of the commanding general, and participation of the commissioners. Knowing that malignants, the tremor being off, are at work to discredit and misrepresent the case (as I had anticipated), I feel obliged to Colonel Davis for having thrown together the materials and facts.

"W. J. Worth,
"Brig. Gen. commanding 2d division.
"Monterey, October 12th, 1840."

"Terms of the capitulation of the city of Monterey, the capital of Nueva Leon, agreed upon by the undersigned commissioners, to wit: Gen. Worth, of the United States Army; Gen. Henderson, of the Texan Volunteers; and Col. Davis, of the Mississippi Riflemen, on the part of Maj. Gen. Taylor, commanding-in-chief the United States forces; and Gen. Requena, and Gen. Ortega, of the army of Mexico; and Señor Manuel M. Llano, governor of Nueva Leon, on the part of Señor Don Pedro Ampudia, commanding-in-chief the army of the North of Mexico.

"*Article* 1. As the legitimate result of the operations before this place, and the present position of the contending armies, it is agreed that the city, the fortifications, cannon, the munitions of war, and all other public property, with the undermentioned exceptions, be surrendered to the commanding general of the United States forces now at Monterey.

"*Art.* 2. That the Mexican forces be allowed to retain the following arms, to wit: The commissioned officers, their side-arms; the infantry, their arms and accoutrements; the artillery, one field-battery, not to exceed six pieces, with twenty-one rounds of ammunition.

"*Art.* 3. That the Mexican armed forces retire within seven days from this date beyond the line formed by the pass of the Rinconada, the city of Linares, and San Fernando de Pusos.

"*Art.* 4. That the citadel of Monterey be evacuated by the Mexican, and occupied by the American forces to-morrow morning at 10 o'clock.

"*Art.* 5. To avoid collisions, and for mutual convenience, that the troops of the United States will not occupy the city until the Mexican forces have withdrawn, except for hospital and storage purposes.

"*Art.* 6. That the forces of the United States will not advance beyond the line specified in the 3d article before the expiration of eight weeks, or until the orders from the respective governments can be received.

"*Art.* 7. That the public property to be delivered shall be turned over and received by officers appointed by the commanding generals of the two armies.

"*Art.* 8. That all doubts as to the meaning of any of the preceding articles shall be solved by an equitable construction, and on principles of liberality to the retiring army.

"*Art.* 9. That the Mexican flag, when struck at the citadel, may be saluted by its own battery.

> "W. J. WORTH,
> "Brig. Gen. U. S. Army.
> "J. PINCKNEY HENDERSON,
> "Maj. Gen. commanding the Texan Volunteers.
> "JEFFERSON DAVIS,
> "Col. Mississippi Riflemen.
> "J. M. ORTEGA.
> "P. REQUENA.
> "MANUEL M. LLANO.

(Approved),
"PEDRO AMPUDIA.
"Z. TAYLOR, Maj. Gen. U. S. A. commanding.
"Done at Monterey, Sept. 24th, 1846."

This publication defeated the unjust and ungrateful attempt to crush Gen. Taylor by arraying against him the war feeling of the nation, which had been thoroughly aroused by his own victories.

Viewing the transaction at this distance, it would seem that the capitulation was justifiable; and it reflects this honor on the republic, that, in the full career of conquest, a victorious army pressing a retreating and supplicating enemy, a general who had never been defeated, with the sanction of advisers who had never flinched from peril or responsibility, accepted the first overture for peace. In a moral point of view, and as an illustration of national character, inspiring confidence in our military men, showing how strongly and correctly they appreciate the duties of the citizen, and are ever ready to relinquish bloody laurels for the public welfare, the capitulation of Monterey is a richer heir-loom for the nation than the victories of that memorable campaign. If it turned out afterward that some of the representations made to the commissioners by the Mexican general were false, it reflects no dishonor upon us. When parties consent to negotiate, good faith, and not perfidy, is to be presumed.

General Quitman disapproved the capitulation. He had always condemned the policy of President Polk, which General Taylor presumed, and justly presumed, he was acting upon when he accepted overtures from Ampudia. Quitman's fixed opinion was that the war should be carried on chiefly by volunteers; that they should never be inactive; that it should be a war, not on Mr. Polk's feeble maxim, "to conquer a peace," but a war *for conquest and occupation*. He regarded, and justly regarded, the great bulk of the Mexicans as a bastard and robber race, incapable of self-government, and only fit for servitude and military rule. Viewing the war on our part as eminently just, he considered that the whole Mexican territory should be subdued, annexed, and governed by the sword, under American laws, until the population should be sufficiently tutored and improved by immigration to be incorporated with the republic. His plan was a prompt movement, with an effective force, on San Luis de Potosi, and thence to the capital. These views are foreshadowed in the following letter:

To Hon. Robert J. Walker, Secretary of the Treasury.

"Camp Allen, near Monterey, November 12th, 1846.

" My dear Sir,—Your prominent position in the administration, and our long and intimate acquaintance, induce me to address you without reserve upon some matters of the highest interest to the country and to the present administration.

" I forbear to say any thing of what has passed in the army, except to disclaim having ever given any countenance to the unfortunate and ill-advised convention of Monterey. I was present, by invitation of General Taylor, at the conference between the opposing generals, but my opinion was not asked, nor had I any participation in the results.

" I believed the city and army entirely in our power, and would have opposed terms which must result in converting a brilliant and decisive victory into a drawn battle.

" It is not my purpose, however, to comment upon circumstances which have tended to place this temporary volunteer army in a state of inaction for a large portion of the season best calculated for prosecuting a successful campaign in Mexico. I have been informed that officers high in rank have recommended the policy of ceasing farther offensive operations, of holding on to the conquered Mexican provinces, and standing on the defensive. This policy, in my opinion, would be disastrous, if not disgraceful to the country, and would result in protracting and adding to the expenses of the war, to say nothing of the contempt of our national character which it would engender in Europe and even in Mexico. National insult is at least one cause of the war. Will the occupation of territory unimportant, in a revenue point of view, to Mexico, compel her to atone for national insult? Will not such a policy tend to prolong the war? It will soon be known to Mexico. Under it, secure from attack, she need not even defend her salient points in advance of our line, and may quietly and safely await the development of her resources until, on her part, some favorable blow may be struck. All the occupied points of our defensive line being equally accessible to her, she may choose her own time and season to throw upon any one of them an overwhelming force and cut off our garrisons or defeat our detachments. Suppose, in pursuit of this policy, we occupy the line from Tampico through Victoria, Linares, Monterey, or Saltillo and Monclova, to Santa Fé, 25,000 men would be required; 5000 at Tampico; 5000 at Victoria; 5000 at Monterey and Saltillo; 5000 from Monclova to Santa Fé; and at least 5000 to protect the depôts and transportation in rear; and even then Tampico and Monterey would be exposed to the whole force of the Mexican army before relief could be had from other points. If, however, we had an efficient army of but half this force *in the field*, threatening Potosi, or any other vulnerable point in advance of our line, it would most effectually cover the whole strategic line in rear of its line of movement, and force the enemy to concentrate his forces and meet us in the field, or uncover the way to his capital. I do not intend positively to designate Potosi as the proper objective point to our operations, but to give my opinion that the war should be prosecuted by penetrating the country on some practicable line with an adequate force, say 12,000 men, well equipped. From the information I have been able to pick up, I have no doubt such a force could take Potosi against 30,000 Mexicans. The obstacles in the way are said to be deficiency of permanent supply of water. I have no doubt this is exaggerated. At least, I am satisfied it can be overcome in several modes, which I will not weary you with detailing. With such an enemy as we have to contend against, we can never succeed in impressing them with respect for our power and national character except by dealing upon them hard blows: we can only obtain their respect through their fears. Besides, this mode of prosecuting the war would be better suited to the character of the provisional force we have in the field, to the ardent and energetic disposition of the people of the United States, and would be more in consonance with our pretensions, or rather claims, as one of the principal powers of the civilized world. Besides, the heavy expenses incident to a war are calculated to have the most serious effects upon the administration in power unless they are compensated by brilliant results.

M 2

The field is, in my opinion, open for these, if judiciously planned. An army of volunteers will always be brought into the field at great expense. Of these sent into this country there has been an average loss, from disease and incapacities of various kinds, of about thirty per cent.; yet, in my opinion, those now in the field constitute the very best forces we have. They are generally well commanded, subordinate, and brave almost to a fault. Should this campaign be wasted in inactivity, the same expense and loss will have to be encountered before a proper force can be placed in the field. Be assured, Mexico will never make peace upon any terms which an administration dare accept until she has received some harder blow.

" My friends think that some injustice has been done to me in accounts of the battle. The prominent part which my brigade acted certainly deserves better notice."

CHAPTER X.

Discontent of Gen. Taylor.—Expedition to Victoria.—Holt's Journal.—Division of Quitman's Command.—The Mississippi Regiment.—Tampico.—Siege of Vera Cruz.—Quitman's first Battle.
—Alvarado Expedition.—Marches for Puebla.—Question of Rank.
—Correspondence with Gen. Scott.—Quitman's Freedom from Jealousy.—Social Relations.

On the fall of Monterey Gen. Worth and his division
occupied the city. Gen. Taylor, with the other divisions,
encamped in the Bosque de San Domingo, a beautiful
wood three miles north of the city. They lay supine
for three months, although it was apparent to the army,
and the general desire, that a push should be made for
San Luis Potosi, and thence to the capital. Three routes
were proposed: 1. By Saltillo and Encarnacion; 2. By
Saltillo and Parras, through Durango; 3. By Victoria
and Tula. But there was no cordiality between Gen.
Taylor and the secretary of war. On the contrary, the
former believed that there was a concerted plan to embarrass and disgrace him. He bitterly complained of
interference with his command, and especially of the direct communication opened by the secretary with Gen.
Patterson, directing him to detach a large body of troops
and march upon Tampico. This order to a subordinate,
in the presence of his superior, was in flagrant violation
of all military rule, and neither the exigencies of the
service, nor the difficulty of communication between the
seat of government and the frontier, supply a satisfactory excuse. The example was pernicious, and became the
source of irritation and suspicion. "The President and

the secretary of war," says Stevens, a warm friend of
the administration, "experienced as statesmen, were to-
tally inexperienced in military affairs, and it was a violation of the plainest principles to endeavor to organize
campaigns without reference to those who had made
campaigns their special study."

On the 6th of November Gen. Taylor notified the Mexican authorities that the armistice would terminate on
the 13th. On that day Gen. Worth and his division
marched for Saltillo. On the 2d of December Gen. Hamer died, and, in the absence of Maj. Gen. Butler, the
command of the division devolved on Gen. Quitman.
Gen. Taylor having planned an expedition to Victoria,
the capital of Tamaulipas, a strong position on the line
of occupation between Monterey and Tampico, dispatched Gen. Twiggs with his division on the 12th of December. The 2d infantry and the 2d Tennessee Volunteers,
stationed at Camargo, were ordered to form a junction
with Twiggs at Montemorelos. On the 14th Gen. Quitman, with the 1st Tennessee regiment, Col. Campbell, the
1st Georgia, Col. Jackson, the 1st Mississippi, Maj. Bradford, and the 1st Baltimore battalion, Maj. Buchanan, in
all 1500 men, took up the line of march on the same
road which had so recently led them to victory. A narrative of this march and of the country is here abridged
from the journal of John S. Holt, Esq., military secretary
of Gen. Quitman.*

---

* Mr. Holt was an officer of the Wilkinson County Volunteers.
He has since represented Natchez in the Legislature, and is now a
prominent member of the bar of that city. When Gen. Quitman left
Victoria for Tampico he sent to Mr. H. the following note :

"Victoria, Mexico, Jan. 5th, 1847.

"DEAR SIR,—I pray you to take with you this note as a testimony of my sincere esteem and affectionate regard. You have been
acting as my military secretary for some months past, during which
time your conduct and deportment have been so exemplary, and you
have displayed so much intelligence and promptness in the execution

This journal gives us a new view of the Rio Grande provinces, and shows that they are well watered, fertile, and capable of sustaining an agricultural population. They belong by nature to our Gulf states, and must, in a few years, be annexed.

"The men were in fine spirits. Those who, when they had marched before, were lean and sickly, let out their belts a notch or two, and, slinging their rifles and muskets over their shoulders, took the route-step with a springiness which, however, was changed before night. Crossing the hollow where the army was drawn up, and below where, during the battle, Webster's mortar was placed, turning the point of bushes, and then ascending the hill, we had in our front a full view of the city, toward the left of which we were moving, and on our right, looming over the plain, the long line of wall composing the Black Fort. Standing in it are the dark and crumbling arches of the old unfinished cathedral, on the top of which the Mexicans made their bomb-proofs. Soon we rose the swell where the ricochet cannon ball cut down the seven Tennesseans, and we had to march past them. Pah! how it made the soul shrink in, to see the broken limbs, the blood, to hear the groans, and to see that one sitting on a rock, holding in his bowels, and singing a psalm!

"Farther on we passed the mud fort where the work of vengeance commenced. A dispute was raised as to which of the regiments was foremost in this most gallant action of the battle; whichever it was, they were in the same brigade, and had the same general.

"Still farther on a short distance, and on our left, was the Taneria, passing which, and going down a hill, we crossed the channel that conveys the water from the bridge of La Santa Purissima, the *tête du pont* of which proved so destructive to the regulars.

"Crossing this duct, and going about three hundred yards farther, we came to the wide channel of sand and

of your duties, as to win my highest regard and to deserve my sincere thanks. Wherever your lot may be cast, be assured of the friendship and esteem of J. A. QUITMAN, Brig. Gen. U. S. A."

rocks, in the centre of which runs the Rio Monterey, a large creek which bounds the back of the town. Passing this, as we did below the town, we had on our right the fort called Rincon del Diablo, and as some of the men saw it, and remembered what a 'devil's corner' it was, a long whistle would alone serve to convey the wonder, surprise, fright, impatience, and every other feeling which then agitated them.

"Mounting the steep bank on the farther side of the creek, we turned our backs upon the city, and had in front, about five miles off—though we appeared at its very foot—the Cerro Silla (Saddle Mountain), or, as we called it, the Comanche-saddle Peak.

"About four miles from Monterey, above the chapparal, rises the white spire of the village church of Gualupe. Through this little village we marched; the inhabitants, being used to us, had their stores open, and at the corners women sold corn bread and sweet bread, while the men tugged up to the side of the road their little donkeys loaded with sugar-cane or oranges.

"At half past two P.M. we arrived at the Rio Monterey, where it again crosses the road, and, fording it, camped on the top of the hill beyond.

"Tuesday, 15th. We left camp about seven o'clock this morning.

"To-day we passed through Cadereyta, a large town situated on the farther bank of the Rio Monterey, which we had again to cross. Our road ran through the plaza, that necessary part of every Mexican town, where are collected most of the sight-worthy objects. The houses surrounding this one were of one and two stories in height, and in its centre stands a column about twenty feet high, erected, we were told, to the memory of General Cadereyta. There was also, upon one side of the square, the commencement of a church, which bids fair to be a fine one, and in front of it were its bells, suspended to some stout beams, waiting the completion of their belfry. The materials of which this church, and most of the larger houses in this country are constructed, are a white, soft, and very porous limestone. Nothing can excel it for fortifications, as it will receive a ball without splintering, and is in fact a sort of fossil sponge or mineral cotton-bale. The Block Fort is built of it. The more common houses are of sun-dried brick about eighteen inches long, eight inches broad, and four in thickness, called *adobes*. The whole country being a sort of mixture of brick-kiln and cement, they are made without trouble.

"Surrounding the town is a deep ditch, which we crossed by a wooden bridge. For what it was dug, unless for a fortification, I can not conjecture, for it is too deep for purposes of irrigation. There is one thing I would here note particularly. The Alcalde of Gualupe had promised General Quitman to send him a guide, and, singular to relate, he kept his promise. I wonder if he lost caste for telling the truth once!

"About three miles and a half from Cadereyta, we came to the large hacienda of Santa Figinia (or Virginia), situated in the bottom watered by the Rio Guajuke, which, after passing near a mile through a lane of brush fence, we crossed and pitched our camp. It is a clear, swift mountain stream, about a hundred feet broad. We found encamped here a good many arrieros, with their trains of mules, on their way to Monterey with corn. The dexterity of these men, and the docility and intelligence of their animals, are very surprising. The pack-saddles are placed in a row when taken off, and when the mules are driven in from the bushes, whither they have wandered in search of food, they arrange themselves, each in front of his own saddle; and should one be so unfortunate as to forget his place, those on either side soon freshen his memory with their heels. What a lesson for schoolmasters! In loading, the arrieros place a blind over the eyes of the mule, and throwing on each side of the pack-saddle a fanega—which is three bushels, weighing about one hundred and fifty pounds—tie them together so firmly by a few magic turns of their rawhide ropes, that when the hoodwink is taken off and the mule realizes his situation, he generally, with a little wonder in his look, follows his brethren very peaceably, without any bridle, though he is at perfect liberty to run away or kick up if he can.

"On the journey some arrieros go before, leading often a white mare, which the mules follow as though charmed; others follow on their prancing little mustangs, the long spurs jingling, and with their short whips beat the erratic into the path again, vociferating, *sst mula! sst, sst mula!* with an emphasis and cadence peculiar to themselves.

"But that which involuntarily sets the mouth on a broad grin is to see a ranchero going from market on his donkey. Seated on the rump of the little animal, as far back as he can get, his spare, leather-encased legs, terminated like mauls, dangling down, and holding in his hand a short stick worn smooth, he presents a most ludicrous appearance.

"Sometimes they come in tied by halters to each other's tails, a boy driving the leader; and often you see an immense pile of green corn-stalks moving along without a wagon or, apparently, any thing else to carry it; but by watching closely you may occasionally catch a glimpse of the feet of the poor, patient little animal bearing the load which covers it, head, ears, all—thus very much resembling some two-legged animals with their load of vanity.

"Wednesday, 16th. We left camp early this morning, and very tired, for this was our third day's march, and old campaigners say it is always the hardest. After this the muscles begin to recover from their soreness. We were told at the last camp that we would find no water for a long distance after leaving there, except on creeks five miles off; but we were agreeably surprised at finding five creeks crossing the road before we arrived at the Rio de Ramos, where we camped. When within about two miles of the camping-ground we passed through the village, or ranch, of La Santa Purissima, a small cluster of miserable mud huts, into each one of which, however, our ranch-man doubtless examined minutely.

"This ranch-man, as he is called, is a singular being, belonging to one of the regiments, whose monomania, or hypochondria, or whatever it is, perhaps excels that of any other of all the crazy officers in the army. There is not a rancho, or any thing in the shape of one where humanity can dwell, in a mile of the road, but that his long, sallow, anxious face protrudes within the door, and his big, hungry eyes go wandering over the rafters and all about the house, in search of edibles of any shape or character whatever; first into this one, then gliding out into that, like the restless spirit of hunger, he haggles with some old crone for an egg, or holding back from the suspicious Mexican the string of dried beef, and half hiding it, in his selfishness, lest some other spy it and out-bid him, he trades with the eagerness and sternness of necessity, and then his spider-like legs bear him' off through the chapparal toward the marching line, chuck-ling at the bargains he has made, and gloating over the prospect of the good big supper he will make off of it. Wandering from the road in this way, he undergoes, in his monomania, more real peril than he would like to do for a more worthy object.

"The Rio de Ramos is the prettiest and largest creek we have yet seen. At the ford there is a fall of about eight feet in three hundred yards, which renders it rather ticklish wading. About four o'clock in the evening, while walking on the banks, I was surprised to see some dragoons emerge from the chapparal and ride into the ford; then came others, and finally General Taylor and staff, and Captain Sibley's supply train, escorted by the command of Lieutenant Fowler Hamilton, all of whom we had left in Monterey.

"Thursday, 17th. General Taylor left camp before us this morning. Traveling at our leisure, we had a very pleasant march, and camped within two miles of Monte Morelos, at which place are concentrated the troops from Camargo and those which preceded us from Monterey. We crossed three creeks to-day, and, when within a mile and a half of camp, overtook General Taylor and Captain Sibley's train going up a hill so long and steep that it was necessary to double teams; our train having the same difficulty, they did not all arrive in camp until after dark. General Taylor went on to town, and our di-vision encamped on an irrigating ditch called Garrapa-tas, supplied, I presume, from the Rio Garrapatas (Tick River), which we crossed some distance back. Well does Camp Garrapatas deserve its name, for the ticks cover it, crawling about on the grass, first upon one blade, and by their weight bending it down, then on to an-other, and with their spraddling legs hurrying up the stiff seed-stems and the thorn-bushes to look out for something to bite.

"About four o'clock in the evening four dragoons passed us in great haste, bearing a dispatch from General Worth, at Saltillo, announcing that a large force of Mexicans was advancing on him, and that he expected to be attacked in three days.

"Friday, 18th. Generals Taylor and Twiggs, with the division of the latter, which is the best rested, having been here for several days, accompanied by Bragg's battery, started this morning for Saltillo, leaving General Quitman in command of the rest of the troops, with orders to advance to-morrow toward Victoria, where, it is represented, there is a Mexican army, and which is about half way between Monterey and Tampico.

"General Quitman commenced by dividing the troops into two brigades, the 1st under Colonel Campbell, of the 1st Tennessee regiment, and the 2d under Colonel Jackson, of the Georgia regiment, Colonel Davis, of the Mississippi Rifles, being absent in the United States.

"All the general staff officers have to be changed, and, among others, the quarter-masters, the one heretofore acting as quarter-master general having to go with General Taylor. The wagons, mules, horses, extra tongues, even to the very nails and screws—all the paraphernalia of a large army—he has had in his charge, have to be counted and passed over, with the requisite papers, to another.

"The 1st Tennessee regiment moved into town to-day. General Quitman also moved his quarters within half a mile of town, toward the mountains, into an alley of poplars, part of which has been destroyed.

"The town of Monte Morelos is small, and situated at the foot of the Sierra Madre, on the Rio Morelos, a swift mountain creek. This beautiful valley is apparently very fertile, and, though not now much cultivated, it appears, from the numerous irrigating ditches now half filled up and grown over with grass, and from the long alley of trees, to have been at one time in a state of high improvement.

"Since the day we left Monterey, our march has been between two ranges of mountains. On our left, about fifteen miles off, the Sierra Seralvo lies like a dark cloud upon the horizon, and we march sometimes under the very shadow of the Sierra Madre, whose tall peaks tower high on our right, and which extends as far as the eye can reach—far away, until it becomes absolutely tantalizing, for we are told that our road lies all the way at its foot, and every hill we mount as we progress brings in view some new portion in the distance. We have noticed every night fires on the top of the Sierra Madre opposite to our camp. It has been very cold for four days. The changes of the weather in winter are much more sudden and violent here than with us at home, owing to the northers, which fall as swift and withering as misery upon the poor.

"Saturday, 19th. The 1st Tennessee regiment and part of the train left Monte Morelos very early this morning. It was very cold, and, though the creek rushed along smoking as if it had just boiled up from a volcano, it made our bones ache as we waded it, and the water came as high up as the thigh, and it seemed to cut like a knife, and the round stones on the bottom rolled over when stepped upon in a most disagreeable complaisant manner. After marching near two miles, we came to the camp of the 2d Tennessee regiment, which forming in our rear we marched on about a mile and halted to let the other brigade catch up; we then moved on, and, after a pleasant march, arrived at Rancho Nogales, which is about the fourth of a mile to the left of the road, and nine miles from Monte Morelos. Here we camped, being informed that there was no more water for five leagues. To-day we crossed two creeks.

"Rancho, or ranch, has become with our army the common designation for every sort of Mexican house, in every position, whereas, with the Mexicans themselves, it has a particular signification. Not only because of the sterility of the soil, but because also, in consequence of the uncertainty of the rainy season, the inhabitants are obliged to resort to irrigation to make sure their crops, no portion of this country is cultivated but the creek bottoms. Fixing their houses in some rich bottom, they ascend the creek a distance necessary to insure the water always on a level with their fields, then, building a stout stone dam across it, convey the water by means of ditches around hills and through valleys, sometimes for several miles, to where they wish it. Often, on the march, we have found a ditch high up on the side of a barren hill. Having this ditch to run on the higher side of their fields, which are divided by means of smaller trenches into beds, when the crop needs irrigation they open gaps here and there, and, letting the water flow, a man goes before with a hoe, and damming in this place, and opening a trench in that, soon waters a large spot of ground. To divide the great expense of making dams and trenches, and for the additional purpose of mutual protection in this border country, several of these *labores* generally lie together, and the houses of their owners also together, forming a village, and this is called a rancho. Those places owned by the more opulent persons, and where sugar and corn are cultivated on a large scale by means of *peones* and hired persons, are called haciendas, from the verb hacer, to make; thus being what we, in English, would call factories. The difference between the two, rancho and hacienda, appears, then, to be both in the number of the owners and the quantity produced. Rancho Nogales appears to be more of a place for cattle-minders and goatherds than a regular rancho. Situated on the side of a large hill, we have from it a view of an immense basin, shaped like a tin funnel mashed about the centre, formed by the hills connected with this, to which there is no apparent outlet. We can see our *voluntarios* ranging among the chapparal, although just off a march, seeing what can be seen—a prominent trait in American character. In the bottom is a creek, small, but affording enough of water.

"20th. Rather a desolate march to-day to the Rio Ramos, a fine clear stream.

"21st. Passed through Linares, a town of 7000 inhabitants, surrounded by fields of corn and sugar-cane.

"22d. Camped on a fine creek 10 miles beyond Linares.

"To-day one of our Mississippians, foot-weary and straggling in the rear of the column, got up behind a ranchero for a ride, giving him his rifle to carry. The Mexican soon dextrously twitched him off the horse and rode away with the weapon! The country to-day was rolling and rocky, abounding with deer, pheasants, and peccanes, an animal between a pig and a porcupine.

"23d. A hilly country; water scarce, but, for the first time on this march, plenty of muskeet-grass, covering the ground like a mat, knee-deep; camped on the River Parida, amid rich cane and corn fields, and parrots by the thousand screaming around us.

"Dec. 24th. Left the camp about seven o'clock this morning. El Pilon, or Sugar-loaf Mountain, was pointed out to us as the landmark of Villa Gran, which is about six miles off. This peak, rising to a great height above those which surround it, is quite conspicuous.

"Gen. Quitman, Lieut. Lovell, his aid, and the rest of his staff, together with Lieut. Meade, of the Topographical Engineers, Lieut. Thomas, commanding the battery, and Col. Kinney, the Texan, rode ahead to take breakfast in state at Villa Gran.

"Gen. Quitman has acted wisely in accepting these invitations, for he thus quiets the fears, and, by showing confidence, gains the confidence of the inhabitants. There is not another general in the volunteer or regular service who has as much high moral influence over his officers and men, or one who has a more excellent aptitude for procuring respect for his country from the enemy. By only acting out the impulses of his good heart, he could gain the love of all; but by uniting to these wisdom and firmness, and meting out even-handed justice, he has gained the highest respect. No man has done more for the volunteer service than he. By restraining and punishing, severely when necessary, the excesses of the bad; by acting as a polite gentleman to all; and, though the most essentially military in appearance and manners of the volunteer generals, never putting on that tragico-devilish voice and action thought by so many others to be a necessary component of the true military character; in fine, bringing the character of martinet down to that of a just judge, a humane man, and an amiable and polite gentleman, his men come to him in confidence as to a friend, and his brigade has become as celebrated for good conduct in camp and on the march as it was for terrible courage in the conflict.

"Dec. 25th (Christmas). The road to-day was tolerably good; the hills, if in any thing differing, were more abrupt, but there were still the same stunted chapparal, disagreeable prickly-pear bushes, and infinity of stones of all sizes, from the minute pebble to the lofty mountain.

"Soon after leaving camp, a deputation from Hidalgos waited on the general for the purpose of surrendering their town, on which we were advancing. When within about two miles of the town, we passed through an extensive forest, bordering the banks of a fine creek. It must have been quite a mile and a half in breadth, and it was delightful to pass from the glare of the hot sun (although on Christmas-day) into the cool, quiet shade. I wonder if the grave is not, to some good men, like this wood was to us?

"About noon we passed through Hidalgos. The town is as small as Villa Gran, and looked very desolate and ruinous. In place of a stone column, as at Cadereyta, there was in the centre of the plaza a palm-tree, standing solitary, far from its companions of the grove. It completed a sad picture.

"After leaving Hidalgos we passed two creeks, one near the town, the other about two miles off, called the San Jose, upon which we camped.

"The nights in this climate are beautiful; and which, of all the nights in the year, should be more so than this —Christmas-night!

"Dec. 26th. We left camp early this morning, and, after going about nine miles, and finding there was no other water for twelve miles farther, camped on the Rio Mecca, or Rio de la Purificacion, near a ranch called the Chopo. Saw a good many very large rabbits about the camp: their color is gray, and they are about three times as large as our common rabits. The river upon which we have camped is very swift, and much larger than any other we have yet crossed.

"27th. An alarm to-day. Our men on the *qui vive*, and anxious for a fight. No such luck. 3 P.M. emerged from the hills into an extensive plain, in which stands the hacienda of Don Simion Porl, a French physician, the largest and best cultivated plantation we have yet seen. The sugar here is made into pilensi (little sugar-loaves) resembling maple-sugar, which are transported on mules to the large cities to be refined. The orchards were luxuriant with the orange, lime, lemon, and shaddock, planted regularly and watered by little artificial rills. A detachment of 250 Mexican cavalry camped here last night, and left early for Victoria.

"28th. Having no cavalry, and feeling the need of it, Gen. Quitman to-day organized a troop, and placed it under the command of Lieut. Patterson, an active and enterprising officer of the 1st Mississippi regiment. They went immediately on a scout.

"29th. The road to-day was good, and plenty of water. A deputation from Victoria came out and surrendered the town. We marched in, formed on the plaza, and took possession of the government-house, where Gen. Quitman took up his quarters.

"Dec. 30th. Our march to this place has been made over a country never before penetrated by our army—a barren, rugged country, filled with inhospitable and hostile inhabitants, who, before we passed, would have called upon the rocks and stones to blast us from their presence. Through this there passed an army of volunteers —a kind of force thought almost incapable of control— commanded, it is true, by officers, but the bands of authority were placed upon them by their own permission, and, like the green withes upon Samson, might have been snapped in a moment, as tow when touched by the fire. We had, as incumbrances, immense quantities of baggage, extra supplies, mules, wagons, and all the paraphernalia necessary for the transportation and continued support of our force.

"But, to crown this formidable list of obstacles, we were at this critical period placed under the command of a brigadier general of volunteers, a man who, but three or four months before, had been in his first battle—who, although his masterly mind and cool courage had been tried in the actual conflict, had never yet been tested as to his powers of endurance, his capacity for a long-continued draw upon his military resources, his capability for supporting a burden under which men of far longer experience have found their shoulders ache, and which they have been obliged to resign. Gen. Taylor, in this instance, was sagacious, for, under Gen. Quitman, the rugged steep was patiently surmounted; the enemy retired; that worse enemy, the hate of the inhabitants, was conquered; volunteer troops proved themselves to be most efficient, and, controlled by wisdom and kindness, forgot their superior physical power, and extorted an approving glance even from their denouncers. On the whole march we lost not a man, or even a mule—a thing, we doubt not, unparalleled in the marchings in Mexico. Gen. Quitman seldom dismounted from his horse to take his rest until every part of the army and train were safe in their places in camp.

"January 4th, 1847. Gen. Taylor arrived from Monterey with the troops he had taken back with him. Col. Jefferson Davis came with him.

"Gen. Patterson arrived from Matamoras with the 3d and 4th regiments of Illinois troops, the Tennessee horse, and Lieut. Gibbon's section of artillery.

"Jan. 6th. Major Williams, of the Georgia regiment, is acting governor of the town, and affairs go on quite smoothly.

"Gen. Taylor visited the Illinois Volunteers yesterday, and the way the boys crowded around him threatened immediate suffocation. By way of salutation, I verily believe the old general pulled at his cap five thousand times, and I was looking every minute to see him pull the front-piece off. The general was mounted on a large and gentle mule, while his orderly rode a splendid dragoon horse, and was himself dressed in a clean and handsome uniform, while the general had on that same old black frock-coat, and a big Mexican straw hat. Mr. Fannin, the orderly, got about six salutes to Taylor's one, the 'Suckers' taking him for the general, and wondering why they called him *old* Taylor. When at last they found out that the old ranchero was the sure-enough general, they inferred from his plain appearance that it would be nothing amiss to offer him a hand to shake, and they went at it with such good-will, that by the time the two regiments finished squeezing it, there could have been little feeling left in it. As he rode off, there were many who wondered whether that was the animal on which he charged the Mexicans."

"We have now at this point a very pretty little army. Gen. Taylor is here with all his staff—Gen. Twiggs, with the 1st, 2d, 3d, and 7th regular infantry—the 2d dragoons, mounted riflemen, and Bragg's battery, all numbering 1900 men. Gen. Patterson has the regiment of mounted Tennesseans, two regiments of Illinois infantry, two companies of artillery, and a company of sappers and miners, making in all a little over 1700 men. Gen. Quitman has the two regiments of Tennessee infantry, 1st Mississippi do., 1st Georgia do., and the Baltimore battalion, and his total will not fall short of 2100 effective men—so that all together we can present to an enemy 5700 men."[*]

On the 15th it was announced in general orders that General Taylor would return to Monterey, to continue on the frontier, and the rest of the command would proceed to Tampico, under orders from Major General Scott. General Taylor decided to take the 1st Mississippi regiment with him, much to the regret of General Quitman, but fortunately for the glory of that celebrated corps. Soon afterward they took a brilliant and decisive part in the great battle of Buena Vista, and their heroic leader won imperishable fame.

The battle of BUENA VISTA belongs to the general history of the war, but as a Mississippian I may be pardoned for referring to the brilliant and decisive part taken in it by the Mississippi Rifles under the command of Col. Jefferson Davis.

The battle had been raging some time with fluctuating fortunes, and was setting against us, when Gen. Taylor, with Col. Davis and others, arrived on the field. Several regiments (which were subsequently rallied and fought bravely) were in full retreat; O'Brien, after having his men and horses completely cut up, had been compelled to draw off his guns, and Bragg, with almost superhuman energy, was sustaining the brunt of the fight. Many officers of distinction had fallen. Col. Davis rode forward to examine the positions of the enemy, and con-

---

[*] Letter from "Chapparal," in New Orleans Delta.

cluding that the best way to arrest our fugitives would
be to make a bold demonstration, he resolved at once to
attack the enemy, there posted in force, immediately in
front, supported by cavalry, and two divisions in reserve
in his rear.   It was a resolution bold almost to rashness,
but the emergency was pressing.   With a handful of
Indiana Volunteers, who still stood by their brave old
colonel (Bowles), and his own regiment, he advanced at
double-quick time, firing as he advanced.   His own
brave fellows fell fast under the rolling musketry of the
enemy, but their rapid and fatal volleys carried dismay
and death into the adverse ranks.   A deep ravine separated the combatants.   Leaping into it, the Mississippians soon appeared on the other side, and with a shout
that was heard over the battle-field, they poured in a
well-directed fire, and rushed upon the enemy.   Their
deadly aim and wild enthusiasm were irresistible.   The
Mexicans fled in confusion to their reserves, and Davis
seized the commanding position they had occupied.   He
next fell upon a party of cavalry, and compelled it to fly,
with the loss of their leader and other officers.   Immediately afterward a brigade of lancers, 1000 strong, were
seen approaching at a gallop, in beautiful array, with
sounding bugles and fluttering pennons.   It was an appalling spectacle, but not a man flinched from his posi•
tion.   The time between our devoted band and eternity
seemed brief indeed.   But conscious that the eye of the
army was upon them, that the honor of Mississippi was
at stake, and knowing that, if they gave way, or were
ridden down, our unprotected batteries in the rear, upon
which the fortunes of the day depended, would be captured, each man resolved to die in his place sooner than
retreat.   Not the Spartan martyrs at Thermopylæ—not
the sacred battalion of Epaminondas—not the tenth legion of Julius Cæsar—not the Old Guard of Napoleon

ever evinced more fortitude than these young volunteers in a crisis when death seemed inevitable. They stood like statues, as frigid and motionless as the marble itself. Impressed with this extraordinary firmness, when they had anticipated panic and flight, the lancers advanced more deliberately, as though they saw for the first time the dark shadow of the fate that was impending over them. Col. Davis had thrown his men into the form of a re-entering angle (familiarly known as his famous V movement), both flanks resting on ravines, the lancers coming down on the intervening ridge. This exposed them to a converging fire, and the moment they came within rifle range each man singled out his object, and the whole head of the column fell. A more deadly fire was never delivered, and the brilliant array recoiled and retreated, paralyzed and dismayed.

Shortly afterward, the Mexicans having concentrated a large force on the right for their final attack, Col. Davis was ordered in that direction. His regiment had been in action all day, exhausted by thirst and fatigue, much reduced by the carnage of the morning engagement, and many in the ranks suffering from wounds, yet the noble fellows moved at double-quick time. Bowles's little band of Indiana Volunteers still acted with them. After marching several hundred yards they perceived the Mexican infantry advancing, in three lines, upon Bragg's battery, which, though entirely unsupported, held its position with a resolution worthy of his fame. The pressure upon him stimulated the Mississippians. They increased their speed, and when the enemy were within one hundred yards of the battery and confident of its capture, they took him in flank and reverse, and poured in a raking and destructive fire. This broke his right line, and the rest soon gave way and fell back precipitately. Here Col. Davis was severely wounded.

The V movement has been recently criticised as neither original nor meritorious. The reverse is true. At Waterloo there was a movement somewhat similar, but differing in essentials. By looking at a detail map of that great battle, it will be seen that some Hanoverian cavalry were thrown out before the position occupied by a body of infantry, at the intersection of two main roads, near Quatrebras. Some French hussars, as soon as the cavalry of the allies had passed beyond the wood which covered their movement, charged, and drove them at full speed back on the supporting infantry. The infantry formed along the ditch of the two roads, so as to occupy two sides of a square, the apex toward the enemy; and when the pursuing hussars were sufficiently uncovered, the two lines obliquing, concentrated so deadly a fire upon the French they were compelled to retreat. This case—the only one cited—is not only different, but is, in fact, the very opposite of what occurred at Buena Vista. They formed a salient, we a re-entering angle. Theirs was the ordinary disposition of troops who, not having time to "form square," "re-fuse one wing" to repel attack; ours the novel proceeding of inviting cavalry inside of infantry lines. If such a movement was ever made before, I can not find it in military history from Plutarch to Napier. The great Wellington, who knew something of the art of war, and who kept his eye upon the map and traced the operations of Taylor and Scott, pronounced this movement new and masterly.

The other criticism, that there was no peculiar merit in it, because it was a palpable necessity forced upon Col. Davis by the nature of the ground, is fallacious. If a soldier, driven by necessity, seizes upon the accidents of ground to defend his position, and thus achieves victory instead of suffering defeat, he would be entitled to the highest military praise; and such has been the award from Cæsar to Turenne, and from Jackson to Taylor. In our case, moreover, it was not an absolute necessity. It was a bold experiment, a desperate hazard voluntarily encountered (by an officer who knew his men and the weapons they carried), to save from capture our unprotected batteries, then holding the key of the battle-field.

The reports of Gen. Taylor, Gen. Jo. Lane, and other distinguished officers, bear testimony to the great talent, coolness, and courage evinced on the field by Col. Davis, and the intrepidity of his troops.

Maj. Gen. Patterson, now in command of Victoria, marched forthwith to Tampico, from which point the troops were transported to the island of Lobos, where Gen. Scott organized the army of invasion. Quitman's command (a part of Patterson's division) consisted of the South Carolina, Georgia, and Alabama regiments.

1847. On the 9th of February the troops disembarked near Vera Cruz, and on the 10th the investment commenced. Patterson's division had the honor of the first brush with the enemy. Gen. Pillow drove before him, after a brisk fire, a strong detachment of skirmishers, and seized the hacienda Malibran and a magazine near by. On the 11th, Gen. Quitman was ordered to relieve Pillow. An extract from his report succinctly details the operations of the day:

" My command, the Georgia regiment, Col. Jackson, in advance, was moved to the heights at an early hour in the morning. The enemy appeared on the sand-hills in front of us in considerable force. While the South Carolina regiment was forming the enemy opened a fire at long range, but soon pushed forward strong parties of infantry, whose escopettes were quite annoying to a portion of our line. At the same moment a considerable body of cavalry made a demonstration on our right. A brisk cannonade from the city opened upon us, and there was reason to expect a serious effort to drive us from our position. I had just completed my dispositions for a movement against the enemy, when Maj. Gen. Patterson and staff rode up. He approved of my arrangements, and left their execution to me. Capt. Davis's rifle company, Georgia regiment, was thrown forward as sharpshooters. Lieut. Col. Dickinson, of the South Carolina regiment, was directed to advance with two companies to the right, to cover the rifles and watch the Mexican cavalry, about 500 strong, manœuvring on our right. Capt. Davis soon became actively engaged. He was joined by Capt. Sumpter, with his company of South Carolinians. Under the effective fire of these companies the Mexican infantry were soon driven from their advanced positions, but still continuing to menace our right. Maj. Gladden was sent forward with the companies of Capts. Moffatt, Secrist, and Marshall, of the Carolina regiment. This movement, with the effective fire from our skirmishers, compelled the enemy to retire from the neighboring heights, though not without some loss on our side. Lieut. Col. Dickinson, while gallantly leading the advance detachment, was severely wounded by a musket ball in the breast, and likewise several officers and privates of the several regiments. Col. Dickinson, though suffering much, refused to leave the field. My whole command displayed the utmost coolness and anxiety to meet the enemy."

The general-in-chief determined to reduce Vera Cruz by bombardment. His batteries were judiciously located,* and, after having vainly summoned the city to

---

* Three of them by Lieut. Beauregard (now brevet major, U. S. Engineers), a native of Louisiana, distinguished in almost every battle from Vera Cruz to the Belen Gate, and honorably mentioned by the general-in-chief, and by Quitman, Smith, Shields, and others in their reports. Gen. Pierce, just before his election to the presidency, in a private letter to the author, thus referred to this officer:

"Do you know Major (formerly Lieutenant) Beauregard, of the engineer corps? His father's residence is near New Orleans, and he was there when I last heard from him. If you do not, I wish you to make his acquaintance. He is a man of rare attainments, and, like many Louisianians whom I have met in the army and elsewhere, he combines the best qualities of a gentleman and a soldier.

surrender, he opened upon it in the afternoon of the 22d.

On the 25th a prisoner informed the general-in-chief that Santa Anna was advancing with 6000 men to raise the siege. Gen. Patterson was ordered to push one of his brigades to the extreme left to maintain the ground occupied by the first and second infantry, who were transferred to another position. Gen. Quitman was selected for this post of honor. The report, however, proved erroneous, and next day the city surrendered.

Gen. Scott, having planned an expedition by sea and land to Alvarado, a city in one of the most fertile districts of Mexico, and which had contributed largely to the commissariat of the enemy, directed Maj. Gen. Patterson to hold a brigade in readiness. "Besides capturing the city and forts," said the general-in-chief, "the object is to conciliate the good-will of the inhabitants along the route, and to encourage them to supply the army with mules and fresh provisions—much wanted for our advance into the interior."

Gen. Quitman was designated for this important undertaking, and reported at once to head-quarters. His instructions were as follows:

"Head-quarters of the Army, Vera Cruz, March 30th, 1847.
"SIR,—You are designated with your brigade, a section of Steptoe's field battery, and a squadron of dragoons, for a land expedition, in co-operation with a naval force, in the direction of Alvarado, and you have been placed in communication with Commodore Perry, commanding U. S. Home Squadron, on the subject. * * *
The general objects of this expedition are to capture the city of Alvarado and places in its vicinity, including the works near the mouth of the river leading from that

"Pray write me all that concerns yourself, and come in the summer and visit our mountains, farm-houses, and battle-fields.
"Very sincerely your friend,   FRANK. PIERCE.
"Col. J. F. H. Claiborne."

city—in all of which you will zealously co-operate with, and, no doubt, be powerfully aided by the naval force. The rule of co-operation between land and naval forces is, that the commander of each branch of the service shall consult freely with the other commander, and when the object and manner of attack shall be jointly determined upon, each commander in good faith and to the extent of his power shall carry out his part of the service. Consequently, the commander of neither branch of the service can, strictly speaking, give orders to the other branch. But great deference will always be shown by one command to the other. I presume that the time for reaching the objects of attack has been settled between Com. Perry and yourself; you will commence your march accordingly. With great confidence in your zeal, abilities, and judgment, and wishing you full success, I am, sir, etc., etc. WINFIELD SCOTT."

Quitman's official report will show the result of this expedition.

"Head-quarters 2d Brigade, Volunteer Division, Camp, Vera Cruz, April 7th, 1847.

"SIR,—I have the honor to submit a brief report of the expedition to Alvarado, with which I was charged by orders from the commander-in-chief.

"My command, consisting of the regiments from Georgia, Alabama, South Carolina, a squadron of dragoons, under Major Beall, and a section of artillery, under command of Lieutenant Judd, left their camp about 3 o'clock P.M. on the 30th of March, and advanced that evening to the mouth of Madelin River, when we encamped. I had previously arranged with Commodore Perry a plan of co-operation for the expedition against Alvarado, in which it was stipulated that, whether resistance were made or not, the land and naval forces would effect an entrance at the same time, and act conjointly with each other. In crossing the Madelin River, on the morning of the 31st, I was greatly indebted to the assistance of the navy, in preparing a bridge of boats, under the energetic direction of Lieutenant Whitwell, first lieutenant of the Ohio ship of the line. The march on the 31st lay partly along the beach, through deep sand, and partly over a plain country, in rear of Lizardo. On the 1st of March [April] we again struck the beach, and pursued it to the mouth of the Alvarado River with the infantry and train. I reached the town of Alvarado with the cavalry on the evening of the 1st of March [April], about half an hour after Commodore Perry had landed there. In the mean time, when about fifteen miles from the town, I had received a note from Midshipman Temple, of the steamer Scourge, informing me that the town had surrendered, and requesting the commander of the land-forces to hold it. This note is annexed to this report. Immediately upon my arrival Commodore Perry expressed to me his disapproval of the act of Mr. Hunter, the commander of the Scourge, in landing; and has, I learn, signified it more publicly by the arrest of that officer.

"My command was posted in the town during my stay there. On the 2d, Commodore Perry, in the steamer Spitfire, proceeded up the river to the town of Tlacatalpa, having invited me to join him. My presence being required in camp, I sent with the expedition Lieutenant Derby, of the topographical engineers. Commissioners from that town conferred with the commodore and myself at Alvarado. They had made an unconditional surrender of their town and the neighboring country to our arms, and promised to furnish a number of horses, at least 500, to the quarter-master's department, at low prices. The town of Alvarado contains about 1200 to 1500 inhabitants, most of whom, however, had fled on our approach. With the surrender of the town there fell into the hands of our naval and military forces twenty-two pieces of artillery, some ammunition, and military equipments of minor value, all of which were left in the possession of the naval forces on our departure, as the common capture of the naval and land forces. On the morning of the 4th of April my command left Alvarado, and reached its camp at Vera Cruz on the forenoon of the 6th, having again been indebted to the active and prompt assistance of First Lieut. Whitwell, of the navy, and the officers under his command, in crossing the Madelin at its mouth. I have the pleasure to report that, although the leading objects of the expedition had been anticipated by the surrender of the city,

N 2

the other objects designated in my instructions have been fully accomplished. The Mexican population to the southward of this point have been conciliated by the exemplary conduct of the troops. On my departure from Alvarado I had the gratification to receive the thanks of the alcalde, the cura, and the principal men, for the protection afforded to them and to their property. I feel perfectly assured that our march has made a favorable impression upon the inhabitants. Communications have been opened with the people of the fertile country near the River Alvarado, and negotiations opened for supplies of horses and beef cattle, in which the country abounds. Lieutenant Mason, of the engineer corps, was detailed to accompany the expedition. He joined my staff, and performed, at his own request, the duty of superintending the pioneers in the repairs of the roads, and greatly facilitated the march by his attention to this matter. His report to me, which is transmitted, will show the description and calibre of the captured guns. Lieutenant Derby, of the topographical engineers, volunteered to act generally on my staff, and was zealous and active in the duties assigned him. For the order and good conduct of my command I am also greatly indebted to the active assistance of Captain Deas, assistant adjutant general, and to the respective commanders of the regiments and separate commands. Commodore Perry, with his accustomed liberality, regards all captures as made jointly by both commands. I can not close this report without expressing the great gratification which an official intercourse with this patriotic and efficient naval officer has occasioned. I also beg leave to present the valuable services which I received from that efficient officer, Captain Irwin, assistant quarter-master, who had been detailed in that capacity under my command.

"I have the honor to be, very respectfully, your obedient servant,   J. A. QUITMAN,
         "Brig. Gen. U. S. A. commanding, etc.
"Lieut. H. L. Scott, A. A. A. General."

Commodore Perry, in his official report to the secretary of the navy, says : "On this expedition I have had the good fortune to become acquainted with Gen. Quitman and many of his officers, and have been gratified to observe a most cordial desire, as well with them as with the officers of the navy, to foster a courteous and efficient co-operation."

And now, the strong fortress of San Juan d'Ulloa and the city and harbor of Vera Cruz being in our possession, commenced a campaign which, considering the inequality of force, the defensible nature of the country, the populous cities, formidable fortifications, and pitched battles won by our arms, has scarcely a parallel in history. The events of this great drama have been detailed by able writers, and should be studied in the military reports. They can only be briefly referred to in this memoir.

On Quitman's return from Alvarado a portion of the army had marched from Vera Cruz for Jalapa, and it was rumored that they would encounter the enemy at Cerro Gordo. He found no transportation for his brigade, but resolved to march; and so eager were his "brave fellows to advance, they cheerfully carried their knapsacks, forty rounds of cartridges, and seven days' rations, over the burning sands. They only got up in time, however, to hear the booming of the last guns. The Mexicans were in full retreat."*

At Jalapa he rejoined the command of Maj. Gen. Patterson, encamped three miles west of the city. The term of service of the Tennessee Cavalry, the 3d and 4th Illinois Infantry, the Georgia and Alabama Infantry, and the 1st and 2d Tennessee Infantry being about to expire, they were sent to New Orleans to be honorably discharged. Maj. Gen. Patterson, being thus without a command suitable to his rank, was ordered to accompany the returning volunteers. The four volunteer regiments, viz., one from South Carolina, one from New York, the

* From Quitman's letter to Colonel John D. Elliott.

1st and 2d Pennsylvania, and a detachment of mounted Tennesseans, were formed into a brigade under Gen. Quitman. Of these, the 1st Pennsylvania regiment, Col. Wynkoop, was left to garrison Perote, and the 2d Pennsylvania regiment, Col. Roberts, to garrison Jalapa. With his command thus reduced, re-enforced, however, with Wall's battery, he was ordered to form a junction with Gen. Worth, then in advance. On this march, May 12th, he received his commission of major general, dated April 14th. He now considered himself the senior of Brevet Major General Worth, but fearing that the service might be injured by a contest for rank, and with a high appreciation of the talents of that veteran officer, he modestly withheld the claim, and cheerfully acted under his orders. They maintained throughout the war the most friendly relations.

General Worth reached Amozogue, eight miles from Puebla, on the 13th of May. Santa Anna, who lay in the vicinity with a large body of troops, having ascertained that Quitman was in the rear with a small force of volunteers, encumbered by a heavy train of wagons, detached 3000 cavalry to intercept him before he could form a junction with Worth. This movement was discovered, and Gen. Worth sent Col. Garland, with Duncan's field battery, to counteract it. They soon, by a few well-directed discharges, compelled the enemy to retreat. Santa Anna had expected to find Quitman some miles back, in the defile of Piñal. He was not apprised of the celerity and order that characterized the volunteers on the march. When they first heard Duncan's guns they were within three miles of Worth, in a compact column of march. The moment they perceived the enemy the line was formed, and they were ready to receive his charge. Squadron after squadron approached and wheeled into line in front. It was an imposing spectacle. Three cheers from the volunteers evinced their readiness to meet the shock of a superior force. Having closely observed our steady line of bristling bayonets, they concluded that "discretion was the better part of valor," and moved off to the adjacent mountains. In an hour afterward the junction was effected, and the advance of the army of invasion marched into the city of Puebla. It was an inspiring event. Ninety miles in advance of the main army, with only 3000 men, they entered a hostile city having a population of 80,000, which, only three years before, had defended themselves against Santa Anna and 3000 veterans, and now knew that he was in their vicinity with 6000 men to aid them in resisting the invaders. A vast concourse of scowling Mexicans thronged the streets, the roofs of the houses, and the balconies when the Americans entered the plaza and planted our national standard on the government buildings, but not an arm was raised for the defense of their beautiful city.

On the arrival of the general-in-chief Quitman applied for a command more proportioned to his rank.

General Quitman to General Scott.

"Head-quarters Volunteer Brigade, Puebla, May 29th, 1847.

"Sir,—I this morning received orders from general head-quarters establishing orderly hours, and thus announcing to me officially the presence and command of the general-in-chief. Since the receipt of these orders I have been informed that the regiments heretofore under my command have received direct orders from Brevet Major General Worth, have been paraded in readiness to march or to fight under his immediate orders, without any information, intelligence, or orders of any kind having been communicated to me. Finding Colonel Burnett's regiment under arms without my authority, I ordered him to dismiss the men to their quarters, but to keep them in readinesss to form in case of necessity. Having, however, in the mean time, received information from you through my aid, Lieutenant Lovell, that the order to parade the regiments was sanctioned by the authority of the general-in-chief, I have countermanded my directions to Colonel Burnett, and left him subject to the former order he had received from General Worth. If these measures have been taken under the authority of the general-in-chief, I consider myself stripped of my command.

"This evening I have received an order from Brevet Major General Worth to detail a company for guard at General Scott's head-quarters.

"You will readily perceive the very embarrassing circumstances in which I am placed, and the necessity I am under, however reluctantly, to trespass upon the time of the general-in-chief to ask his farther orders to extricate me from these embarrassments.

"I have the honor to be, very respectfully, your obediant servant,   J. A. QUITMAN, Maj. Gen. U. S. A.

"Capt. H. L. Scott, A. A. A. G., Head-quarters of the Army."

General Quitman to General Scott.

"Puebla, May 30th, 1847.

"Sir,—I have heretofore inclosed to your address two letters, the former dated at this place May 16th, the latter dated yesterday, the receipt of neither of which has been acknowledged.

"Supposing that the former may have been interrupted in its transmission, I inclose a copy; the latter, I am informed, was handed to you. I had determined to await the leisure of the general-in-chief for an answer to these letters, before making application to him for a command suited to my rank.

"In the mean time, I have received this day General Orders No. 162, the second paragraph of which, in effect, assigns me to the command of the two regiments of volunteers now here in the field.

"It is but due to the general-in-chief to state that I regard myself as senior officer under him, unless Brevet Major General Worth has been assigned to duty according to his brevet rank by the President, of which I am not informed.

"Under the order alluded to, my command will consist of but two regiments, while my juniors in rank, entitled only to brigades, are in command of divisions consisting of five and six regiments each. And this army would present the singular spectacle of brigadier generals commanding divisions, colonels and lieutenant colonels commanding brigades, and a major general commanding less than a brigade.

"I will not at this time present my views of the humiliating position in which such a distribution of the forces would place me; but I earnestly appeal to the sense of justice of the general-in-chief, and to his known respect to the institutions and laws of our country, the common source of the power and rights he as well as I possess, to assign to me a command in the army proportionate to my rank."

From General Scott.

"Head-quarters of the Army, Puebla, May 31st, 1847.

"Sir,—I have just received your letter of yesterday, inclosing a copy of one dated the 16th inst., which, as you have supposed, miscarried.

"I also received, the night before the last, your letter of the 29th inst., which I considered as substantially answered by my order of yesterday. Some confusion was unavoidable under the circumstances of my arrival, the consequent change in the general command, and the false alarm of the 29th.

"It takes a commander several days to learn the distribution of the troops made before his arrival, the approaches the enemy may avail himself of, the points of defense, etc., etc. Being much indisposed, I was slow in acquiring that knowledge, and, in the mean time, left much power in the previous commander of the advanced corps.

"I regret that you have addressed me the letter of the 30th, being much occupied with the ordinary business of the army and the high duties of the campaign, with all of which I should be happy to make you acquainted if you would call. I have no leisure for a laborious correspondence with the officers I have the honor to command, and who are near me.

"I have heretofore announced to this army in orders,

and reminded you by letter, that Brevet Major General Worth was assigned to duty here, in Mexico, according to his brevet rank.

"Since you marched from Jalapa a brigadier general of the United States army in the command of volunteers, I have been officially advised of your merited promotion, as I understand the law, to the rank of major general, attached to the new regiments authorized by a recent act of Congress, not one of which has arrived, though all of them were originally intended for this army. Portions of several of them, amounting to about 4000 men, have been, I learn, ordered to the Rio Grande frontier; should two or more of those regiments come under my immediate orders, they shall be assigned to your present division. That division, I am aware, is at present not embodied, being divided between Jalapa, Perote, and this place. Foreseeing that it would be so divided, I declared Major General Patterson to be a supernumerary with this army. You, at the date of that order, was only a brigadier general. The two regular divisions with me have also left detachments at Vera Cruz, Jalapa, and Perote, and have otherwise been much reduced.

"Not having with me the necessary number of troops to fill up your division without breaking up the other two, which I would deem inexpedient, if not highly unjust, to oblige you I might consent to send you to the new regiments ordered to the Rio Grande frontier, if it were practicable for you to go there in safety. But I do not think it practicable, and hope, therefore, under all the circumstances, you will remain in your present position, though somewhat anomalous, and let this army have the benefit of your valuable services. Casualities or changes, which could not have been foreseen at Washington or by me, and which have been entirely unavoidable, have placed you in that position. As a good soldier, a good man, and a good patriot, you will, I hope, cheerfully bend to circumstances. I should part from you at this time with deep regret. Your post is still one of honor, and you can fill it with distinction. Remain, then, and give me your cordial aid and support."

Gen. Quitman to Gen. Scott.

"Puebla, June 3d, 1847.

"SIR,—I have the honor to acknowledge the receipt of the letter of the general-in-chief of the 31st ult. His wishes not to be burdened with a farther correspondence on this subject prevailed with me for a time; but farther reflection convinced me that, while my opinions remained unchanged, he would more highly appreciate a frank reply. The position of this army, in the midst of a hostile population, and almost before the gates of their capital, leaves me, for the present, no alternative but to adhere to its fortunes, however my rank may be degraded or my rights as an officer overlooked. So deeply am I impressed with this conviction, that I would follow the destinies of this army as a volunteer sooner than abandon it at this moment. I have, therefore, no choice but to remain in the truly anomalous position in which the recent order places me; but I would be faithless to the trust which the President has reposed in me, and to the rights with which the laws of my country have invested me, were I to submit to the humiliating position assigned me in the army without entering my respectful protest against the construction placed by the general-in-chief upon my commission as major general, and against the order which limits my command to the volunteer troops in this army.

"I hold a commission as major general in the service of the United States; its language is the same as that ordinarily used in the regular army, without any other qualifications or limitations. If we refer back to the Act of Congress of the 3d of March, under which the President was authorized to appoint two additional major generals, we will find nothing in it which limits their command to the additional forces to be raised under the Act of the 11th of February preceding. The terms of the acts of Congress appear to me palpably inconsistent with such a construction, because they provide that no division shall consist of less than two brigades, of at least three regiments each, when but ten regiments are raised by the Act of the 11th of February, thus requiring at least two additional regiments from the regular or volunteer troops to constitute the minimum command of the major general. Moreover, these acts authorized the President to organize this additional military force into divisions and brigades indiscriminately with regular and volunteer troops; and, when thus organized, they may be commanded by any of the general officers of the army. I will not dwell upon the confusion and difficulty which would arise in the service if this construction be not correct.

"To present fairly and explicitly my objections to the limited command assigned to me by the second paragraph of General Orders No. 162, it is necessary to refer to the present organization of this army.

"The 1st division, commanded by Brevet Maj. Gen. Worth, consists, as I learn, of the 4th, 5th, 6th, and 8th regiments of infantry, the 2d and 3d regiments of artillery, and Lieut. Col. Duncan's battery; the 2d division, commanded by Brig. Gen. Twiggs, consists of the 2d, 3d, and 7th regiments of infantry, the 4th artillery, the rifle regiment, and Capts. Taylor and Talcott's batteries, besides the troops left behind in garrison. The division assigned to me consists only of the New York and South Carolina regiments, besides the 1st and 2d Pennsylvania regiments left in garrison—the 1st at Perote, under Col. Wynkoop, as commander of that department; the 2d, with other troops, under Brevet Col. Childs, of the artillery, as commander of the department of Jalapa; over neither of these regiments have I any authority; thus leaving my command to consist virtually of but the two first-named regiments. The brigades of the 1st division are respectively commanded by Col. Clarke and Brevet Col. Garland; those of the 2d, by Brevet Brig. Gen. Smith and Brevet Col. Riley. Each of these brigades has more effective men in the field than my whole actual command. This inequality, when taken in connection with my rank and the respective grades of the other officers, is so striking as to give me just cause of complaint; for, if it be considered highly unjust to any, or a portion of the officers now in command, under the temporary organization which now exists, to limit them to their appropriate command, how much more so to deprive a higher officer of the command unquestionably due to his rank?

"Heartily reciprocating the personal respect which

the general-in-chief has ever manifested toward me, and grateful for the kind expressions of his letter, I very reluctantly again advert to the question of rank heretofore presented by me. Believing, as I do, in common, as I am informed, with a large portion of the officers of the army, that the President of the United States alone has authority to assign an officer to duty according to his brevet rank, I owe it to myself and to the service to question the right of a brevet major general to command me, except in the cases specified in the 61st Article of War. Until I am advised that such assignment comes from the high source required by law, neither the order of the general-in-chief referred to, nor his letter addressed to me from Jalapa, gives me the desired information on this point.

"I should have been well content if the power had been reposed by law in the discretion of the commanding general; but, conscientiously believing that it is not so vested, a sense of duty requires me frankly to express my opinion upon this subject now, that the question may be settled by the proper authority, and that conflict of opinions hereafter may not produce inconvenience or do injury to the public service."

Notwithstanding this conflict in respect to rank, and a difference of opinion as to other grave matters, the relations between Gens. Scott and Quitman continued friendly and agreeable.* Quitman was ambitious; he had a proper conception of his own military talents, but no mean jealousy of the great commander under whom he served ever had a lodgment in his bosom. That was re-

---

* "Head-quarters, Puebla, August 2d.
"GENERAL,—If you have no pressing engagement, the general-in-chief will be glad to encounter you this evening in a game of chess.
"Very respectfully, T. WILLIAMS, A. A. C.
"Major General Quitman."

"Puebla, August 6th.
"GENERAL,—I am directed by the general-in-chief to request you to drop in, by the merest accident, at 9 o'clock this evening, to take a glass of hot punch. Very respectfully,
"J. HAMILTON, A. A. C.
"Major General Quitman."

served for presidential plotters at Washington and very small generals in Mexico. He had, nevertheless, the independence to differ with him on important questions of policy and strategy; but this independence never deprived him of the confidence of Scott.

CHAPTER XI.

Review of our Relations with Mexico.—Scott's Proclamation.—Disapproval of the President.—Ingersoll's Report.—Spirit of the South
and West.—Condition of Mexico.—Obstacles encountered by Taylor and Scott.—Mr. Trist.—His Mission.—Rupture and Reconciliation with Gen. Scott.—Gen. Pillow.—British and Mexican Intrigues.—Secret Conference at Puebla.—The Gomez Letter.—
Report of the Court of Inquiry.—Gen. Scott's Letter.—Quitman's
Position.

THE celebrated proclamation of Gen. Scott, issued at
Jalapa, on the 11th of May, 1847, for the consideration
of the Mexican people, set forth that war had been commenced on the part of the United States to counteract
the schemes of President Paredes, who was aiming to
overthrow the republic and establish a monarchy under
the protection of one or more of the European powers.
"Duty, honor, and dignity," said the proclamation,
"placed us under the necessity of not losing a season of
which the monarchical party in Mexico was fast taking
advantage." This paragraph President Polk condemned, and Mr. Marcy, the secretary of state, on the 15th of
June wrote to Gen. Scott that it was by no means "to
be considered as an authoritative exposition of the views
of the President," who had all along professed to depre-
cate the war as having been *forced* upon him by the attack of the Mexicans upon Gen. Taylor in April, 1846.
This pretense was more in accordance with the temporizing character of Mr. Polk than with the facts, or the
frankness of our national policy. As far back as 1837,
President Jackson announced that an immediate decla-

ration of war against Mexico would be justifiable, and recommended reprisals and blockades to enforce our just demands. From that period down to the arrival of Gen. Taylor on the Rio Grande, in 1846, we had been subjected by Mexico to almost every insult and injustice that one nation can offer to another. All these were enumerated by the Hon. C. J. Ingersoll, of Philadelphia, chairman of the House Committee of Foreign Affairs, in a report of great force and vigor, in which, however, there was too much effort to please the Puritanism of the President, and to secure his own re-election by a Quaker community.

The truth is, the American people, especially of the Southwestern and Western States, demanded war, and were determined to have it—just as much so as when the same people insisted on war with Spain to affirm our right to the free navigation of the Mississippi. The annexation of Texas, it was foreseen, would be followed by war, and it had substantially been declared by Mexico in the manifesto of President Parades of April 23d, 1846, before the commencement of hostilities on the Rio Grande.

But had none of the real or pretended motives that have been assigned for the war existed, the grounds upon which Gen. Scott placed it were sufficient. We should be faithless to our mission, and to our own interests, to permit the acquisition of territory or the re-establishment of monarchical institutions on this continent, under European auspices or intervention.* That

* The doctrine of European non-intervention, commonly attributed to President Monroe, originated with Mr. Jefferson. August 12th, 1790, when secretary of state, he thus wrote to Gouverneur Morris, our minister in Paris: "The consequences of their [the British] acquiring territory on our frontiers are too obvious to need development. We wish you to intimate that we can not be indifferent to enterprises of this nature; that we should contemplate a change of neighbors with great uneasiness; and that a due balance on our borders is not less de-

single sentence of the Jalapa proclamation to which Mr. Polk excepted comprehends the proper policy of our government, and expresses frankly the necessity for armed intervention that existed then, and which is imperative now. A country in perpetual insurrection—holding in contempt the comity of nations—under the dominion of brigands—overrun by savages in some quarters—in others perpetrating, with its own soldiery, more than savage enormities on its own citizens and on the citizens of other nations—refusing satisfaction for our pecuniary claims and national outrages—and liable, at any moment, to complicate our relations with European powers, is no safe neighbor for the United States. Humanity and interest, the stability of our institutions, and a wise forecast for the future, demand of us more than the intervention of an abortive diplomacy. Civilized communities provide guardians for the helpless and imbecile, and defenses against the lunatic and the outlaw. Mexico is, and long has been, in this relation to us, and as her next neighbor and nearest friend, and for our own safety, we should establish these relations with her, with or without her consent. American protection and immigration would soon restore peace, and be the guarantee for her future prosperity.

These were the views of Gen. Quitman when Gen. Scott's proclamation appeared, and he entertained them to the end of his life. The American executive, however, frightened by the howl of faction, and anxious to conciliate the New England sectarians, was determined on peace. What had been achieved on the Rio Grande frontier was due to the valor of our troops, coldly supported by the national government. Gen. Taylor had desirable to us than a balance of power in Europe has always appeared to them. We wish to be neutral, and we will be so if they will execute the treaty fairly, *and attempt no conquest adjoining us.*"—*Life of Morris*, vol. ii., p. 32.

fended Fort Brown, won two pitched battles, captured Matamoras, Camargo, and Seralvo, and penetrated the Mexican territory to Monterey, with but little aid from the government. He had carried that strongly-fortified city by assault after three days' hard fighting, only to be censured for granting terms to the defeated. The capitulation of Monterey, accepted by the hero of Palo Alto and Resaca de la Palma, had been disapproved by President Polk. He reiterated his determination to prosecute the war with energy, but, with singular inconsistency, considered 4000 men sufficient for the reduction of Vera Cruz ! Politicians wholly ignorant of campaigns planned campaigns. Neither Gen. Scott or Gen. Taylor were in favor, but when consulted they recommended the employment of not less than 30,000 effectives to carry on the war. What a satire on the army of 4000 suggested by the executive !

The appointment of a lieutenant general to take precedence of Scott and Taylor was urged by the President, and it was understood that the appointment would be conferred on the Hon. Thomas H. Benton, then a senator from Missouri, a man of unquestionable talents and energy, but without military education or experience. At the same time, N. P. Trist, chief clerk in the State Department, was sent out, with secret instructions, as commissioner to attend the army ; an appointment uncalled for, of questionable legality, without precedent in our own service, and in imitation of very bad precedents in Europe. The commissioner was, as might have been anticipated, received coldly by the general-in-chief and by the army. The former indignantly remonstrated against his mission, his presence, and his proceedings. The latter regarded him with suspicion, and deprecated any interference at that juncture with the arbitrament of arms. His operations are to this day, to some extent, matter of conjecture. Though treated with severity by the executive on his return to the United States, he never disclosed enough of his secret instructions and proceedings to rebuke his employer or to vindicate himself. His integrity and good sense, which had previously stood high, were called in question. Neither the odium of his mission, or the frown of the President, as unexpected as it was ungrateful, prevailed on him to explain. He became the target of his own party and the sneer of the opposition. A protegé of Jefferson, who had been the friend of his father ; in the confidence of both Jackson and Van Buren; a citizen of Virginia, educated in its most fastidious notions, both personal and political; of honorable official antecedents, and with a distinguished career in prospect, he submitted to injustice and misconstruction from friends and foes, and became at once a scapegoat, and "a dead cock in the pit." He refused to testify upon certain points before a court of inquiry, and his philosophy was proof against the ribaldry of the press. Mousing politicians badgered him in his retreat, and the chief magistrate, sole author of the ignoble mission, interposed no word in his defense. What was the extent of his powers, what his secret instructions, and how far he was sustained by the President until the mission became hateful to the nation and fatal to the popularity of all concerned, will be a problem until Mr. Trist himself gives the solution. And for this history must wait before it can be determined whether his silence was owing to dread of power, the hope of reconciliation and reward, or, most probably, to that scrupulous sense of honor which prefers suffering, and even death, to the loss of self-respect. The first Lord Shaftesbury, who abandoned the king for the Parliament, when appealed to to disclose the royal secrets, with a chivalry of feeling that atones for much of his political profligacy, said : "There

VOL. I.—O

is a general and tacit trust in conversation whereby a man is obliged not to report any thing to the speaker's prejudice, though no intimation may be given of a desire not to have it spoken of again."* This is the true rule of conversational intercourse and of trust, and Mr. Trist, it is presumed, has never felt himself at liberty to violate it, even though treated with marked ingratitude by the high functionary who most profited by his silence.

Mr. Trist, before leaving Washington, was fully apprised of the hostile feeling entertained against General Scott by the President and secretary of war, and his coincidence of feeling had recommended him to their favor.† This was well known to General Scott. The commissioner reached Vera Cruz in May, and, arrogantly ignoring the American general-in-chief, opened negotiations with the enemy. This was, of course, resented, and led to an open rupture, and to a correspondence discreditable to both, and which not even the provocation he had received can reconcile with the dignity of the general-in-chief. On hearing of the quarrel, the American secretary of state, in a letter characteristic of his bland temper and enlightened judgment, directed Mr. Trist to discontinue his vituperative correspondence with Gen. Scott, and make a full communication of the objects of his mission. This dispatch established harmony between the parties. Mr. Trist had been directed by the President to exhibit his secret instructions to Gen. Pillow, and to confer confidentially with him. Gen. Pillow had privately been employed by the same high authority to confer with Mr. Trist, and to "protect the honor of the existing administration"—a covert implication against the American general and his comrades in arms, which Gen. Pillow himself should have been the first to disdain. These gentlemen communicated to each other their mutual powers

* Locke's Memoir.   † Ripley, vol. ii., p. 97.

and secret instructions, and held frequent conferences with Gen. Scott, to which no other officer was admitted. Communications were opened with the enemy through the agency of the British minister, who dispatched his secretary to the American head-quarters at Puebla to confer with this extraordinary triumvirate. The spectacle, even at this distance of time, is humiliating. It shocks our national pride, this intervention of an antagonistical diplomacy with a treacherous enemy, from whom no`justice or good faith could be expected but at the point of the sword. Great Britain had intrigued against us in every quarter of the world; her diplomatists and capitalists had encouraged and sustained Mexico in her course of outrage against the United States; she had exerted all her art to prevent the annexation of Texas, with the view of establishing a refuge on our southern border for fugitive slaves, in harmony with her former Indian policy which had so often deluged our northwestern frontier with blood. From the moment the war commenced, her metropolitan press, the organs of every faction, had pronounced Mexico impregnable, and predicted disaster to our arms. Yet, notwithstanding this, the American executive, the head of a great republic, elected, too, by a party never accused of Anglo-mania, permitted his generals and secret agents to be in frequent and confidential communication with British ministers, consul generals, attachés, and speculators, and, as one of the parties avers, "the army halted or advanced, attacked an out-work or consented to an armistice, as these agents of Great Britain advised!"* If this be true, there has not been, since the treason of Arnold, any thing so disgraceful in our military history. It was more degrading than the surrender of Hull. No part of the ignominy, however, attaches to our gallant army,

* Gen. Pillow.

which at every halt, though often rendered imperative
by the necessity for re-enforcements and by strategy,
manifested their impatience to advance upon the capital.
Officers and men, regulars and volunteers, unseduced by
the luxuries and pleasures of Jalapa and Puebla, fretted
at delay.

1847. On the 17th of July the general-in-chief invited a
consultation with his generals, when a scheme previously
agreed on between himself, General Pillow, and Mr. Trist
was announced, under an injunction of confidence, viz.,
the employment of money to purchase a peace!

How General Scott ever brought his imperious and
martial mind, so long regulated by the rules of a profession the most scrupulous as to punctilio and propriety,
to favor a process so mercenary and demoralizing, can
not be explained. Ripley, in his able work, ascribes political motives to him, which will not stand the test of
criticism, and are too ungenerous to be tolerated in the
absence of proof. If visions of ambition influenced him,
he was aware that they were to be realized only in the
palace of Montezuma. Nothing less than the occupation of the capital would have satisfied his countrymen.
It is more reasonable to presume that he had become
disgusted with the service. His constitutional irritabil-
ity had been aggravated by advices from Washington.
He had neither the ear of the President or the secretary
of war. They had proposed to commission a civilian,
with a rank superior to his own, to supervise his operations. A secret agent had been sent to head-quarters to
consult with one of his brigadiers, and without his approval communications had been opened with the enemy.
Every thing indicated the determination of President
Polk to accomplish a speedy peace. His secret agent,
with the approval of General Pillow, his secret representative, proposed the use of money; and the general,

worried and disgusted, probably considered this the shortest way to relieve himself from a position where he was dogged by emissaries and threatened with superiors —a fire in front and " a fire in his rear."

Whatever his motives, when his officers assembled he frankly announced the plan, and as frankly sustained it. General Pillow, known to be the confidential friend of the President, and really more *his* secret agent than Mr. Trist, concurred with the general-in-chief. Worth, owing to a personal misunderstanding with Scott, had not been invited. Smith was absent. Twiggs considered it " a political question," and declined an opinion. Quitman and Shields strongly condemned the plan, and Cadwalader coincided with them. The council broke up without any definite conclusion, and with the understanding that the meeting and the subject matter was to be considered strictly confidential.*

* The public attention was first attracted to this matter by a letter in the St. Louis Republican signed " Gomez," dated Puebla, Aug. 6th. The most material passages are here published :

" I observe from the papers that an idea is prevalent among the more intelligent portions of the United States that General Scott is vested with high diplomatic powers. Whatever may have been the case previous to the arrival of Mr. Trist, since then all such powers have been vested in Mr. Trist alone. He was sent here as a confidential political friend of the administration, as the disburser of the three-million fund, and with the expectation that, by a judicious application of it, *a peace could be speedily purchased! from a people over whom our standard had floated victorious in every engagement we had had with them.* I mention this, because I believe that the administration, fearing the infamy that will attach to a peace procured upon such terms, have cunningly devised the plan to create, and allow the impression to become prevalent, that General Scott possessed the diplomatic power, and that upon him must rest the responsibility of any such termination of the war.

" A short time since things were in a fair way thus to be ended. The application of this fund was to be, upon certain contingencies, in bringing about the appointment of commissioners to treat with us for peace, and those who had secured this result were to be the recipients of certain portions of the fund. To this Mr. Trist was committed in full, and, so far as consent went, General Scott in part. A council of war was decided upon and called. It convened at the head-quarters of the army on Saturday evening, the 17th of July last past. Those

This letter was generally ascribed to George J. M. Davis, a lieutenant of Illinois volunteers, on the staff of

who were present at the council were, the general-in-chief, Major Generals Pillow and Quitman, Brigadier Generals Twiggs, Shields, and Cadwalader.   The justly distinguished General Worth was not present, in consequence of a most unfortunate disruption of the friendly relations that had existed for thirty-five years between him and General Scott.   But of this more anon."

The principal topic of discussion at this council was *whether the application of a portion of the $3,000,000 fund to the* PURCHASE *of a peace would be justifiable under the peculiar circumstances of the case.* The deliberations on this point are thus described in the letter of Gomez:

"The general-in-chief, with his usual bland, impressive, and, I may add, eloquent manner, first went over the whole ground, bringing, in support of his position, every argument to which tact, much reflection, and a strong mind could give birth.   To these considerations he added the great and pressing anxiety urged in all their communications by the administration to terminate, *by any means*, if possible, this war. Upon his concluding, the opinions of the different generals present were called for, according to rank.   General Pillow's was the first given, and was favorable to the plan proposed.   General Quitman followed, but objected in toto to it, on the ground that it would inflict a stain upon our national escutcheon that centuries could not wipe out.   Of the brigadier generals, Twiggs was the first to express his views, and, by regarding it to a great extent as a '*political question,*' he declined giving any opinion.   General Shields was next required to give his views; he at once rose from his seat, his whole countenance lit up with animation, and in that bold, fearless, uncompromising manner that so strikingly illustrates his whole public career, denounced the whole scheme in the most unqualified terms.   He insisted that the application of this fund for any such purpose was not only immoral, but debasing.   That, while for purposes of self-defense it was, according to the usages of modern warfare, justifiable in one nation to employ as spies the subjects of the other belligerent power, yet there was no state of circumstances that ever had or could exist, that would warrant our bribing or hiring the officers or functionaries of that belligerent power, for the sake of benefiting us, to cut the throats of their own subjects.   And he boldly declared that, rather than see the country of his adoption thus disgraced, he would prefer by far to witness the continuation of the war for ten years, and in every battle we fought lose five thousand men.   The one would admit a remedy; the other was an evil, from the consequences of which, as a nation, we could never recover.

"General Cadwalader simply remarked, that General Shields had exhausted the subject, and he fully concurred with him in the conclusions to which he had come.   Thus terminated the council of the evening of the 17th of July.   What followed is soon related.

"The next day General Shields had a long interview with Mr. Trist.   What occurred at that interview I have no means of ascer-

General Shields, but in a letter to Gen. S. he denied any connection or knowledge of it whatever. It was reprinted in the Baltimore Sun, and became the subject of a court of inquiry, which made the following report:

"In obedience to the confidential instructions of the secretary of war, the court has proceeded to investigate the several points of inquiry specified in those instructions.

"It has summoned before it all the officers of the army present at the council of officers held at Puebla on the 19th of July last, except Lieut. Col. Hitchcock, who can not, it is presumed, add any thing material to the testimony of the general officers examined; and it has obtained no information concerning the deliberations of that occasion, and the proposition therein made by Major General Scott, commanding the American army, to apply certain public moneys to a purchase of a peace with Mexico, other than was already possessed by the department.

"The court is not of opinion, upon the evidence before it, that the military operations of the United States army were, in fact, influenced by any such arrangement as that which was discussed at the meeting in question.

taining, but the subsequent acts of Mr. Trist can leave but little doubt upon that subject. Two days afterward, Mr. Trist withdrew all papers connected with *this* manner of terminating the war. And from that hour to this an immediate march upon the capital, so soon as General Pierce came up, was determined upon, and all hopes of an early peace abandoned.

"I have been thus particular in relating the proceedings of what I regard by far the most important council of war that has convened since the existence of hostilities between the United States and Mexico, because I believe my country has been saved from being plunged into an abyss of infamy from which there would be no extrication; and for the reason that those who, regardless of consequences to themselves, have averted that blow, should receive the credit of it. For myself, I sincerely hope that the hand that shall ever be extended in offering as a bribe, either directly or indirectly, any portion of this three millions to Santa Anna or any other Mexican, for the purpose of procuring a peace, may, before it accomplishes its object, fall palsied by his side, and that a mark more distinguishable than that placed upon the brow of Cain may be indelibly fixed upon his, that so long as his unworthy life is spared he may be the object of execration of all his indignant countrymen."

"The court has not been able to obtain *legal proof* as to the payment of money, or the understanding to pay money for the purchase of a peace; nor as to what effect any such understanding was agreed or contemplated to have upon the operations of the army of the United States; nor as to whether any written memorandum of agreement on the subject was made or received by any officer of the army; nor as to the parties by, to, or through whom any proposition on that subject may have been made or received by any officer of the army.

"The court having, in consideration of the nature of the subject of inquiry, deemed it inexpedient to examine on those points, or attempt to examine, in Mexico, any persons other than officers of the American army.

"In the progress of the investigation it appeared that the only persons, citizens of the United States, who had it in their power to furnish legal proof on these points, were Major General Scott and Mr. Trist, the Commissioner of the United States in Mexico.

"Mr. Trist, as the record shows, has declined to appear before the court.

"General Scott presented an informal statement of some of the facts in the case, but declined to testify as a witness; and, as the court did not feel itself justified in considering him as a party under charges, it is constrained to leave that subject for direct correspondence, as proposed by General Scott in that statement, between him and the department; and it accordingly submits the whole matter for such farther action, if any, as the President may deem to be called for by the interests of the army or the government."

Circular letters were addressed to the generals by the secretary of war. General Scott replied:

"Head-quarters of the Army, Mexico, Jan. 28th, 1848.

"I have received your letter of the 24th ult., inclosing a slip cut from some newspaper that purports to give the deliberations of a council of war held at my quarters in July last, respecting a large bribe to the Mexican government to be paid out of the 'three millions appropriated by Congress,' and you demand of me, in the name of the President, a report of this newspaper rumor.

"I have never held in Mexico what could be properly called a council of war—that is to say, a meeting of officers to *vote* on any military subject whatever ; but to insure an intelligent concert and hearty good-will in carrying out views and plans, I have frequently called together many of the principal officers of the army, to lay before them the number and condition of the opposing forces, the next movement or attack contemplated by me ; my motives and proposed manner (in detail) of executing the given purpose ; and, in order to take all the chances of avoiding errors, I have always concluded my expositions by inviting free suggestions. It is due to myself to add, that I can not recall a single material change or modification of plan the result of such conferences.

"There was a meeting of some of the principal officers of the army at my quarters in July, to which the anonymous letter-writer in the newspaper probably alludes. When I add that the meeting was strictly confidential, it will be evident that the individual who violated his plighted honor did so for the purpose, as far as falsehood might serve, to inflict discredit and dishonor on others.

"The subject discussed at that meeting was certainly of a delicate nature, too much so to be reduced to writing under any chance of the miscarriage of the paper. Mr. Trist, however, has the whole matter written out in cipher, to be, I presume, submitted at the proper time. But neither Mr. Trist, our sole commissioner, nor anybody else, as far as I know or believe, either at that meeting or any where else, ever proposed or suggested to use a dollar of the three-million fund either as a bribe or for any other purpose not to be expressed on the face of a public treaty."

General Pillow, in his reply, detailed the consultations he had held with Mr. Trist, and afterward with General Scott and Mr. Trist. He states that he was at first opposed to the employment of money to secure a peace, but was converted by the arguments and the precedents cited by General Scott ; that the objections he suggested as to accounting at the proper offices in Washington for

O 2

money thus expended, were obviated by the ingenious
expedients of the general-in-chief; that he therefore
went into the conference of the 17th of July and advocated the proposition; that, subsequently, negotiations
were carried on by Mr. Trist, with the knowledge of
General Scott, with Santa Anna, which he disapproved;
that he would have nothing more to do with propositions or negotiations; *that these negotiations restrained,
modified and controlled the subsequent movements of the
army, and occasioned many disasters*, etc.

This remarkable statement of General Pillow was not
sustained by the evidence before the court, or by the
letters of the several generals to the secretary of war.
They, one and all, denied any knowledge of the payment
of money, or any belief that the movements of the army
had been influenced by the negotiations of Mr. Trist.

In 1857, General Pillow, being a candidate for the
Senate of the United States, reiterated his charges in a
public address, and set forth the services he had rendered in counteracting, as far as practicable, the errors of
General Scott. This drew from him a letter, and from
General Hitchcock, long a member of his military family,
an elaborate and rather crushing reply. General Quitman was thus drawn before the public:

"*To the Editor of the Natchez Free Trader.*

"I have just read in the New Orleans Delta the reply
of General Pillow to the letter of General Scott, written
in answer to some charges against him, contained in
General Pillow's recent address to the people of Tennessee.

"In the personal controversies between these gentlemen, as well as that between Generals Pillow and Hitchcock, I desire to take no part. Although my statement
in relation to the Puebla meeting has, upon several occasions, been called for, I have abstained from appearing
before the public heretofore, and would not do so now,

but that General Pillow, in his late reply to General Scott's letter, has thought proper to introduce a mere abstract from the statement submitted by me to the War Department in 1848, on the call of President Polk. I take no exception to the course adopted by General Pillow in this particular. He had a right to publish a part or the whole of my evidence; but, since I have been brought upon the witness stand, I deem it due to myself that the whole correspondence between myself and the War Department, on this subject, should be published.

"The reader will perceive that this correspondence refers alone to the proceedings of the meeting of officers at Puebla. In this communication I do not feel called on to go beyond the matters therein referred to, except to say that, subsequently to the meeting, General Pillow informed General Shields and myself that he had changed his opinion in relation to the subject submitted to the meeting, and now was opposed to the measure. As to any understandings or stipulations, outside of the proposition presented by General Scott to the council or meeting, I never heard of them while I remained in the army.   J. A. QUITMAN.

"Monmouth, October 25th, 1857."

"War Department, Washington, December 24th, 1847.

"SIR,—I invite your attention to the article herein inclosed, from the Baltimore Sun (first published in a Western paper), pretending to give an account of the proceedings of a council of war, and representing that it was held at the head-quarters of the commanding general in July last, and that you were present, in which it was proposed to give General Santa Anna, or some other Mexican, for the purpose of purchasing a peace, a portion of the three millions appropriated by Congress.

"Nothing could have appeared more improbable to the government here, which is fully aware that not the slightest authority for any such proceeding has in any way emanated from it, than this story, yet I am pained to be obliged to say that suspicions do to some extent prevail, and appear to be gaining ground, that there is some foundation for the rumor.

"You will, I trust, agree with me in regarding it of the greatest importance to those alleged to have been present on that occasion, as well as to the government, that this rumor, assumed to be unfounded, should be met with an authoritative denial ; but should it be that any thing has taken place which could have afforded even a colorable pretext for putting forth the statement herewith sent to you—if any such proposition as is therein mentioned has been offered or entertained—if any has been acceded to, and any steps taken to carry it into effect, the President directs that you communicate to this department all that you know, and all that you can ascertain in relation to the whole matter.

"Very respectfully, your obedient servant,
"W. L. MARCY, Secretary of War.
"Major Gen. Quitman, U. S. Army, Washington City."

"Washington City, January 10th, 1848.

"SIR,—I have the honor to acknowledge the receipt of your communication of the 24th ultimo, inviting my attention to an article from the Baltimore Sun inclosed, purporting to give an account of the proceedings of a council of war held at Gen. Scott's head-quarters in Puebla, Mexico, in July last. In your note you advise me that the President directs that, if any thing has taken place which could afford even a colorable pretext for putting forth the statement alluded to, or if any such proposition as is therein mentioned has been offered or entertained, etc., I should communicate to the department of war all that I know, and all that I can ascertain in relation to the whole matter.

"Were I alone personally concerned, I should not have a moment's hesitation in making known whatever may have come within my knowledge connected at any time with the public service; but it seems to me, without wishing to be understood as admitting or denying the statements of the anonymous writer of the article alluded to, that your letter involves a very delicate question in regard to my duty as a subordinate officer. It is this— whether I can with propriety divulge matters which occurred in a council of war of which I was a member, or expose the opinions of officers, communicated at such meeting under the implied obligation of secrecy which attaches to their deliberations on such occasions.

"I am at present inclined to think that this obligation

remains unimpaired, upon the subordinate officer, until he is relieved from it by the consent of the party or parties concerned, or until he is required by legal process to testify in relation to the matter.

"Entertaining these opinions, I feel it my duty most respectfully to decline answering the questions propounded in your letter, and I request that my objections may be laid before the President for his consideration. Should he, after considering them, still insist upon a full answer, I ask leave to be permitted again to deliberate upon the matter before making up a final conclusion upon the subject.

"I have the honor to remain, very respectfully, your obedient servant,

"J. A. QUITMAN, Major General U. S. A.
"The Honorable W. L. Marcy, Secretary of War."

"War Department, Washington, March 2d, 1848.

"SIR,—I have received your letter of the 10th of January, in reply to one from me of the 24th of December. Your reply has been laid before the President. He has duly considered the reasons which you have offered as an excuse for not responding to the inquiries submitted to you by his direction in my former letter. He considers it important that he should have full and accurate information on the matters presented to you in my letter, and in his view of the subject he feels it to be his duty to again invite your attention to these inquiries, and to ask a full disclosure of what you may know in regard to them. The character of the replies received from Major Generals Scott and Pillow to letters similar to the one addressed to you, renders it, in his opinion, the more important that he should be made acquainted with what is within your knowledge relative to the matters alluded to in my former communication.

"The President appreciates the embarrassment which has induced a hesitation on your part to comply with the request which he directed me to make, yet he does not doubt that you will, on further reflection, view the matter as he does, and regard it as your duty to the government to make a full statement of what you may know of the transactions embraced in the inquiries contained in my letter of the 24th of December. The official acts of officers in the public service should not, as he conceives, be withheld from the executive branch of the government.

"I have the honor to be, with great respect, your obedient servant,

"W. L. MARCY, Secretary of War.
"J. A. Quitman, U. S. Army."

"United States Hotel, Washington, March 9th, 1848.

"SIR,—I have received your note of the 2d instant, in which you inform me that the President, after duly considering my objections to make a full disclosure in answer to the inquiries submitted to me by his direction in your letter of the 24th of December, still requires that I should state fully whatever may be within my knowledge in relation to the transactions embraced within those inquiries.

"While my opinions, in the abstract, remain the same as those announced in my former letter, the fact, since ascertained, that Generals Scott, Pillow, and Twiggs have answered similar inquiries, has removed the objections that I should otherwise have had to disclosing matters which, though connected with the public service, came to my knowledge confidentially.

"However reluctant I may be to make the disclosures, it would be presumptuous in me longer to refuse a compliance with the demands of the President. I therefore submit herewith a statement of the material facts within my knowledge which occurred at the meeting of officers supposed to be alluded to in the publications to which you have called my attention.

"About the middle of July last I was summoned to attend a meeting of officers at General Scott's headquarters, in Puebla, Mexico. I there met the general-in-chief, Generals Pillow, Twiggs, Shields, and Cadwalader, and I think Colonel Hitchcock, inspector general. General Worth was not present, and General Smith's absence accounted for by General Scott's remarking that he, General Smith, had been consulted on the matter.

"The general-in-chief first dwelt upon the great importance of peace to our country, and the anxious desire of our government to bring it about. He said that, influenced chiefly by these important considerations, and his belief that a movement upon the capital would cut off all prospects of an amicable adjustment of difficulties, he had halted thus long at Puebla; that General Pierce, with a considerable body of troops under his command, was shortly expected to arrive; that our numbers were now weak for the formidable enterprise before us, and that the expected re-enforcement would be of great importance. He therefore requested the opinion of the officers present upon the propriety of awaiting the arrival of General Pierce.

"He desired to consult them upon another subject of great delicacy and much importance. That the prospects for peace were now slight, but that he was informed by some foreign residents in Mexico that this desirable result could certainly be attained by the application of a considerable sum of money; that the Mexican leaders expected the negotiations to be attended by a *douceur ;* that they were not in the habit of moving without it; that the use of money for such purposes was justified by the practice of other nations; and that, considering the great good it would, in this instance, bring to our own country, he regarded the means as moral and proper, and did not perceive how any sensible man could think otherwise. He farther added that Mr. Trist had no power or instructions to use the three millions voted by Congress, or any part of it, to such a purpose; that sum must be accounted for on the face of the treaty; that, however, if it should be considered advisable, he, General Scott, had credit, upon the assent or request of Mr. Trist, to raise a million or a million and a half of dollars to apply to this purpose, a sum sufficient to insure the success of the negotiations; that he had already expended ten or twenty thousand dollars, which he regarded as 'bread thrown upon the waters.' He then presented and read a note from Mr. Trist on this subject, assenting to, if not requesting, that the scheme should be adopted. He concluded by inviting the opinions of the officers present upon the measure. After some pause General Pillow expressed his opinion in favor of awaiting the arrival of General Pierce, and proceeded to express in detail his concurrence with the views of the general-in-chief on the propriety of raising and applying the money as proposed, pledging his influence, as an officer and a citizen, to sustain the measure.

"I followed. Alluding to the importance of commencing our march upon the capital during the partial suspension of the rainy season, I still concurred in opinion that we should wait the arrival of General Pierce's command, if it could be expected in a few days. On the other question, I declared my decided opposition to the secret use of money for the purpose of procuring a treaty of peace. Without undertaking to discuss the morality of such a measure, I held that all our dealings with other countries should be high-toned and above-board, not requiring concealment from our own people nor from the world. That such a transaction, involving the payment of a large sum of money, however secretly it might be conducted, neither could nor should be concealed from the people of the United States; that whatever might be the views of casuists upon the subject, there was among the people of the United States a high tone and nice sense of public morality, which would lead them to denounce and condemn a treaty obtained by corrupting the rulers of a sister republic, etc., etc.

"General Twiggs expressed his concurrence in the propriety of awaiting the arrival of General Pierce. The other subject he regarded as political, and not military, upon which he had not formed, and would not express, an opinion, etc.

"General Shields followed, and expressed his decided opposition to the scheme. He enlarged upon its impropriety. He hoped that money would never be used to purchase a peace by corruption. It was, in fact, a plan to bribe the government of Mexico, and he would sooner see our country in war for ten years than resort to this mode of purchasing a peace. Not doubting the patriotic intentions of the commanding general, he thought it his duty as a friend to caution him against the assumption of such responsibility, etc.

"General Cadwalader, being called upon finally, said that he agreed with General Shields and myself.

"Colonel Hitchcock's opinion was not asked nor given.

"I had no knowledge or intimation, before the meeting, of its objects, nor do I know, nor have I ever heard, that the project was prosecuted any farther. Indeed, I supposed it was entirely dropped and abandoned. I know not by what means or from what source this matter became public.

"I took no notes of the transaction at the time, and have made this report of it entirely from memory, and, of course, may have stated the language inaccurately.

"The occurrence made an impression on my mind at the time, and I think the substance is above correctly stated. Your obedient servant,

"J. A. QUITMAN, Maj. Gen. U. S. A.
"Hon. W. L. Marcy, Secretary of War."

CHAPTER XII.

Advance from Puebla.—Valley of Mexico.—Approaches to the Capital.—The Chalco Route, and the Controversy it occasioned.—Duncan's Reconnoissance.—Mason and Beauregard's Reconnoissance.—Remarks.—The proposed Assault on Mexicalzingo.—Battle of Contreras.—Battle of San Antonio.—Battle of Churubusco.—Death of Colonel Butler. — Lieutenant Colonel Dickinson.—Kearney's Charge.—Overtures from the Enemy.—Quitman at San Augustin.—The Armistice.

THE expected re-enforcement having arrived, the army marched from Puebla for the valley of Mexico. Quitman's division consisted of the New York, South Carolina, and 2d Pennsylvania regiments, a battalion of marines, Steptoe's battery, and Gaither's troop of horse. On the 10th of August they reached the mountain range which separates the department of Puebla or Cholula from Mexico; and as they emerged from the cloudy canopy, before them the beautiful valley lay like a vast garden, dotted with bright lakes, fields of emerald, and the white domes and glittering spires of the villages which environ the capital. Through the transparent medium of that elevated region they discerned here and there large bodies of cavalry in motion on the plain.

This remarkable interior basin is closed on every side by a mountain barrier, varying in height, at different points, from two hundred to over ten thousand feet. It is circular in form, the diameter of the edge or crust of the rim being about fifty miles. It contains some 830 square miles of productive land, for the most part under a high state of cultivation. Six large lakes stretch in an almost continuous line from south to north, occupying about one fifth of the valley proper. On their shore extensive fields, spread out on a nearly perfect level, reach back to the mountains. Ten extinct volcanoes, distinctly presenting their craters, rear their cones in the southern part of the valley. Glancing over the mountains to the south is seen Ajusco, its scarred and blackened peak elevated more than 11,000 feet above the level of the sea. To the east and southeast Iztaccihuatl and Popocatepetl, the Titans of the plains, mingle their smoke with eternal snows glittering in the sun, their outlines and inequalities so sharply defined as to make them seem almost within reach, yet looking cold and glacier-like, while every thing else is glowing under a tropical sky. Nine populous towns are supported by this great valley, each of them environed by picturesque villages. But the object of greatest interest is the city of Mexico itself. It was originally surrounded by Lake Tezcuco, whose waters have been receding for many years, owing chiefly to the diversion of the River Guatitlan into another channel, and the clearing of the mountain sides diminishing the contributions formerly poured into it by various streams. This recession, however, has added to the defenses of the city. The lake is not navigable. The ground on all sides is low, intersected in every direction by wide and deep ditches, which, from the superior elevation of lakes Chalco and Xochimilco, are always filled with water, and the city can only be approached now, as in the time of Montezuma, by narrow causeways between aqueducts.*

1847. On the 11th of August the American army descended into the valley of Mexico in the following order. Gen. Twiggs, with his division in advance, encamped at Ayotla; on the 11th the division of General Quitman came up and encamped at Buena Vista; General Worth

* Smith and Hardcastle's Reports.

came next, and occupied the town of Chalco; and next General Pillow, who pitched his tents near Gen. Worth. The general-in-chief established his head-quarters at Ayotla, upon the northern border of Lake Chalco, fifteen miles from the capital—a point whence he could reconnoitre the enemy and best deceive him as to his ultimate line of approach. From that point four different roads communicate with the city. 1. The national road, the most direct. On this, seven miles from Ayotla, the enemy were in force at the Penon, a high solitary hill overlooking the plain for several miles in every direction. Entirely surrounded by water or impassable marshes, the road or causeway lies immediately at its base. Two long lines of breast-works for infantry ran along the base of the hill, and above these were fifty pieces of cannon arranged in batteries, so as to sweep away the columns of an approaching enemy.

2. The next most direct route is by Mexicalzingo. Before reaching that town the road contracts into a narrow causeway three quarters of a mile long, a marsh on one side, formed by Lake Xochimilco, and on the other very low grounds, with a net-work of deep ditches and canals, the whole within range of the formidable batteries of the town and field-works recently erected.

3. By the large town of Tezcuco, known as the northern route, branching off at Buena Vista, and leading through the most populous section of the great valley. This had been strongly fortified at different points, and was occupied by a strong body of the enemy under Gen. Valencia.

4. The route south of Lake Chalco, winding along the base of the mountains which bound the valley to the south. This road, in use in the days of Cortez, had been almost abandoned, was deemed impracticable for an army, and had been left unguarded.

A bitter controversy after the war sprung out of these routes. Gen. Pillow and the historian Ripley insist that on the 14th of August the general-in-chief had positively determined on the route by Mexicalzingo, which could only have been carried by an enormous sacrifice of men; that the movement would have put the whole army in jeopardy in case of a defeat; and that he was only dissuaded from it by the remonstrances of Worth and Pillow, and their report of the practicability of the Chalco route, based on a reconnoissance made by Lieut. Colonel Duncan, at the instance of Worth, on the 13th inst., and communicated to head-quarters on the afternoon of the 14th, when the orders, which that morning had been given for the advance on Mexicalzingo, were countermanded. The statement is absurd upon its face, unless we presume an ignorance, recklessness, and incompetency on the part of the general-in-chief not to be presumed. The facts, as I gather them, are these. While the army lay at Puebla, the engineer officers—a corps of which any nation may be proud—were engaged in preparing maps for the army chiefly from the maps of Humboldt. Much information was collected at head-quarters from various persons of different nationalities, but no concerted movement of the army, from the siege of Vera Cruz to the downfall of the capital, was ever based upon information not verified by actual reconnoissance. Gen. Scott established his head-quarters at Ayotla, whence *four* roads branch off to the capital, *for the express purpose of obtaining information.* Why would he restrict his reconnoissances to *two* routes only—the Penon and Mexicalzingo? He arrived at Ayotla at 3 P.M. on the 11th, and at daylight next morning Capts. Lee and Mason and Lieut. Stevens were reconnoitring El Penon, and Maj. Smith and Lieuts. Beauregard and Tower were on the hill of Calderon. *At 3 P.M. on the same day*

Capt. Lee and Lieut. Beauregard *examined the north shore of Lake Chalco as far as the village of San Francisco,* near the causeway separating said lake from Lake Xochimilco, *and ascertained that the old road on the southern shore, though narrow and rough, might be made practicable, thus corroborating information received at Puebla.* On the 13th Capt. Mason and Lieuts. Beauregard, Stevens, and M'Lellan were dispatched toward Mexicalzingo. Lieut. Stevens went to work near El Penon to complete the observations of the preceding day. Capt. Lee and Lieut. Tower were engaged near Lake Chalco. Capt. Mason reported at head-quarters the same evening, and it was the general impression that Mexicalzingo would be assailed, unless the reconnoissance of the ensuing day should recommend a different movement. With this view Capt. Mason and Lieut. Beauregard were directed on the 14th to report to Gen. Worth, who lay near Lake Chalco. But on the 13th, while the engineer officers were thus engaged, Lieut. Colonel Duncan, at his own suggestion approved by Worth, had examined the southern shore of Lake Chalco as far as Tuliagualco, half way between the towns of Chalco and San Augustin, nearly opposite San Francisco, where Lee and Beauregard had gone, as before stated, on the evening of the 11th. Finding the road practicable that far, and *hearing* that there were no obstructions beyond, he returned to Chalco at 2 P.M., and was forthwith dispatched to head-quarters by Gen. Worth, with a strong recommendation of the route. This valuable information, communicated by a reliable officer, agreeing with the information had at Puebla, and with the intelligence *previously obtained* at San Francisco by Lee and Beauregard on the 11th, at once decided the general-in-chief. The four routes would doubtless have been examined simultaneously on the 12th had the engineer officers been sufficiently numerous. It by no means follows that the route by Mexicalzingo had been decided upon because it had been reconnoitred *before* the Chalco route. On the contrary, every movement that was made denotes to an impartial mind the original intention of the general-in-chief, in halting at Ayotla, to perplex and deceive the enemy. It was a stroke of strategy successfully carried out; one of the *coups* of the campaign which the general-in-chief, probably for reasons known to himself, carefully concealed from all but the confidential officers of his staff.* It succeeded in deceiving Santa Anna to the last. He had hoped to encounter our army at El Penon, and he lay there, impregnably intrenched, with the flower of his army, until we were in motion round Lake Chalco. And thus the general-in-chief was enabled to concentrate his entire force at San Augustin without the loss of a man, at the same time compelling the enemy to abandon their strongest defense and their preconcerted place of battle.

The route round Lake Chalco was unquestionably the proper one, and the credit of ascertaining it has been claimed exclusively for the late Lieut. Col. Duncan—a truly gallant officer—in a spirit of disparagement to the general-in-chief. Gen. Worth, in a letter to Duncan, dated Tacubaya, March 31st, 1848, labors to make this impression. But his letter, at last, only shows that the general-in-chief was masking his intentions until he obtained thorough information, and of this very Chalco route. Gen. Worth, after reciting what he and Col. Duncan had done, says: "Though Gen. Scott evinced a disposition to gather information as respected this route (Chalco) on the 12th, and, no doubt, *preferred* it, he, nev-

---

* Gen. Scott, Inspector Gen. Hitchcock, Capt. Lee, and other officers, positively aver that the attack by Mexicalzingo was never decided upon.

ertheless, gave out specific orders for a different route on the 13th, satisfied, I have as little doubt, of its impracticability. On taking leave of Gen. Scott at Ayotla, having my final orders, when in the saddle I took the liberty of requesting him to forbear his movement until I could report the result of your examination; to which he implied *assent*. As I have said, Gen. Scott *directed* me to send and examine *the Chalco route*, etc., etc." This admits all that I contend for.

Ripley likewise argues that the attack on Mexicalzingo would have been full of difficulty and peril, if not of defeat, and insinuates a want of generalship in Scott for contemplating a movement which he considers in violation of the principles and precedents of military science. Upon this point it may be conceded that the whole campaign was in violation of precedent. When the American general, with only 10,000 men, a large proportion of them new levies that had never seen fire, and but imperfectly drilled, left Vera Cruz, Jalapa, and Puebla, with its 80,000 inhabitants and 100,000 hostile rancheros and guerrillas in his rear, and plunged into the very heart of a great empire to attack its capital, occupied by 180,000 people, defended by 35,000 soldiers, and environed by formidable fortifications bristling with cannon served by skillful artillerists, he found no precedent for so daring a movement in military history. When a general undertakes such a campaign, he must be expected, in the course of it, to depart, more or less, from the strict rules of strategy, and rely sometimes on the exigencies of the crisis and the inspiration of his genius.

But would the attack on Mexicalzingo necessarily have been disastrous? Upon a critical examination of the engineer reports, it will be seen that, though naturally strong and tolerably fortified, there were few guns in position, and few troops to defend them. It was altogether isolated, and had no connection whatever with the strong force at El Penon. From that point no assistance could be had, especially if, at the moment of attack, a simultaneous demonstration had been made in front of El Penon itself. To come to the relief of Mexicalzingo, Santa Anna would have been compelled to march by way of the capital, or to attack the invaders in the rear, a movement—which doubtless entered into the calculations of Gen. Scott—that would have brought the two armies into the open field, and insured the fall of Mexico by a single battle! Under any circumstances the attack on Mexicalzingo would not have been as hazardous as the attack by Napoleon on the Austrians at Arcole; and what is there that Frenchmen, or any other people, have done that Americans can not do?

Up to this moment Santa Anna had expected to be attacked at El Penon, and he was not undeceived until the 15th, when our army, Worth's division in advance, was in motion on the southern shore of Lake Chalco. On the 18th the advance division took position near the hacienda San Antonia, and the rear divisions were concentrated upon San Augustin, nine miles from the capital. The Mexicans had, in the mean time, withdrawn from their original positions, the eastern approach being no longer threatened, and were strongly intrenched at San Antonia, and behind a line of works stretching off to the left in the marshy grounds of Lake Xochimilco. Having avoided El Penon to spare his army, the general-in-chief now resolved, for the same reason, not to attack the strong position of San Antonia, but to make his way across the pedrigal to the San Angel road. On the 19th Gen. Pillow advanced to open the road, which was a mere mule-path through a field of volcanic scoria. At

VOL. I.—P

the intersection of this path with the road, Gen. Valencia had thrown up breast-works, surmounted with 22 pieces of cannon, commanding both the path and the road. Avoiding this formidable battery by a detour to the right, our light troops made their way over the field of lava, and gained the high road at a point between Valencia's position and that of Santa Anna at San Angel. And then commenced the battle of Contreras, one of the most complicated and brilliant of the campaign. The enemy lay in a strongly-intrenched camp, defended by a formidable battery, with every advantage of ground, with an immense superiority of numbers, and hourly re-enforcements from the city. Pillow's and Twiggs's divisions, floundering through the field of lava, the officers all on foot, advanced rapidly to the attack. Smith's and Riley's, Pierce's and Cadwalader's brigades were exposed to a heavy fire of artillery and small-arms for more than three hours. But though they fought well, no decided impression had been made on the enemy's position, because, independent of the impassable ravine in front and to the left of the camp, our infantry, unaccompanied by cavalry or artillery, could not advance in column without being mowed down by the grape and canister of the batteries, nor advance in line without being ridden over by the Mexican lancers. Under all these disadvantages they maintained the positions they had originally gained, and resisted several charges of cavalry. At this juncture the general-in-chief directed Col. Morgan with his regiment (till then idly held in reserve by Pillow*) to move forward and occupy Contreras, and arrest the re-enforcements continually coming to the enemy. He soon afterward ordered Gen. Shields, with the New York and South

---

* When ordered to hold his regiment in reserve, Morgan, who desired to push on, said, in a very audible whisper, "D—n your reserves."

Carolina regiments (Quitman's division), to follow and sustain Morgan. With great difficulty Morgan, at 5 P.M., reached the hamlet which Cadwalader and his brigade had held with unflinching firmness. Santa Anna was found posted immediately in his front, at the distance of 1000 yards, with some 8000 men and two heavy pieces of artillery. At the same distance in his rear was the intrenched camp of Valencia, with 6000 men and 22 pieces of cannon. In the mean time Gen. Smith arrived. The countenance of Cadwalader, full of anxiety for his men, lighted up, and he said to Gen. S., "Welcome, sir. I presume you will take command." "With pleasure," was the prompt reply. "And now, while my brigade is coming up, let us look at our position and Santa Anna's." While thus engaged, the veteran Col. Riley, with his brigade, came in, to the joy of all, for it had been currently reported that he had fallen. It was now nearly night, but Gen. Smith was inclined to get rid of Santa Anna at once. Capt. Lee and Lieut. Beauregard were ordered to examine the ravine in front of our position, and the brigades of Riley and Cadwalader were formed in close columns of divisions, at half distance, left in front, the first to attack the right of Santa Anna's line, the latter the centre; his own brigade to act with Riley or otherwise, as circumstances might dictate.

Riley's and Smith's veterans were in position in ten minutes, but before Cadwalader's column of new troops could be formed, fortunately, perhaps, it became so dark the design had to be abandoned.* The night was dark

---

* Gen. Smith—one of the best tacticians in the army—yielded, in this instance, perhaps, too much to his anxiety to engage the enemy. The contemplated attack was injudicious:

1. Because he had no accurate knowledge of the intervening ground, and what he did know indicated the presence of deep ravines running parallel to our line of battle. This the map now before me establishes.

as pitch, and the rain fell in torrents.   At 11 P.M., Gen. Shields, with his command, reported to Gen. Smith, waiving his seniority, and thus paying a delicate homage to the acknowledged science, experience, and military talent of the junior general.   He reserved to himself the difficult task of holding the hamlet, with his New Yorkers and South Carolinians, against ten times his numbers.

In the mean time, Lieuts. Beauregard, Tower, Brooks, and Canby had examined the ground; and at 3 A.M. on the 20th, hungry, cold, and wet, the rain still pouring down, Smith silently advanced to dislodge Valencia from his intrenchments.   After wading knee-deep in mud and water, he halted some 500 yards in the rear of the Mexican position to close up the columns and examine his arms.   At dawn of day, Riley, conducted by Lieut. Tower, had gained an elevation behind the enemy, whence he rushed to the assault, stormed the intrenchments, and planted his colors in seventeen minutes.   The official reports are full of eulogies on the gallantry of officers and men in this brilliant affair.   The general-in-chief pronounced it one of the most decisive victories on record.

---

2. Before he could have reached the enemy, it would have been too dark to distinguish friend from foe.

3. Military men would object to the order of battle, Cadwalader's men, composed entirely of new levies, having been designated to attack the centre, the strongest position of the enemy.   But Gen. Smith knew the prowess of American volunteers, and this objection may be waived.

4. The moment our troops could be discerned or heard on the rising ground in our front, Valencia would have opened upon our rear with his 22 pieces.

5. It was risking the battle upon a movement the favorable issue of which would not have been commensurate with the hazard incurred and the odds against us.

6. The map indicates that if the attack was made at all, it should have been made on the left of Santa Anna (his right resting on a deep ravine running toward Smith's position), to cut him off from his base of operations at San Angel and Churubusco, especially as his two pieces of artillery, being on the left of that line, would otherwise have taken our columns in flank.

Our whole force, including Shields's brigade, numbered only 4500 rank and file; the enemy had 7000 men behind batteries, and 12,000 in sight and within striking distance, both on the 19th and 20th. The result was, an open road to the capital; 700 of the enemy killed; 813 prisoners, including 4 generals and 88 other officers; 22 pieces of cannon and a vast store of munitions of war; thousands of small-arms, innumerable standards, and over 700 pack-mules. Our loss did not exceed 60. Among our trophies was the recapture, by Capt. Drum, of the 4th artillery, of two brass six-pounders, lost by another company of the same regiment while bravely contending against vast odds at Buena Vista. They had long been mourned by that gallant regiment; they were now received with every testimonial of affection: officers and soldiers wept over and caressed them, the whole command joined in the wild hurra, and the general-in-chief, riding up, cheered louder than all, and received the congratulations of his troops.

While the enemy were retreating to Churubusco, Worth promptly attacked and carried the strong work at San Antonia, and pushed on with Twiggs and Pillow in hot pursuit. At this point these divisions, respectively pursuing from Contreras and San Antonia, arrived nearly at the same time. Twiggs was arrested by the strong fortifications thrown up around a large convent; the two others by the *tête du pont* defending the passage of the Churubusco River. The concentration of our forces at this point brought on the battle of Churubusco. Worth and Pillow carried the *tête du pont*, after a severe struggle, at the point of the bayonet, the volunteers of Cadwalader's brigade, led by the intrepid Trousdale, vying with the regulars. Twenty minutes thereafter, after a desperate conflict of two hours and a half, the convent surrendered to Twiggs, just as Capts. Alexander and J. M. Smith, and Lieut. O. L. Shepherd, 3d infantry, had cleared the way with the bayonet.

Two hours and a half before this, while the battle was at its height, Gen. Shields had been detached with his own and Pierce's brigade* to the left to turn the enemy's works, to oppose the extension of their troops from the rear upon and around our left, and to prevent their escape when driven from their positions.

Shields made his way a mile beyond Coyacan to an open but swampy field, in which is situated the hacienda De los Partales. On the edge of this field, beyond the hacienda, is a road leading from Churubusco to the capital; this was occupied by the Mexican reserve of 4000 infantry, strongly posted behind a ditch and breast-work in rear of the town. Shields determined to throw himself between these troops and the capital, but, finding their right supported by 4000 cavalry, he withdrew to the cover of the hacienda and resolved to attack in front. He selected the Palmetto regiment as the base of his line, and it moved forward rapidly but firmly under a fire of musketry as terrible as infantry ever faced.

The New York regiment, led by Col. Burnett,† recoiling at first under the tremendous fire, subsequently charged with a wild and irresistible enthusiasm. Within 100 yards of the ditch its gallant leader fell, and Lieut. Col. Baxter (who had two horses shot under him) assumed the command, ably seconded by Capts. Dyckman

---

* Gen. Pierce had been severely injured the day before by the falling of his horse in the pedrigal, and could neither ride nor walk. He was deeply chagrined by the accident, and had the sympathy of the whole army, who knew his cool, modest, and unquailing courage, moral and personal, manifested throughout his career, and every way worthy of his heroic lineage.

† To this gallant officer has lately been awarded the gold snuff-box presented to Gen. Jackson shortly after the victory of New Orleans by the ladies of New York, and by him bequeathed to be presented to the New Yorker who should most distinguish himself in battle.

and Hungerford, and as noble a corps of officers as ever went into a fight. Sergeant Romaine, who carried the national standard, had his right arm shattered, but supported it with his left until he received his mortal wound, and the colors fell. They were seized by Corporal Lake, who, rushing to the front, was immediately shot down. Orderly Sergeant Doremus took possession, and bore it through the storm to the Mexican breast-work, where he proudly planted it amid the cheers of the brigade. The flags of South Carolina and New York there floated in glorious fraternity.

In this sanguinary conflict Gen. Shields lost 240 from these two regiments alone, not exceeding 600 men. The enemy fought well, as they did at every point on this bloody field, standing in position till driven back by the bayonet.

Col. Butler, of the South Carolinians, had left his sick-bed against the remonstrances of his friends to lead the Palmettos to the combat. Early in the engagement his horse was shot under him. Soon after he received a painful wound in the knee, and yielded the command to Lieut. Col. Dickinson. Taking the Palmetto flag from the hands of Sergeant Beggs, Dickinson placed himself in front, and Beggs was immediately shot down. Col. Butler now came up to resume the command, and was killed by the side of Dickinson while standing under the flag. Dickinson himself soon fell mortally wounded,* and Maj. Gladden received it from his hands and committed it to Lieut. Baker, who being unable, from debility and exhaustion, to carry it, Maj. Gladden placed it in the hands of Patrick Leonard, and led his regiment to the charge. His men fell rapidly, but not one wavered, from first to last, under the concentrated fire of the enemy. In the whole history of war there has never been

---

* He died some weeks afterward.

a more striking example of indifference to death, the result of stern resolve. Each man fought for the honor of Carolina. Several companies were almost annihilated. Some had not men enough left to bury their dead, or bear their wounded to the ambulances. The uniforms of some of the officers were literally torn from their persons; the color-bearers were shot down, but the flag, bathed in their blood, was always seized as they fell and borne to the front. Proudly it floated through the tempest of death until the victory had been won, and then, all torn and blood-stained, it drooped over its own glorious dead! The regiment entered the battle with 273, rank and file, and when it was over it mustered 169! It had no missing; its dead and wounded made up the deficiency. Cadets of a noble state, sons of a sunny clime, branded by their country as traitors for defending the Constitution and their rights from usurpation and outrage, yet dying cheerfully for that country in a foreign land—the world may learn that such a race, in defense of their own homesteads and institutions, can never be subdued!*

And thus terminated the battles of Contreras, San Antonia, and Churubusco, fought on the 19th and 20th, almost continuously, aptly consolidated by the general-in-chief under the general title of the *battle of Mexico*. We contended against 32,000 picked troops, strongly intrenched, supported by powerful batteries, by their choice of ground, under the eyes of the capital, and with the certainty of refuge if defeated. We made 3000 prisoners, including two ex-presidents, six generals, and 208 other officers; killed or disabled 7000, and captured 37 pieces of ordnance, besides immense supplies.

After this great battle, well fought on both sides in every part of the field, there was an open road and no obstacle to the advance of our army. We were in pos-

* For a further notice of the Palmettos, see Appendix.

session of every thing except the last line of works encircling the city, and the garita of San Antonio Abad was only defended by a two-gun battery. The Mexican army was paralyzed. Universal consternation prevailed in the city. Worth and Pillow had formed a junction with Shields at the hacienda Portales, prepared for a vigorous advance. Harney had collected Kearney's, Ker's, M'Reynolds's, and Duperu's companies of dragoons, and was pursuing the fugitives. They rode over and trampled down the flying masses on the narrow causeway, charged within arm's length of the battery in the face of its fire, dismounted and would have carried it with their sabres, but, unhappily, the bugles, under peremptory orders from the general-in-chief, sounded a recall, and the heroic band, bleeding at every pore, and in the very moment of their triumph, was compelled to fall back.

The general-in-chief, in his official dispatch, says that, "On the same evening, with but little additional loss, we might have occupied the capital. But Mr. Trist, the commissioner, as well as myself, had been admonished by the best friends of peace—intelligent neutrals and some American residents—against precipitation, lest by wantonly driving away the government and others dishonored, we might scatter the elements of peace, excite a spirit of national desperation, and thus indefinitely postpone the hope of accommodation. Deeply impressed with this danger, and remembering our mission—*to conquer a peace*—the army very cheerfully sacrificed to patriotism—to the great wish and want of our country— the *eclat* that would have followed an entrance, sword in hand, into the great capital. Willing to leave something to the enemy, of no immediate value to us, on which to rest their pride and recover their temper, I halted our victorious corps at the gates of the city,

and have them now cantoned in the neighboring villages."

These are the reasons assigned by Gen. Scott for this
unlucky halt, which, instead of being "cheerfully" accepted by the army, filled it with surprise and mortification.
It was well known that on the night of the 20th the British
secretary of legation, the British consul general, and several other parties interested in Mexican finances, had visited Gen. Scott and Mr. Trist at San Augustin, and strongly recommended a suspension of arms and a renewal of
negotiations. The "peace policy" of Mr. Polk, prompted by a weak desire to propitiate a party whose clamor
against the war sprung from a mean jealousy of the
Southern States, hung like a nightmare over the army,
and dimmed the lustre of its most brilliant operations.
It paralyzed the energy of the general-in-chief, and converted a march of triumph into a march of blood.

And where was QUITMAN during these stirring events,
when so many of his compeers were winning imperishable renown?

He had taken post, it will be recollected, with his command, on the 10th instant, at the hacienda Buena Vista,
five miles to the rear of Ayotla. His division marched
with the rest of the army round Lake Chalco, and on the
18th he pitched his tents near San Augustin, the head-
quarters of General Scott, and the general dépôt of the
army. On the 19th, while several corps of the army
were engaged with the enemy, at different points, on
what is now termed the field of Contreras (Shield's
brigade, a part of his division, being thus employed), he
was directed, with his remaining brigade, to make his
way toward the conflict. But, when coming in view,
the general-in-chief, learning that our dépôt at San Augustin was threatened by General Alvarez, ordered Quitman to return. This noted partisan, with a strong body

of cavalry, had followed our army around Lake Chalco, but had not ventured an attack. The duty assigned to General Quitman, though highly important, was not the service he desired, but his application to be relieved was promptly but firmly rejected. In his official dispatch, General Scott says: "I regret having been obliged, on the 20th, to leave Major General Quitman, an able commander, with a part of his division—the 2d Pennsylvania Volunteers and the veteran detachment of United States Marines—at our important dépôt San Augustin. It was there that I had placed our sick and wounded; the siege, supply, and baggage trains. If these had been lost, the army would have been driven almost to despair; and considering the enemy's very great excess of numbers, and the many approaches to the dépôt, it might well have become emphatically *the post of honor*."*

* *Pencil Memorandum by General Quitman at San Augustin.*

"August 20th, 1847.

"On the 19th my division arrived at San Augustin, and there I received orders requiring it to remain in reserve in charge of the dépôt, baggage-wagons, and teams at that place. Twigg's division, which had been in my van, was ordered to pass on with Pillow's, which was immediately in advance of me, for the purpose of opening a road to turn the works at San Antonia. In front of them, where the way debouched from the ridge of land, the enemy were posted in force, having some twenty pieces of cannon. As soon as our troops came within range, they opened their batteries and continued them all day. In the morning I called to see General Scott, and said to him that his orders detailing me to guard this place had cast a gloom over my division. He said 'the language was unmilitary.' I said it was true that we had been in the rear from Vera Cruz. He replied, 'Not so.' I said that I meant we were not in a position to gain any credit. He said he 'should always place his strongest divisions in front, no matter who commanded them.' He showed considerable excitement, and I left him after I had said that I also had some reputation and a character to maintain, and that he must pardon my sensibility respecting orders which left me and my division no means of distinction.

"About an hour afterward I received a note from Captain Scott, directing me to take command of this place as governor or commandant, etc. The firing from the enemy's works continuing, I was

The assignment of this duty, though it chafed Quitman's temper at the moment, was a striking evidence of the confidence reposed in his sagacity, prudence, and courage. General Taylor had exhibited the same confidence when he trusted to his discretion after the storming of Fort Teneria, and again by confiding to him the occupation of Victoria and the frontier, at that time threatened by Valencia and Urea with 5000 men. Gen. Scott manifested it by selecting him for the first separate command after the surrender of Vera Cruz, the expedition to Alvarado, by intrusting him with the defense of San Augustin, and, as we shall hereafter see, in other signal instances. His peculiar trait was to grapple himself upon the esteem and confidence of all with whom he associated. He scarcely ever lost, even by political combinations and changes, a friend once gained, and no man won friends more readily.

On the morning of the 22d, the general-in-chief having established his head-quarters with Worth's division at Tacubaya, appointed Gens. Quitman, Smith, and Pierce to meet the Mexican commissioners to arrange the terms of an armistice. At the same time he handed to Gen. Quitman his own draft of the terms of the convention. Quitman was altogether opposed to this cessation of hostilities, not only from a distrust of the Mexican officials, but because he held that our proper policy and manifest destiny was to seize and occupy the country. At the special request of Gen. Scott, however, he reluctantly consented to act on the commission. It would have been more consistent with his opinions and usual practice to have refused to participate in a transaction he was unable to prevent. Strange to say, this service was

verbally ordered to send out one or two regiments to the support of the troops in advance. I directed General Shields to advance with two battalions of his brigade."

an object of desire in certain quarters, and some generals took offense at the general-in-chief for passing them by. His selection was admirable. Pierce, Quitman, and Smith were not only gallant soldiers and men of honor, but they had long been distinguished in the public service as jurists and statesmen.

The armistice was proclaimed August 24th, and Mr. Trist and the Mexican commissioners renewed their negotiations for peace.

On the 26th, Gen. Quitman wrote Gen. Scott from San Augustin, that the Mexican officers, and many citizens whom he had met with, unanimously expressed the opinion that no treaty of peace between the United States and Santa Anna would be ratified by the Mexican Congress, and that, even if so ratified, a majority of the states would pronounce against it.

He believed that the armistice should never have been proposed, and even two days after it had been agreed upon he doubted the wisdom of prolonging it.

CHAPTER XIII.

The Armistice.—Mexican Treachery.—Credulity of Gen. Scott.—
Resumption of Hostilities.—Battle of Molino del Rey.—Queries.—
Council at Piedad.—Defenses of the Capital.—Chapultepec.—Pillow's Advance.—Quitman's Assault.—Detour of Shields.—Quitman on the Rock of Chapultepec.—Advance on the Belen.—Leads
the Charge.—Surrender of the City.—The American Flag.—Appointed Governor of Mexico.—His Popularity.—Returns to the
United States.—Reception in New Orleans.—Welcome home.

UPON the part of the Americans this agreement was
rigorously observed, the general-in-chief even forbidding
his engineers to make reconnoissances, but it was daily
infringed by the Mexicans, who employed the opportunity to reorganize their army and strengthen the defenses of the capital. In the mean time Mr. Trist entered
into negotiations with the minister of foreign relations,
and subsequently with commissioners, whose functions,
however, were limited to the mere reception of propositions. The first meeting took place on the 27th, when
Mr. Trist presented the projet of a treaty which he had
brought from Washington. Delay was asked and granted. Pretext upon pretext was resorted to. The whole
army saw the fraud that was being practiced upon us.
But the Polk policy, Puritan influence at home, and the
insidious representations of British officials, who were
constantly at head-quarters flattering Gen. Scott and ca-
joling Mr. Trist, prevailed. The American chief, when
every one else was impressed with the falsehood of Santa
Anna, reposed on his good faith, although warned that,
though professing the most pacific views, he was actual-

ly planning a night attack on one of our divisions. Incapable of dishonoring the plighted word of a soldier himself, he did not perceive or comprehend the treachery of the Mexican, whose antecedents, and the general conduct of his government in its relations with the United States, should have rendered Gen. Scott less credulous. As it was, the illusion continued until the designs of the enemy became transparent, and on the 17th of September the hostile relations of the parties were resumed.

Our first demonstration was against the Mill of the King (Molino del Rey), a massive range of stone masonry, one mile due north of Tacubaya, and about one thousand yards east of the castle of Chapultepec. It was, in fact, an outpost of that formidable fortress, forming a part of its inclosure, and each reciprocally commanding the approach to the other. West of the Molino, at the distance of 450 yards, stood another spacious and strongly-built stone structure called the Casa Mater. Between these an effective battery had been located, and the intervals were lined with infantry. Near by hovered the ubiquitous Alvarez, with his swarm of Pintos. This strong position—doubly strong by its secure communication with the castle of Chapultepec and the capital—was occupied by over 14,000 troops of the line and national guards, and commanded by Santa Anna in person. General Scott had been induced to believe by "intelligent neutrals," but probably by emissaries of the Mexicans, that, during the armistice, the Molino had been converted into a foundery, and that the casting of cannon was then actually going on. This was the motive assigned for the attack.

Generals Scott and Worth made a survey of the position on the 7th, but formed no adequate conception of its defenses, which had been skillfully masked. Captain

Mason, of the engineers, and Lieutenant Colonel Duncan, of the artillery, continued the reconnoissance, as the event shows, with imperfect results, but upon their report General Worth made his arrangements for the attack. The details of this disastrous battle are well known. It began at daybreak, and lasted two hours. Worth's force consisted of 3100 men of all arms. They fought with desperation. He drove the enemy from all his positions, but our loss was frightful. The return of casualties runs up to 787, including a long list of distinguished officers, who fell in the assault of the Casa Mater, which, instead of being, as Scott and Worth supposed, an.ordinary field intrenchment, proved to be a citadel, of old Spanish masonry, with bastioned intrenchments and impassable ditches.

The information as to the foundery turned out to be false. But it is contended that the battle was neither unnecessary or fruitless, because the Molino, being an outwork of Chapultepec and commanding its defenses, its fall contributed to our subsequent success, and that the general effect was to destroy the confidence of the Mexicans in their ability to hold any position, however strong. The general-in-chief had contemplated a night attack, and expected to penetrate the Molino at the point of the bayonet with little loss. General Worth, however, after Mason and Duncan's reconnoissance, deferred the attack until daybreak, and, rather in a spirit of bravado, gave notice with Huger's guns of the approach of his assaulting column. If he relied on artillery, would it not have been better to rely on it exclusively, employing the heavy metal we had captured at Contreras and Churubusco? And, instead of attacking the centre, where the enemy was strongest and our loss consequently terrific, would it not have been wiser to fall on his left or right wing at dawn of day with the bayonet, and enter the buildings with the fugitives?

Be this as it may, the leading Mexican journals derived comfort from this bloody affair, and declared that a few such victories as we claimed at the Molino would convert our anticipated conquest into a chastisement and a curse.

Santa Anna threw a strong force into Chapultepec, and concentrated the remainder of his army within the city and at its several garitas. Our engineer officers were busily employed in reconnoitring the defenses of the city. On the 11th of September the general-in-chief convened a meeting of general officers at Piedad, which the engineers likewise attended.

The general-in-chief said that he desired to have the opinion of his officers as to the best point of attack on the capital; that, after the casualities we had met with in our several engagements in the valley of Mexico, it became a matter of vital importance to strike a decisive blow on that part of the capital which offered the greatest probability of success with the smallest chances of loss, and that the decision must be made at once. He added that his own predisposition was for an attack on Chapultepec and the western gates of the city (the Belen and San Cosme), but that he desired the opinion of his officers uninfluenced by any impressions he had formed.

General Pillow followed in a long harangue, filled with his peculiar notions of strategy, and the attack and defense of fortified places, and concluded strongly in favor of an attack by the southern gates.

General Quitman modestly said that, having no personal knowledge of the relative strength of the defenses, and claiming only a superficial acquaintance with military science, he would reserve his opinion until he heard the engineer officers.

Major Smith, Captain Lee, and Lieutenants Tower and

Stevens gave the result of their observations, and concluded in favor of an attack by the southern or San Antonio gate, which decided Generals Quitman, Shields, Pierce, and Cadwalader, notwithstanding the deference they felt for the views of the general-in-chief.

General Twiggs expressed his concurrence with General Scott.

Colonel Riley wished to know which front would require the least time and labor for the construction of the batteries?

Major Smith answered, "The western." "Then," said the bluff old soldier, "I go in for more fighting and less work."

Neither General Worth nor General Smith were present, the former being engaged in selecting the sites for batteries, and the latter on special duty at San Angel.

General Scott then called on Lieutenant Beauregard, whose conduct at Vera Cruz, Cerro Gordo, and Contreras had strongly attracted his attention. That young officer observed that, inasmuch as he differed *in toto* with his brother engineers, he felt great diffidence in expressing his views; that ever since the night of the 7th he had been reconnoitring the southern front of the city; that he had seen its defenses hourly increasing in profile, development, and armament; that, in his opinion, the garita San Antonio was now stronger than Churubusco. The approach was open to the view and to the guns of the enemy, cut up with deep ditches, and almost entirely under water; that, moreover, there was no possibility of attacking there by the flank or rear—our most successful tactic with the Mexicans. Santa Anna expected an attack in that quarter, and had made his preparations to receive us, and it is a maxim in war "never to do what your enemy expects or wishes you to do." That all military authorities agreed that the best way to attack a large city, not sufficiently armed and garrisoned, is simply to make the strongest demonstration practicable at one of its points, and then, by a rapid movement during the night, to attack suddenly about daybreak some other point more or less remote, at the same time keeping up a simulated one at the point where the first demonstration had been made; that, as the general-in-chief had stated, by so doing we would have the advantage of making the real attack on that part of the city which offered the greatest facilities for the construction of batteries (if required), and the movement of troops; and that, by first seizing Chapultepec, we secured a pivot to move upon any part of the circumference of the city, even though eventually we might find ourselves compelled to attack those same southern gates.

General Scott having asked if any other officer present had any opinion to submit, General Pierce said, after what he had just listened to, he asked permission to change his opinion. He was now in favor of the attack by Chapultepec. The general-in-chief then, rising to the full majesty of his stature, said: "We shall attack by the western gates; the general officers will remain for orders; the meeting is dissolved."*

The outworks of the CITY OF MEXICO had been closely examined by Captain Lee and Lieutenants Beauregard, Stevens, and Tower, in a series of reconnoissances

---

* This circumstantial account is from a paper indorsed by General Quitman—"Minutes of the Council at Piedad."

A fortnight afterward, when our army was within the city, while General Scott was riding with Generals Twiggs and Smith on the San Cosme road, meeting Lieutenant Beauregard with Colonel Hitchcock and Mr. Trist, he said, in a tone of feigned severity, "Young man, I wish to reprimand you, and I wish the whole army was present; but these generals represent it. Why did you advise me to attack by the western gates? You now see the consequences! We have taken this great city and the halls of Montezuma, after a few hours' hard fighting, and with only a loss of 800 men. Be careful in future, sir, of such bad advice to your seniors."

full of hazard and adventure. The city is built on a
slight elevation near the centre of an irregular basin, and
is girdled with a ditch—for the most part a canal of sufficient capacity for navigation. There are eight en-
trances, or gates, strongly defended. All the approaches
to the gates are narrow causeways, flanked on each side
by deep and wide ditches. These causeways had been
recently cut in various places, to render access more difficult, and they were completely swept by the front and
cross fires of the batteries at the garitas or gates. The
roads connecting one causeway with the other and the
bridges at the intersections had been broken, and the
marshy plain around was inundated. In the rear of the
Belen gate (a strong work, with parapet and ditch on
one side of the aqueduct, and a redan on the other), at
the distance of 1712 feet, stands the citadel, a square
bastioned work, whose guns commanded the Tacubaya
causeway. Projecting out from this like a huge spider
from its centre, 4656 feet from the Belen gate, frowns
the castle of Chapultepec, on a rock 150 feet high, only
accessible over a rugged and difficult path on its western and southwestern sides.* The buildings were of
solid Spanish masonry, and the whole had been fortified
with great skill and upon the most approved principles.
General Nicolas Bravo, one of the most distinguished
officers of Mexico, with the ablest of her artillerists and

* *Memorandum of Distances made for General Quitman by Major John
L. Smith, Engineer Corps.*

From interior extremity of citadel to garita below......1712 feet.
" garita to bend in road and aqueduct.............. 135 "
" this bend to first bridge................................. 800 "
" first to second bridge.................................2207 "
" second bridge to the battery......................... 214 "
" battery to intersection of road at Chapultepec...1300 "

Entire distance...6368 "
Deduct distance from citadel to garita....................1712 "
Leaving as distance from garita to Chapultepec........4656 "

engineers, and 6000 picked troops, was intrusted with its defense.

To deceive the enemy as to the real point of attack, on the night of the 11th Lieutenant Beauregard was ordered to locate Steptoe's battery, which opened at daylight against the works at the garita San Antonio, or southern gate of the city. General Twiggs was in position near by to sustain this demonstration.

Pillow and Quitman had been selected to command the assault on Chapultepec, the former to attack the western ascent, the latter the more formidable works on the southeast. Batteries in aid of both were located during the night of the 12th. At 8 P.M., the two generals and General Worth, who was to support Pillow, repaired to head-quarters to receive their final instructions. Their movements after the fall of the castle were to be determined upon subsequently, it being understood, however, that an attack upon the capital would immediately follow the fall of Chapultepec. There was a protracted discussion as to the best mode of proceeding, during which General Pillow strongly urged a peculiar plan of his own; but the general-in-chief, after listening in polite and patient amazement, gave his own orders with an exactitude not to be misunderstood, leaving, of course, a certain latitude of discretion for unforeseen contingencies.

Worth was directed to support Pillow, one brigade of his division being deemed sufficient, and he supplied him with a storming party of 260 men and 18 officers, led by Capt. M'Kenzie, of the 2d artillery.

Smith's brigade was ordered to support Quitman. His storming party was composed—1st. Of 120 men, volunteers from his own division, under Major Twiggs, of the marines. 2. A pioneer party of 40 select men from the volunteer division, led by Captain Reynolds, of

the marines. 3d. 250 of Twiggs's veterans, and 13 officers selected out of the rifles, the 1st and 4th regiments
of artillery, and the 2d, 3d, and 4th regiments of infantry, all under the command of Capt. Casey, of the 2d infantry. This party was organized into six divisions, cor-
responding to the different regimental detachments of
which it was composed. The first was led by Captain
Roberts, of the rifles; the second by Lieut. Hoskins, 1st
artillery; the third by Capt. Dobbin, 3d infantry; the
fourth by Lieut. Hill, 4th artillery; the fifth by Lieut.
Westcott, 2d infantry; the sixth by Capt. Paul, 7th infantry. These storming parties were supported by Watson's battalion of marines.

Sept. 13th, 1847. The signal agreed on for the joint attack was the simultaneous cessation, for five minutes, of
the fire of our heavy batteries. At 8 A.M. on the 13th
this signal was given, and both columns were put in
motion.

General Pillow started from the Molino, materially
supported by Magruder's battery, and was soon engaged
with the Mexican sharp-shooters in an open wood. These
being speedily dislodged, he rapidly pushed his men to
the foot of the acclivity, where he was paralyzed by a
glancing ball. The intrepid Cadwalader now took command, and over rocks, chasms, and mines he led his
troops up the steep ascent in the face of a fearful fire of
cannon and musketry. They gave the enemy no time to
explode their mines. Those who attempted it were shot
down. As the general-in-chief graphically expresses it,
"There was death above as well as below the ground."
Thus fighting inch by inch, leaping from rock to rock
over the fiery jaws of a volcano, and still struggling upward and onward, this band of heroes scaled the main
work on the summit of the castle, and their exulting
shout rang high above the roar of artillery and the crash

of small-arms, which hoarsely resounded upon the rock below like the surge of a heavy sea.

In this assault Pillow had the advantage of starting, as it were, from within the enemy's works, and found himself on an equality with him up to the very moment of scaling the walls at the crest of the mount. He started from the Molino, an adjunct of the castle, and Magruder's battery completely commanded the wood and low grounds on that side of Chapultepec.

Quitman, on the contrary, had to advance on the Tacubaya causeway, exposed at every step to a sweeping discharge of grape from the formidable outworks at the base of the hill, far more destructive than the plunging fire from elevated fortifications. The principal battery mounted five guns, and was supported by a strong detachment of musketry posted on the east. The causeway had been cut at intervals to render approach more difficult. There was little shelter for his men from the storm of grapeshot, and deep ditches on each side, and morasses cut up with canals, left no margin for manœuvring. By a daring reconnoissance on the 12th, Quitman had acquired a knowledge of these difficulties, and made up his mind to rely chiefly on the bayonet.* Under a tremendous fire from the five-gun battery, the breast-works, and the castle, Quitman steadily advanced by a flank, the storming parties in front, to a ruined building within 200 yards of the battery, which afforded partial shelter. Here Quitman, perceiving that a strong body of the enemy had concentrated on our front and right, directed General Shields, with the New York and South Carolina regiments, and the 2d Pennsylvania regiment, Lieut. Col. Geary, to advance obliquely on the left and breach the wall at the foot of the hill, and thus aid

* For the details of this affair, in which Lieut. Lovell greatly distingushed himself, see Appendix.

on that flank the assault of the stormers.   It was a masterly conception, resulting from a new aspect of affairs,
that demanded an instant change in the plan of attack.
He perceived it in a moment, and halted his stormers
under the ruins, while the volunteers plunged into the
morass.   Under a heavy fire of grape and musketry they
struggled forward.   Captain Van O'Linda, of the New
Yorkers, was shot dead.   Lieut. Col. Baxter, of the same
regiment, fell mortally wounded.   Col. Geary received a
severe contusion.   General Shields's arm was shattered
by a musket ball, but he refused to quit the field.   The
New Yorkers and Pennsylvanians pushed for the redan,
through which they entered the inclosure, and were seen
rapidly climbing the ascent to take a glorious part in the
strife then raging within the castle.

> "Steady they step adown the slope,
>   Steady they climb the hill;
> Steady they load—steady they fire—
>   Marching right onward still."

The Palmettos, more to the right, and more exposed to
the fire, suffered severely.   Led by the intrepid Gladden, they advanced silently, in perfect order and without
firing a gun, until, like a storm-surge on their native
shore, that breaks over the beach and sweeps far inland,
carrying drift and barriers before it, they broke across
the breast-work and ascended the hill to support the
stormers of Pillow's division.   There these regiments of
Quitman's command joined in the assault, and, when the
gallant Seymour, of Pierce's brigade, tore down the
Mexican flag, the standard of the New York regiment
was hoisted in its place.   Immediately thereafter the
Palmetto banner floated by its side, and Bravo, the veteran commander of Chapultepec, surrendered his sword
to Lieut. Brower, of the New Yorkers.

While Shields was executing this important move-

ment, and as soon as it was seen that he had crossed the
outworks, Quitman ordered the assault. The stormers
advanced in the order in which they have been named.
Major Twiggs was shot dead. Capt. Casey was severely wounded, and the command devolved on Capt. Paul.
Capt. Roberts led the advance, and, with a shout that
shook the earth, they rushed upon the battery. And
then

> " There rose so wild a yell
> Within that dark and narrow dell,
> As though the fiends from heaven that fell
> Had pealed the banner-cry of hell."

The sabre, the bayonet, and the clubbed rifle soon did
their work of death, and the grim victors paused while
their general ascended to the castle to reconnoitre the
positions of the enemy.*

---

* Capt. Casey, who led the stormers until he was disabled, in his
report says: "From the desperate nature of the service, and their
zealous co-operation, I would recommend all the officers composing
the storming party to the general-in-chief. Capt. Roberts, by his position as commanding the leading division of the column, more particularly attracted my attention. From what I myself witnessed, and
from the testimony of others, he, by his activity, zeal, and gallantry,
merits the highest praise."

Injustice was done to these heroic men in some of the official reports, which occasioned the following appeal, never heretofore in
print.

"City of Mexico, 3d Oct., 1847.

"GENERAL,—The undersigned officers of the storming party from
General Twiggs's division, with great reluctance, have the honor to
ask a court of inquiry for the investigation of the facts connected
with the storming and taking of the five-gun battery in the rear of
Chapultepec.

"General Twiggs, in his order congratulating his division of the
army for its successes before this city, credits to General Smith's brigade the assaulting and taking of this work; and in the report of
Capt. Paul, who succeeded Capt. Casey in the command of the storming party of this division, Capt. Paul reports that he charged and carried the same battery, supported by Capt. Roberts, etc., etc. Both
the order from Gen. Twiggs and the report from Capt. Paul contain
errors in fact, which, without correction, are calculated to injure the
officers and the assaulting party who stormed and carried this work.

"We regret extremely, General, that we feel constrained to ask
this investigation; but, in justice to ourselves and the brave men who

VOL. I.—Q

What a spectacle presented itself, as he gazed with eagle glance from that lofty eyry! On one side the battle-field, where so many

were with us, it seems that the truth should appear. It will *then* be shown that this battery was assaulted and carried by the stormers commanded by Capt. Roberts without the aid of any other force.

"We have the honor to be, with high regard, etc.,

"B. S. ROBERTS, Capt. Rifles.
"S. D. DOBBIN, " 3d Infantry.
"J. A. HASKIN, 1st Lieut. 1st Art'ry.
"D. H. HILL, Lieut. 4th Artillery.
"JAMES STUART, 2d Lt. M'nt'd. Rifles.
"B. E. BEE, 2d Lieut. 3d Infantry.
"J. B. RICHARDSON, Lieut. 3d Inf'try.
"GEO. C. WESTCOTT, Lieut. 2d Inf'try.
"FRED. STEELE, Lieut. 3d Infantry.

"For Major General Winfield Scott, Com. Army."

There was influence in high quarters, and other considerations, perhaps, that prevented this investigation. But among the papers of Gen. Quitman I find the following letter, written, evidently, with no view to publication, but as it is to vindicate the truth of history, it should make a part of the record of Chapultepec. Col. Roberts was a great favorite with Quitman, and the just sensibility of a soldier, and his sentiment of state pride this letter evinces, are worthy of high consideration.

From Lieut. Col. B. S. Roberts to Gen. Quitman.

"Washington, June 23d, 1852.

"MY DEAR GENERAL,—I have recently been called upon by a committee of gentlemen from my native state to furnish them with a historical account of the services I rendered in the battle of Mexico, which I can not with propriety do, except as they have been mentioned in the official reports of my commanders. In these reports, however, there is apparent conflict, and they would not be clearly understood without explanations that military propriety would forbid my making. For example, Gen. Smith reports that the flag raised on the capital was raised by 'a non-commissioned officer' of the rifles. Gen. Twiggs makes the same statement. These reports are not correct in spirit or in fact. *You* detailed *me* for *that* service, and *I* rendered it, raising that flag mainly with my own hands, and I was, in fact, the first American who entered the palace and cleared it of the leperos.

"Gen. Smith, Gen. Twiggs, and Gen. Scott all report, in substance, that Smith's brigade became stormers at the fort of Chapultepec, and entered the works with the storming party. This is not so. I applied to Gen. Smith to re-enforce me on finding the batteries impregnable, and he positively refused to aid in the storming, and said I must go to *you* for orders, his were to support me. You were then at the stone ranch by the road-side, and I went to you, repeating that my party was so cut to pieces that I must be re-enforced. You replied,

"The same wild road,
On the same bloody morning, trode
To that dark inn, the grave!"

Above him, the flags of his own division, mutilated in
the strife, but floating proudly, the symbols of a conquering race. Before him, the splendid capital of an
empire whose traditions and vicissitudes constitute the
romance of history. He felt the grandeur of the moment, and saw, with the eye of a soldier, the brilliant
destiny in reserve for him. The Tacubaya causeway
was the nearest approach to the imperial city, and the
Belen gate and the citadel, though bristling with cannon, and guarded by Santa Anna and the flower of his
army, would fall before the energy and enthusiasm of
his troops. He did not pause for consultation or for orders, but deriving his authority from the force of cir-

*Captain Roberts, you must storm and carry the battery within ten min-
utes!'* I said I could do so if given the command of marines and all
that remained. Your reply was, *'Take the command.'* I did so; rallied, on my way back, the stragglers and the marines, and took the
work. I assert, and can not be contradicted, that none of Gen.
Smith's brigade (except the stormers) had any thing to do in the assault, neither did they come into the work until it had been in my
possession some fifteen minutes. History demands that these things
should be set right.

"In Capt. Paul's report to Gen. Riley, he claims, in spirit, to have
led the stormers, and has got the reputation of having taken the battery in the rear of Chapultepec. I required him to alter the report he
made to you, setting the matter right.

"General, I have always been convinced that there were unworthy
and unmanly attempts to deprive your division of the fame of capturing the city of Mexico. The attempt on the part of Gen. Smith and
Gen. Twiggs to turn to the credit of Smith's brigade the service rendered by the stormers under your personal orders and direction should
be rebuked.

"I will thank you to write me, at your earliest convenience, the
facts of this case. They are, that the storming party alone captured
the 5-gun battery in the rear of Chapultepec; that you assigned me
to the command of it on the field; that the flag carried by that party
was the one raised on the capital, and that it was raised there by me.
My friends in Vermont think it is due to the truth of history that
these facts should appear, and that my native state may know what
service Vermonters rendered under your command."

cumstances, and yielding, as Wellesley did at Salamanca,
to the inspiration of the moment, he placed himself at
the head of his column, and stormed, in succession, two
batteries, about midway between the castle and the citadel. The desperate work before him was now apparent. There stood the Belen, with its powerful batteries; just in its rear, the citadel, capable of throwing an
enormous amount of metal—an enfilading fire from the
guns of the Paseo—a long line of musketry on the Piedad road, and a swarm of sharp-shooters lurking wherever there was shelter and concealment. Of all these
obstacles he was apprised. Reorganizing his column—
mingling the Palmettos with Loring's rifles in advance—
supported by the 2d Pennsylvania regiment, the marine
battalion, Seymour's regiment of Pierce's brigade, a detachment of the 6th infantry under Major Bonneville,
and the residue of Smith's and Shields's brigades, he advanced to the desperate work before him, silent and resolved, with no music but the thunder of cannon and the
rattling roar of small-arms. When within two hundred
yards of the Belen, Major Loring fell, severely wounded.
At this juncture Gen. Quitman seized a rifle, attached
his handkerchief to it as a flag, and waving it over his
head, ordered the assault. With one wild cheer they
followed their leader through a hurricane of fire, and at
20 minutes past 1 drove the enemy from his guns. Quitman, black with smoke, and stained with blood, leaped
upon the battery and called for a flag. Lieut. Sellick, a
young and dauntless Carolinian, vaulted to his side, and
amid the iron tempest from the citadel, proudly planted
the Palmetto banner. Like the famous Jasper of the
Revolution, he fell under its folds.

Gen. Smith, aware that they were performing an act
in a great drama that history would never forget, held
up his watch, and called on all to note the time. The

ensign of conquest floated on the walls of the capital.

Our troops in advance of the garita were now directed to fall back to the partial shelter it afforded until batteries could be constructed to support the attack upon the citadel. During the night, by extraordinary exertions, and at much personal hazard, Lieut. Beauregard located a number of batteries for our heavy pieces ; but at break of day, on the 14th, a flag from the citadel proposed to surrender. The Mexican chief, with his troops, had withdrawn from the capital.* Leaving the Palmettos posted at the Belen, and the 2d Pennsylvania regiment in the citadel, with the rifles in front, and Steptoe's battery in the rear, Quitman conducted his column to the Grand Plaza, and formed in front of the national palace. He gave orders to plant the flag of our republic upon its dome, and precisely at 7 A.M. it was saluted by his division.†

At 8 A.M. the general-in-chief, with his staff, in full

---

* "Mexico, September 13th, 1847.

"*Major General Quitman:*

"DEAR SIR,—By your request, and also for your information, I beg to state, that on this night, before twelve, Gen. Santa Anna abandoned this city, taking with him about five thousand cavalry and upward of four thousand infantry, and twenty-six pieces of artillery, besides several cart-loads of ammunition.

"I have the honor to be, with high respect and esteem, your most obedient servant, R. L. GRAVES.

"P.S.—The above information I am enabled to give you from my observation, having come into the city during the armistice, and being unable to get a pass from Gen. Santa Anna (which was then required) I was forced to remain in the city."

† Gen. Quitman thus describes this event: "When forming my division on the plaza, I perceived several non-commissioned officers hastening towards the palace with their regimental colors. I cried out, 'No, my brave fellows, take back your colors. The first flag on that palace must be the flag of our country.' Capt. Roberts, of the rifles, was then directed to bring forward a stand of national colors and plant them upon the palace." For more on this subject, see "*American Flag in Mexico*," published by order of the Senate of the United States.

uniform and escorted by cavalry, appeared on the Grand Plaza, and was received by Quitman with the highest military honors. He had intended to enter the city first, with Worth's division, by the longer and easier route of the San Cosme causeway, and had there concentrated his strongest array. But this intention had been defeated by the bold, impetuous, and masterly operations of Quitman.* Captivated, however, by the brilliant *coup-de-main* of the Mississippian, and the great military qualities he had exhibited on these last three eventful days, the general-in-chief immediately appointed him Governor of the City of Mexico.

And now, at last, the soldier's dream of ambition was realized. He stood over the ashes of Montezuma, and ruled where Cortez, the prodigy of the sixteenth century, had held his regal sway. First in the fortress of Chapultepec! First on the walls of the capital! First in possession of the city! First to erect our national standard on its loftiest tower!

"Oh, war! thou hast thy fierce delight,
Thy gleams of joy intensely bright!

---

* In his official report, General Scott says:

"I had been, from the first, well aware that the western, or San Cosme, was the less difficult route to the centre and conquest of the capital, and, therefore, intended that Quitman should only manœuvre and threaten the Belen or southwestern gate, in order to favor the main attack by Worth—knowing that the strong defenses at the Belen were directly under the guns of the much stronger fortress, called the *citadel*, just within. Both of these defenses of the enemy were also within easy supporting distance from the San Angel (or *Niño Perdido*) and San Antonio gates. Hence the greater support, in numbers, given to Worth's movement as the *main* attack.

"Those views I repeatedly, in the course of the day, communicated to Major General Quitman; but, being in hot pursuit — gallant himself, and ably supported by Brigadier Generals Shields and Smith, Shields badly wounded before Chapultepec and refusing to retire, as well as by all the officers and men of the column—Quitman continued to press forward under flank and direct fires, carried an intermediate battery of two guns, and then the gate, before two o'clock in the afternoon, but not without proportionate loss, increased by his steady maintenance of that position."

Such gleams as from thy polished shield
Fly dazzling o'er the battle-field!
Such transports wake, severe and high,
Amid the pealing conquest cry!"

INCIDENTS OF THE THREE DAYS.

In the desperate conflicts on the causeway and at the Belen, Quitman had incurred all the hazard of his storming parties. Every member of his staff was wounded. Lieutenant Wilcox, one of his most efficient aids, says: "The general was greatly exposed. Our brave fellows were falling fast when he directed me to order up the storming party. I found Captain Casey severely wounded. He referred me to Lieutenant Gantt. As I approached to give the order he was shot dead. I then gave it to Lieutenant Steele. Rejoining the general, I found that General Shields, Adjutant General Page, and Lieutenant Tower had all been wounded."

HIS RESOLUTION AND PERSISTENCY.

That gallant officer, Captain D. D. Baker, of the marines, writes: "During the 12th we were under fire all day, but General Quitman's bearing and indomitable spirit pervaded our ranks. On the night of the 12th he defeated an attempt to re-enforce the garrison of Chapultepec. On the 13th he led his troops against the batteries under a tremendous fire, and aided to carry the castle with the bayonet. My brave commander, Lieutenant Colonel Watson, shortly before he fell, directed me to communicate with the general, and I found him, with Captain Drum, engaged in turning a captured gun against the enemy. He detained me a few moments to assist. After we had stormed the battery, I met him on the heights of Chapultepec. He said to me, 'Adjutant, your marines behaved nobly. But we must now push for the Belen.' 'General,' said I, 'the citadel is in your front.'

'I am aware of it, sir, but we must try it.' He placed himself at the head of his men, fought his way along the aqueduct, stormed the garita, and at half past 1 P.M., a tempest of grape, canister, and musketry roaring around him, he stood upon the captured battery, waved his handkerchief on the point of his sword, and claimed possession of the city."

NARROW ESCAPE.

A short time after the garita was stormed, while Generals Quitman, Smith, and Shields, and several of their aids, and Lieutenant Beauregard were conversing, a howitzer shell from the citadel struck the upper edge of the aqueduct immediately above their heads, exploding at the same time. The concussion knocked them all down, but none of them were wounded. The gallant Major Loring says: "General Quitman was at the head of my regiment at the time I was shot. We were the nearest American soldiers to the city of Mexico and their army at the time I was wounded. After I fell, he armed himself with one of my rifles in their charge upon the Garita de Belen, fired his last cartridge, then tied his handkerchief to its muzzle, and waved his gallant soldiers over the breastwork—being the first to mount amid the terrible carnage that followed. I'll venture to say there are few instances in history where one so high in rank and advanced in life has thus had, and availed himself of, the brilliant opportunity of wreathing around his brow so distinct a title to the honor of being regarded the 'bravest of the brave.'"

DEATH OF CAPTAIN DRUM.

"About this time," says Lieutenant Beauregard, "Captain Drum and Lieutenant Benjamin passed with their pieces (one 24-pound howitzer and one long 18-pounder) on each side of the aqueduct, firing as they advanced, in the face of a heavy fire of grape and canister, solid shot and shells. After the seizure of the garita Drum took possession of an 8-pounder, turned it round on its own platform against a battery near the citadel, and, after having several sets of men cut down, fell himself mortally wounded by a shot that broke both his legs. And thus perished one of the most promising and popular officers in the service. A few moments afterward his lieutenant, Benjamin, boldly pushing his piece toward the citadel, fell, to rise no more, on the corpses of the brave gunners that lay thickly around."

A BRAVE SERGEANT.

During the advance one of Benjamin's men, becoming terrified under the awful fire of grape and canister, took refuge in one of the arches of the aqueduct, and when called back to his gun, moved very reluctantly. The sergeant, who had just been wounded in the leg, bandaged it with his handkerchief, and, hobbling to the man, repeated the order. The fellow still moving slowly, the impatient officer drew his sabre and thrashed him back to his duty. It was indeed a terrible post, and never did men stand by it more firmly.

INTREPIDITY OF GENERAL SMITH.

"After taking the garita," says Lieut. Beauregard, "while waiting for the approach of night to enable us to construct our batteries, screening ourselves as best we could from the heavy fire of the citadel, Gen. Persifer F. Smith performed one of the most daring acts ever witnessed. Between the battery at this point and the aqueduct, there was an opening of some twelve feet for the passage of vehicles between the city and Chapultepec. This was completely swept by the guns of the citadel,

which kept up an incessant discharge of grape and canister, and by the Mexican sharp-shooters from behind the
arches of the aqueduct.   It was a matter of life and
death to cross this passage from one side of our position
to the other.   One of the riflemen started to cross it,
and, instead of going over in a direct line and in double-
quick time, he crossed diagonally and leisurely.   As a
matter of course he was shot down.   He raised himself
several times on his elbow, but could not get up.   Gen.
Smith ordered a party to bring him in.   Several soldiers
stepped forward, but recoiled from the fatal passage,
through which poured a torrent of projectiles.   Upon
the order being repeated they advanced a step, and
stood apparently paralyzed.   Gen. Smith got up, un-
buckled his sword, and, without saying a word, went to
the wounded soldier and stooped to raise him up.   In a
moment a dozen officers and men were at his side, and,
wonderful to say, they all got back safely, the enemy
having, fortunately, intermitted his fire.   They brought
in a corpse.

"As though to show the chances of war, soon after
this a solid shot *ricochet* killed five or six of our men
who were under the arches of the aqueduct, and had felt
themselves perfectly safe."

A MIDNIGHT ADVENTURE.

"During the night of the 13th," continues Lieut. Beauregard, "Gen. Quitman and I were groping along in
the dark, in front of our position, in search of a suitable
site for a second battery he desired to have.   The general pertinaciously insisted that the ground before us was
high.   I expressed my doubts, when suddenly he disappeared head foremost, and I had scarcely heard his plunge
before down I went myself neck-deep in the Piedad Canal!   I could not forbear rating the general about his

'high land,' and asking what he thought of it now. He readily admitted that 'it was rather lower than he had taken it to be.' We did not give up, however, but scrambled out and located our battery, and by daylight had our guns in position and our matches lighted. This was very hard work, but was done with the aid of my gallant friends, Lieut. Coppie, 1st artillery, and Lieut. Wood, 3d infantry.

A FASTIDIOUS OFFICER.

"Upon the offer to surrender the citadel Gen. Quitman dispatched Lieut. Lovell and myself to confer with the officer, detaining the flag as a hostage. The officer in charge offered to pass over every thing to us, but demanded our receipts. It was with difficulty we made him comprehend that receipts on such occasions were written with blood and signed with the bayonet."

NEW STYLE OF PRINTING.

During the storming of the Belen Lieutenant Wilcox was struck down, and supposed to be killed. His revolver, hanging to his belt, saved his life. The ball struck its barrel, and was picked up as flat as a dollar, with the name of the maker and the place where it was made legibly stamped upon it.

A FAITHFUL TEAMSTER.

"While we lay under shelter at the garita an ammunition-wagon came trotting down the road. Knowing that the enemy would open upon him we signaled to him to turn back, but he did not notice our signs and came on. The road being too narrow to turn, we directed him to unhitch. While doing this two of his team were killed. We called to him to get under cover. 'No, be Jasus,' said he, 'I must save my mules.' And,

notwithstanding the shower of grape, he got off safely
toward Chapultepec."

QUITMAN IN BATTLE.

A distinguished officer of the 2d Pennsylvania regiment, writing from the City of Mexico to the Philadelphia Inquirer, says:

"This battle at the garita was the hottest point of
the whole war. It lasted *from noon until dark* of the
13th of September. A few hundred of us congregated
around the gate which gave us entrance to the city.
We had one field-piece there, taken from the enemy
when we drove them from the gates to their citadel.
In using that field-piece we were entirely without protection, and were exposed to the fires of the citadel (one
of the strongest in the world), of a cross battery, and of
thousands of men in position on the Paseo.

"The conduct of Major General Quitman was truly
sublime. I never witnessed so much chivalrous heroism,
united with so much concern for his men, and with so
much cool intellectual battle wisdom. While he calmly
dared every thing, his mind was supreme, presiding over
every thing, and making provision for every emergency.
At all points he was exposed, and he would suffer no
man to expose himself to shield him. On one occasion,
when it was necessary for him to pass along a line of
desperate exposure to effect an object, I approached
him and asked permission to do what *he* was about to
do in person, to bear his message, intimating to him that
my own fall would be, in the crisis of the moment, of no
importance compared with his. His reply was, while he
puffed away at his cigar, 'No, take care of yourself; it is
necessary for *me* to do it.' And he *did* do it. At another time, about the middle of the afternoon, when our
own gun was silenced (for we had run out of ammuni-

tion), and the fire of the enemy was fast dealing death around, I asked him to let me be one of a select party at once to storm and take the citadel, and by one dreadful sacrifice, if needs be, put an end to this one-sided work of blood. His reply, again, was in the same spirit, 'No, I will not permit my brave men thus to be sacrificed. I must take care of them as well as conquer the foe. All I now design is to maintain, with as little loss as possible, my present position until night. When night covers us we will bring up our guns; will have an abundance of ammunition; we will construct a battery, and before to-morrow's sun is an hour high we will plant our country's flag on the capital of Mexico—Mexico will be ours!' All this was said in the calmèst manner, while he quietly smoked his cigar, without the least emphasis or excitement, with no discernible manifestation of boast or vainglory, and with the enemy's balls falling as hail around him.

"We did maintain our position; we did construct our battery, making all right; we did bring up more captured guns, and with them an abundant supply of ammunition. And soon after the day's dawn, before the sun's rays had lighted up the scene of desolation around us, the white flag of the enemy approached—the citadel and city were surrendered, and, before the sun was an hour high, the flag of our country floated in triumph over the national palace—the Halls of the Montezumas, whence I now write.

"The manner of General Quitman, even in the midst of the most exciting danger, is the calmest you can conceive of. His orders are as quietly communicated as if he were conversing with a friend at the dinner-table. His presence, his mild, benevolent face, his daring courage, his concern for all but himself, his mind providing for every thing, inspire universal confidence, and seem to animate all who follow with the same indomitable heroic spirit of him who leads."

THE WARRIORS' REUNION.

Colonel John D. Elliott relates the following touching incident:

"Soon after the termination of the Mexican war, while on a visit to Washington city, we made the acquaintance of Major Loring. During our sojourn, General Quitman, who had been in attendance upon a court-martial at Frederick, arrived in the city and took lodgings at the United States Hotel. On hearing of his arrival we repaired, in company with Major Loring, to his quarters.

"The hero of Chapultepec earnestly grasped the extended hand of his guest, and, with moistened eye, for a moment stood speechless in the presence of one whose right arm had been lost in the effort to save the life of his commander. It was their first meeting since the gallant major had been borne from the field of battle in the storm upon the Garita de Belen.

"We gathered, from what was said, that General Quitman was in the act of giving some word of command to the major, when the practiced eye of the latter, and his knowledge of projectiles, discovered the elevation of a piece of cannon, charged with grape, about being discharged directly upon them. They were both standing adjacent to the arched wall of the aqueduct, when the major, without time to speak, forcibly impelled General Quitman beneath the arch in time to screen him from the destructive fire, but not to save himself from the deadly blow, which cost him the loss of one arm and nearly his life. Such self-sacrificing devotion, such noble impulse, deeply impressed the heart of the fearless veteran, and now, for the first time, he sought language to convey in person some feeble testimony of its appreciation."

"On the evening of the 12th Sept.," says Sergeant
Devit, 3d artillery, "a detachment from the 3d was ordered to man four iron guns on the Tacubaya causeway.
One piece, a 24-pounder, was confided to me. One of
my shots took effect near the flag-staff of the castle, and
tore off a section of the roof. Stepping up to me, Gen.
Quitman said, 'Well done, sergeant. We shall get that
flag first.' A few moments after this Gen. Shields came
up, and sprung upon a ridge on the side of the road,
where an opening in the pulque bushes had been made.
Gen. Quitman insisted on his coming down, because he
had noted it as directly within range of one of the Mexican guns. Gen. Shields had scarcely moved when a ball
from the castle struck the very spot where he had stood,
covering both of our generals with dust. Gen. Quitman
said, 'Shields, you owe me one;' and Gen. Shields pleasantly related the anecdote of Napoleon, who, when a
young officer at Toulon, remarked, when a cannon ball
covered the paper on which he was writing with dust,
'We shall need no more sand.' "

"When we were under a very heavy fire on the causeway before Chapultepec," says Corporal John Bold, of
the Palmettos, "a volunteer belonging to another regiment was shot down. He called for assistance, but no
one moved. Gen. Quitman, hearing his call, sternly cried
out, 'Gentlemen, I fear there are some of you in the
ranks that I can not trust.' I instantly stepped forward; my comrade, Anderson, joined me. The general,
and Lieut. Bell, of our regiment, took our muskets, and
we brought the man in. 'You deserve your muskets,
gentlemen,' said the general, shaking us by the hand.
'You do your duty as soldiers and Christians.' "

ENTRANCE INTO THE CITY.

"After leaving a garrison at the garita and at the citadel," says Lieut. Beauregard, "we marched toward the main plaza of the city with only about three or four regiments and Steptoe's battery. We arrived and formed in line of battle in front of the cathedral as its clock was striking 7 A.M. The American flag was then hoisted on the palace of the Montezumas.

"The sight we presented marching into that immense city, being nearly all of us covered with mud, and some with blood, some limping, some with arms in scarfs, and others with heads in bandages, followed by two endless lines of gaping leperos and rabble, was any thing but glorious in appearance.*

"The novelty of our position had renewed my failing energies, and Gen. Quitman, not having one of his personal staff about him at the time (as they were transmitting his orders in every direction), requested me to go and inform the general-in-chief of our entrance into the city, and of our having taken possession of the palace. I rode toward the San Cosme garita through the deserted streets of that large capital as silent as the tomb—every house being strongly barricaded—with nothing to disturb this death-like stillness but the clattering of my horse's hoofs on the pavements. I could not then help remembering the description by Prescott of Cortez's flight from the city during that celebrated 'Noche Triste,' about 317 years before, by the very road I was then traversing."

* Lieut. Wilcox says that General Quitman had but one shoe on. He lost one the night before in the canal.

INTERVIEW WITH THE GENERAL-IN-CHIEF.

"At the Almeda, or public garden, I came upon the head of Worth's command stationed there at the time; they appeared as astonished to see me coming from that direction as I was to find them there, for I was not aware of their true position until then. When I told them of our having occupied the palace, they appeared somewhat surprised at our temerity and success. I continued on, and met General Scott and staff near the angle of the San Cosme and Chapultepec roads; it must have been about $8\frac{1}{2}$ hours. He appeared delighted to see me. When I had communicated my message, his first question was, 'Whether we had been in any hurry to forestall Gen. Worth in the occupation of the palace?' I told him that we had never been aware of the position of Gen. Worth, and that I had only just ascertained it. Moreover, that we had never heard of the surrender of the city until we had entered the citadel, where we met an English gentleman who had come to give us the information, and to tell us to be on our guard, as it was reported that as soon as our troops would become disorganized by the excesses and depredations inherent to the violent possession of such a large city, a rising of the leperos would take place, during which, Santa Anna, who had only retired to the small village of Guadalupe, three miles to the north of Mexico, would suddenly return and attack us when thus unprepared to receive him, and it was hoped every one of us would be exterminated. This scheme had been arranged, but it was frustrated by our doing the very reverse of what they expected us to do."

INSURRECTION OF THE LEPEROS.

"I returned with the general-in-chief and staff to the palace, where we arrived about 9 hours, when a salute was fired by Steptoe's battery, and all the necessary orders given for the proper occupation of the city, Gen. Quitman being appointed governor; but before they could all be carried into execution the outbreak spoken of took place, and by 12 hours had become so intense that Santa Anna thought the favorable moment had arrived for carrying his scheme into execution. Unfortunately for him, the head of his column came directly upon Duncan's battery, which opened upon it a destructive fire, and drove it back faster than it had come. This revolt continued until the next day about noon, and at one time looked very unfavorable. I again had the pleasure of seeing here the gallant Cerro Gordo division (with which I had so often served, that I almost considered myself as belonging to it), led on by its worthy general (Twiggs, or 'Old Orizaba,' as he was called), doing its fighting in the streets, storming houses, etc., as it did every thing else, '*sans peur et sans reproche.*'

GEN. WORTH AND LIEUT. COL. DUNCAN.

In his report of the actions before the gates of Mexico, Gen. Worth says:

"A portion of Garland's brigade, which had been previously deployed in the field to the left, now came up with and defeated the enemy's right; the enemy's left extending in the direction of the Tacubaya aqueduct, on which Quitman's division was *battling* and *advancing.* Pursuing the San Cosme road, we discovered an arched passage through the aqueduct, and a cross route practicable for artillery, for a considerable distance over the meadows, in the direction of the battery and left of the enemy's line, which was galling and endeavoring to check Quitman's advance. Lieut. Col. Duncan, with a section of his battery, covered by Lieut. Col. Smith's battalion, was turned off upon this route, and, advancing to within 400 yards of the enemy's lines (which was as far as the nature of the ground would permit), opened an effective fire—first upon the battery and then upon the retreating troops, great numbers of whom were cut down. Having thus aided the advance and cleared the front (being favorably situated) of my gallant friend Quitman as far as it was in my power, this portion of my command was withdrawn."

Gen. Quitman, who was ever ready to acknowledge the success of others, thus refers, in his report, to the same incident:

" On our approach to the garita, a body of the enemy, who were seen on a cross road threatening our left, were dispersed by a brisk fire of artillery from the direction of the San Cosme road. I take pleasure in acknowledging that this seasonable aid came from Lieut. Col. Duncan's battery, which had been kindly advanced from the San Cosme road in that direction by General Worth's orders."

Upon examining the matter critically, however, it does not appear that this diversion could have had any material effect. The distance, instead of 400 yards, as stated by Worth, was 883 yards, according to a map of the city of Mexico and its defenses, made by Lieut. Beauregard, and now in the office of the chief engineer, Washington city. The position was not on the flank of said battery (which had its flank protected by a parapet forming a traverse in that direction), but on a line forming nearly an angle of 30° with that flanking direction; and there were at least two pieces in the Mexican battery, heavier than any in Duncan's, firing through embrasures. Duncan, though one of the boldest officers in the service, could get no nearer, owing to the canals which intersected his line of approach in every direction, and, at that long range, the heavier metal of the enemy (always well served) would have been more likely to drive him away than he to " clear Quitman's front." The fact is, the fire was ineffective, owing to the range and the calibre of his guns.

GEN. PILLOW'S REPORT.

In his official report of the storming of Chapultepec, Gen. Pillow (who personally saw but little of it, having been struck down in the beginning of the action by "an agonizing wound") remarks :

"The advance of Gen. Quitman's division, which was to have assaulted upon the left of the position, having fallen under the fire of a battery on the outside of the outer wall, and, being unable to scale it in consequence of the want of ladders, were obliged to march several hundred yards to the south, and to enter the very breach through which portions of my command had passed at the commencement of the action. The consequence was that command did not get into position in time to render me material assistance in the assault ; though, owing to the delay at the summit of the hill, occasioned by the want of ladders, portions of Gen. Quitman's command, who passed through the breach in the outer wall under my own observation, had time to come up and enter the inner works about the same time with parts of my own command, which had for some time previous completely enveloped the work and called out for the ladders."

There was no necessity for this passage, which has been construed to the disparagement of Quitman and his column. Nor is it accurate. Gen. Pillow's arrangements for the attack on Chapultepec have been severely criticised. His original plan of attack is said to have been wholly unmilitary, but, of course, was superseded by the instructions of the general-in-chief, who, early on the evening of the 12th, in consultation with Capt. Lee and Lieuts. Tower and Beauregard, of the engineers, had arranged his plans, which shortly afterward were communicated to Gens. Quitman and Pillow.

Gen. Pillow's call on Worth for re-enforcements, so much in the spirit of "Come, help me, Cassius, or I sink," was unnecessary, for he already had a superabundance of troops swarming up and around the hill, and the call for more only multiplied the casualties.

And, in the opinion of military men, he committed a material error in assigning *his* ladders to new levies, who were thrown into disorder, and the ladders were not forthcoming when needed, thus delaying the final assault, and exposing his men to a prolonged and destructive fire.

Let us now examine the passage from his report.

1. From what he says, it would be inferred that Quitman had erred more egregiously than himself about the "ladders." The inference is that Quitman, though ordered expressly to storm certain batteries, had ignorantly or culpably neglected to provide the indispensable ladders. The fact is, they had been carefully provided and intrusted to Capt. Reynolds, who says, "We were provided with muskets, *ladders*, pickaxes, and crowbars." Maj. Casey, in his report, refers to his ladders and other storming apparatus. There was no delay, therefore, on that account—no change of operations for the want of "ladders," as Pillow intimates. See also Major Casey's report.

2. From the language of General Pillow, it may be inferred that the regiments led by Shields and Geary, when making the oblique movement Quitman deemed it expedient to order, were wandering, confusedly, over an unknown track; and he states positively that "they entered the walls of the fortress through a breach made by his troops, and did not get into position in time to render him material assistance in the assault."

In answer to this sweeping statement, it may be observed that General Quitman, by an elaborate reconnoissance, had a thorough knowledge of the ground. He knew the difficulties to be overcome. There was no delay whatever in the execution of his work. The oblique movement to the left was the result of the unexpected

concentration of the enemy in a new position. It was
a masterly conception of Quitman, and was gallantly executed by Shields and his volunteers. They waded
through the morass in the face of a terrific fire, and
calmly preserved their own until they had penetrated
the walls. "The Palmetto regiment," says General
Shields, "being in advance, gained the wall without firing a shot, *broke through it*, and ascended the hill in a
body." When ordered by Lieutenant Colonel Johnson,
of the Voltigeurs (who had just stormed the castle, and
was senior officer at the moment), to form his regiment,
Major Gladden, of the Palmettos, replied that "it was
already formed." It had never broken its ranks—an instance of discipline and steadiness under fire and in the
assault that no veteran regiment in any service ever surpassed.

Major Gladden, who led the Palmettos, says, "Upon
arriving at the wall, *I set to work*, and, after considerable
difficulty, succeeded *in making a breach* in it."

3. According to General Pillow, they rendered him
no material assistance in the assault. What says General Quitman?

"Simultaneously with these movements on our right,
the volunteer regiments, with equal alacrity and intrepidity, animated by a generous emulation, commenced
the ascent of the hill on the south side; surmounting every obstacle, and fighting their way, *they fell in and
mingled* with their brave brethren in arms *who formed
the advance* of Major General Pillow's column. *Side by
side*, amid the storm of battle, the rival colors of *the two
commands* struggled up the steep ascent, entered the
fortress, and reached the buildings used as a military
college which crowned its summit. Here was a short
pause; but soon the flag of Mexico was lowered, and
the stars and stripes of our country floated from the

heights of Chapultepec high above the heads of the brave men who had planted them there. *The gallant New York regiment claims for their standard the honor of being first waved from the battlements of Chapultepec.* The veteran Mexican general, Bravo, with a number of officers and men, were taken prisoners in the castle. They fell into the hands of Lieutenant Charles Brower, of the New York regiment, who reported them to me."

General Scott, in his report, expressly recognizes the services of Quitman's command in "the final assault, after having gallantly carried the works at its southeastern base."

General Shields says, "The Palmettos ascended the hill in a body *to the support* of the storming parties from the other division. The New York regiment *united with* the storming parties of the other division."

Major Burnham, who led the New York regiment (its colonel, Burnett, having been wounded, and its lieutenant colonel, Baxter, killed), says, emphatically, "It was the first at the ditch, first in the enemy's works, and *first* to place the national flag on the conquered castle."

Major Brindle, who took command of the 2d Pennsylvania regiment, Colonel Geary having been wounded, says, "In ascending the hill, moving by the right of companies, the regiment gallantly charged *the works on the summit.* The ascent was made under a brisk fire of small-arms by the enemy, which was returned by our advancing columns with such effect as *to cause their immediate retreat.* It is due to the regiment to state that, although others entered simultaneously with them, they were among *the first* inside."

Captain D. D. Baker, of the marines, says, "Quitman brushed away the strong defenses at the base of Chapultepec, and carried the castle at the point of the bayonet."

Pillow's report of the action bears date September 18th, 1847; Quitman's, September 29th, 1847. The presumption is that Quitman had seen or been informed of this passage in Pillow's report when he drew up his own, and claimed for his command an equal share of the honor of the final assault, after having first accomplished a more exposed and more difficult enterprise. He accomplished what from the first he designed to do. In his report he alludes to his contemplated assault upon *the castle*, as distinct from the batteries at its foot.

General Pillow's command performed the part assigned it—a perilous and difficult part—most brilliantly, and this defense of their brothers in arms is not intended to rob them of the laurels they so nobly won.

THE QUESTION OF PRIORITY.

It has been a matter of controversy which was first carried, the castle, or the works at its base, and how far Pillow's attack assisted Quitman, and *vice versa*. The question is of little value, but it can not be doubted that Quitman's command stormed the batteries, and was in the fortress on the hill in time to take part in the fight. The *simultaneous* advance made by the two divisions undoubtedly operated in favor of both in its effect on the enemy. In a strategic point of view, it must, of course, be conceded that the fall of the *castle* would bring with it the evacuation of the *lower batteries*, which were commanded by the former. But the fact is that these batteries were stormed before the fortress surrendered. The proof is conclusive. The Mexicans at the leading battery, directly on the line of advance of Quitman's storming party, stood obstinately to their guns until they were overpowered by the bayonet and clubbed rifle. A portion of those that retreated fled along the causeway toward the Belen; another portion, and a portion of those that had been formed in line of battle along the aqueduct, sought safety *inside* of the wall at the base of the hill, whence they were subsequently driven by the guns of the castle after it had surrendered to Quitman and Pillow. This one fact is conclusive as to the question of precedence, independent of the positive testimony already quoted.

QUITMAN'S ADVANCE ON THE BELEN.

The general-in-chief, in his report, says he only intended that Quitman should manœuvre and threaten the Belen gate while the main attack should be made by Worth on the western or San Cosme route, and that, during the day, he repeatedly communicated these views to General Quitman.

There is no evidence in the papers of General Quitman to show that he ever received such instructions. He marched from Chapultepec, in broad daylight, on an elevated causeway, in full view of the whole army, storming battery after battery, and finally carried the garita by assault at 20 minutes past 1 P.M. "During all this time," says Lieutenant Beauregard, "I was near him, in constant communication with him, conversing freely as to what he proposed to do, and he never hinted having received such instructions." If he had received them even after the storming of the garita, is it probable that he would have kept a large portion of his exhausted command, who had been two days under fire, employed in constructing batteries to attack the citadel next morning? It is a violent presumption to suppose that Quitman, under any circumstances, would have disobeyed the orders of the general-in-chief. He understood the value of subordination, and, a thorough stickler for his own rights, he never disputed the rights of others.

Capt. Baker, of the marines, says, "About dark, after the fall of the garita, while I was taking a cup of coffee with Gen. Quitman, Lieut. Hardcastle brought congratulations from Gen. Scott, and desired him to withdraw for the night from his exposed position. The answer was, 'I will not retire without a peremptory order.' Lieut. H. then inquired of the general what he wanted for the night? He replied, 'Intrenching tools and ammunition.' When the lieutenant rode away Gen. Quitman rose and said, 'Baker, the capital is mine; my brave fellows have conquered it, and, by G—d, they shall have it!' Next morning he took possession of it."

Lieut. Wilcox, one of his aids, says, "As he was going up to the castle, after we had stormed the batteries, he left orders with me (and, I presume, the other members of his staff) to have the troops ready for an advance upon the city. This was the first word I had heard on the subject. I remember having seen several officers from Gen. Scott while we were advancing along the aqueduct, but whether they gave orders to Gen. Quitman I can not say; he communicated none to me. The orders given to him were, as a matter of course, almost invariably made known to his staff. I remember having a brief interview with Maj. Kirby, one of the officers referred to. He said nothing of orders from Gen. Scott."

Gen. Quitman was sensitive in regard to the matters here referred to, and propounded a series of interrogatories to Capt. Danby, of Arkansas, one of his aids, distinguished for his gallantry, activity, and intelligence. His testimony covers the whole controversy, and settles every doubtful point.

"Little Rock, Arkansas, July 21st, 1852.

"GEN. J. A. QUITMAN: DEAR SIR,—I have examined your interrogatories, propounded with the view of eliciting such facts in the history of the storming of the fortress of Chapultepec and the gate of Belen as might be in my possession and transpired under my observation, and will, with pleasure, respond to all of your interrogatories as briefly as I can with justice to all parties concerned.

"I have to say, in reply to interrogatory

"1st. 'When and at what time were you received on my staff?'

"I was introduced to you in a restaurant in Tacubaya, where you had called to get your breakfast, about eight o'clock in the morning of the 12th of September, 1847. You had just arrived, if I mistake not, from Capt. Drum's battery, which was then firing on the fortress of Chapultepec from the road leading from Tacubaya to the city. Immediately on making your acquaintance I offered my services as a volunteer, and on your staff, was accepted, and proceeded with you to Capt. Drum's battery. I did no service of importance on the 12th.

"2d. 'What verbal orders did you receive from me on the 13th before you were wounded, and the particular place and point of time when you received each?'

"The *first* order I executed for you on the 13th of September was to direct Capt. Hunt, with a section of Duncan's battery, to move up. He was between Drum's battery and Tacubaya. He moved up as directed, and received orders from you at Capt. Drum's battery. The *second* order was a similar one, a very few minutes after, to Major Twiggs to move up with his storming party. He also advanced and received orders from you at Drum's battery. The *third* order was not long after this, when you directed me to go across the meadow between where we were (Drum's battery) and Chapultepec to gather up all the stragglers, close up the column, and direct the volunteers to advance on the fortress of Chapultepec and carry it by storm. The *fourth* order was when we both had ascended the hill at Chapultepec, you directed me to go down the causeway leading from Chapultepec to the city of Mexico, and ascertain and report to you the movements of a body of Mexican troops, who appeared to have marched out from, and were ascertained to be retreating again toward the city, after the fall of Chapultepec. The *fifth* order was received from you immediately on my

return and report to you of the execution of the *fourth*
order; it was received on the causeway leading from
Tacubaya and Chapultepec to the gate of Belen and the
city, not far from where the Tacubaya road crosses the
aqueduct, and between the crossing and the city. On
my return from executing your *fourth* order I heard the
cry of '*Gen. Quitman's division, to the city! Gen. Quitman's division, to the city!*' Immediately on my reporting to you, I was directed by you to proceed again to
the then surrendered fortress of Chapultepec, and repeat
to all of your command whom I might see the order of
'*Gen. Quitman's division to the city.*' The *sixth* order
I executed was on the Belen causeway, near the *Casa
Colorada* (Red House). This was to direct Maj. Bonneville to take possession of the *Casa Colorada*, and there
gather and take command of all stragglers. The *seventh*
order was after we had advanced from the *Casa Colorada* toward the city, when you directed me to ride back
to the head of the causeway near Chapultepec and direct
all stragglers to move up on the right or south side of
the aqueduct; and also to direct Gen. Smith to move
up and join you with your reserve, which was commanded by him. Just before I reported the execution of this
order to you, and immediately outside of a work thrown
up by the Mexicans between the *Casa Colorada* and
the city, I received a wound which disabled me and prevented my reporting to you. I may have received other
orders from you on the 13th of September, but these are
all which I can now recall to my memory. It would be
impossible for me, after this lapse of time, to give the
precise time of receiving any of the orders enumerated
above; indeed it would have been difficult for me to
have done so the next day, as I took no particular note
of time, having lost my watch when I was taken prisoner. I would give it as my opinion, however, that the
first order (to Capt. Hunt) was received about 8 o'clock
in the morning, and the *last* order (to Gen. Smith) was
soon after 11 o'clock in the forenoon of the 13th of September.

"3d. 'At the time the volunteer regiment passed over
or through the wall, could you see any of Gen. Pillow's
division ascending the hill? Was not the battery in

front of my column carried before the Mexican flag was lowered on the castle?'

"I did not see any of Gen. Pillow's division ascending the hill at the time our volunteers passed the wall, though I presume they ascended the hill about the same time with our volunteers. The battery in front of your column *was* carried *before* the Mexican flag was lowered on the castle.

"4th. 'What flag was first on the walls of the castle?'

"I can not say which of the different flags was first on the walls of the castle, though the first flag I saw there was that of the New York regiment. It is just, however, that I should say that, immediately after seeing the flag of the New York regiment, I saw several other flags on the castle. The first thing which attracted my attention to the other flags was an apparent scramble as to which flag should be run up on the fortress after the hauling down of the Mexican flag. The Mexican flag was hauled down some time, in my opinion, at least five or ten minutes, before the firing ceased and the Mexicans were subdued.

"5th. 'Which way did the body of the Mexican troops retreat?'

"I was not in a position to see, and, consequently, do not know which way the body of the Mexican troops who escaped from Chapultepec did retreat; but it must have been north of the Belen road, and on the other side from where we were. It is impossible that they could have escaped down the Belen road, because our storming party, aided by General Smith's command, carried the works just at the end of, and which commanded the entrance into that road, and took a large body of prisoners (amounting to some hundreds) between those works and Chapultepec on the hill.

"6th. 'Did the firing continue until I had entered the works and ascended the hill, or while ascending the hill?'

"A scattering fire did continue until after you had entered the works, and had ascended, or was ascending the hill. This fire was from the timber (or woods) on the hill-side on our left as we ascended the hill.

"7th. 'At what point were you wounded?'

"I was wounded at a point just before we reached a

breast-work outside of the gate of Belen, and the only one, I believe, between the *Casa Colorada* and the Belen gate.

"8th. 'At what point did you first hear the orders given by me to advance toward the city? Or when and where did you first learn my intention to attack the city? On your advance up the hill did I direct you to inform my command that they should form on the causeway to march on the city? When you ascended the hill what was going on in our division? Where then was I? and where was I, and what doing, when you last saw me?'

"I first heard your orders to advance on the city on the causeway leading from Chapultepec to the city, not far from where the Tacubaya and Belen road crosses the aqueduct; for an account of the orders then received, see my answer to your *second* interrogatory. It is given in my account of the *fifth* order, and therein referred to and explained. When I ascended the hill to execute your *fifth* order you were at the head of as much of your column as you had collected, and had commenced your advance on the city by the Belen causeway. When I last saw you on that day you were in advance of where I received my wound. I had, as I have before stated, been back to the rear, and ordered up Gen. Smith with your reserve, and was, when I received my wound, coming up to report to you that I had executed that order. At this time you were advancing toward the city; I think about where Drum's battery was at that time.

"9th. 'Were was General Shields then, and General Smith?'

"The last I saw of Gen. Smith on that day was a few minutes after I last saw you. He was advancing at the head of his column to join you, as he had been ordered by you through me. This was a short time after I had received my wound. Gen. Shields passed where I lay a few minutes after Gen. Smith. He had his arm in a sling from a wound he had received that morning. He stopped and conversed with me some minutes. I desired him to report to you that I had been disabled, so as to prevent my joining your staff again, which he politely promised to do, and, smiling, bid me '*Good-morning.*'

"10th. 'Were you not much about my person until you were carried from the field? and did you, at any time, hear of my receiving any communications from the general-in-chief, or any other source, in relation to his intention to make the principal attack by the San Cosme causeway?'

"I was much about your person—indeed all the time I was not absent carrying orders for you to your different commands. During the whole day, until I was carried from the field, I heard nothing of your receiving any orders, or communications of any kind, from the general-in-chief or from any other source. I did not hear it intimated in any quarter that the principal attack was to be made on the gate of San Cosme. My impression was, at that time, and still is, that a joint attack was contemplated, as it certainly was carried out, on both the gates of Belen and San Cosme. But whether that was the contemplated plan or not, I am certain that you received no orders or communications from the general-in-chief on that day until you had taken the gate of Belen. What orders you might have received after that I can not be cognizant of; for shortly before the gate was carried I was wounded, and shortly after it was carried I was taken from the field."

The general-in-chief, with a brilliant suite, escorted by the cavalry, entered the city at 8 o'clock, the band of the 2d dragoons playing "Hail Columbia." As the cortége appeared on the Grand Plaza the general was received with acclamations, and "Yankee Doodle" from the different bands raised the national feeling to the highest pitch. Without dismounting from his charger—like a conqueror acknowledging the valor of his generals on the field of battle—Gen. Scott proclaimed Gen. Quitman governor of the city of Mexico, with high civil and military powers. His staff consisted of Capt. F. N. Page, assist. adjutant general; Lieuts. M. Lovell, C. M. Wilcox, and R. P. Hammond, aids; Capt. Charles Naylor, superintendent of the palace, Capt. G. T. M. Davis, secretary; Mr. Levi, interpreter.

A formidable insurrection had been organized, to be initiated by the leperos, or rabble, of the city, and seconded by Santa Anna, if circumstances were favorable. There were several hours of bloodshed and confusion, but the prompt and decisive measures adopted soon restored order. Gen. Scott and Gov. Quitman both commanded the confidence and respect of the better class of Mexicans. The municipal authorities co-operated in every measure for the preservation of tranquillity. The American Star, published in the city of Mexico, of the 20th of September, says:

" In our opinion, confidence is now perfectly restored; there is scarce a place of business that is not open; and what more clearly than any thing else demonstrates the fact that contentment reigns in a great measure over the scores and scores of families that begin to promenade the streets. Whenever you see the softer sex walking the streets in confidence, you may set it down at once that things are as they should be.

" The shops are again opened, and security and public confidence are perfectly restored. The theatre was opened on Sunday, the 26th ult., and the crowd was immense, the building not being capable of containing the numbers who thronged the avenues."

This was the result of the liberal but firm and vigilant administration inaugurated by the American governor. In the neighboring city of Puebla, which had been temporarily evacuated by our troops, as though to show the contrast between American and Mexican rule, the greatest disorders prevailed. A letter from a responsible source, dated Puebla, September 22d, says:

" The guerrilleros have disgraced the name of man— they are monsters. The letter says there is scarce a foreign family or a foreigner that has not received more or less injury from them, and, in many instances, of the most aggravating nature. Independent of the outrages committed upon the persons and property of the Mexican citizens, they have gone into the houses of foreigners, and devastation and dismay have followed their every step. They broke into the store of a German jeweler near the Diligencias, and, after robbing it of near $25,000 worth of property, put a rope around his neck and took him to the Alameda for execution. They then went into the house of an American lady who has lived many years in Puebla, and whose husband is now in Mexico, and, putting their swords and lances to her breast, were about to kill her, when she delivered what money was in her hands and they left. But were we to enumerate all their enormities we would have place for nothing else. Suffice it to say, that their actions are disgraceful in the extreme, and has put a blot on the national character that will be hard to wipe out."

Among General Quitman's papers there are numerous evidences of his popularity in Mexico. There are many letters, written after his return to the United States and up to the period of his death, from very influential citizens, expressing the warmest interest in his fortunes, and a deep sense of obligation for the moderation, and respect for the national feelings and misfortunes of Mexico, that had characterized his course while exercising the arbitrary functions of his position. There were overtures made to him to remain in Mexico, and as long as he lived strong hopes expressed that he would become identified with her destiny. He was known to be in favor of an armed occupation of the country, and his plan was not without powerful supporters even in Mexico.*

* The following letter, from a very observing man, will be found interesting. The internal condition of Mexico is much the same as it was then, only it has deteriorated, and calls more loudly for American intervention.

"New York, April 29th, 1857.
"General ——, whom I saw much of at the capital, has sailed for Europe. He returns here expressly to visit you *incog.* He is a man of fine talent and education. He confirmed, in various conversations with me, the general impression prevailing in Mexico that your division won Chapultepec and the capital. Most of the Mexican functionaries concurred in this opinion. And they all spoke of your hu-

R 2

Having restored order to the capital, and believing that the war would be prolonged, Gen. Quitman now ap-

manity, justice, and delicacy while administering the government of the city of Mexico. General Scott has a great reputation in that country. You stand next to him. I spent two days at the castle of Chapultepec with Colonel Piedras, *estada mayor* of General Comonfort. He pointed out to me the Mexican positions during the attack, and said their main dependence was on the battery you carried by assault. He referred to your reconnoissance as 'audacious — the most audacious thing of the whole war.' The old castle is now, as before, a military college, and we found one of the professors tracing out for his cadets the marks of our artillery. Captain Rodal, of the engineers, informed me that they deemed the Belen impregnable to assault. He says the heavy metal at the Ciudadella and at the Park was concentrated upon you.

"My jaunt from Acapulco to the capital was very pleasant. The road, though rugged and mountainous, is exceedingly picturesque, provisions and water abundant. Acapulco, in the State of Guerrero, is the birthplace of General Alvarez, president of the republic. The state or department terminates some sixteen miles south of Guernavaca. In his native province Alvarez is much esteemed, and has unlimited control. Outside of it all classes regard him as an Indian, and of ordinary intellect. He has a large estate. I met his excellency in Ignala, a beautiful little city of 8000 inhabitants between Acapulco and Mexico. He had some 900 troops, and was expecting an attack from the Pronunciados, led by Colonel Vicario, whom I subsequently fell in with at the village of Alpuyeca. This rencontre took place twenty-four hours later, and the Pronunciados were dispersed. Alvarez is an Indian of the Pinto race, so called from their skins being spotted with a species of leprosy peculiar to the department of Guerrero. They make good soldiers, and are described as 'muy valientes.' General Comonfort, President *ad interim*, resides in your old apartments in the palace. He often refers, in very pleasant humor, to his honorable predecessor, Governor Quitman! The foreign population of Mexico respect him much, though many leading Mexicans deny his capacity. His late decree, confiscating the *bienes* of the *clero*, has diminished his popularity and caused great excitement. This is the prime source of the pronunciamentas that have recently been made and of the blood that has flowed. The motto of the Pronunciados is, "*La Religion ó la Muerte;*" their banner is a bloody cross. After a battle they usually disperse and become guerrilleros, and harass the roads, cutting off all communication between the capital and the departments. Intelligent people of all parties feel that there is only one power that can rescue them from the anarchy that prevails. The regular troops are but half paid, and ill fed, and poorly clad, and general discontent exists. Whole regiments are often in revolt. Mexico was never so happy, never so well governed, property was never so secure as when the American flag floated over her capital. While I was at the capital there were twenty-two pronunciamentas in one day, the 20th of November. They were put down, how-

plied to the general-in-chief for the command of a full division, in consonance with his rank as major general— a right which it will be recollected he had waived at Puebla when the exigencies of the public service were imperative. Gen. Scott did not consider himself able to make the arrangement, and he asked and obtained orders to report in person to the secretary of war in Washington for the purpose of being permanently assigned to duty.*

On the eve of his departure from the city the municipal authorities called in a body to manifest their respect and good wishes. The officers of his division assembled at the palace, where he was addressed by Col. Burnett, of the New York regiment, as follows:

"GENERAL,—Having learned that you were relieved as the commander of our division, the officers have imposed upon me the pleasant duty of expressing our feelings to you as toward a general, father, and friend.

"We have served with you in the most interesting campaign of this long war of victories—a war calcu-

cver, by the energy of Don Jose Vaz, governor of the district. Since then all the churches are guarded by troops, to prevent a general pillage by the populace. The leaders of the opposition to Comonfort and Alvarez are Spaniards, of whom there are many all over the republic, restless, intriguing, and ambitious men. They pay, and often officer the Pronunciados. They monopolize much of the trade and wealth of the country, and are disliked by the people generally, whom they regard with contempt. I do not think the existing difficulties between Spain and Mexico will occasion war; but should it occur, the party in power, doubtless, would rejoice to see an influx of Americans. If you could visit Mexico you would be warmly received. Such a visit would give you grand ideas. Ten thousand men, such as you led to the Belen, would obey your call and follow you at a word. Half a million of Mexicans would receive you with open arms."

* "Head-quarters of the Army, Mexico, October 26th, 1847.
"Special Orders, No, 146.
"Major General J. A. Quitman, much distinguished for gallant and efficient services, will proceed to the United States and report, in person or by letter, to the Department of War.
"By command of Major General Scott,
"H. L. SCOTT, A. A. A. G."

lated to produce results of the last importance to our
country, liberty, and the world.

"Those who at first denounced it at home as an immoral and aggressive war, even *these* have come and
united with us by the sentiment, ' Our country, always
right, but, right or wrong, our country.'

"The great results that must flow from this war, in
adding to the area of freedom and communicating the
habits, customs, and laws of our beloved republic to the
masses of Mexico are yet unseen by the world, but they
can not remain long hidden in the womb of time; they
must soon develop themselves, to the delight of every
Christian, republican, and philanthropist.

"Among the most prominent *you* have performed
your part. Your fame was known to us before our association as officers, and its lustre has brightened as the
sun from morn till noon. We have seen you upon our
wearisome marches, ever watchful for the comfort of men
and officers, and anxious to produce harmony, so essential to effective discipline. We have seen you at Chapultepec, as cool as now when we meet you in friendship,
directing the storming of that formidable work, regardless of personal danger, but looking to the safety of your
soldiers. Not a muscle moved in that stern and manly
face but to smile when the colors of your division and
our beloved country were thrown to the free winds
above the conquered castle; we have seen you at the
Garita de Belen as the hero of that long and sanguinary
engagement; we have witnessed your acts as the first
Anglo-Saxon governor of the city of the Montezumas—
every where inspiring that confidence in your soldiers
which produced such brilliant results, and receiving from
the whole army their approbation of your able and consistent course as the governor and the civilian.

"We will not confine ourselves to our own sentiments.
The enthusiasm so frequently manifested by the rank
and file of your division—those whose strong arms and
stout hearts have obeyed your orders through us—indorse our sentiments in perfect unanimity with their
approbation.

"The soldiers of this successful war will receive, as they
deserve, the grateful acknowledgments of their country.

A gallant soldier should ever be the pride of his country, and particularly the citizen soldier. Besides leaving the comforts and luxuries of home, the delights of the family hearth, he sacrifices his interests in the prosecution of his business or trade; and eminently so have *you* sacrificed your every interest at home to serve your country.

"We, as officers of your division, can only repay you upon your sudden departure with an expression of our feelings. We shall meet you again after the war as fellow-citizens, and our present sentiments, written upon our hearts as upon adamant, will lose nothing by the hand of time; uniting *then* with a gratified people, your present sacrifices may be somewhat compensated by the only boon of the patriot—the grateful acknowledgments of your country. We shall then have deposited our standards with the authorities of our respective states, but ever ready to rally under our victorious banners as the prestige of success, and ever ready to be directed by our gallant general, whom we now part with as a father and a friend."

This speech was frequently interrupted by the company present, who expressed their approbation of the sentiments by warm applause. When this had subsided Gen. Quitman replied in substance as follows:

He said that when he looked around him and found himself in the presence of the gallant officers who had participated so largely in the recent brilliant events before the city, and heard himself addressed by the senior officer of the division, yet leaning upon his honorable crutch, in remarks so full of the elegant feeling of the heart, he was overwhelmed with emotion, and felt himself wholly unable to do justice to the occasion. Circumstances had rendered it necessary, as a matter of high duty, that he should apply to the proper authority for some permanent assignment to duty, where he might be best enabled to serve his country. Had he consulted personal feeling merely, he would have been gratified to remain with the brave associates of his cares, his perils and fortunes in war, but he regarded it the soldier's part to seek the path were duty called him. That path now separated him from the gallant officers and men to whose good conduct and services he took this occasion to say he felt himself wholly indebted for whatever reputation or honor he might have acquired in this campaign. It was theirs, not his. They were entitled to his regard, his esteem, and his friendship. He would bear these feelings with him wherever his lot should be cast.

In conclusion, he expressed his heartfelt regret at his separation from them, and hoped that they would receive for themselves, and bear to the gallant rank and file under their commands, his friendly farewell."

Gen. Quitman, Gen. Shields, and many other distinguished officers, most of them suffering from wounds, arrived in New Orleans, in the Steamship Alabama, on the morning of the 24th of November. National salutes were fired in their honor from the Place d'Armes and Lafayette Square.* At night they visited the American Theatre, and were received with acclamations. The Picayune of the 25th said:

"A generous enthusiasm was aroused among our citizens yesterday, of all classes, by the presence of the distinguished officers who had just returned from Mexico. In truth, from the moment of the arrival of the Alabama the night previous, an excitement was awakened which has yet known no abatement. The stirring narratives of the great deeds of Churubusco and of Chapultepec reached us almost contemporaneously with the personal representatives of those glories. The public mind was attuned to sympathy by the glowing relations of Gen. Scott, and close upon them there appeared Quitman, and Shields,

---

* In the crowd of officers of his own division who came over with Gen. Quitman, besides Gen. Shields, were Col. Burnett, Major Dyckman, and Lieut. Sweeny, of the renowned New York regiment. Col. Burnett was dreadfully wounded at Churubusco in several places, and his recovery was miraculous. Tetanus had supervened, and he was repeatedly in those terrible convulsions that usually precede death. Major Dyckman received a musket ball which passed from shoulder to shoulder. Lieut. Sweeny lost his arm. Of the fifty officers then in the city, nearly all had been wounded; and it was noticed as a singular coincidence, that of the many who had lost an arm, it was the left arm, except in two instances.

and Garland, and Harney; but why need we again enumerate those who return to us all fresh from fields made immortal by the prowess of our countrymen? What heart so poor as not to share in the exultation with which we first read of feats of arms unparalleled in military annals and then gaze upon the representatives of those who participated in those feats—themselves distinguished actors therein? The whole town was alive with feeling, and the St. Charles was, throughout the day and night, overrun with citizens flushed with pride and eager to catch a glimpse of those who had so helped to swell the national renown. How freshly we then remembered the perils and the glories of the Belen gate, the desperate assault of Chapultepec, and the 'older and yet unsurpassed honors of Cerro Gordo! And there, in the midst of all, were moving the pale and mutilated forms of those who, so dearly to themselves, had helped to pay the price of so much glory to the nation. The sympathies of the whole mass with these wounded gentlemen in vain sought adequate expression. No eloquence can reach the pathos of poor dumb wounds."

On their return from the theatre they were serenaded at the instance of the municipal authorities, and then accepted the hospitalities of Col. Wm. Christy, a veteran of 1812. The morning following they were waited on, says the Delta, by the mayor and members of the councils, and by crowds of citizens.*

* In quoting from the Delta and Picayune, we are reminded of the extraordinary and unrivaled energy exhibited by those journals during the war. They were represented in Mexico by gentlemen of great ability, who bore a gallant part in the various engagements, and then described them with rare fidelity and eloquence. Mr. George W. Kendall, one of the founders and editors of the Picayune, after having steadily urged the necessity for the war, accompanied the army to Mexico, volunteered on the staff of Gen. Worth, and distinguished himself at Churubusco, Molino del Rey, and Chapultepec, where he was wounded. His letters to the Picayune were subsequently reproduced in a splendid volume entitled "The United States and Mexico."

The principal correspondent of the Delta was Mr. James L. Freaner, a printer by trade, a native of Maryland, but an early adventurer to Louisiana and Texas. He went to the Rio Grande with the Loui-

Gen. Quitman, accompanied by several officers of his staff and many personal friends, left New Orleans on the 25th of November, and, on his arrival at Natchez, was received with every demonstration of honor. He was saluted with cannon captured at Alvarado, and afterward escorted into the city by a civic and military procession, where Wm. T. Martin, Esq., in a strain of impassioned oratory, welcomed the hero home. "How wonderful is it," said the orator, "that this very city, bearing the name of a noble fragment of the Aztec race, who, driven from Mexico by the sword of the Montezumas or of Cortez, found shelter on this bluff, where their proud name is still preserved—how wonderful is it that from their ashes should have appeared an avenger of their wrongs, and that our Quitman, from fair Natchez, was the instrument, in the hands of Providence, 'to spoil the spoiler!'"

At the banquet that followed, the following toast—a compendium of the war—was proposed by one of the boldest and most daring men of his time, the late Gen. Felix Huston:

"Gen. Quitman: 'Second to none;' *six* hours before any other chieftain, he fought his way into the heart of Monterey! *eight* hours before any other leader, he stormed the garita and entered the city of Mexico!! The *first* to plant the stars and stripes over the Halls of the Montezumas!!!"

siana regiments, and when they were disbanded he entered Capt. Jack Hays's famous company of the Rangers. At the battle of Monterey he slew an officer of lancers in single combat and seized his charger. He thus gained the sobriquet of "Mustang," under which signature he wrote his celebrated letters. He subsequently died in California.

END OF VOL. I.